Love UNDYING

Love
UNDYING

MICHELE
PAIGE
HOLMES

Copyright © 2025 Michele Paige Holmes
Print edition
All rights reserved
No part of this book may be reproduced in any form whatsoever without prior written permission of the publisher, except in the case of brief passages embodied in critical reviews and articles. This novel is a work of fiction. The characters, names, incidents, places, and dialog are products of the author's imagination and are not to be construed as real.

Interior Design by Cora Johnson
Edited by Cassidy Wadsworth, Lorie Humpherys, and Macie Adams
Cover design by Alyssa Howard and Rachael Anderson
Cover Image Credit: Photography by Alyssa Howard. Cover model: Hannah Fackrell
Published by Mirror Press, LLC
ISBN: 978-1-952611-50-6

HEARTHFIRE ROMANCE SERIES
Saving Grace
Loving Helen
Marrying Christopher
Twelve Days in December
Love Unbound
Love Undying

HEARTHFIRE SCOTTISH ROMANCE SERIES
Yesterday's Promise
A Promise for Tomorrow
The Promise of Home

HOLIDAY HARBOR SERIES
A Holiday Affair
Home Sweet Holiday
The Heart of Holiday

Dedication

To my daughters Carissa, Alyssa, and Hannah, who are each so different yet have a deep and abiding love for one another. May you always stay close and be there for each other as sisters should. What a privilege it is to be your mother!

Part One

> "Real love and truth are stronger than any evil or misfortune."
>
> —Charles Dickens

One

Caerlanwood Estate, Scotland
October 1831

SOPHIE BENT TO wipe the bright stain of berries from Matthew's mouth, cheeks, chin, and generally everything in that vicinity, right down to the collar of his shirt. "Did you enjoy your tart?" she asked, laughing as his tongue darted out, attempting to claim the last of the treat from the cloth in her hand.

He nodded and rubbed his stomach. "Can I have more?"

"May I?" she corrected, then shook her head. "Not yet. The men still need to eat. Then, if there are leftovers, you may have another." Turning from Matthew, Sophie held a hand up to her forehead, shielding her eyes from the rapidly descending afternoon sun. In the distance she saw Graham, shirtsleeves rolled to his elbows as he worked one end of a crosscut saw. Part of the harvest festival, a long tradition at Caerlanwood that he had reinstated, was preparing for winter—accomplished by the various teams of men who competed throughout the day, cutting peat and as many logs as they could from the trees felled over the all-too-short summer months.

Summer was fleeting. Sophie pulled her shawl tighter around her as the chill of evening crept ever closer. Though the temperatures had cooled significantly, she didn't mind, as the cooler weather had changed Caerlanwood's gardens and trees from lush greens to a brilliant display of yellows, oranges, and reds. She'd loved every one of the nearly five months she'd been here, but so far October was her favorite.

Though it was the season when the world braced for winter and animals and people alike retreated to places of warmth and safety, she felt almost like it was spring and the world was alive with possibility. For her it was, with her love for Graham and the children and now the new life growing inside of her that would make his or her appearance late next spring. She'd only known for certain the past two days, after she'd missed her second cycle of menses, and she'd yet to tell Graham. She wanted the moment to be just the two of them, alone, and to be perfect. She worried he still had fears about being a good father, though he was a wonderful one to Ayla and Matthew.

In the months since their marriage, the four of them had become more of a family. They took all of their meals together, and Graham joined them on their adventures as often as he was able. Sophie and the children helped him with the projects to restore Caerlanwood whenever they could, working in the gardens, painting walls, hanging curtains and tapestries over windows and in halls that had long been bare.

Ayla still had not spoken, though her nightmares had all but ceased, and she responded to conversation by nodding or shaking her head and using hand gestures or facial expressions. A time or two Sophie had even caught her smiling.

Progress.

Evenings were Sophie's favorite. After the children were in bed she and Graham spent long hours alone in their room, reading to one another, talking—sometimes on opposite sides of a subject—touching, loving in a way neither had ever realized was possible only a few short months ago. On clear evenings they often wandered down to the beach and walked along the shore hand in hand, or sometimes they brought a blanket and headed for their favorite place among the dunes. Life was beautiful, nearly perfect. And she was, oh, so happy.

SOPHIE WRUNG THE water from the cloth then laid it over the side of the bathtub. "Lean forward," she said, placing her hands on Graham's bare shoulders.

He obeyed then gave a moan of contentment as she began kneading the muscles in his shoulders and back. "That feels even better than the warm water."

"Good," Sophie said then, after a minute, paused her ministrations. "Perhaps I ought not to extend such mercy when it's obvious that you overdid it today, even after my many warnings."

"Ye wouldna' be so cruel," Graham drawled in the Scots brogue she adored. It appeared more often lately, as the months they'd spent in Scotland had transformed him from the English duke with too many cares to the Scottish laird who loved his family and home and all living on his land. It wasn't only Caerlanwood that had suffered beneath his father's neglect and abuse, but the people living here as well. Graham was doing all he could to make amends, right down to ensuring that the occupants of every cottage had enough fuel to keep them warm through the winter.

Sophie tilted her head, pretending to consider. "If I did withhold my care, it might teach you that you needn't be the one cutting peat for every single family living on Caerlanwood land."

"It wasn't *every* family." Graham rolled his shoulders, as if inviting her to continue the massage. "Just those I feared would not have enough if I didn't help."

"And how many turns with the crosscut saw did you take?" She began kneading his muscles again, enjoying the feel of his warm, smooth skin beneath her hands.

"Too many," he admitted. "What's a laird to do, but to be braw and carry on."

"Is that what today was all about?" She knew it wasn't but poked him anyway. "A contest of strength? Just who were you trying to prove yourself to?"

"My bonny wife, of course. She's such an intelligent lass, so kind, so knowledgeable about . . . anatomy." He turned so that he was facing her. "A man in my position has to continually prove his worth if he is to keep his wife." He reached for Sophie before she could move out of the way.

"Graham, my nightgown. I just put this on." She frowned as she looked down at her now wet sleeve. She had bathed before him and dressed for bed afterward.

"*Why* did you put it on? Seems a waste when you knew I'd just wish it off shortly."

"I was cold."

"I can help with that." Graham rose from the tub and hauled her against him, wrapping his arms around her.

Sophie let out a huff of exasperation, even as her body was already responding to his nearness, her heart synching with his yet again. "Now all of me is wet."

"Allow me to assist with that as well." Graham stepped out of the bath, then swept her into his arms and carried her to the bed.

Soon she wasn't cold anymore.

SOPHIE'S EYES FLEW open, and she sat up in bed, ears straining to discern what had awoken her. *Ayla?* Beside her Graham slept, his chest rising and falling peacefully. Odd, since Ayla's infrequent cries usually woke both of them.

There were no cries now, but Sophie eased herself out of bed and put on her wrap. She headed for the hall, smiling to herself as she passed the bathtub and their discarded clothing, remnants of their earlier lovemaking. It had turned out that Graham wasn't nearly as tired as she'd believed him to be.

She left their room and felt her way along the dark hall to the nursery where light from the full moon illuminated the nursery enough for her to see both children sleeping peacefully. Matthew's rocking horse stood beside his bed, and his hand hung off the edge, resting atop the horse's head. Ayla lay curled on her side, her doll tucked safely in her arms.

They were both the picture of innocence and childhood. *Exactly as children should be.* Content that all was well, Sophie retraced her steps and was approaching her own bed when the cry, accompanied by what sounded like someone pounding on the front door, came again.

Graham was out of bed at once. He tugged on pants and boots in record time, then reached to the top of the wardrobe, where they kept two loaded guns and a set of keys they didn't wish curious children to access. He tossed the keys to Sophie. She caught them then flew to her bedside table, unlocked the drawer, and removed her own weapons. She hoped never to have to use either the gun or the knife, but she would if it meant protecting herself and her family.

"What do—" she started to ask as she turned around, but Graham was already gone.

Sophie rushed from the room to follow but stopped long enough to close the children's door. Whatever the disturbance, they need not have their sleep interrupted too.

In the dark she crept down the stairs still in need of repair, the sounds of a woman's hysteria reaching her before she'd come halfway.

"They shot him! And Ethan's alone at the cottage. They breached the gate, and they won't be far behind."

Lucy. Gooseflesh sprang up along Sophie's arms and the back of her neck, pinpricks of fear and foreboding. She ran down the rest of the stairs and into Graham, who was coming up two steps at a time.

He squeezed her hand as he passed. "Take Lucy, rouse everyone, and leave by the kitchen door. Run into the woods as far as you can and hide. I'll bring the children."

"Hurry!" Sophie pled. She ran to the bottom and located Lucy by the sound of her crying. "Are you hurt?"

"Adam is," Lucy said tearfully, then doubled over, clutching her stomach as liquid gushed onto the floor beneath her. She gasped. "No! It's too early."

"Is it your baby?" Sophie wrapped her arm around Lucy.

She nodded. "This is what happened last time, and it went quick. But it's too soon. I'll lose them both, them *all*, on the same night." She grabbed Sophie's arm. "They shot Adam, and Ethan is at the cottage by himself."

"We'll send someone to get Ethan." The thought of the toddler alone frightened Sophie too. "*Who* shot Adam? Can you tell me what happened?"

"I don't know which one shot him," Lucy said, tears streaming down her cheeks. "From the window I saw maybe five or six men. Adam took his time answering their shouts and summons to open the gate. I don't know what was said when he went outside, only that Adam had turned back toward the cottage when one of the men shot him. Adam fell— and didn't get up again." Lucy's hand covered her mouth.

Sophie turned Lucy toward her and pulled her into a hug. "It may be that Adam is all right. If those men believe him dead or seriously wounded they're not likely to bother with him again. The smartest thing for Adam to do was to stay down."

Lucy bobbed her head and sniffled violently. "He's a smart one, my man."

"He is." Sophie took Lucy's hand. "We need to be smart, too, and hurry."

They took three steps before Lucy gave an agonized moan and leaned forward. "This baby's coming."

We're not going anywhere. Not out in the woods, anyway. "You'll have the baby here, then," Sophie said with a calm she didn't feel as she turned Lucy back toward the stairs. "You can use my bed."

With her arm around Lucy, supporting her more with each step, they climbed the stairs, encountering Graham at the top, holding a sleepy Matthew in one arm and Ayla in the other.

"Lucy's about to have her baby," Sophie blurted before he could ask why she wasn't with the others. "She can't make it to the woods, and she can't give birth on the lawn."

"Lock yourselves in our room. Don't let *anyone* in. I'll send the children with the servants and be back."

"Be careful," she admonished, the words sounding hollow.

"Stay upstairs," was his terse reply.

As he disappeared, Sophie turned her attention to Lucy, who was groaning between sobs.

"You need to leave," Lucy said, her breath short. "They're here for *you*."

"Who is?" The gooseflesh reappeared, raising the hairs on the back of Sophie's neck. "My father?"

Lucy nodded. "And Viscount Newsome."

"I am married. They can do nothing." Sophie attempted to push aside her fear. After so long, she hadn't believed they would come for her. Was her father really so vindictive? One daughter's death hadn't been enough for him?

Inside the room she locked the door, set the gun on the bedside table, and helped Lucy onto the bed. She was propping pillows behind her when more shouts and pounding came from below. A minute later banging sounded on the bedroom door.

"Open the door, Sophie. Let the children in."

She ran to the door.

"He told you *not* to open it!" Lucy cried from the bed.

"I know my husband's voice. Graham is on the other side." Sophie threw back the bolt, then reached her hands out to take Matthew from him as Graham pushed open the door and strode into the room.

"They're here. There's no time to leave. *Stay* upstairs, keep your gun with you, and don't let anyone into this room." Graham deposited Ayla, looking much more awake now, on the edge of the bed, then ran into the hall.

Shifting Matthew to her hip, Sophie secured the door once more, then turned to face Ayla and Lucy.

"Lucy's going to have her baby tonight. Isn't that exciting?" Sophie forced a smile she did not feel. "Ayla, Matthew, you two may rest over here on the window seat." Sophie carried Matthew over to the seat, then tucked a blanket around both children as soon as Ayla had made her way over as well.

Lucy groaned and arched her back. "Birthing's a messy business. We'll need some hot water and towels."

Sophie headed toward the fireplace, grateful there were still embers and enough wood to build the fire up again, and that she was skilled at such a task now after her months here. There was water in the pitcher too. "Tell me what to do," she said, then added a silent prayer. *Show us all what to do.*

Two

London, England
October, 1831

OLIVIA CLAYBOURNE SAT on the floor of the cupboard, her knees tucked to her chest in the tight space. Her eyes had long ago adjusted to the dark, and her ears listened attentively to the conversations on the other side of the door.

The Dowager Palmer had guests tonight, a small dinner party of only a dozen or so, but they were among London's elite, and Olivia hadn't wanted to pass up the opportunity to overhear some important piece of gossip. One never knew. Having spent the past five months out of society and in hiding, she had to get her news where she could.

Tonight's was most dull. One gentleman—older, she assumed—insisted upon complaining about his many physical ailments to anyone who would listen, and likely those who would not. Two ladies were in eager conversation about the recent, rushed wedding of an acquaintance's daughter and whether or not there would be a baby coming before too many more months had passed.

The dowager had earlier promised to bring up at least some of the topics on the list of requests that Olivia had given her, but thus far she had not.

Olivia covered her mouth as she stifled a yawn and tried

not to think of the bedroom upstairs, where she might have been stretched out before the fire reading any number of books.

She'd never cared much for reading until her forced exile had driven her to find means of entertainment outside of her usual pursuits. Deprived of her friends, parlor games, walks in the park, balls, or social outings of any kind, she'd had little choice but to begin haunting the libraries of whatever house she was temporarily stashed away in. To her great surprise, she'd discovered that she enjoyed reading quite a lot. *Sophie was not the bore I believed her to be.*

Sophie. Olivia felt a pang of longing as she thought of her older sister—her only sister now. Torie, the eldest of the three, had been dead for two and a half years. It felt both like yesterday and forever since they had all been together. *We never shall be again.*

But I still have Sophie. Or at least she hoped she did. Mother had insisted that Sophie was somewhere safe as well, though Olivia didn't see how she could be, with the Duke of Warwick interested in her sister. Viscount Newsome had been bad enough, but a murderous duke . . .

"Newsome, you say?" a man's voice asked, snapping Olivia back to the conversations happening on the other side of the door. "Despicable man, if you ask me, but his cunning has earned him friends in high places."

"*Friends* seems a somewhat generous term," the dowager said. "It seems more likely that there are those concerned with not becoming his enemy."

A few grunts of agreement followed this statement.

"London is free of him for a few days at least," another man said. "He was at White's last week, boasting that he'd finally located the Duke of Warwick."

"Newsome's a fool if he thinks to take on the duke. Raymond won't think twice about shooting him."

Love UNDYING

"He'd be doing us all a favor," the first man muttered. "Not that I condone murder," he added hastily, as if perhaps realizing he had said too much.

"What does Newsome intend to do now that he's found his nemesis?" the dowager asked casually, as if she were merely entertained by such gossip.

"Nothing good. After all, the duke has caused Newsome no end of problems on Saint Kitts."

"Not to mention that he stole Claybourne's daughter right out from under the viscount's nose," a female voice added. "I was there that night. It was quite the scene."

"Pish posh."

Olivia imagined the dowager batting both her hand and eyelashes at the suggestion that Sophie had been stolen by anyone. *As if.* Her sister was brave and bold, and smarter than anyone else she knew. Sophie had run away. No duke or anyone else was controlling her now. Or so Olivia desperately wanted to believe. In truth, she was worried. Sophie had been gone for so long, and even Mother didn't know where she was, though she still insisted that Sophie was safe.

"The Claybourne girl ran away—both of them did, I've heard," the dowager said. "Can't blame them, with a father like theirs."

"Regardless of what actually happened, Newsome holds the duke responsible for his troubles on Saint Kitts as well as Miss Claybourne's sudden disappearance. He was more than foxed last week at White's when he was bragging about his plans to finally bring Raymond down. According to Newsome, the duke's been holed up in Scotland somewhere."

Scotland. Was that where Sophie was? And if so, would she still be safe if Newsome came after her? Olivia could hardly wait for her mother's visit tomorrow. Maybe when confronted with this news, she would finally tell Olivia what she knew about Sophie and the duke. Maybe Sophie would even return to London if there was trouble.

Just so long as it is not Newsome who forces her to it.

If Sophie didn't return soon . . . *I'll not see her before we leave.* Their passage on the *Columbia* was booked for late November. Mother had insisted she needed that long to finish arrangements here—to procure enough finances so she and Olivia could survive on their own in America, at least long enough to find Jonathan, and to ensure that Father never found them. Hopefully he would tire of chasing false leads of her whereabouts. But thus far he had not, necessitating that she never remained at any one location too long.

From London to Derbyshire, to Lancaster, to Nottingham and Norfolk, then back to London, she had traveled everywhere over the past months. All while seeing precisely—nothing. She hadn't even been permitted to look out the windows of the many conveyances that had carried her on her journeys. She spoke to almost no one, received no visitors. Wrote no letters—or none that she was ever able to send. Servants were told she was a distant, sickly relation, come to recover from some contagious illness, and she was not to be disturbed. She'd become invisible, and she hated it. But soon that was to change. Olivia stared through the dark at the wall opposite her cramped quarters. *Soon.* She and Mother would be on a ship bound for America, New York, and Jonathan.

How surprised he would be to see them. How angry? He had every right. *But I'll soothe that anger. I'm keeping my promise, Torie. It just took longer than I thought it would.* Jonathan, too, had vanished—over two years ago, only weeks after Torie's death. It had taken Olivia over a year to find out what had become of him.

And then, as she'd had to so many times before, she'd had to wait.

Three

Caerlanwood Estate, Scotland

GRAHAM RAN DOWN the steps to the main floor. The front doors were still barred, despite the pounding on the other side. Boyce the butler stood at his post, his skinny legs poking out beneath his nightshirt. Any other time the sight would have been comical, but now it only increased Graham's panic.

"Heard we have visitors. Thought I'd best be ready to greet them," Boyce said, as if they were expecting someone for tea.

"I'll not be answering the door for them," Graham said. "And neither will you." He jerked a thumb toward the kitchen. "I want you out with the others."

"And leave you alone to protect your lady and the bairns?" Boyce shook his white head. "Some butler I'd be."

"Butlers in England obey orders." Graham looked for a place to stash Boyce in a hurry if need be.

"From a whelp they've known since he was knee-high to their britches?" Boyce shook his head. "I'm an auld man now. If it's my time to go, I'd just as soon do it defending ye—and yer lady." His gaze, clear and sober and every bit aware of what he was offering, sought Graham's.

"Don't die," Graham ordered, reluctantly acquiescing to the older man's request. "I can't handle another death on my conscience."

"That's why I'm here," Boyce said. "Evens up the odds a bit—"

"Open up, Raymond! We know you're in there." Raised voices carried through the heavy door, and Graham glimpsed the flash of torches through the window.

"Open up, or we burn the place down!"

The window to his left shattered, and Graham jumped to the side, trying to avoid the airborne shards of glass. A second later a burning torch sailed toward him, landing on the floor, only just missing the rug or a chair that would have easily been caught up in the flame.

Graham grabbed the torch and flung it back through the broken window, then stomped at the cinders littering the floor.

The stone wouldn't burn, but the floors, the roof, the rugs, and the furnishings would. *Sophie and the children.* It wouldn't take much for a fire to take hold, and then they'd either be trapped or forced out into the open where the men waited. These men might torch the house, regardless. *My chances are probably better if I face them. I could take two out right away.* But that would still leave the others to kill him. *I can't leave Sophie and the children alone.* He would have to try to stall the intruders and hope some of the servants had gone to the stables to find Griggs and the other men.

A second window shattered, followed by two balls of fire. Graham snatched up a rug and beat them out, Boyce aiding him as best he could.

Graham nodded to him. "Looks like I need your services after all. Open the door."

Boyce shuffled forward as Graham stepped back into the shadows, both weapons pointed toward the entrance. Boyce raised the bar and pulled one of the heavy doors toward him, careful to stay behind it.

A torch held high in the first man's hand led the intruders' way—six of them, including Sophie's father and Newsome, the coward, at the rear. He crossed the threshold, and fury built in Graham at seeing the man in his home.

"Not a step farther," Graham warned. "Hands out where I can—"

A loud metal *bong* reverberated through the hall as the man standing beside Newsome, the same man Sophie had hit with the pitcher in Gretna Green, crumpled to the ground.

The torch-bearing man nearest Graham pulled out a gun and lunged forward. Graham fired. The man fell, his torch going with him, catching hold of the rug at once. Boyce ran out from behind the door, a large skillet in his hands, which he attempted to beat out the fire with.

Another gun fired, and hot pain shot through Graham's shoulder.

"Enough!" Newsome said. "I want him alive."

Graham dropped the weapon he'd already fired, then used both hands to steady the one he still held. Warm blood seeped through his shirt, but he didn't dare take his gaze from the men.

"Another murder to add to your others." Newsome *tsk*ed, staring at his man Graham had felled. "It's a shame you can only hang once."

"Get out," Graham said. "Get out of my house and off of my property, or I'll add to that number."

"Not while you have *my* property here," Lord Claybourne snarled. "Where are they?"

They? Who else was he after besides Sophie?

"Threats, threats." Newsome took another step forward. "You can kill me if you wish, but then you'll be killed too—and who will see to your pretty little wife if you're dead?"

Boyce straightened, the skillet held in front of him like a shield. "We will. The staff here willna let anything happen to her."

Newsome nudged the man at his side. "Take care of him. He's obstructing justice."

"*No*," Graham said. "Boyce. Leave. That's an order."

Boyce hesitated.

"Get out with the others," Graham said, hoping Newsome would believe Sophie one of those others, that she was already gone from the premises.

After another second's hesitation, Boyce gave a curt nod and side-shuffled away. Graham knew a second of relief when he had gone from the room without being hurt.

"Is your loyal staff all of such an age?" Newsome asked, his tone amused.

Graham didn't bother answering. "As you just noted, Sophie is my *wife*. We were wed in a church, in front of witnesses, of her own free will. Legally you cannot remove her from my property."

"Oh, I know." Newsome smirked. "And I wouldn't want to do anything outside of the law. We're here to see justice served. Isn't that right, Constable Jenson?"

"Aye. Justice served." The man beside Newsome looked back and forth from Newsome to Graham, then cleared his throat. "You are hereby under arrest for the murders of Oliver and Stewart Higgins."

They aren't here for Sophie? Graham couldn't quite feel relieved. They were up to something. He kept his tone casual. "It's a little late to be bringing that up after so much time has passed."

"We have a *witness*," Claybourne added, his tone almost gleeful.

"That is fortunate," Graham said. "As anyone who *actually* saw what happened that day knows I am not guilty of murder." *I wasn't even the one who shot Stewart.*

"Just as we have witnesses to what you've done here

today." With the toe of his boot, Claybourne nudged the man who'd come at Graham, currently bleeding out on the floor. "Poor bloke was just trying to do his job when you shot him for no reason."

"He came at me with a torch and his weapon drawn and pointed at me—this after you shot my gatekeeper, breached my gate, and threatened to burn my home. I'd say those are reasons enough," Graham said, though arguing was fruitless. Men like Claybourne and Newsome bent justice to their side every time.

"You'll find it difficult to support that abolition bill you've been promoting from prison," Newsome said with mock regret.

So they knew about that. *Most unfortunate.*

"Even harder when you're dead," Claybourne added.

Constable Jenson cleared his throat and held a shaking hand out toward Graham. "I'll need you to surrender your weapon and come with us."

"I need *you* to get out of my house," Graham repeated. "You cannot expect me to think that justice will prevail when you're led by two of the most untrustworthy men in all of England, responsible themselves for numerous deaths."

"Slaves don't count," Newsome said casually. "But the murder of two well-known and respected white men is a different matter."

"Get out," Graham repeated a third time, willing his eyes to stay focused. He needed to stem the bleeding in his shoulder, but he didn't dare let go of his gun. Just a few minutes more, and he might have help. If Boyce or Finella or Maime could get to the stables, Griggs and the others would come. The tenants would aid him as well. He'd put all of them on alert months ago that something like this might happen.

"You heard him. Get *out.*" Sophie entered the crowded

foyer, blood-stained hands gripping her gun and training it on Newsome.

Whose blood? Graham fought panic. *You were supposed to stay upstairs.* His horror only increased as he caught sight of Ayla, peeking out from the stairwell. He redoubled his efforts to remain upright and alert, fear for them temporarily restoring his faculties.

The viscount laughed. "Had I known your only defenses were an old man and your wife, I could have come alone."

"I wish you had," Sophie muttered. "Father," she said coldly without looking at Lord Claybourne.

"Where is your sister?" He took a step toward her.

The fourth man still standing snarled and broke from the group, a knife in his hand as he leapt toward Sophie. She fired at him, but he ducked to the side, and the ball entered his arm instead of his chest. With a howl of pain, he lunged forward, grabbed her hair, and jerked her head back.

"Let her go!" Hot anger surged through Graham at the same moment a stone of utter helplessness slammed into his gut. *I have to protect her. I can't.*

Sophie ceased fighting as the blade pressed against her throat.

"You call this justice?" Graham demanded of the constable. "She has done nothing but defend herself against an unwarranted attack. Let her go."

"Release her, Mr. Granger," the constable said, his voice timid.

Granger shook his head. "This is *my* justice." He held out the arm that wasn't pressing the knife to her throat, revealing a mangled, scarred hand, streaked red from the blood seeping from the new wound in his arm. "*She* did this."

The twisted face flashed in Graham's memory. *I should have killed him when I had the chance.* He wanted to reassure

Sophie, to save her, but he was powerless all over again, just like the boy who couldn't protect his mother or sister. "She was defending herself when you attacked her then too," Graham said, his voice deceptively calm. "You should be grateful that she shot only your hand."

Constable Jenson seemed anything but calm as he mopped his forehead with a handkerchief and looked from one man to the other. "Gentlemen, as I told you at the gate, this is not the correct way to handle things. Your Grace, if you will put your weapon down and come with us, we will release your wife and leave your property." He looked to Newsome as if for support or approval of this offer.

"Not so fast," Lord Claybourne said, stepping closer to Sophie, the sneer on his face the antithesis of fatherly affection. "Don't release her until she's told us where Olivia is."

"I don't know where she is," Sophie said, meeting her father's gaze with one filled with equal loathing. "But if I did, I wouldn't tell you."

"Olivia has never been here," Graham said, forcing his focus to the men when he wished to look at Sophie.

Newsome flicked a hand toward Sophie and Granger. "Let her go. We've no need of her. Used goods, she is. It's Raymond we came for."

"And Olivia," Lord Claybourne insisted.

The man holding Sophie growled his displeasure. Graham tensed. Could he shoot him and avoid hitting Sophie?

Granger turned his knife, then released Sophie suddenly, shoving her forward.

She stumbled but didn't fall, then ran to Graham's side. "You're hurt." She faced the constable. "He cannot go anywhere until we've attended to this wound."

Newsome shook his head. "We've delayed long enough. And who knows but there are other men here, waiting to ambush us as we leave."

"I'm going to search for Olivia." Lord Claybourne started toward the back of the hall.

"She *isn't* here." Sophie glared at him. "And never was. But little wonder if she left home too, after what you did to Torie. And what you intended for me." She turned her glare on Newsome.

"We leave *now*," Newsome said, waving Sophie's glare off. "What's it to be, Raymond? What else should I do to gain your cooperation?" The viscount's slow perusal of Sophie was in direct contrast to his earlier expression of disinterest.

Graham gritted his teeth against pain and the desire to howl with frustration. How could he have allowed himself to be placed in such a position of vulnerability again? Even worse, he'd endangered Sophie. The children. Everyone here. *There will be no help for us.* The tenants were spread out, and it would take a while for them to gather. Griggs and the others at the stable were his only chance. *And even then . . . I don't want anyone else hurt.*

If I go with them, that will get Newsome and the others away from here. Graham agonized as he weighed the decision. Once he put his gun down he'd have no chance of helping anyone he loved. *What chance have I now?* Two of the men were down, but he was still outnumbered four to one and weakening by the minute with every drop of blood that drained from his shoulder. "I'll go with you." Graham lowered his gun, and the constable and the other man beside Newsome—also one they had seen in Gretna Green—stepped forward, took his weapon, and pulled his arms roughly behind him. Graham winced, and the room spun dangerously.

"You're hurting him," Sophie exclaimed, her voice breaking. "Let him go. He doesn't have a weapon, and he's injured. He's not a threat."

Ignoring her, they pulled him toward the door. Claybourne hung back, then headed for the stairs.

Ayla! Utter helplessness and despair flooded Graham's senses. He hadn't felt this weak since he was a boy. He *couldn't* feel this way now. *The children and Sophie need me.*

You can do nothing for them. His father's mocking voice pulsed through his head.

"Where are you taking him?" Sophie grabbed the constable's arm.

"London," Newsome said, his pleased smirk still in place.

"He'll stand trial for his crimes," the constable said, then added hesitantly, "You may join us if you're concerned about his treatment."

"No!" Graham turned his head to give her a warning look. "Stay *here.* Write to Willliam. He'll know what to do."

Newsome laughed. "Are you certain about that? Who do you think told us where to find you?"

Graham felt as if he'd been punched.

"William would never betray you." Sophie ran along beside them, trying to work her way to the front of the trio. When they had to pause near the door, for the other members of their party to pick up the man Boyce had struck with the pan, she succeeded.

"On the contrary," Newsome said. "Lord Fitzgerald was all too eager to provide most-detailed instructions on how to get here." Newsome lowered his voice and leaned close to Graham. "It's amazing what a man will do when his wife and unborn child are threatened. I imagine you can understand that—or at least part of it. It doesn't appear that you've planted a brat in her yet."

Sophie's stricken expression met Graham's, and he felt another invisible punch to his gut. She didn't say anything. She didn't have to, incapable as she was of lying to him. *She's carrying our child.*

She stepped forward and kissed him. "I love you."

He didn't say anything. He wished she hadn't. *More leverage for Newsome.*

Graham knew another moment of panic as she untied her wrap and shrugged out of it, then laid it across his shoulder.

"Use this to stop the bleeding when you get in the carriage." She leaned forward again to whisper, "This is *only* for you, to keep you safe. *No one* else unless it's a matter of life and death. Stay alive."

Clad only in her nightgown now, she turned away to address the constable, revealing the thin line of blood crossing her neck.

Granger actually cut her. I'll kill him. Fury surged through Graham, and he jerked free, shoving Newsome aside with his injured shoulder. A jolt of pain, followed by a gush of blood, sent Graham stumbling forward instead. Sophie caught him.

"This bleeding needs to be stopped. You cannot pin his arms back. I want assurance that my husband will be given the proper medical attention." She spoke with the authority of a queen, though she faced her enemies barefoot and wearing only her nightgown.

The constable, seeming even more shaken now, nodded. "I'll see to that." He took Graham's arm again but did not pull it behind him.

Sophie pinned the constable with her gaze. "And fair treatment. He must be allowed to use his hands to stop the bleeding."

The constable eyed Graham uncertainly. "So long as he is cooperative."

"You can always join us if you are that concerned." Newsome had straightened and leered at her, his gaze fixed on the gown that did little to hide her figure beneath.

"*Go inside,*" Graham said, fighting the rage building

inside of him. His heart felt like it would beat out of his chest. He *would* be guilty of murder before this was over.

As if suddenly aware of her precarious situation, Sophie stepped aside. She turned toward the house as her father stormed from it, cursing as he hopped awkwardly on one foot, his other elevated and limp. His face was bright red and blotchy, his hair and clothing soaked.

"Olivia *must* be in there. They were waiting for me. I slipped on a crumbling stair and fell, then someone above dumped scalding water on top of me."

Newsome snorted, and the constable hurried his pace down the drive Graham wished he hadn't been so hasty to repair. *But the stairs . . .* He hoped Lord Claybourne had broken his ankle in the fall.

"All the more reason to leave. We have what we came for," Newsome said. "With Raymond out of our hair, we can do as we please on Saint Kitts."

"But—" Claybourne hobbled along, attempting to keep up. "I thought you wanted—"

"Your daughters are more trouble than they're worth," Newsome said, cutting him off. "What I want now is to see Raymond's neck in a noose."

Graham was shoved none too gently into a waiting carriage and followed Sophie's instructions as soon as he was seated and his arms released. He bunched up her wrap and pressed it against the pain coming from a spot between his shoulder and his chest. As he did, something hard bumped against his palm. Half-delirious as he was, he nearly pulled the cloth away to see what it was but stopped himself just in time.

The hilt. Of her wee knife. Clever woman. She hadn't wanted him to be without a weapon.

As they rolled toward the gatehouse, no one tried to stop them. Dawn was just beginning to pink the sky when Graham glimpsed Griggs out the window, carrying Adam up to the house.

"And will there be justice for my gatekeeper and his family if he dies?" Graham asked, staring at the constable.

"He was obstructing justice," Newsome said. "He's had his reward."

Let Adam live, Lord. Graham didn't want to think about Lucy being a widow. He prayed her child would arrive safely too. Perhaps it already had, given the blood on Sophie's hands.

They left Caerlanwood's grounds and traveled past the bridge. The pain in his shoulder throbbed, and Sophie's wrap stuck fast to him as the blood dried. Moving his fingers slowly, Graham managed to find the knife in the pocket. Its pressure against his palm was reassuring.

Across from him Newsome gloated, and beside him Granger sneered. *I could slit* his *throat before anyone could stop me.* Granger deserved it. Twice he'd attempted to hurt Sophie. This time he *had* hurt her.

Anger and hatred simmered inside Graham as he mentally reviewed the sins of Granger, Claybourne, and Newsome. Each deserved to die. But he could only choose one. And he would have to strike quickly. *Who has done the most harm?*

His thoughts fed his anger, rapidly moving toward a boiling point, and one hand fisted in his lap as his other pressed harder on the hilt of the small knife Sophie had provided.

Sophie. He closed his eyes, and her face appeared. How dare they threaten her. How dare they invade Caerlanwood. He couldn't allow it. He *wouldn't.* He would do this for her, because of her. After all, she'd provided him the means.

Slowly he began sliding the knife from the pocket.

This is only for you. No one else. Sophie's words—strange

when she'd spoken them—suddenly made sense. She had not intended that he use the knife for revenge.

Graham squeezed his eyes shut. His fingers stilled on the handle, and he brought his other hand up to cover them, lest they move again. *Stay alive.*

For many years he hadn't cared whether or not he did. But now—

I can't leave them alone.

Then you must control your anger. Katherine's voice in his head now.

Graham drew in a long, slow breath and relished the pain that accompanied it. It was no less than *he* deserved for going down the path of his father. Still, it wasn't an easy path to abandon.

Newsome deserves to die. Granger would have killed Sophie. Claybourne is responsible for her sister's death and showed not a shred of mercy or kindness to Sophie today.

Kill them. Do it. His father was speaking now.

I love you. Those three words somehow overpowered all others. He pictured Sophie's face, and his thoughts of violence scattered, winging outward in all directions, much as shards of glass had flown from the shattered window.

I love you. Somehow she did. Heaven knew why. But he couldn't give her another reason not to. He couldn't leave her and Ayla and Matthew. He was smarter than that. Smarter than his father. *Intelligent like Sophie.* Intelligent people controlled their emotions. They fought back, but wisely, not when they were outnumbered five to one in a crowded coach.

They were nearly to Annan. He remembered the afternoon he and Sophie had spent there, when she'd first used his given name, when she had stood up for him. What a remarkable woman he'd married. He would be the biggest fool to trade her love for an act of anger. He glanced at Newsome.

Even if it was justifiable. When this was all over, he'd take her to the Blue Bell Inn, and this time they'd stay for a cèilidh. *How long will it be until then?*

He was both dismayed and relieved by his growing distance from Sophie and the children.

Everything is well at home, he assured himself. Everything would be well.

Newsome kicked him. "What are you smiling about?"

"It's a beautiful day, and I am on my way to London." *I am winning. I am beating this. I am* not *my father.*

But damn if the viscount isn't a nuisance.

Four

SOPHIE PLACED THE cool cloth across Lucy's brow and tried to hide her concern at the lines of pain creasing Lucy's eyes and the tears rolling down her face. "You did so well."

Lucy moaned and gripped Sophie's hand hard enough that she feared it would be bruised. "I don't remember it hurtin' so bad after last time."

"I imagine that every birth is a little different." Sophie bit her lip, hoping that assumption was correct. Lucy's baby had indeed come quickly, slipping into this world and Sophie's hands almost as soon as they'd settled Lucy into the bed. But the blood, so much blood, she hadn't expected. And it still didn't seem wont to stop, even now, well after the delivery of the afterbirth. Sophie had returned to her room, intending to pack quickly and bid the children farewell, but Lucy hadn't been sitting up in bed with her new daughter in her arms. Instead she'd been curled on her side, groaning, while Ayla held her baby and looked on worriedly.

"Adam is here now, and Maime is downstairs caring for him. Everyone says she's the best healer for miles around." She was also the best midwife, and Sophie had sent Matthew with the urgent request that Maime come attend to Lucy as soon as possible. But in her absence . . . *I'll not let Lucy or her child die.* She glanced to the window seat, where Ayla held the bundled infant close.

Lucy groaned again and brought a hand to her stomach. "Why does it still hurt so?"

"I don't know," Sophie admitted, but she intended to find out—that and much more before her own time to deliver a child came. Thoughts of Torie and what her last minutes must have been like had been plaguing her all morning, even with all else going on. Had Jonathan been at Torie's side? Had her sister known she was dying? Had she lived to see the child she delivered? Sophie had heard that her sister and her child, a little girl, had been buried together. How must Jonathan have felt lowering that casket into the ground after closing the lid on his wife and daughter? *I should have been there.*

"Ethan?" Lucy asked between shallow breaths.

Sophie brushed at the tear trailing down her cheek. "Finella went to the cottage to get him. They'll be back soon." She believed that with all her heart. If Newsome had left her alone, surely he'd no cause to harm a child. Only Adam had been in his way, trying to sound a warning and dissuade the men from entering Caerlanwood.

Lucy nodded, her face no longer flushed, as it had been earlier when delivering her child, but pale now. Beyond offering words of comfort and bathing her sweat-soaked brow, Sophie felt helpless to alleviate her suffering. *And Graham's. What is he suffering now?* Had she made the right choice not going with him? What kind of wife was she to send her husband off into the care of a madman? Mad *men.* Her father and Newsome had no scruples. *And the man with the knife . . .* Sophie's hand went to her neck, her fingers brushing the blood caked there.

Graham was right in telling her to stay. She would have only been a liability to him. *But here*—she could and would do something. Just as soon as Lucy was safe and Ethan had been found.

And the man in the front hall removed and buried, and the blood and glass cleaned up, and the children comforted.

She had yet to explain to them why Graham was gone and that she must go too. As soon as possible. Today. This morning.

Ayla knew at least some of it as, unbeknownst to Sophie until afterward, she had watched from the stairs and then had the presence of mind to pour scalding water on the man—*father*—trying to come up them. Today's events had the potential to undo the months of progress Ayla had made, but Sophie couldn't think about that right now. She had to help Lucy first and then Graham. Then, together, they could help the children.

A gasp tore from Lucy's throat as more blood gushed onto the fresh linen Sophie had replaced.

"Why she not have her baby?" Maime demanded as she marched into the room, sleeves already rolled to the elbows and a colorful scarf waving in the air above her head with each step. She dropped a basket on the end of the bed and, before Ayla could rise, snatched the infant from her and handed the bundle to Lucy. "Put her to your breast. It'll hurt something fierce just about everywhere, but it help the bleedin' stop."

Sophie stepped back as Maime pulled the blanket away from the infant and a tiny arm and hand waved spastically. A lusty cry followed.

"That be good too," Maime pronounced as she gently turned the infant's head toward Lucy. "Fill her lungs with air and make your body ready to give milk."

A second, lustier cry, followed by a few of Lucy's own until, at last, the infant had latched on and Maime stepped back with a huff of air. "That better." She turned to Sophie. "Always put the child to the mama's breast first thing."

"I didn't know. I'm sorry," Sophie said, fearful she'd done irreparable harm.

"Now you do," Maime said matter-of-factly.

Sophie gulped back the fear rising in her throat as she watched Lucy struggle to feed her newborn daughter. How much time had passed since she'd been born? *How long was I downstairs? I should not have left her.* But she'd heard the gunshots and raised voices and hadn't been able to ignore the feeling that Graham was in trouble. He had been. *He still is.*

Sophie's gaze flitted to the blood-soaked sheets. Was Lucy in danger now too? *Is it too late?* Was this what had happened to Torie, since she'd had no physician to help with the birth? "Will Lucy be all right?"

"We see 'bout that." Maime busied herself at the opposite end of the bed. She placed a hand on Lucy's stomach and pressed down. Lucy cried out, and Maime frowned as another gush of blood seeped onto the bed.

Maime straightened and looked down on Lucy. "You listen to me. Your man downstairs hanging on after I dig a lead ball outta his back. I tell him to be strong for you. Now you be strong for him. We gonna pack your womb, and it ain't gonna feel good. But if we don't do it, this child won't have no mama."

Lucy nodded. "Adam is all right?"

"He will be," Maime declared. "You will be too. Just hold that child and look at her sweet face and think how you wanna be here for her."

Lucy nodded again and reached for Sophie's hand.

"I'm right here," Sophie murmured. "I won't leave you."

For the next half hour she watched and listened carefully, following Maime's every action and instruction.

Lucy's face went even more white after Maime began working on her, and a time or two Sophie had to close her eyes as she battled the queasiness rising within her. But she stayed by Lucy's side, alternately trying to comfort and soothe Lucy and fetch whatever Maime needed and help her as requested.

When they were done, Lucy's pale face was streaked with tears, but her bleeding had slowed considerably.

"Keep that child at your breast," Maime ordered. "She gonna help your womb contract."

Lucy nodded, then turned to Sophie. "You need to go," she whispered, her voice hoarse from her earlier screaming to get their attention.

"I do," Sophie said, resisting the urge to run from the room this very second. "But not yet. Not until you have Ethan safely returned to you." She met her dear friend's gaze. "You risked everything to alert us this morning. I can stay a little longer."

"The world needs more Sophies," Lucy said, her eyes filling.

"And more Grahams," Sophie added. *The things we could do together.*

"Amen to that," Maime added as she helped Sophie gather the soiled sheets. "That man be a good one. You go to London and bring him back here."

"I intend to," Sophie said. She would go to London and stay with William and Elizabeth. He would help her find a good lawyer to represent Graham. He would be proven innocent.

And if he's not?

She banished the thought. *He will be. He is innocent.* Truth and the right would prevail. They had to.

SOPHIE SHOVED FILE after file into the valise until every scrap of paper had been collected from Graham's desk. She had records from the plantation as well as Caerlanwood and Graham's estates in England. She had receipts and ledgers; she had letters, the largest stack found in the back of the bottom drawer of his desk—bundled together and with a note on top that simply said, "Katherine."

Sophie had no idea what she might discover in all of those pages, but it seemed prudent to take them. If a lawyer was to build a case in Graham's defense he needed proof of innocence. *Something* important had to be here. She would begin reading them on the journey to London. And if nothing was to be found, she would visit his other estates and search there.

Valise in hand, she exited the room. Boyce stood just outside, waiting for Sophie as he had all day, acting as her personal guard in Graham's absence. She found the gesture touching, and the sight of him again filled her eyes with tears. She blinked them quickly away. Having held them at bay throughout the long night and morning, she'd no time to give in to such now. Every minute here was another away from Graham, with him miles ahead already.

Griggs appeared in the hall. "The carriage is ready, Your Grace."

She winced at the formality but supposed she had best become used to it, if she was to be in London for any length of time. "Thank you, Griggs." Sophie held the bag out to him. "Will you see that this is placed on the seat inside, please?"

He took it from her with a nod.

"If you'll give me but a moment, I must say goodbye to Lucy and the children."

"The children?" His brow furrowed.

"Yes." Sophie turned away. "I already told them that I am going, but I promised to say goodbye before I left." She hurried upstairs and into the bedroom that had held so many happy memories until today.

Lucy sat up partway in bed, her tiny daughter held in her arms. Ethan played with Matthew's blocks on the floor. Beside Lucy, Adam lay on his stomach, sleeping fitfully. Maime slept too, snoring lightly from a chair at his side. Getting him upstairs had taken a concerted effort, but they had deemed it worthwhile for the family to be together and Maime able to attend to both without traipsing up and down the dangerous staircase.

"He be all right," she had assured both Lucy and Sophie. "My poultice draw out the infection."

Even if she hadn't been assured of Adam's recovery, Sophie could delay no longer. Every minute she thought of Graham, worried for him, feared for his life. But seeing Lucy and Adam together, with Ethan and their baby girl, seemed a good portent of things to come. Sophie fought to hold back a strange combination of fearful and joyous tears.

"She's so beautiful." She dropped into the chair beside Lucy and looked closer at the tiny face with the even tinier fist bunched up beside it. "She's such a miracle."

Lucy reached out and grasped her hand. Sophie winced.

"I'm sorry!" Lucy withdrew her hand, but Sophie reclaimed it.

"It is fine, and I shall endeavor not to repay the favor too dearly when you help me through this greatest of travails next spring."

Lucy's eyes widened. "You are with child?"

Sophie nodded. "And so I must leave now to collect his father. Like you," she glanced at Adam's still form, "I've no wish to have my child grow up without one."

Lucy nodded, tears glistening in her own eyes. "Thank you for staying with me. Godspeed."

Sophie squeezed her hand lightly, then stood. "Write to me at William and Elizabeth's home. Finella will know how to get a letter there."

"I will," Lucy promised as she looked down at her baby. "I'll tell you all about Sophie Grace and how she is faring."

Sophie brought a hand to her mouth. "That's a lovely name."

"After a lovely person." Lucy smiled at her.

"Thank you." Blinking rapidly, Sophie left the room and crossed the hall to see the children, but they were not upstairs.

Frustrated at every minute of delay, she ran carefully down the steps, calling for them. She didn't have time to waste. It was past noon already. She intended to make it as far as she could today, but if she didn't leave soon, she would be fortunate to spend the night in Annan.

"Try out front," Boyce said, trailing behind her. "I believe you will find them there."

"Thank you." Sophie pivoted and headed for the front doors, noting the bare and freshly scrubbed floor. The stablemen had wrapped the body in the partially burned rug and taken it away, and the maids had cleaned the room until it practically shone. The windows—those that weren't broken—had all been opened to let in plenty of fresh air and to clear the scent of death.

Outside the children were nowhere to be found, but voices coming from the carriage drew her closer. The footman came to assist her as she put one foot on the step and peered inside.

Ayla and Matthew sat there, dressed in their finest clothing, Ayla clutching her doll, and looking at her expectantly.

Sophie placed a hand over her heart that felt like it might break yet again. "You can't come," she said gently as she climbed inside and sat across from them. "It is going to be a very long journey, and when I get to London I won't even be with Graham. I don't know how long it will be before court or—"

"He saved me," Ayla said, in a quiet, clear voice. "Saved us." She gestured at Matthew.

The tears that had been threatening all morning spilled over. Sophie covered her mouth then reached out, pulling Ayla into a hug. Instead of stiffening in her arms, Ayla returned the hug with a fierceness equal to Matthew's on the first day they'd met. After a moment they pulled back to look at one another, but there were no smiles between them, in spite of the joyous moment.

"He saved me," Ayla repeated. "Now I'll help him."

"There's nothing you can—" Sophie broke off. There *was* something Ayla could do. She could testify about the men who were whipping her and the way Graham had stepped in to stop them.

"I come too," Matthew added.

Sophie sat back on the seat and considered them both. Matthew was definitely too young to be allowed into a courtroom. She wasn't even certain Ayla would be permitted. And if she was, would the court even consider the testimony of a female child of African descent? If they did, it could be brutal for Ayla. *I shouldn't allow them to come.*

"I *will* help him," Ayla repeated, a fiercely determined look in her eyes that Sophie recognized all too well.

"We *all* will," she said, hugging both children and praying that she was right. She glanced at the valise on the seat beside her, realizing she wouldn't be doing a lot of reading on the journey now—not of documents, at least. But she'd packed something else too, more as a measure of comfort than anything else. Sophie reached for the bag, opened it, and pulled out the familiar volume.

"Since we have a long journey ahead of us, who wants to hear *The Swiss Family Robinson* again?"

Five

London, England

LILIAN CLAYBOURNE LEANED forward in her chair and clasped her youngest daughter's hand, relishing this small touch and seeing Olivia before her, safe and well. "Sophie is in London."

"At last!" Livie jumped up, her mother's hand apparently forgotten as it fell away. "Just in time, too. We leave in one month."

"Perhaps not." Lilian pressed her lips together.

"What do you mean?" Eyes narrowing, Olivia dropped into her chair again. "Do not ask me to postpone going to America, Mother. I'll go mad if I have to remain shut up, away from everything and everyone any longer, and I've told you why I *must* go to Jonathan. I gave Torie my word."

"I know, dear." Lilian held in a sigh. Worry over Olivia's devotion to and growing affection for her former brother-in-law was often near the top of her list of concerns, right below keeping Olivia hidden and safe from her father. But today that paled in comparison to their current troubles. Lilian would have taken her daughter's hands again, but Olivia held them tucked in tight at her sides.

"Sophie may need us. Her husband—"

"She *is* married then?" Olivia's nose scrunched as if she

could not quite believe this piece of news. "To whom? The duke?"

Lilian nodded. "And according to Lady Fitzgerald, Sophie loves him *very* much."

"Sophie—in love?" Olivia shook her head. "I should like to see that. You haven't spoken with her?"

"Not yet," Lilian said, privately agreeing with Olivia. Seeing Sophie—bookish, headstrong, independent Sophie—in love was something she was most eager to witness. "With your father in town, it isn't wise to visit her. I was only able to come to see you today because the dowager sent an invitation to the house inviting me to luncheon with her and several other ladies. I made certain to leave the invitation out where your father would see it."

"I wish he would leave for good," Olivia muttered.

Lilian felt the same, though she held her tongue. Once, long ago, she had believed she might come to love her husband. But that hope had faded with the years; it had completely disappeared when he had set out to ruin their oldest daughter's marriage, the result of which had cost Victoria her life. Lilian couldn't forgive him for that. Nor could she forgive herself for not stopping him. But she *could* stop him from hurting their two remaining daughters. And so she had. She was.

Until now. If Sophie really did love her husband, and he was taken from her as Victoria had been taken early from Jonathan . . . It didn't bear thinking of, yet Lilian had to consider that possibility. And do all in her power to see that things were put to rights.

"The duke has been arrested for murder. He is being held in Newgate. It was a plot orchestrated by Viscount Newsome and your father. That I did not learn of it beforehand suggests that they may suspect me of aiding Sophie and even, perhaps, of hiding you."

"But the duke *has* killed someone, has he not?" Olivia's eyes grew troubled. "If convicted he will hang, and Sophie will be a widow."

Lilian nodded. "If what Lady Fitzgerald has said is true, Sophie will be heartbroken as well."

"Sophie has always been a good judge of character. She wouldn't love someone who is a bad person," Olivia said as if attempting to convince herself.

"I do not believe the duke is deserving of his reputation. Were that the case, I would not have asked him to help Sophie last spring. But I did ask, and he came to my aide. Were it not for him, she would have been forced to wed the viscount. Now it is the duke who is in need of help—and Sophie as well, if she truly cares for him—and I feel I must do what I can. It is entirely possible that it will take longer than the time we have before we are to leave."

Olivia leaned forward, her face in her hands. "I want to scream."

"Unwise," Lilian said gently. "There really is a luncheon going on downstairs, and the ladies would all wonder at the goings-on upstairs."

"I said I *want* to, not that I would." Olivia sat up and heaved a dramatic sigh. "Promise me that when we have done all we can—when we have helped Sophie and her duke—that you will do just as much to help me find Jonathan in America?"

"I promise," Lilian said readily, though she wasn't convinced that was the best idea at all.

Elizabeth rose from her chair near the fire as Sophie entered the room. Her expression fell upon seeing Sophie's. "No better luck today?"

"No." Sophie sank onto the sofa, the despair she fought

daily threatening to overwhelm her. "Two wouldn't even see me. The one who did explained that there was no reason for him—or any other lawyer in London—to take on Graham's case."

"Because Newsome has threatened them all," Elizabeth said, her eyes flashing with anger.

"It's not just that," Sophie said. "Everyone knows there is a witness who claims to have seen Graham kill the Higgins brothers. That, coupled with his poor reputation—thanks to his father—makes the outcome seem a foregone conclusion."

"No lawyer wants to fight a battle that's already lost." William came into the room, stopping to greet Elizabeth with a kiss on the cheek.

Sophie turned away, the sorrow she felt almost too much to bear. What she wouldn't give to share a tender moment like that with Graham again. Three weeks she'd been here and had not been permitted to see him. Three weeks of seeking out nearly every lawyer in London, trying to find one to represent him—without any success. She'd started with the best, according to William's recommendations. As each rejected her plea, she had worked her way farther down the list, certain that someone would be willing to take the case. But that someone had not made himself known yet, and she was running out of time. The trial was set for two weeks from today. The Old Bailey court met on a strict schedule, and this was the last session of the year, so there was no hope of postponing the date.

If she didn't find a lawyer to represent Graham . . . she wouldn't let herself think of the alternative. She simply had to find someone who would help him, help *them*. More than one life was being affected by his incarceration.

Matthew had become almost as silent as Ayla in the weeks they'd been here, his temperament affected by both Graham's absence from his life and Sophie's neglect. But that couldn't be helped; every minute she had been focused on freeing Graham. When she wasn't meeting with lawyers, she spent her time poring over the documents and letters she'd brought with her from Caerlanwood. Those seemed more important than ever, as whatever counsel she did find to represent him would now have little time to prepare his defense. The timeline she had pieced together and the supporting paperwork would be needed.

"Sophie, I saw your mother today."

Elizabeth's words pulled Sophie from her list of troubles and back to the present. A painful throb—equal parts guilt, sorrow, and anxiety—struck her already beleaguered heart.

"Only this week did she learn of your presence in London. It seems that when your father is in town, she stays at home much of the time, in the solitude of her room playing the part of a grieving mother who has lost all three of her daughters. Only when he is away does she dare venture out—and then only with utmost care and discretion. He is in town now, so she is unable to come to see you."

How much was acting, and how much was true grief? Had Mother truly lost Olivia too? Or had she orchestrated her disappearance as well? Perhaps her sister had gone off to parts unknown with some other duke. "And Olivia? Have you any news of her?"

Elizabeth shook her head. "Your mother did not mention your sister, but in our brief time together, she plied me with all sorts of questions about you, inquiring about your well-being, happiness, and the state of your marriage. She seemed most concerned and asked me to relay her affection. She intends to visit you as soon as she is able. I heard from another source—our maid Matilde, who is acquainted with some of the servants in your parents' home—that there was quite a row between her and your father when she learned you are here and that he had known and had not told her."

William stepped away from Elizabeth and came to sit beside Sophie. "I do have some good news. I've finally secured permission for you to visit Graham."

"Today? Can we go right now?" Sophie stood, wringing her hands.

"Tomorrow morning," William said. "It won't be a very long visit—a quarter hour—but I accepted on your behalf."

"Thank you, William." She sat once more, her mind spinning. She desperately wanted to see Graham. But she also feared it, as she had no good news for him, nothing encouraging to share.

"It is good that we have until tomorrow morning," Elizabeth said. "That gives us time to put a basket together for him. You can bring him food, blankets, and warm clothing."

"You're right." Sophie stood again, already mentally composing a list. "I can finally give him Maime's ointment for his wound, gloves for his hands, thick socks—" She would bring him as much as she could. No weapons, of course. She'd only attempted that when he had been taken, wanting him to have something for self-defense if her father or Newsome had decided to take justice into their own hands—even more than they had already. William had since reported that her knife had been turned over to the doctor who'd treated Graham's wound. Graham had known of it and had not used it. Insignificant to some, perhaps. But Sophie understood the importance. He was not his father and was coming to understand that himself. She was so proud of him and desperate to see him and hold him in her arms and be held in return.

"Whatever items you intend to bring to him, you might wish to consider bringing two or more of each," William suggested.

"Why?" Elizabeth asked.

"Because Graham will give them away to those worse off than himself," Sophie and William answered together.

This elicited the first genuine smile she'd felt for some time. *Graham is a good man.* Somehow, some way, they would find a way to prove that to London and to the world.

Six

SOPHIE BROUGHT A gloved hand to her face, covering her mouth and nose against the foul stench of Newgate as she followed the guard through the dim stone hallways, past numerous cells holding those in as dire predicaments as Graham. How many others were also innocent?

A rat scurried past, and her stomach roiled, but she pressed the basket she carried to her middle and continued walking without so much as an outward flinch. *I will not be sick. I will not be sick.* She would not waste the precious minutes she'd been granted with her husband. Their child growing within her would simply have to be calm this morning, contrary to most recent mornings when he or she had rendered her useless for much beyond an intimate acquaintance with a chamber pot.

She'd hardly eaten anything at dinner last night and nibbled only a dry biscuit before coming here, hoping to stave off her usual nausea. William had planned to accompany her—a comfort if she did succumb to the morning sickness—but at the last minute had not been granted access. This left them both uneasy, but she could not delay and chance missing the opportunity to see Graham. She could do this on her own. She had to.

"Right 'ere." The guard stopped in front of one of the many

doors, inserted the key, and pushed it open. The iron hinges squealed in protest.

It was even darker inside the cell, but Sophie entered, eyes straining to see. "Graham?"

A groan sounded from the far side, and she moved toward it. Behind her the door shut with a clang, and the key turned in the lock. *What if this is a trick? What if—*

"Sophie?"

Her heart leapt at the sound of his voice. She dropped the basket and hurried forward and into his arms the next second.

"You shouldn't be here. You shouldn't touch me." He tried holding her away, but she clung tighter, his thinner frame and sour scent unfamiliar. Yet it was he. Beneath the beard and soiled clothing, it was her Graham.

At last she stepped back, her eyes adjusted now, and had a long look at him. His clothing was tattered and dirty, and he favored the wounded shoulder. He was scruffy and unkempt— the antithesis of his usual grooming habits. Even when working at Caerlanwood, outdoors or on a repair inside, he'd always managed to look neat and fashionable, as one owed the greatest respect. He'd always had the air of a duke, whether or not he wished it.

But now . . . She studied his eyes, and though they were haunted, she caught the same spark of determination she'd seen in them the first night they'd met and every day thereafter. Graham was strong and sure and solid. Even here, in this most wretched of places.

"I'm not certain I like your new style," she teased, fingering the filthy sleeve of his shirt. "If you've a mind to change it, I brought you some other clothes."

"Yes, please." A weak smile broke out across his face, and then he was pulling her close again. "How I've missed you."

Sophie's eyes blurred. "And I you. How did we ever live without each other before we met?"

"I have no idea." His voice sounded as choked as hers.

Reluctantly Sophie stepped back from his embrace and pulled herself together. As much as she wanted to simply stay in his arms, she couldn't. They had much to discuss. "We haven't a lot of time. Let me show you what I've brought."

Graham released her, and she busied herself unpacking the basket. "How is your shoulder?"

"The prison doctor dug the ball out, but it hasn't healed well." He attempted to roll his shoulders forward, then winced and stopped halfway through the movement.

She pulled out a jar of ointment. "Maime sent this with me when I left Caerlanwood and said that applying it will help."

"Wonderful," he said sincerely.

Sophie helped him strip off the shirt, letting it fall to the floor. She poured some of the fresh water she had brought onto a cloth and sponged off his torso, arms, and shoulders. When she came to the angry wound—poorly stitched, from her estimate—she took extra care cleaning it, then applied the thick paste and a clean bandage. "I'll leave this jar with you if they'll allow it. Use it until it's gone."

She helped Graham into the clean shirt she'd brought, then added a wool jacket over the top, fastening each of the buttons all the way up to his neck. November in London was cool, but the damp cold down here was even worse.

"You'd think I was a little child," he muttered but sounded grateful for her fussing.

"You've had plenty of experience with *my* buttons. I figured it was time you had a turn."

"This doesn't count." His eyes sought hers, and the renewed spark in them filled her with hope.

"No," she agreed, her voice as low and sultry as if they were at home in their bedroom. "It does not. I shall remember that there is a debt owed when we are alone again and endeavor to fulfill it by *un*buttoning your every article of clothing."

"I live for that moment and dream of it every night." Graham held her against him again.

Sophie closed her eyes and savored the cadence of his heartbeat. *He is alive. He is still himself.*

A single knock sounded on the door. "Five minutes," the guard called.

Sophie cursed. Graham chuckled and raised his brow. "What is this new habit you've developed in my absence? I hope you choose better words around the children." He frowned suddenly. "Why are you *here*? Didn't I tell you to stay at Caerlanwood?"

"Were I imprisoned in London, would *you* stay at home?" Sophie patted the front of his jacket and gave him a knowing smile.

"That's different," Graham said.

"Because I'm a woman?" She picked up the basket again and began pulling things out of it.

"Yes." Graham's frown deepened.

"And here I thought we'd made more progress." Sophie shook her head in mock distress.

"It's my responsibility to protect you," Graham insisted. "I can't do that right now. I can't do that here. But at least if you're at Caerlanwood, I know you're far from London and Newsome and your father. I know you're with the children and can imagine you all there, safe and well. What must they think with both of us having left them so abruptly?"

"It was rather abrupt," Sophie agreed. "We left mere hours after you, as soon as Lucy was safely delivered of her baby and Maime had tended Adam's wound." She handed Graham another jar. "Drink this broth. When you've finished, I have a loaf of fresh bread and some cheese for you."

"I am glad to know all is well with Lucy and Adam, but what of *our* bairn?" He whispered the last as if afraid someone might overhear. There was a new fear and intensity in his eyes when he looked at her.

"All is well," Sophie assured him, placing a hand over her flat stomach. "I intended to tell you the day you were taken. I was going to write our news in the sand at the beach, then convince you to come walk with me where you might see it."

A corner of his mouth lifted in a wistful smile. "That would have been nice." His mouth turned down again. "Who is caring for Ayla and Matthew in our absence?"

Sophie lifted the jar to his mouth. "Drink and listen. They may not allow me to leave these things, and you need the nourishment."

Still frowning, Graham brought the jar to his lips. She nodded approvingly.

"Ayla and Matthew came with me. Had I left them behind, I fear they might have attempted the journey on their own—or Ayla would have, at least. She intends to testify on your behalf."

Graham choked and leaned forward with a coughing fit. "She *what?*"

"She is *speaking.*" Sophie clasped his arms and leaned closer, trying to impart the joy of this exquisite miracle. "After you were taken she came to me and told me that you had saved her and that she wanted to help you. Her voice is the sweetest, Graham. She is such a strong girl. I couldn't leave her behind, and if she came Matthew had to, as well. We have all been staying with William and Elizabeth, and we are quite safe. He has retained a considerable number of additional servants for the sole purpose of protection, given the incident with Elizabeth when Newsome threatened her."

"She is well?" Graham's brow creased with concern.

"Yes." Sophie nodded, eager to reassure him and assuage his fears that extended to so many he felt responsible for. "Elizabeth was forced into a different carriage as she was leaving Lady Somerset's home after tea. William received a ransom note, stating that he must provide directions to your current location. If he failed to provide such or gave false information, she would not be returned to him."

"I am grateful he complied," Graham said, his expression haggard instead of relieved.

"Elizabeth was returned unharmed, after spending the better part of the day sitting alone in a carriage as it drove around the city. She never saw who her captors were, other than the footmen who forced her into the vehicle. William sent a letter warning us, but it did not arrive in time. He has been here every day, asking to see you and trying to gain permission for me to visit. He is a true friend and deeply regrets his part in this."

"It isn't his fault. Were I faced with the same . . ." Graham pulled Sophie close again. "I would do anything to see you safe."

As I will do anything for you. She didn't speak the words out loud. He wouldn't like them but would insist he wanted her far away instead, where her father and Newsome could not get her. But she was being careful. William waited outside for her, and she never traveled anywhere without one or more of his men escorting her. She never traveled anywhere without a weapon now either.

Graham released her, then gulped down the rest of the broth and handed her the empty jar. "It is wonderful that Ayla is talking, but you cannot allow her into that courtroom. They will destroy her."

Sophie took his hands and looked up at him, imploring. "We have no choice. Newsome's witness is going to testify. Ayla is our only hope for rebuttal. Who knows what lies this other man will tell? But Ayla's voice will be the innocent truth of a child's. It is your best hope."

Graham shook his head. "I'll not destroy her to save myself. Do not bring her into that courtroom, Sophie. If you do, I will stand up and demand that she be removed. She cannot face that roomful of cruel, biased men, many of whom champion the practice of slavery."

"But—"

"*No.* Think of her beauty and how that might attract Newsome or any others like him that are there. It would not matter to them that she is a child. We must keep her hidden from men like that at all costs."

"Time," the guard called. The key jingled in the lock.

Tears of fury and sorrow filled Sophie's eyes. How could they have argued during the precious minutes they had? She pushed the loaf of bread and the cheese into Graham's hands, then laid the quilts across his shoulders. "There are stockings and gloves folded within those."

The door hinges squealed again.

"Thank you," he said stiffly. "Promise me, Sophie. Promise me Ayla will not come to the court."

She looked up into his eyes, and the worry and fear she saw there undid her. "I promise." She threw her arms around him and kissed him. "I love you."

Graham leaned forward so their foreheads touched. "And I you, Sophie. I love you so very much. Please stay safe."

The guard pulled on her arm. Sophie shrugged him off and shot him a look filled with disdain. She picked up the empty basket and stepped away from Graham and toward the open door, then paused to look back at him. "If I don't see you again before then, I'll see you in court. Ayla won't be there, but *I* will."

Seven

Sophie looked up from the papers spread in front of her as William entered the library of his London townhome. "What is this tale Elizabeth has just shared with me?"

"It is no tale, but truth. Since no one will agree to represent Graham, I am going to speak on his behalf."

"They'll never allow it," William said. "If that were the case, if anyone could represent his defense, I would."

"I know you would." Sophie gave him an appreciative smile. "That means a great deal, especially considering all you and Elizabeth have suffered already because of Graham and me."

"Newsome caught me off guard last time," William said. "It won't happen again."

"If you were to try and represent Graham, my father and Newsome would retaliate," Sophie predicted. "They don't like to lose—look at the lengths they have gone to getting even with Graham."

"It's about more than getting even," William said. "They're concerned about the future of slavery. Graham is a threat to that, to their very livelihood. His stealing you away was only part of the equation."

"Regardless, you are unable to be his counsel, which leaves only myself to possibly help him. Hear me out, please, before you insist I cannot do this."

"Very well." William held his hands out, as if in surrender.

"Women in court are uncommon but not unheard of. *Seventy-six* women have acted as prosecutrices this year alone. I read of each one in the Old Bailey records."

"Accusing someone of a crime and testifying in that regard is not the same as acting as a lawyer presenting a defense case."

"I realize that," Sophie said, trying not to feel insulted by William's comment. "I plan to make a complaint, on behalf of my husband—also rare, but not unheard of—against the Higgins brothers who wrongfully took over Katherine's plantation after her death. I have both her will, showing her conditions that Graham was to inherit the plantation and that slavery never be permitted there again. I also have the deed, given to Graham by the attorney who shared Katherine's will with him."

"Go on," William said, sounding more curious than doubtful.

Encouraged by his change in demeanor, Sophie continued. "I'll present these documents to the court, along with a few others—letters from his sister, stating that Ayla is her first husband's child, and another, after that husband's death, telling Graham that she fired Higgins and he was never to set foot on her property again. I also have the letter from the solicitor to Graham, notifying him of Katherine's death and that he had been named guardian of her children. I have the receipt for the ticket he purchased to Saint Kitts and the date he sailed. All of this leads us up to the date of his supposed crimes, which I will relate to the court as they actually happened that day, with Graham acting well within his rights to protect Ayla, as he had been charged.

"His claim against the Higgins brothers is that they both trespassed on his property and abused those living there, over whom they had no jurisdiction, and that they attacked him when he asserted his legal rights on the property. I have documented everything possible." Sophie pointed to a trail of papers lining the table. "This is my timeline with each of the facts I must present and a letter or affidavit to back them up."

William took several minutes to study the work she had done before commenting again. "This is all very thorough, but without a witness to state firsthand what actually took place the day the Higgins brothers died, to refute the prosecution witness . . ." He shrugged. "I don't know that this will be enough. And even if you have changed your mind about allowing Ayla to testify, it is not likely the court will allow it."

"I have not changed my mind." After her visit with Graham last week she had shared with William the promise she'd made regarding Ayla. He had agreed with Sophie that without Ayla's testimony, it would be a very short trial with an almost assured outcome, not in Graham's favor.

William had urged her to prepare Ayla to testify, while he continued the search for a lawyer to take Graham's case.

"I gave Graham my word. I cannot go back on that."

"Even if it means his life instead?" William had asked.

"It won't," Sophie had insisted, though at the time she'd had no idea what she was going to do to save him.

It had come to her that night, as she was reading through Katherine's letters once again. The mention of a familiar name had sent Sophie running to Ayla's room and waking her, though the hour was late.

Ayla's answer to her question had proved that there was another witness who could be summoned—a vast relief to them both. Sophie had penned a letter that very night and sent it on its way with the sunrise.

"We have a different witness," Sophie said, smiling up at William as he leaned over the table. "She arrived today."

"She?" He glanced around the room, as if expecting to see said witness.

"Is upstairs resting," Sophie said. "She made the journey in record time, on horseback part of the way—at her age, can you imagine? The bridge near Caerlanwood is washed out again."

William straightened, then crossed his arms and leaned against the desk. "Tell me."

"Maime," Sophie said, speaking the name almost reverently. "She worked for Katherine, and it was she who opened the door the day Graham came to Saint Kitts to collect Ayla and Matthew. It was she who alerted him to what was happening to Ayla. Maime followed him to the yard and saw the whole thing. She remembers everything in detail, and she's willing to face that court of men and tell them."

William stepped away from the table and took a turn about the room, massaging his temples as he walked, as if his head pained him. "It still remains to be seen if they will allow you to make this complaint and then if they will accept the testimony of a female, former slave. It is possibly better than a female, former slave *child*, but it also may be that Ayla would have drawn more sympathy. Or perhaps they would reject both. But," he drew in a breath, "it is possible this just might work. It may be our best hope."

"It is our only hope," Sophie said. "We are out of time. Graham's trial is in two days."

William pulled out a chair and sat across the table from her. "Let's get to work, then."

Eight

SOPHIE'S HEART STUTTERED as she watched Graham enter the courtroom flanked by a guard on either side, as if he were a dangerous criminal. So much depended on the next hour, on her ability to make the complaint on his behalf, and on the judge and jury's willingness to listen to Maime's testimony.

Graham looked better than when she had last seen him at Newgate, though he was still too thin. William had arranged for him to shave and had brought him a fresh suit of clothes, which hung loosely on him.

Sophie forced her gaze to the front of the courtroom and rose with the others as the judge entered. She was alone on the front bench, the place usually reserved for the defendant's counsel, when there was such.

In strategizing with William, her position up front had seemed the best way for her to gain the judge's attention, though it was not without risks. It was entirely possible he might throw her out altogether. It seemed he wished to now as he peered down at her from the bench.

"Who are you?"

Sophie forced herself to speak calmly, though she wanted to rush her explanation before anyone could stop her. "Your Honor, I am here to issue a complaint on behalf of my husband, His Grace the Duke of Warwick."

Murmurs of disapproval issued from the jury box as the judge peered over the bench at her, his forehead creased in a stern expression. "Your husband is currently on trial in the present case, is he not? This is not the time for him to be making complaints against anyone."

Sophie lifted her chin and looked directly at the judge. "Your Honor, this complaint is against the deceased, Oliver and Stewart Higgins, and it has a great deal to do with the matter at hand."

"Given that they are already dead, I do not see much point to any complaint. It is apparent that if there were grievances between your husband and the Misters Higgins, your husband has already taken action."

Sophie pressed her lips together in a thin line, barely able to restrain herself from decrying this unjust comment. What little hope she'd had for a fair trial fled. Perhaps Graham was right in his assessment of England's judicial system and its inability or unwillingness to discover truth and support justice.

Sophie silenced her panicked thoughts and worked to compose herself. "That has yet to be proved, Your Honor. All I am requesting is the opportunity to present, on my husband's behalf, a complaint of wrongs done to him and others by the deceased. Given that my husband is on trial for murder, this is possibly the only opportunity I shall have to present these complaints, and I assure you that the information I have is most pertinent in today's proceedings."

More murmurs erupted among the jurors until a scowl from the judge silenced all. He glanced toward the back of the courtroom, then to Sophie once more.

"Is your husband incapable of making this complaint on his own? He is already here, and it seems he could speak for himself." The judge looked over at Graham, as if expecting him to answer.

Sophie sent him a pleading glance and gave a slight shake of her head before addressing the judge again. "My husband was taken from our home very abruptly, and he did not have time to gather the necessary documents. Additionally, the past weeks of his imprisonment he has been recovering from a gunshot wound and suffering malnutrition while living in deplorable conditions. He is not in a position or of a mind to present this claim at present."

Snickers from the jury box and throughout the courtroom followed her declaration. She dared not look in Graham's direction but bit her lip, concerned she had made things worse for him.

"Let us hope he is at least of a mind to stand trial," the judge said with a roll of his eyes.

"I would like my wife to speak on my behalf," Graham said, his voice clear and strong.

Tears stung the back of Sophie's eyes as she looked at him again and gave him a wobbly smile. The one he returned was confident, and it bolstered her courage.

I can do this. I have to—for him.

The judge's attention focused on the back of the room once more, his lips pursed and fingers tapping together. "Very well," he said at last. "You may make your *brief* complaint after the prosecution has finished."

"Thank you, Your Honor." Sophie sank into her chair slowly, though she felt like collapsing. *The hardest part is done. They have agreed to listen to me.* Sharing what she had prepared would be easy in comparison.

The prosecutor stood and began his explanation of the charges, followed by an incorrect summary of what had happened the day the Higgins brothers died. He concluded by calling a Roland Higgins, cousin to the deceased, to the stand.

The man walked with a swagger, and Sophie longed to slap the smirk from his face.

"Tell us what you witnessed on the eleventh of April, 1829," the prosecutor said once the man was comfortable in the witness seat.

"That man there," the witness pointed a stubby finger at Graham, "shot both of my cousins. And for sport he struck an axe through Stewart's head."

Sophie clenched her teeth to keep from shouting that he was lying. She'd heard the recounting of that day, first from Ayla and just this week from Maime, and their identical reports vastly differed from this.

"Do you know why the defendant shot your cousins?" the prosecutor asked.

Roland Higgins shrugged. "He didn't care for the way things were being run on the plantation. But with his sister dead and him overseas, someone had to step in and keep the place going. The way I see it, he was in Oliver's debt for helping out."

Helping? Sophie sat on her hands to keep from jumping up and wringing the man's neck. Instead she looked down at her notes and tried to steady her breathing. Becoming angry would not help Graham's cause. She had to be calm, precise, focused.

At last the odious man was dismissed and the prosecutor concluded his case against Graham. The judge turned his attention briefly to Sophie as she stood, his words again attempting to dismiss her. "It would seem that whatever grievances your husband had with the Misters Higgins are irrelevant now, and as this court values time—"

"With all due respect Your Honor, his complaint has *much* to do with the matter at hand and his own innocence." Sophie imagined William's wince at her word choice. *They must not think that I am defending Graham.* She hurried to amend her mistake. "We have proof that Oliver and Stewart

Higgins trespassed my husband's property and made use of it for a period of nearly four months, when their presence was expressly forbidden. I have written proof—" she snagged a paper from the documents she had brought, "from my husband's sister and former owner of his plantation, that Oliver Higgins had been dismissed from service there over a year prior and was never to set foot on the property again. In addition, the Higgins brothers violated the law with regard to specific legalities associated with my husband's plantation, as set forth in his sister's last will and testament." *Bless you, Katherine, for being so thorough.*

Sophie held up the will, and held her breath as she met the judge's gaze. She'd purposely not mentioned what legalities had been violated. William had advised her to avoid the topic of slavery as much as possible, as it was likely that the jurors themselves were slave owners.

The judge's attention was again fixed behind her. Sophie longed to turn and look herself, to see what—or who—held his attention, but she guessed easily enough. *Newsome? Or my father?* If the viscount had frightened nearly every lawyer in London there was little doubt he held the judge in his pocket as well. *And the jury?*

The judge cleared his throat. "The court will allow you ten minutes."

"Thank you, Your Honor," Sophie said humbly, though she seethed at the time limit when the prosecution had been allowed as much as it desired. "On the twentieth of February, 1829, my husband sailed from London." Though Graham had not been her husband at the time, William had emphasized the importance of reminding the court frequently that she was making a complaint on her husband's behalf—*not* acting as a lawyer might for his defense.

"He sailed just nine days after learning of his sister's death and becoming guardian of her two children. He arrived in Saint Kitts on the eleventh of April, 1829, and, immediately upon disembarking, traveled to what was now *his* plantation. I have the deed here, given to my husband by the lawyer his sister Katherine had retained prior to her death. If it would please the court, may I present it?" She lifted the paper from the desk in front of her, but the judge waved it off.

Undaunted, she continued, "According to the instructions left by my husband's sister in her will—" Sophie held up the document but did not even bother to ask when the judge shook his head, "my husband expected the plantation to be operating under the leadership of those Katherine had left in charge. But upon his arrival, he discovered very different circumstances. If it would please the court, my husband has a witness to these circumstances."

"It would please the court to be done with this and get on with the verdict and sentencing," a familiar voice called from the gallery.

Newsome. Sophie worked to keep her composure. *If they won't allow the witness . . .* "Your Honor, my husband's complaint relates *directly* to the matter he is on trial for."

"Bring the witness forward," the judge barked.

Thank you. Sophie pressed her fingertips into the desk to keep from clasping her hands in joy—or prayer.

A collective gasp rippled through the room as Maime shuffled in. She took the stand, stated her name, and spoke the oath.

Sophie sent her a grateful smile. "Maime, will you please tell the court the events of the eleventh of April, 1829, as you witnessed them."

"I will." She launched into her story, relating how Oliver and Stewart Higgins had been part of the mob that had killed Graham's sister and had then enslaved those employed on her plantation once more. "On the morning of the eleventh, Oliver was whipping Ayla, the former white master's own flesh and blood, for taking a cup of milk for her little brother." Maime related that Graham had asked Oliver to stop and had then restrained him when he would not. Higgins had used his free hand to draw his gun, but Graham was faster. "Oliver Higgins died while attempting to shoot His Grace."

"He run over to Ayla and cut her down then set her on the ground and ask if she all right," Maime continued. "Then Master Higgins's brother come at him from behind. He swingin' a shovel, and it woulda killed His Grace, but he turn at the last second and the shovel just slice his cheek. He still got the scar." Maime pointed to Graham.

"Higgins keep swingin' that shovel, and the duke reach for his gun, but it gone. Both of them. Some boys doin' Higgins's bidding taken it. They wave it around, shouting. So now His Grace has no gun, no nothin', and he got Stewart comin' at him, still swingin' that shovel."

The courtroom had grown silent, and even the judge's gaze was fixed on Maime.

She's a good storyteller. But might that hurt their case? Would they think she was telling a story instead of the truth?

"The duke, he get backed up to the house. He got nowhere to go, and Stewart talking about feeding his innards to the dogs. His Grace got nothin', then he see the chopping block and axe, and he grab it and throw. It hits Higgins in the head, and he fall."

"He died of a gunshot wound!" Newsome again.

This outburst earned him a frown from the judge.

"His Grace don't have no gun," Maime insisted. "Those boys got it, and one of 'em shoot Higgins as he fall. Then they all yell, 'Make free!' because no one got any love for those two who take over after Miss Katherine die. They mean, even to little ones like Ayla."

"Thank you, Maime." Sophie hurried on, aware that she had used her allotted time. She turned to face the jury. "So you see gentlemen, Oliver and Stewart Higgins wrongfully took over my husband's plantation, both trespassing and using property that did not belong to them. Additionally, they went against numerous dictates in the previous owner's will. They also enslaved and abused her daughter, the biological child of her first husband, the Marquess Kempton.

"When my husband traveled to Saint Kitts it was with the intent to collect this child, his niece, and his nephew. My husband was not aware that the Higgins brothers would be at his plantation, nor was my husband aware of the many wrongs that had been done there. He acted first in defense of a child and then of his own life. He requests recognition by the court of the wrongs done to him that day and in the months previous, between the time of his sister's death and his arrival in Saint Kitts, as well as recognition that his actions on the eleventh of April, 1829, were those of self-defense and the defense of a minor child entrusted to his care."

Sophie ceased speaking and waited, wanting to look at Graham but not daring. *Please. Please. Please.*

"The witness is dismissed," the judge said curtly. Maime stepped down from the box and exited the room, where William waited to whisk her away to safety. Silence reigned a full minute after she had left before the judge spoke, his gaze directed to the room at large, or perhaps to the one sitting at the back of it.

"Inasmuch as slaves are rejected as witnesses, because they are held for nothing by the civil law and excluded from all legal responsibilities, the jury will disregard the testimony just given."

"Maime is not a slave. She is a free woman," Sophie challenged. "Therefore, her testimony should be admissible."

The judge glared at her, then cleared his throat and slammed his gavel to quiet the escalated murmurs around the room. "When Jack Kempton was alive, she was his slave and is still regarded as such in the view of this court. Therefore she is not permitted to bring evidence."

"What of *this* evidence, Your Honor?" Sophie snatched up the pile of papers and waved it at him. "Does the court permit truth, and the proof thereof in the form of documents, at least?" Her temper was threatening to get the best of her, but if she didn't speak up, she'd never get another chance.

He did not bother to respond, instead keeping his gaze fixed on the back of the room. "The jury will now convene to decide a verdict."

Sophie remained standing, frozen in place as the men in the jury conversed among themselves, and whispered conversations began in the benches behind her. It seemed both forever and only minutes before a paper was handed to the judge.

He did not look up as he read it. "The defendant is found guilty as charged in the murders of . . ."

The room spun, and Sophie's legs buckled. She gripped the edge of the desk to stay upright.

". . . sentenced to be hanged two days hence . . ."

They can't. He's innocent. Not Graham—

The judge's gavel slammed into the block a final time. Graham was hauled roughly to his feet and ushered toward the side door.

"Graham—" Her voice caught, and her legs buckled again. Someone caught her and held tight even as the room began to fade.

Sophie fought against the arms holding her, then twisted to face her captor. Her mother stood behind her, hands supporting Sophie, eyes brimming with tears.

"Mama." Sophie sobbed and fell into her embrace.

Nine

UNFAMILIAR SURROUNDINGS FILLED Sophie's vision as she opened her eyes. White frilly curtains gathered at each corner of the four-poster bed where she lay, with a matching canopy overhead. She sat up quickly, and the room seemed to darken and sway.

"Drink this. It will help ease your headache." A teacup was pressed into her hands.

Sophie blinked, then focused her gaze. "Livie?"

Her sister smiled, then leaned forward and hugged her, taking care not to spill the contents of the cup. "It's so good to see you. I've missed you."

"And I you," Sophie said, realizing it was true. Much of their life in London she had not missed, but Livie's chatter and enthusiasm she had. "Where are we?"

"In London at the dowager Palmer's house. I've been staying here the past six weeks. Mother arranged it. Since the night you left she's been hiding me with different family and friends, both in the city and out. So Father couldn't find me and force me to take your place and wed Newsome."

"Oh, Livie, I'm sorry you've had to hide." Sophie reached a hand out to her. "I never meant to cause you problems or to cost you your season."

Livie waved as if unconcerned. "I didn't miss it at all—or

too much, at least." Her pained expression said otherwise. "I've been having plenty of adventures playing hide and seek from Father while you were off having yours with the Duke of Warwick."

Graham! "What time—what *day* is it?" *How could I have slept?* "Is Graham—"

"He is alive." Livie clasped Sophie's free hand. "You were not asleep for long. The trial was this morning. There is time yet to help him."

Sophie's eyes filled with tears, and their instant ache reminded her of the many she had shed already that day. Mother had gathered her papers then helped her from the courtroom and into a carriage, where she had cried herself to near hysteria. Graham was going to hang. *Nothing I said or did helped him.*

"What am I to do?" She handed the teacup to her sister and wrapped her arms around herself, pain from the aching hollow in her stomach spreading to every point in her body.

"You are going to do what women have been doing for centuries." Mother strode into the room carrying a tray of bread, jam, and cheeses. "You are going to use your womanly wiles to your advantage."

Sophie sniffled. "You've confused your daughters. I've never had wiles, only a mind I thought useful, though it failed me today."

Mother shook her head. "You did not fail, Sophie. There was foul play afoot from the beginning. It was not even an *un*fair fight, no fight at all, as the outcome was determined before anything that happened in that courtroom." She set the tray on the bed in front of Sophie. "Eat. I want every last bite of that gone. You can't go see Viscount Newsome looking pale and fragile as you do right now."

"*Newsome.*" Sophie shuddered, and her stomach flipped

with revulsion. *I am not fragile.* Troubled though she was, her mind rebelled at the suggestion.

"Going to see the viscount is necessary if you wish to save your husband's life." Determination shone on Mother's face as she looked between Sophie and Livie. "I made the mistake of not standing up for your sister, and we've all paid for that dearly—most of all sweet Torie." The ever-present pain shone in her eyes. "But no more. I won't—*we* won't—let your father or any other man ruin or dictate our lives. God may have made us the weaker sex, but he gave us the mightier minds. You're going to make a deal with the devil and beat him at his own game."

Sophie sat up straighter, a tiny spark of hope flickering. "What do you have in mind?"

Mother perched on the edge of the bed and looked directly at her. "You're going to make an offer Newsome can't refuse—yourself in exchange for your husband's freedom."

Sophie gasped. "I can't—how could you suggest that I—"

"I only said *offer.*" Mother placed her hand on Sophie's. "Do you really believe I would give my precious daughter over to that abhorrent, vile excuse of a man?" She shook her head. "*Never.* That is why I enlisted the duke's assistance last spring—to save you from Newsome." She patted Sophie's hand. "I will ensure you are safe. But Newsome must believe that he is getting what he wants—you."

Sophie sighed, her initial hope deflated. "I am but one small part of what he might once have wanted, which was the merger of his and Father's plantations, giving him greater governing power on Saint Kitts. But the real issue here is slavery, the abolition of which Graham has been leading the charge for. He has been funding and backing various bills to end slavery—some of which have come close to making it to the House for debate. Offering myself to Newsome in exchange for Graham's freedom is not an equivalent, as a free

Graham will continue the fight—and if slavery topples, Newsome's empire does as well."

"That may be true," Mother said. "But you are still underestimating your power as a woman. Newsome has wanted you for several months now. If he believes he is finally going to have you, it will seem like the ultimate victory—one too great to pass up."

"What Mother is attempting to say tactfully is that men do not always think with their brains," Livie put in.

"Thank you, Olivia." Mother sounded anything but grateful as she turned an exasperated expression upon her. "I see you have made good use of this time on your own these past months to further your education."

Livie shrugged. "Nothing Sophie wouldn't have done." She grinned at her. "You were right. Our uncle has the most exceptional library, particularly the medical section."

Mother sighed. "Since you are both so well informed, you know that a woman can often persuade a man to do something he otherwise would not. It would seem worth trying, given that this is your husband's life we are talking about. Or do you not care for him as I believed?"

"I love Graham very much," Sophie said. "And I would— I will—do anything I am able to see him live. But using any feminine advantage I possess will come last. There are other things that may be more persuasive." Her mind was sifting through ideas already, points of truth—mostly—that might be used to convince Newsome that it would be better for him, were Graham to be released.

Mother nodded. "Excellent. The more tools at our disposal the better."

The doorbell chimed in the hall below.

"Dry your tears and wash your face, Sophie, then join us downstairs when you have finished eating."

"Us?" Sophie asked.

"Lord Fitzgerald, Livie, the dowager, and myself. It will take each of us working together if we are to save the duke. We have fewer than forty-eight hours before his sentencing is to take place and while your father is away in Yorkshire, believing that he has at last discovered Livie's whereabouts." Mother and Livie exchanged conspiratorial grins as they walked toward the door. Mother paused to look back. "There is also the matter of where we all must go when we have accomplished our goal of freeing your husband. England will not be safe, nor Scotland, I believe, for some time. And I cannot keep hiding Livie forever. I've booked passage for all of us, but if we fail the ship will not wait."

Passage? On a ship? "To where?" Sophie asked, but Mother had already left the room.

GRAHAM LOOKED UP as the cell door swung open and William entered. *Not Sophie.* He had waited all day, since being returned here after his ill-fated trial, hoping for a visit from her. *Let me see her just once more. Let me tell her I love her and how proud I was of her today. Let me tell her goodbye.* Graham tried to mask his disappointment. "How is Sophie?"

"Hello to you too," William said with a grim smile. "No, how is William, your oldest and dearest friend?"

"I'm sorry." Graham ran a hand through hair that was already standing on end from similar, repeated actions all afternoon. "How are you?"

"I've been better."

"We all have. Except Newsome." Graham resumed the pacing he'd been doing before William's arrival.

William grunted. "His deeds will catch up to him."

"As mine did to me." Graham frowned. "Sophie?" he asked again.

"She is devastated," William said flatly. "But she is also Sophie. Already at work on a dozen ways to get you out of here—in one piece."

Graham stopped his pacing and stared at William. "What is she planning?" What could she possibly do?

"I have instructions from her that you are to follow exactly."

Graham nodded, though he felt no hope for release, only concern for Sophie. "Why did she not come herself?"

"She is otherwise occupied at present," William said evasively, heightening Graham's concern.

"When my time is up in a few minutes and I leave, you are to request—loud enough for the guard to hear—that you would like to have a visit from clergy so you can make a confession."

"That would take a while," Graham grumbled.

William nodded. "Exactly. After you make the request, I'll say that I will talk to the warden about it."

"What else?" Graham asked. *What is Sophie up to?*

"If you are asked to sign your plantation over to Newsome in exchange for your freedom, you are to agree."

Graham pulled back. "Are you mad? And give him control over all those people? I would rather hang than live and know I was the cause of such monumental suffering." He shook his head. "No."

"Time," the guard called.

William grabbed Graham's arm. "You will not be causing anyone's suffering—unless you hang. And then it will be all those on your plantation, along with Sophie and your unborn child, Ayla, Matthew, and myself who suffer greatly. Trust me. Trust Sophie. And pray."

"Where is she?" Graham placed his own grip on William when he would have pulled away. "What is she doing? You must tell me."

William shook his head. "It is best that I don't. Only do what I have requested. Do not make her endeavor for naught."

What endeavor? Give Newsome my plantation? Newsome— "Is she—did she go to see Newsome?" *To plead for my life? To bargain with him?*

William pursed his lips, refusing to answer, but his solemn expression was answer enough.

Graham hadn't thought he could feel worse than he had, shortly to face a noose. But this—

Had he eaten anything today he surely would have been sick. He might be anyway. Acid and bile turned over in his stomach as he thought of Sophie at Newsome's mercy. "Tell me she didn't go alone at least, that her mother is with her or a servant or—"

The door opened, and William clapped Graham on his uninjured shoulder, then stepped away. "Godspeed, my friend."

"God ain't where he's goin'," the guard lurking in the doorway said with a laugh.

"Perhaps he might be," William said with a pointed look.

Nearly too late Graham recalled his role. "I must set myself at rights with the Lord." The door shut on his words, but he pressed his face to the small, barred window. "I would like a visit from clergy—to hear my confession."

"I'll speak with the warden," William assured him and started down the corridor.

"Mayn't be enough time left for the Black Duke's confessional," the guard chuckled. "His list of crimes is long."

"Indeed." William grimaced. "Nevertheless it is within his rights to try. I shall see if there is clergy that can be summoned as soon as possible."

His steps faded down the corridor, and Graham stumbled back, collapsing on the cot as he allowed the implications of what Sophie had done—was doing right now?—to sink in. He leaned forward, head in his hands as the tears started to fall. *Newsome has her.* She'd gone to him of her own accord. *To save me.*

He'd failed in the ultimate way. First his mother and sister, and now his wife. All hurt, all taken from him. Because he'd failed to protect them.

Ten

THE SUN WAS already setting as Sophie made her way up the steps to Viscount Newsome's townhome. Beneath her gloves her hands trembled as she reached for the knocker; beneath her gown her heart beat a rapid staccato.

She was greeted by the butler, gave her name, and stated her intent—though the hour was late—of calling on the viscount.

"He is not home at present," the butler said cooly, after an admirable attempt at hiding his surprise. "He is out celebrating, the demise of your husband, I believe."

"I will wait for him," Sophie stated and swept past the butler regally, acting every bit the duchess.

"Very well." He showed her to a small sitting room, then left, whispering something to another servant loitering in the hall. That man took up a post just outside the room, as if to guard her.

Would that he could guard me from his employer. She supposed they believed she might be inclined to theft or some other retribution for the viscount's actions. But they supposed wrong. Burning Newsome's house down, while tempting, would do nothing to further her cause.

Instead Sophie rehearsed what she must say as the clock on the wall crawled slowly past each number. A quarter of an hour passed, then a half, then a full hour. Her back ached from sitting so stiffly, but she did not allow herself to relax. If all went well, she would return to her mother and sister this night. *If it does not . . .* She took comfort from the weapon concealed in her reticule, though using it would not lead to a desired outcome either, but might earn her a place on the gallows beside Graham.

Another hour passed. The clock in the hall chimed just as the butler returned to his post at the front door. A minute later it opened, and Sophie heard the low voices of the butler and the viscount.

Every sense warned her to flee, but she remained as she was, relaxing her posture so that she seemed to be casually waiting.

Newsome appeared in the doorway, his cravat hanging loosely and one shirttail untucked. A slow, sinister smile spread across his ugly face. "What a pleasant surprise."

He is foxed. Sophie returned his smile with one that was almost genuine. A man deep in his cups might be more easily persuaded, or at least more easily outrun if it came to that. "Good eve to you, my lord." She held her gloved hand out to him, missing the bump of her wedding ring beneath, having given it to her mother for safekeeping.

"Your Grace." Newsome took her hand and leaned over it, placing a slobbery kiss across her knuckles.

Sophie resolved to burn the glove when she was through here.

At last Newsome straightened, then looked at the table in front of them and then around the room as if searching for something and perplexed by its absence. "Has my staff offered you no refreshment this entire time you've been waiting?"

"None," Sophie said. "And I do not require any now." Mother had warned her not to eat or drink anything offered to her by Newsome or his staff. The viscount was not to be trusted. "I would prefer to discuss what I came for."

Newsome gave a slow nod, during which it seemed he struggled to right his head again. "To what do I owe this pleasurrre?" His voice slurred the last word suggestively. "Have you come to beg for your husband's life to be spared?"

"Yes, actually." Sophie smiled, as if he had asked her about the weather.

"Excellent." He clapped his hands together, though they did not quite meet correctly. He pulled them apart again, frowning as he flexed each one, as if nursing an injury or uncertain of their function. "Get on with it, then," he said, as he caught her watching his actions. "What are you prepared to offer in exchange?"

Interesting. Perhaps Mother is right.

"I do have something to offer you in exchange for my husband's freedom, but first I wish to point out some things you may not have considered."

"I've considered," Newsome assured her, his gaze roaming over her lazily, making Sophie grateful that she had kept her cloak on instead of giving it to the butler. "I have imagined this very scenario." He continued his perusal while licking his lips as if anticipating a tasty meal.

Sophie did her best to ignore him. "Do you realize that if the duke is hanged, he will then be a martyr for the cause of abolition, and, as a result, many more intelligent, equally powerful men will rise up in his stead and continue his work to an even greater degree?"

"*Pfft.*" Newsome flopped his hand in front of him dismissively, but Sophie didn't miss the beat of concern that flashed in his eyes.

"On the contrary, if Graham were to live, his reputation having been irrevocably damaged by his time in jail and his court appearance, he will no longer be able to associate in any manner with those working to end slavery. He would do more harm than good—even behind the scenes—and instead will need to do all he can to distance himself from the abolitionist movement. Given his withdrawal of support, in addition to the stain on the movement itself because of his, now public, prior involvement, the cause as a whole is likely to flounder for some time, if not fade from the political landscape altogether."

Newsome's fingers drummed on his crossed legs, and his flirtatious, suggestive expression faded. "And you think those theories are reason enough for me to see that your husband— a man who has long been a thorn in my side—does not hang?"

"They are more than theories." Sophie spoke with an air of absolute certainty. "Nevertheless, I recognize that you will need something more in exchange. Collateral, if you will, though this will become yours permanently should you accept."

Newsome's fingers stilled, and he looked at her expectantly. *Greedily. Hungrily.*

Sophie fought off a swell of nausea that had nothing to do with the baby growing inside of her and everything to do with the thought of offering herself to the man before her. Something she could not and would not do.

"In exchange for my husband's release from prison, and a guarantee that he will not be recaptured and hanged at some future time—meaning a not-guilty verdict must be entered with the court—we are offering you Graham's estate on Saint Kitts."

Newsome sat back on the sofa. His brow furrowed with obvious confusion, and perhaps disappointment as well, though Sophie could already detect the wheels of possibility spinning in his mind.

"The deed is here in London, and we can arrange for the transfer tomorrow, once Graham has been released and we have verified the not guilty verdict."

Newsome shook his head. "You expect me to believe that your husband will sign over his plantation to *me*? When he has spent the past few years so tirelessly fighting slavery?"

"Yes." Sophie leaned closer and smelled the alcohol on Newsome's breath. "He *will* sign the deed. He will give up the plantation—and all on it—because it is the only way he can continue the work most important to him. The raising of his sister's children. They are what matter most—more than the fight to end slavery, more than his plantation, and more than me."

You are a good actress. She prayed Graham was right because it was imperative that Newsome believe her. She glanced up at him, her eyes brimming with tears that came all too easily at the thought of losing Graham. She opened her reticule partway and withdrew a handkerchief to dab at the corners of her eyes.

"You heard him when you were at Caerlanwood. I professed my love, and his response was to tell me to stay home—so I could continue to care for the children. It is what he brought me there for. Fulfilling his promise to his sister is more important than anything else. He *will* give you the plantation and walk away from Saint Kitts forever."

Sophie leaned back again but held Newsome's gaze, praying she had not made a grave mistake in revealing Graham's vulnerability regarding Ayla and Matthew. They were his priority, and Newsome must believe that if he was to buy into the plan they had spent the better part of the day constructing.

"Even if I had such power—"

"You do," Sophie said. "I am not blind. I saw the way you cowed the judge and jury." Not that the jury had needed influencing. Her mother had informed her that every member except one owned slaves themselves.

"Even then," Newsome continued. "I have awaited this moment a long time—Raymond's neck in a noose and his wife mine for the taking. Why should his plantation not be as well?"

Sophie stood abruptly. "*Neither* will be yours if Graham is hanged. But you will be a hunted man." Fresh tears blurred her vision, and she blinked them away.

"*Tsk, tsk.*" Newsome stood, facing her. "Hasn't anyone ever taught you that making threats is not the way to negotiate?"

"I wasn't making a threat, merely speaking the truth." *I've failed again.* She turned away, hands shaking as she pulled at the strings of her reticule. *Graham is going to hang. He is going to die. I've endangered Matthew and Ayla for nothing.* She stepped toward the door, her tears falling fast now.

"I admit, this was not the offer I had imagined. But it does intrigue me." Newsome grabbed her arm and jerked her back toward him. "I will require a token of good intent—evidence that you will keep your word."

Was he actually considering it? *Or just toying with me?* She shrugged out of his grasp. "What do you want?"

"Proof of your sincerity. You can seal our bargain with a kiss. Just one, simple kiss." He leaned closer. "It's not asking much."

Sophie forced herself to stay put, when she wanted to shove him to the floor and run. "I am a married woman."

"Not for much longer, if we do not come to an agreement." He stared at her, challenge in his expression that was becoming more sober by the minute. "These are my terms. You'll not speak a word to your husband between now and the time of his release. Nor is he to see you. I will make the arrangements. Tomorrow morning at ten, I will escort you—alone—in my carriage to the prison, where you can see for yourself when he is freed."

"I wish to view the court records as well," Sophie said. "To see a *not* guilty verdict entered." So Graham's freedom would be permanent. "And my husband must be released into Lord Fitzgerald's care." She wanted others there—William and some of the men he'd hired as guards—to ensure Graham's safety. *And mine.* And to dissuade the viscount from anything nefarious.

"Very well. *I* will inform Lord Fitzgerald. You are to tell no one of our arrangement. You will stay here tonight, to guarantee that."

"No." *Never.* Better she were Daniel in the lion's den, without the Lord's protection, than to stay the night in the viscount's home or with him anywhere nearby. "My mother knows I am here and will send the police for me, if she has not already, as I have been gone longer than anticipated."

Newsome's eyes narrowed, his displeasure evident, but he barked a harsh laugh. "Everyone knows your mother is addled. She has been since you and your sister disappeared. No one is going to believe her when you were previously missing for so long. Who knows but that you ran off with some other duke—or viscount." He sidled closer. "I'll see that you have *every* comfort here."

Sophie suppressed a shudder of revulsion and chose her words carefully. The only comfort she wished was to be in Graham's arms again and to know he was safe. "No, thank you." She marched toward the door, sliding her hand into her reticule to grip the pistol.

The viscount jumped in front of her. "I haven't had my kiss."

Did he mean to allow her to leave, then? Keeping her hand concealed she met his gaze. "A parting kiss, and then farewell until tomorrow at ten."

"Ye-es." The word rolled from his tongue in two syllables.

Like the forked tongue of a snake.

"Your every move will be watched between now and tomorrow morning. Any correspondence or visitors to your house will be intercepted. I will call for you tomorrow morning. Bring the deed."

Sophie thwarted his efforts again. "It is safely locked up, and only Graham is able to retrieve it. We can all go to Rothschilds together after he is released."

Newsome grasped her chin and tilted it up. "If you think to deceive me—"

"*Not* when I would lose by doing so." She wrenched his hand away. "I would not have come here if I was not serious in this endeavor. You want your token, your proof that I am in earnest?" Sophie sucked in a breath, leaned closer, and thought of Graham.

Eleven

A TAP ON Graham's shoulder woke him from a fitful, troubled sleep.

"Someone's coming. Sit on your bed with the open Bible in your lap and read out loud. I'll stand in the corner behind the door."

Graham gave a single nod to the other occupant of his cell who had been with him—sitting mostly—throughout the long night. True to his word, William had notified the warden of Graham's request, and within the hour a priest had come, supposedly to hear his lengthy confession.

Thus far the only confessing that had been done was by the man impersonating clergy. In whispered tones, while imitating the invoking of a blessing, and as the guard looked on through the small window in the door, the man dressed in robes had told Graham he'd been hired by Sophie and sent there for his protection.

From whom was easy enough to guess when Newsome's voice was heard in the passage outside.

If he's here, he's not with Sophie. A fraction of the panic that had engulfed Graham over the past several hours receded. He opened the book to the New Testament and began reading in Matthew 5.

"And he opened his mouth, and taught them, saying,

Blessed are the poor in spirit, for theirs is the kingdom of heaven." He probably didn't qualify, though over the course of his lifetime his spirits had been poor more often than not. He stifled a yawn. What time was it? Two? Three in the morning?

The key turned in the lock, and the hinges squealed. Graham kept his face directed toward the Bible.

"Blessed are those who mourn, for they shall be comforted."

"Who do you think will be there to comfort your wife when she's mourning your death?" Newsome strode into the cell, the smug look of victory on his face. "I imagine it will be me, as already tonight she so tenderly bestowed a sample of her affection upon me. And you—not even cold, not even in the grave yet."

Sophie wouldn't. She hadn't. Graham snapped the Bible shut amidst twin flares of panic and pain. *She might.* She'd been desperate enough to see Newsome, to place herself at his mercy.

I will lay down my life for you if necessary. On their wedding night Sophie had asked him to repeat the Murray pledge he had spoken in the church, and then *she* had repeated it, word for word, back to him. He had teased her that she was taking women's rights too far, but in a moment of absolute seriousness and clarity, she had told him that she would do anything for him. Her love for him and his well-being were now the center of her universe. *Anything.*

Anguish filled Graham as he stood and tried to keep his hands from clenching at his sides. *What have you done, Sophie? What did Newsome do to you?* Graham's nostrils flared, like a bull about to charge.

"Do not add to your many sins, my son."

Newsome jumped and whirled around, clearly startled by the imposing figure of the clergyman standing quite near. Clad in his dark robe, he towered over Newsome and, standing in shadow, might have passed for the Grim Reaper had he been holding a scythe.

"Leave him be," he intoned in a low, gravelly voice as he looked at Graham. "God will deal with him justly as well." His solemn gaze returned to Newsome.

Newsome snorted. "Things are quite just right now." He swung his face toward the door. "Get out."

"I cannot," the priest said, his hands concealed before him in the overlarge sleeves of his robe. "I have been summoned to hear this man's confession and to give him penance and absolution—a matter that is going to require every minute allotted to us, as his sins are many. Though not as many as, I sense, are *yours*."

Newsome's glare returned to Graham, frustration evident in the scowl on his face. His jubilance of a moment before had gone. He addressed the priest once more.

"I require a few minutes alone with the prisoner, and I command you to leave."

"I answer to a higher authority, and I will not leave until I have fulfilled my duty here."

Newsome's hand slid to his waist, to the gun resting there. "Do you answer to *this* authority?"

Instead of seeming intimidated, the priest stepped closer. "My son, that is not the way. You will only create more problems for yourself."

Many problems. Permanent ones. How satisfying it would be to see Newsome laid out on the cell floor dead. *But that would make more difficulties for me—and for Sophie and the children.*

"Whatever you wish to say to me can be said in front of the good father," Graham said, watching closely as the emotions marched across Newsome's face. His plans had been foiled, and he was angry.

He wished to bait me—and perhaps would have—and I would have been a dead man. Even more than I already am. Right here. Tonight. Newsome would have claimed self-defense. *But why kill me now when I am already sentenced to hang?* What had changed that Newsome wished to accomplish the deed himself, tonight? Graham forced himself to calm and said a silent prayer of gratitude for Sophie and William and their wisdom in sending this stranger to protect him.

Graham slowly sat on the bed again, took up the Bible, and found his place.

"Your wife said that *if* you were to be freed, you would willingly sign over the deed to your plantation on Saint Kitts. Is that true?" Newsome asked.

Graham closed his eyes and thought of the people there—the families, the children depending on him for their continued freedom and well-being. How could Sophie ask this of him?

Trust her.

"Yes," he ground out. "In exchange for my freedom, the plantation would be yours."

"It seems your wife spoke the truth." Newsome didn't sound as if he quite believed it. "Your sister's children must be *very* important to you."

Graham raised his head slowly, eyes boring into Newsome's, which looked triumphant. *He holds all the cards.* Graham fought against the feeling of helplessness. If he fought back now, he would lose. They all would, which was exactly what Newsome wanted. What he was counting on. *I can do nothing. Sophie must face him alone. She must protect Ayla and Matthew.*

"Sophie is always truthful," Graham said. *To me, at least.* She would be if he was given the opportunity to see her once more and ask what had transpired between her and Newsome.

But what would be the point? *If I am granted only a few minutes more with her...* He only wanted her to know of his love. Graham forced his eyes to the Bible before his anger could get the better of him. "Blessed are the meek, for they will inherit the earth." *Help me be meek, Lord. And I don't need the earth. Just Sophie. And Ayla and Matthew. They are my world.*

The hinges squealed again, then the door slammed, the sound reverberating through the cell. Graham looked up. Newsome was gone.

"You would not have been meek if confronting him alone—nor I, in your shoes." The pretend clergyman checked to see that the window in the door was closed, then lowered his arms, revealing the weapon that had been concealed in one of his wide sleeves.

"I would not have," Graham agreed soberly. "My tendency to act in anger is a true fault."

"It seems your wife knows you well," the man said. "And was wise in sending me."

Graham nodded. "She is my salvation."

Twelve

THE JUDGE FORMED the last character on the parchment, then set the nibbed quill aside and sprinkled the page liberally with sand, to hasten the drying of the new, *Not Guilty* verdict that had been entered in the court record.

"Satisfied?" Newsome asked, looking at Sophie.

"Yes," she said, though she'd feel anything but, until Graham was safely away.

"If word of this gets out—" The judge directed a stern look at Newsome.

"My husband and I intend to quit London today," Sophie assured him. "We have no plans to return. There is no worry of anyone seeing him wandering around."

Newsome dropped a heavy purse on the desk in front of the judge, then took Sophie's elbow and guided her from the chamber.

Once again in his carriage, they set out for Newgate. Sophie's heart felt as if it was keeping time with the brisk clip-clop of the horses' hooves. *Is Graham really to be freed?* She didn't trust Newsome for a second and still worried this was some horrible trick, as had been their kiss last night when he had attempted much more, pinning her against the wall and clawing at her clothing until she had thrust her knee into his groin and shoved him away. By then he'd already made her lip bleed and ripped the bodice of her gown. She'd fled his house not knowing if he would call for her this morning, if he still intended to keep their agreement or not. *Or if he ever intended it.* She never wanted to see him again, and being alone with him in the confines of his Brougham was particularly alarming, with little space between them and nowhere to escape should he attempt to assault her.

Though she'd seen the judge alter the verdict with her own eyes, something still felt terribly off. An ominous warning deep within was blaring that she needed to get away from Newsome, and quickly. But she couldn't. Not yet. Not until Graham had been freed.

The carriage slowed, then came to a halt.

"If you look out this window, you'll see when he is released." Newsome indicated the window on *his* side of the carriage.

Of course. Sophie weighed her options. She would have to switch places in order to see Graham, to verify it was he and not an imposter exiting the prison walls. She would have to slide past Newsome, with either her front or back being pressed far too close to him. Just as he had planned, no doubt.

The choice—no choice at all—made her ill, as did the familiar, morning stirrings in her stomach. *Oh no. Not now.* Sophie brought a hand to her mouth. "I'm going to be sick." She lurched forward, vomiting on their shoes and the carriage floor.

A volley of curses was flung her way as the door opened and Newsome jumped out.

Sophie retched again, then slumped back against the seat, weak and exhausted. She shouldn't have allowed Mother to insist on breakfast this morning. These days that never went well. *Then again . . .* Newsome was no longer beside her.

Lifting her feet over the distasteful sight, she slid to the opposite side. Newsome glared at her with such a look of disgust that she wanted to laugh. Instead she pressed her hands to her middle and moaned. "Something I ate must have been bad."

He stepped farther from the carriage. "Look there," he ordered. "He's coming out now."

Sophie stared down the block as a door in the gate opened and a man walked out. William emerged from a carriage directly across the street, beckoning to him. The man stepped from the shadow of the wall into the light, his features now visible. Dark hair, tall, broad shoulders, trim—too thin—frame, serious expression, mouth set in a line of grim determination. *Graham!* She wanted to vault from the seat and run to him, but Newsome had warned her not to even call out or there would be unpleasant consequences.

Graham's cheeks were gaunt, his gaze wary as he crossed the street, but he was free. Her heart grew lighter with each step he took toward William and the waiting carriage. At last he reached it, and William clasped his hand and pulled him inside. Sophie brushed at the tears sliding down her face. *He is out. He is safe.*

Newsome looked at her sharply. "Stay put. I'll have to get a hackney now, since you've made such a foul mess."

"We could go with them," she suggested. "Lord Fitzgerald's vehicle is large enough."

"You'd like that, wouldn't you?" Newsome sneered. "You planned to be sick, so we could all go together, nice and cozy."

Sophie rolled her eyes at such a suggestion. "If I possessed the ability to vomit at will, I would have used it to ward off your unwelcome advances last night!"

He scowled at the reminder of his thwarted efforts. "You're my collateral now. Until that deed is in my hand, you'll be right beside me."

Sophie peered out the opposite window as William's carriage rolled by. A minute later a smaller, plain coach turned off a side street to follow. Dowager Palmer's? Or Mother's?

"I'm sure they will wait for us if we are late." Sophie spoke as if unconcerned, though she fought panic at the distance growing between herself and the departing carriages.

"Get out," Newsome ordered when the vehicles had turned the corner and were out of sight.

Taking care where she stepped, Sophie climbed down.

"Wipe your shoes on the grass." He shoved her toward a patch of lawn that Sophie could see had already been used to clean his shoes. She obliged him while wishing she *could* vomit at will, given his reaction. Repulsing him could only be a good thing. They were alone now, and she had no weapon today. He had made sure of that before they left this morning, patting her down and checking in a manner that had left her feeling abused and filthy.

No weapon. No womanly wiles. Only my wits. If there was ever a time to employ her mind, it was now—to the matter of staying unharmed.

GRAHAM LEANED AGAINST the plush carriage seat, feeling not an ounce of the relief he ought to have felt at walking out of Newgate. Across from him, beside one of the two hulking, armed guards sharing the crowded space, William turned his mouth up in a grim smile.

"Welcome back."

"Some welcome." Graham glared at the man beside him, a pistol held loosely in his hands. He returned his attention to William.

"Where is Sophie?" What price had she paid for him to be in this carriage, instead of headed for the gallows?

William's lips thinned further. "Riding with Newsome. He wanted her with him until the deed is signed—insurance, he said. Apparently, he doesn't believe you'll go through with it."

"That makes two of us," Graham grumbled. A grunt of disapproval from the hulking brute beside him made him add, "But I will." Sophie's life meant far more than his own. He would do just about anything to keep her safe. A fact Newsome, no doubt, intended to capitalize on.

Graham closed his eyes, inwardly groaning. *Why, Sophie?* Why put herself at such risk? A small part of him—the part that wasn't utterly terrified for her—was furious with her, but as quickly as that flame of anger sparked, he extinguished it. If it had been Sophie in that prison facing death, he would have done anything, given anything to get her out. It wasn't fair for him to hold her to a different set of standards. *She loves me equally.* Graham opened his eyes and tried to resign himself to accept that what had been done to save him had been done. He could either be angry about it, or he could accept her sacrifice and be grateful.

Sophie is intelligent. She knows what she's doing. Trust her. He could practically hear the unspoken words from William as they stared at one another. As the carriage rolled toward the bank, Graham willed himself to a calm that only a few months ago would not have been possible. Even now he felt its terrible strain. *If Newsome has hurt her...*

That would be an entirely different matter.

Thirteen

"THIS ISN'T THE way to Rothschilds." Sophie peered out the dirty window as the hackney took yet another turn away from the New Court financial district where they were to meet Graham.

"We aren't going there." Newsome sneered at her from the opposite seat, still obviously irritated by her earlier expulsions.

Would that I could throw up on him now. But her stomach was empty, probably a mercy given the tension thrumming through her and the erratic manner in which the coachman was driving, tossing her this way and that on the seat. Sophie stared at Newsome, trying not to show her fear. "We agreed to meet Graham at Rothschilds. If you will not take me, I'll walk there myself." She stood and banged her fist on the ceiling. "Stop the coach!"

"The driver won't listen to you." Newsome grinned savagely as Sophie continued pounding. "Before we started out, when you thought I was merely giving him directions, I told him you weren't in your right mind and to disregard anything he heard from you. I paid him extra for the inconvenience of transporting the insane."

Sophie retracted her already sore hand and lowered herself to the seat, as close to the door as possible, though that placed her directly across from Newsome. She steeled her voice with anger instead of the panic flashing through her.

"The deed is at Rothschilds—or have you bribed the banker, as well?"

The viscount leaned back once more and crossed one leg over his knee. "Bribe is such a tricky word. I prefer to think of matters like this as giving a bonus, much as I did this morning to the judge. I paid him handsomely for his time. It was inconvenient for him to change the record and then—to change it *back again,* after we left."

"*What?*" Sophie grasped the door handle and wrenched it down, the click coinciding with another beside her ear.

"I wouldn't do that if I were you. If the fall doesn't kill you, my shot surely will."

Blood pounded in Sophie's ears as she slowly released the handle and eased back to her seat, facing Newsome and the pistol he held pointed at her head. "Why shoot me?" She struggled to keep her voice from quavering. "You'd never get the plantation then."

"Wouldn't I? *Won't* I?" His brows rose in mockery. "Truthfully, I would prefer not to end your life, not when there are so many other, delightful things I intend to do with it. On the other hand—" He waved the gun as if they were discussing a matter of insignificance, but then his expression turned menacing. His hand jetted out, grabbed her chin, and forced her to look at him. "You made a *fool* of me all those months ago in your father's dining room, and I am still angry enough that killing you in cold blood seems a very satisfying option."

He's gone mad. The insane person in the carriage was not she, but the wild-eyed devil before her. He wasn't going to let her go. Why had he bothered releasing Graham at all?

To get his hands on that deed. Newsome was greedy and wanted it all. How could she play that against him?

Sophie pried his fingers from her face and scooted as far back on the seat as possible.

Newsome's finger toyed with the trigger as he tested out several different angles in which he might point it at her. Sophie refused to close her eyes or look away. Her mind scrambled for what to say, what to do, and came up blank. So she sat silent and tense, facing him and praying as the carriage took her farther and farther from anyone who might help.

"I don't like this," Graham muttered as he looked at William, seated across from him in the tiny room at Rothschilds where they awaited retrieval of the box. "Why isn't Sophie here yet?"

"I don't know," William admitted, sounding worried. "You can refuse to sign until she arrives."

"I want to refuse to sign anyway," Graham said. "It's unfathomable—trading my life for the suffering of a hundred others. It's wrong."

William glanced at the men standing just outside the door. "It *isn't* wrong."

William was trying to tell him something, but Graham wasn't sure what. He was missing something important—something obvious?—in the plan that had been constructed to save his life.

"Here we are." The banker returned with the box, but Graham made no move to fit the key William had brought with him into the lock.

"We will wait until my wife and the viscount arrive."

The banker paled slightly. "They are not scheduled to be here, Your Grace. The document is to be delivered to the viscount after you have signed, and only then will your wife be released."

"No." Graham shoved the box aside and stood. He turned toward the door as the two men guarding it entered the room, blocking him.

"William, what is this?" Graham turned to him.

"Not the arrangement I was told of."

"Nevertheless, it is the arrangement that the viscount insists upon," the banker said. "I was given specific instructions, regarding the transfer of this deed. If not completed by noon, his lordship will be taking Her Grace instead. He is to sail for Saint Kitts tomorrow."

Graham whirled around, grabbed the banker, and slammed him against the wall. "Do *you* have a wife?"

"Y-yes," the banker said.

"How would you feel if she'd been abducted by the viscount?"

"I—I—would deed the property to him as quickly as possible to get her back."

Hands on Graham's shoulders jerked him away. He staggered backward as searing pain from his still-recovering wound made his eyes water.

"Leave the bloke alone and sign the papers," the guard who'd grabbed him said. He glanced at the clock. "It's nearing noon."

"Graham," William said, his voice tense. "Sign. Sophie's life may depend upon it."

"I know." Graham sank into the chair and brought a hand to his head. Why had she trusted Newsome? He should have warned her not to, not to go to him, not to make any deal with him—no matter what the viscount promised. It was more than his own life that hung in the balance now, and he would have to barter his sister's work and dream—along with the lives of those dependent upon him for their freedom. "Please forgive me, Katherine." *Forgive me, God.*

Graham's hand shook as he inserted the key in the lock and opened the lid. *For you, Sophie. Because I love you more than anything or anyone.* He lifted the deed from the box.

He set the papers on the desk in front of him and began reading, picturing each of the listed assets. *Mill, boiling house, curing house, main house, offices.* Slave quarters and slaves were not listed on the deed, likely because Katherine had abolished slavery on her land before it came into his possession.

Oddly, her signature was nowhere on the document, yet he knew he'd seen it there before. The night after the lawyer had presented him with the deed, Graham remembered tracing her signature with his finger and thinking of her at her desk writing it.

And now it was gone. He read through the details once more, the acreage deeded to Graham Murray Raymond, Duke of Warwick. *Duke.* He hadn't been a duke when Katherine had drawn up the paperwork, deeding her plantation to him in the event of her death, and before their father had died, leaving Graham to inherit the unwanted title. The deed to *that* property simply read Graham Murray Raymond. He glanced up at William sharply.

William nodded. "Sign."

The banker pushed the inkwell toward him.

Graham took up the quill as his eyes scanned the rest of the document, confirming what he finally understood. He hastily scrawled his signature, granting Newsome ownership of a parcel of land containing fallow fields and a crumbling plantation house and outbuildings that hadn't been lived in or used since the early 1700s.

A little over a year ago, when the property had become available, a Lord Archibald had wished to throw his hat into the sugarcane and, therefore, the slave ownership ring. Graham had taken it upon himself to outbid the man. He had no intention of ever doing anything with the property. He'd simply wanted to prevent the rise of another plantation and additional slaves on the island.

Clever Sophie. She must have found the deed when going through his files and realized she could offer Newsome a plantation on Saint Kitts, without specifying which one. Newsome, idiot that he was, must have assumed he was getting Katherine's plantation.

The relief Graham felt at the way Sophie had deceived Newsome was short lived. She still wasn't safe, and if Newsome discovered what she'd done, that the plantation he was getting was, at present, worthless, she would suffer for her deception. *Is she already suffering now?*

"There." Graham replaced the quill and pushed back from the table. "Let's go."

"You're not going anywhere." The banker snatched the paper and edged toward the door. "A courier will deliver this to the viscount."

"So then he'll have both the property *and* my wife?" Graham stood. "I think not."

The banker hurried toward the door, calling loudly, "Arrest these men! One has escaped from prison, and the other has aided him."

Fourteen

NEWSOME POINTED THE pistol at Sophie's chest as the carriage came to a stop in front of a neglected building on the wharf. "Get out."

She pushed back her fear, folded her arms across her middle, and stared at him. He was angry, insane, but would he really shoot her? What purpose would that serve? Here, on a public street in a hired carriage in the middle of the day? Surely he wasn't that stupid. Neither was she. This, right here, was likely as safe a place as she was going to be with him. There was more danger in getting out here, in a strange part of the city she was unfamiliar with. "You cannot just kidnap me, a married woman—a duchess."

"Who's going to stop me? Your husband?" The viscount shook his head slowly, a sinister smile stretched wide. "Or perhaps your father? He'd be the first in line to hand you over. I know!" He snapped his fingers, or tried to. They didn't quite connect. "Your mother will save you—simpering, useless female that she is. Much like her daughters." Newsome's finger slid over the trigger, moving up and down slowly, caressing the metal. "I can and will do whatever I want—to you." He swung the pistol wide and pulled the trigger.

A ball whizzed by her head and exited the back wall as the acrid smell of gunpowder filled the carriage.

Sophie screamed and jumped from her seat. She flung open the door and leapt to the street, landing painfully on her knees in a heap of skirts as the driver shouted curses and struggled with the reins as he tried to calm his team. In the seconds it took her to rise, the viscount scrambled out behind her. He grabbed her arm and hauled her against him. Sophie screamed again and used her free hand to claw at his face.

"My *many* apologies," Newsome called to the driver. "I told you she was a lunatic! But I have the weapon now. No need to worry." He held the gun up to show the driver as Sophie tried to wrench herself free.

"Let go of me! You're the one who's mad." She looked up at the driver. "Help me, please! I don't want to go with him. He's taken me from my husband and—"

Newsome jerked her around toward him, released her, and struck her face, temporarily stunning and silencing her. Sophie brought a hand to her stinging cheek as she stumbled backward.

Newsome withdrew a pouch from inside his coat and tossed it to the driver. "To cover the damages." Newsome grabbed her arm again.

The driver hefted the bag, then gave a nod and started off.

"You're despicable." Sophie tried to pry his fingers from her arm. She tasted blood and guessed that her lip had split open again.

"Walk." He shoved her forward, toward the door in the decrepit building. "I'm going to hand you a key, and you're going to unlock the door. Otherwise I'll have to use my second pistol, and this time I'll be precise with my aim." He placed a ring with a single key in her hand and nudged her closer to the rusted door.

Sophie's hand trembled as she lifted the key. Her arm throbbed where he held her, and her face and knees stung.

Maybe he would shoot her, but that might be better than whatever he had planned for her on the other side of this door. She couldn't allow him to force her inside. With a jerk of her arm, she flung the ring as far as she could. It skittered down the worn cobbles of the street, stopping several feet away. A carriage approached, then rolled over it and continued on its way.

"You'll pay for that," Newsome promised as he dragged her toward the discarded key. They reached it, and he pushed her down, shoving the pistol into her back. "Pick it up."

Sophie did as he'd commanded, and he wrenched the ring and key from her hand before she could throw it again.

"Help me!" she screamed at the retreating carriage. "Someone help me!"

The viscount hauled her to her feet. "There's no one around to hear you, and if there was they *wouldn't* help. People on this street mind their own business." He dragged her back the way they'd come and thrust the key in the lock himself. Sophie pulled it out again, but the door was already unlocked, and he shoved her roughly inside, releasing her abruptly so that she stumbled into something heavy.

Behind her the door closed and the lock clicked. She whirled around to face him.

The only light came from windows streaked with dirt and salt and that were much too high to climb out of. Sophie backed away from the viscount as she squinted, her hands out behind her as she tried to make out her surroundings. The air was foul, a combination of odors—sweat and urine. *Blood.* The image of Lucy losing so much of it flashed through Sophie's mind.

People. I'm smelling people. Were they here now? Who were they, and what had happened to them?

She bumped into something, and her fingers scraped

against rough wood. Shapes came into focus as her eyes adjusted. She was surrounded by enormous boxes—crates. "What is this place?" she demanded, her voice stronger than she felt.

"A warehouse your father and I use for the merchandise we buy and sell." Newsome strode toward her, the white of his teeth glinting in that dim light as he gave her a wicked smile. "For slaves."

HEART POUNDING WITH fear for her daughter, Lilian Claybourne hurried from the coach near the warehouse that had once belonged to her son-in-law. Sophie's cries for help rang in her ears, and Lilian prayed she wasn't too late. *Don't hurt her.*

Her husband and Viscount Newsome had taken over the warehouse, though they were not in the business of transporting goods as Jonathan had been. Instead, as she'd discovered some months ago after going through her husband's papers in his absence, they dealt in people. Owning slaves, apparently, wasn't enough. They were illegally importing them as well, selling them to plantation owners and others in search of free labor.

Was anyone being kept there now? Aside from Sophie, whom Newsom had roughly forced inside moments ago.

I promised she would be safe. Lilian strove to calm her breathing and her thoughts. Much as she'd like, she couldn't just barge in there and demand that he give Sophie back. *He has a gun. But he won't kill her. He wants her too much.*

The thought brought little comfort.

"Wait here," Lilian instructed the driver, then hurried down the side street with the wrapped parcel beneath her arm. When Newsome's carriage had not followed Lord Fitzgerald's outside the prison, she had waited in hers and watched as Newsome ushered Sophie into a public hackney, which had set out in the opposite direction. It hadn't taken her long to guess where they were going, and from a safe distance she had followed them here.

Lilian glanced up and down the street, searching for one who might do her bidding. As much as she wished to burst through the warehouse doors and bash the bottle beneath her arm over Newsome's head, that wasn't possible, nor would it yield the desired outcome.

Hearing steps behind her, she turned just as a scrawny lad reached grubby hands out, as if intending to steal her package.

"Oh no, you don't." She held it up, out of his reach. "But if you'd like to earn £1, you can deliver this for me."

The child skidded to a stop, and his eyes narrowed suspiciously. "Where to? And what is it?"

"A bottle of very special wine." She unwrapped it and the letter, so he could see. "You wouldn't want to drink it. It would make you *very* ill." She stooped so she was closer to him. "The man inside that building has stolen my daughter. I need *him* to drink it, so he will be sleepy, and I can get her back."

"How you gonna do that?"

"I need you to take it to him, along with this." She showed the sealed letter to the boy. "You must knock a code, or he will not open the door." She used her fist to knock the pattern on the side of the bottle. "You try."

He did, repeating her movements exactly.

"Good. Tell him it is from Lord Claybourne. Will you do that for me?"

"For £1?"

Lilian nodded. She pulled out the money to show him, then considered the child's ragged clothing and thin frame and pulled out an additional coin. "It is an important task worthy of this much, I think."

His eyes grew large, and he bobbed his head.

Lilian smiled kindly. "The man's name is Viscount Newsome. The door is just on the other side of this building."

She handed the boy the letter and, after a second's hesitation, the bottle. "Hurry now. I'll be right here."

He nodded and scampered off. She walked to the corner of the building, peered carefully around, and watched him fist the pattern on the door. As it opened, she shrank back but listened to the exchange and glimpsed the bottle being handed off. She retreated, heart pounding in her ears with the magnitude of her actions. She placed a gloved hand against the side of the building for support and the other over her mouth.

What have I done?

What choice did I have?

Fifteen

"Was this part of the plan?" Graham asked William as they were ushered out of the office at gunpoint.

"No." William's serious expression met Graham's. He lowered his voice. "It would not be prudent for us to both end up in Newgate."

Graham gave a terse nod. If they were to get out of this, their best chance was now, though not this precise moment in a foyer of gaping onlookers. He didn't want anyone else getting hurt. But once they were outside . . .

One of the two men guarding them moved in front to pull open the heavy door. "I'll go first. Walk out one at a time behind me. You first." The man pointed his pistol at Graham. "If you try to run, your friend will be shot." His grin almost made it seem he hoped for that outcome.

The guard turned away and stepped forward through the open door as a woman overburdened with packages plowed into him, sending him backward.

"Oh, my goodness! I'm so sorry," she exclaimed amidst the explosion of loose papers and brown-wrapped parcels. She placed a hand out as if to steady herself. "I told Papa this was too much for me to carry."

Graham stared at the woman, whose face looked a lot like Sophie's. Her eyes shifted to Graham and then to the door briefly before she returned her attention to the man she'd run into.

"Out of the way, lady," he growled.

"I'm terribly sorry, sir." She stepped closer to him, laying a placating hand on his sleeve and creating a gap on her other side for Graham to squeeze through. He grabbed William's hand and shoved him into the space.

"Run!"

"Hey!" The guard tried to step around the woman, but she let out a piercing scream and blocked the way.

"My papers! You're stepping on my papers!"

Graham bolted after William a second before the woman dropped to her knees, her wide skirt taking up the entirety of the Rothschilds entrance as she continued shrieking.

The door of a carriage parked in front of the bank flew open.

"In here," another female voice called.

William jumped for the carriage as shouts rang out behind him. Graham dove in behind him, and they lurched forward before the door was even closed. A shot buzzed past them outside.

Graham pulled the door shut as he and William crouched on the floor. Across from them an elderly woman with white hair leaned forward over her cane and smiled. "Hello, gentlemen."

"Hello," Graham said uncertainly.

"I am Dowager Palmer." Her smile widened. "And this is the most excitement I've had in ages."

NEWSOME UNCORKED THE bottle a boy had just delivered, lifted it to his nose, and inhaled slowly. "Another fine vintage from your father's collection. He took to sharing these with me the past months, a token of apology for your loss, and a way to keep me patient. But my patience has come to an end." Newsome took a long drink straight from the bottle as he read the letter that had accompanied it.

Sophie edged away from him slowly, maneuvering through the maze of crates, a hand to her face as she took shallow breaths, trying to smother the worst of the scents assaulting her and trying to think what to do. He was stronger, but she wasn't slow. If she could put enough distance between them—

Newsome looked up from the letter and tossed it aside. "Your father has been duped again. Your sister was not in Yorkshire, as he was led to believe. Which leaves us with a problem—he still owes a significant debt to me."

Sophie said nothing. *No point in arguing with a madman.* She'd do better to save her breath, but she sent a silent prayer of gratitude heavenward for her mother's foresight in hiding Livie all these months.

"I intend to take his plantation as partial payment," Newsome continued. "But it isn't worth as much as it used to be. The price of sugar is down, and your father owes me a considerable sum." Newsome took another long drink from the bottle, then set it on the nearest crate and winced as he shook out his hands and clenched and unclenched his fists as he had last night when she'd called on him at his home.

Preparing to hurt me? Or was something wrong with him?

"Like the rest of your family, your father is not particularly clever. This latest apology and paltry offering, for yet another failure, is but one example of the small scale on which he thinks—as if I might be plied with something as simple as a good bottle of wine." The viscount took up the bottle again. "Though I do like to indulge in the finer things. Once, you might have joined me in those indulgences."

Sophie moved farther away from him, toward the back of the warehouse, all the while looking for anything she might use to defend herself.

"But now... It's too late for you to be my wife. But a slave, my own personal slave to do my every bidding..." Newsome crooked his finger, beckoning her closer. "That will do to pay the debt."

He never intended to let me go. She knew a moment of rage at her stupidity, and now helplessness, and understood Graham in a way she perhaps hadn't before. "I will *never* be your slave. My father can answer for his own debts. But we had a bargain. My husband is already giving you a substantial sum, by way of his property on Saint Kitts."

"Ah." Newsome took another drink, then raised a finger as if just recalling something. "About that. Your husband—assuming he has already signed his plantation over to me—is presently on his way *back* to prison. Couldn't have him missing his hanging tomorrow now, could we?"

She'd feared the viscount had done something like this, given his earlier revelation that he'd paid the judge to alter the verdict *twice*. But hearing that Graham might have already been taken— Her heart pounded with fear, not as much for herself as for Graham. Was he already back in Newgate? *How will I get him out again?* The unsettled feeling she'd experienced all morning erupted, setting off sensory alarms everywhere from the hairs at the back of her neck to the roiling in her stomach and the quickened beat of her heart. She had to get out of here and get Graham before it was too late. "That was not our agreement." Anger scorched her every word as an overwhelming desire to kill the viscount surged through her.

"Raymond taking you from me last spring, humiliating me in front of that roomful of people, when I had already been promised your hand—and everything else—was not part of the *agreement* I had with your father. It was poor form, and now Raymond's going to pay for it. Tomorrow morning when he hangs, he'll know that you're *my* possession now, and there's nothing he can do about it."

But I can. So long as I'm still living. I can. I will. A crate to her left budged as she moved around it. She paused, waiting for the viscount to draw closer.

"I do love a good game of cat and mouse," he purred. "I'm the cat, and you're the mouse. Only I'm not going to eat you just yet. I'm going to enjoy playing with you first. Then I'll keep you locked up safe and sound until tomorrow after I've seen your husband hang. And then your cage will be loaded onto my ship bound for Saint Kitts. You'll have all the time you want to be barefoot there—bare everything." Newsome laughed. He spotted her on the other side of the crate and took a step closer. Sophie threw all her weight into the wood box, shoving it into his legs and pushing him backward.

She ran toward the door, zigzagging around boxes amidst his cursing. Footsteps sounded behind her as she reached the door and tried the handle to no avail. She beat her fists on the metal and screamed for help.

Newsome lunged toward her, his breathing labored. She rolled out of the way and darted behind a set of stacked crates.

He leaned against the door, as if to catch his breath. Beads of sweat dotted his forehead, though it was cool inside the building. "Come here—little mouse." His voice wasn't sinister as it had been just minutes before. He came toward her.

Sophie tried pushing the top crate over, but it wouldn't budge. Newsome's hand brushed her arm. She feinted right, then hopped back instead, leaving him grasping only air. He staggered forward, off balance, and toppled toward the floor, striking the side of his head on a wood corner as he fell. His body hit the ground with a loud thud. Blood trickled from his head, and he moaned. Sophie ran farther into the room, away from him.

He rolled onto his side. "You'll pay—" His hands clutched his chest, and his face turned ashen. A tremor passed through his body, and he began convulsing.

A trick? Sophie stayed where she was, unmoving and out of his line of vision.

"Help—" he rasped. Just once. The convulsions heightened, then ceased abruptly.

Sophie stared at him, not daring to come closer. If it was a deception, he might shoot her if she came near. She waited, hands pressed to her thundering heart. *Please be dead. Please be dead.* How wrong she had once been to judge Graham for having had the same thoughts about his father.

Graham. He would die if she didn't act quickly. They would put him back in that prison, and she'd never get him out. And tomorrow— Sophie ran toward Newsome, not stopping until she stood over him. He lay still, eyes open, mouth open with spittle dribbling out the side.

Not daring to crouch or kneel, lest he rise up and force her beneath him, she bent over and reached for the nearest pocket in his jacket. Her fingers brushed the cloth of his coat.

Was that a twitch? Her stomach churned. She thrust her hand into the pocket. Empty.

Pounding at the door sent her jumping backward. She stared down at the viscount as the rhythm came again—the same pattern as earlier when the boy had delivered the bottle. *Someone the viscount knows. A colleague?* Whoever it was didn't have a key or hadn't used it yet.

Hurry! Newsome was lying on the second pocket, so she pushed his shoulder until he rolled back enough for her to reach it. Her hand slid inside the fabric, and her fingers closed around the ring and key. She stood and backed away, then ran to the door. She pressed her ear to it, listening, fearful that more trouble awaited her on the other side. For the moment she was safe here. *But Graham . . .* he wasn't. She had to get out, had to risk whatever trouble might be waiting if she was to get to him.

Fingers still trembling, she inserted the key.

Raised voices sounded outside. Male voices. Her hand stilled, and she hardly dared breathe.

"Sophie!"

Mother?

"I know you have her in there, Newsome!"

Graham? Sophie turned the key, and the door swung toward her before she could open it.

Strong arms swept her into an embrace.

"You're here." She pulled Graham closer as tears of relief clouded her vision.

"As are you." His voice broke, and he clutched her to him.

She clung to him, speaking into his shoulder. "The viscount said you were back at Newgate."

Graham lessened his grip to meet her gaze. "That was his plan, but your sister and Dowager Palmer helped us get away from his men. We saw the banker who'd taken the deed get into a coach, and we followed it here." Graham inclined his head to the carriage behind him, where the dowager was visible through the open door.

Mother made a strange sound as she peered past Sophie into the warehouse, then reached a hand out to grasp Sophie's. "I heard you screaming. Did—did he hurt you?"

"No." Sophie shook her head. "I am well enough."

Graham frowned as if he didn't believe her. "We need to get out of here. The guards we escaped may still be searching for us, and we need to be certain your sister is all right. Lady Palmer assured us she would be, but still . . ." He steered them away from the building.

Sophie leaned into him, reluctant to let go even a little and fearful that her imagination had only conjured him. "You shouldn't be here at all. You were—we were—supposed to go straight to the ship after the documents were signed."

"Nothing much went as planned today, did it," William asked, striding past them to enter the warehouse.

"Do you think I could board a ship knowing you were somewhere in this city with Newsome? Do you think I could live with myself if he hurt you, that I'd even want to live?" Graham's voice was gruff as his hands roamed over her head, her face, and shoulders. His fingers stilled when they came to her battered lip. His gaze dropped to the bruises visible beneath her parted cloak. "I'll kill him for this."

"You won't have to," William called from behind them. "The viscount is already dead."

Sixteen

GRAHAM CLASPED WILLIAM'S hand. "I wish you could come with us. I worry about leaving you here to face consequences. Breaking a man out of prison is no small crime."

"Elizabeth is too far along to make the voyage across the Atlantic. And besides—" William grimaced. "You know my feelings on America. I've no desire to sail so far or to see what independence has done to former English subjects. Elizabeth and I will leave for the country within the hour and be sailing for France before the end of the week. Her cousin has welcomed us before and no doubt will again. We'll winter there or possibly stay even longer, depending on the political climate here. I won't return until it's safe, and neither should you, my friend."

"I won't." A pang of longing for the peace of Caerlanwood struck hard as Graham pulled William toward him into an embrace.

"Godspeed," William said. "Write to me when you can. I expect to hear many outlandish tales of a wild people and land."

Graham released him and stepped back, his eyes stinging. "Thank you, William. For today, for everything. For sheltering my family. For your years of loyal friendship."

William nodded, his throat bobbing. "It has been my privilege. I have never known a better man."

"If so, it is in part because of your influence."

"And that of the one waiting for you." William looked past Graham toward Sophie, who stood at the top of the gangplank.

Graham raised a hand in a last farewell, then turned and walked toward Sophie. Her cloak was pulled tight around her against the cold and damp, but she had refused to board until he did. He understood, likewise wishing not to have her out of his sight for a long time to come.

He held out his arm as he approached, and Sophie linked hers through it and leaned into him.

"Will William and Elizabeth be all right?"

"I believe so," Graham answered. "They are going to visit family in France for the time being, and as Newsome is no longer a direct threat..."

They'd left his body as they'd found it in the warehouse, though it had been tempting to truss it up and stuff it into one of the crates that had previously held victims of his abuse. Instead they had locked the door, and Graham had dropped the key into the Thames, some miles from the building. Perhaps Sophie's father had another and would discover his colleague sooner rather than later.

Graham led Sophie past the various crew members on deck preparing the ship to leave and headed for the sanctuary of their private quarters. Maime and the children were already on board and in their room next door. They had all experienced a joyous reunion earlier, with Matthew practically knocking Graham over with his exuberant hug while Ayla had shyly spoken her first words to Graham.

On the other side, Olivia and Lady Claybourne had their lodging. Graham had requested the room between, as he wished to be near Sophie's family and Katherine's children should something go wrong. His net of responsibility now extended from Sophie, Ayla, Matthew, and Maime to include

Lady Claybourne and Sophie's younger sister Olivia. *One man to watch over four women and two children.* A burden, some might say. But reality was that each of those women, and even the children, had fought for and contributed to his rescue, his safety, and his well-being. He literally owed them his life, and he would protect theirs with his.

Sounds from both cabins—of Maime telling the children a story, and of Olivia comforting her mother as she cried—reached their ears.

He paused on the threshold. He ought to bid the children and Maime a good night but guessed he might be called upon to stay a while and read a story. And he needed to speak to Lady Claybourne, to offer understanding and comfort as perhaps only he could. He had no proof, but he guessed that the viscount had not suffered a natural death. Graham had seen the burden etched in Lady Claybourne's features once William had pronounced the viscount dead. But perhaps tonight was too soon to speak with her about the matter.

Sophie looked ruefully toward her mother and sister's cabin. "Mother was so strong throughout all of it, and now it seems she's falling apart. I'll let Livie comfort her tonight, but tomorrow I'll do what I can to cheer her."

Sophie stepped into the cabin, tugging Graham behind her. The sounds from either side seemed even more magnified through the thin walls.

"Not a lot of privacy," Sophie noted. "Or space." A single cot took up most of the room, with barely enough space for their trunk beside it.

He turned to face her before whispering, "But we are together."

He shut the door behind them. Lady Claybourne, who was traveling under the alias Mrs. Cox, had suggested that they all keep to their quarters as much as possible for the first few days of the voyage. Though they'd boarded in separate parties and under false names, an abundance of caution was a good idea, at present.

Graham tugged Sophie onto the bed beside him. "Rather narrow," he mused. "I'm not sure we'll both fit."

She rolled her eyes and gently pushed him down, then snuggled up beside him, her head resting on his uninjured shoulder. "Did you get used to sleeping by yourself again while you were in Newgate?"

"Never. And I never want either of us to speak of that place again." His arm wound around her waist, and he pulled her closer. "I missed you every single second. Most of all at night. I yearned for you, for our bed, for your icy feet pressing up against me, for the sound of the surf crashing on the rocks below and the sounds you make when—"

Sophie pressed a finger to his lips. "Shh. You can't talk like that here, or at least that loudly. My mother and sister will hear. Not to mention the children."

His fingers stroked lightly up her side. "Does that mean you won't be making those noises on this voyage?"

"I won't be doing any—" She sucked in a breath as his hand moved higher. "Oh." A sigh of pleasure escaped her lips and drifted about the room. "I missed you so much. I missed this, missed us—together."

"Me too." He kissed the top of her head. "We can miss it a bit longer. Right now I just want to hold you, and be held."

Sophie's arm across his middle tightened in response. "I love you, Graham. I was so frightened for you—for me, of losing you."

"I know." He held her even closer. "I was frightened too. Last night when William came to see me, when I realized you were with Newsome—" Graham pressed his lips together before he said more. He hadn't meant to bring that up so soon, or maybe ever. *Whatever Sophie did, it was to save me.* And though the thought of Newsome's hands on her made Graham want to break something—preferably Newsome's neck—he was trying to let his anger go.

Sophie leaned up on her arm and looked down at him, as if she'd felt his rising emotion. "I went to the viscount's home to propose the exchange of the plantation on Saint Kitts in return for your freedom. He wanted a kiss to seal our agreement—a token of my goodwill, that I wasn't trying to dupe him."

"But you were." Graham smiled briefly, remembering her clever deception.

"Not as much as he was deceiving us," Sophie muttered. "I was a fool to trust him at all. I should have known that before this morning. I didn't want to kiss him last night, but I needed him to believe me. So I leaned forward, intending to get it over with quickly, but he pushed me against the wall and held me there. He bit my lip and tore the front of my dress. I fought him, shoved his chin back, punched his throat, then pushed him away and kicked, and I ran, out of the room, out of his house, and down the street to the waiting carriage. I had a gun in my reticule, and I would have used it if he'd come after me."

Graham brushed a finger over her battered lip. "I'm sorry to have put you in a position where you felt you must offer anything to that man."

Sophie captured his hand and pressed it to her heart. "It was never my intent to offer him anything of myself. And I wouldn't have given more than a kiss. I wouldn't have broken our marriage vows." Sophie grasped his hand tightly as her eyes sought his.

"I once said that I would do anything to keep you safe, but to do that, to give myself—what is already and *only* yours— would have broken me, and I knew it would have broken you—broken *us*. I did not offer that, Graham. And if the viscount had tried to take it from me, I would have fought him to the death."

"Thank you for telling me that." Graham's voice was gruff as he pulled her back into his embrace. They lay there in silence. He stroked her arm and said another prayer of gratitude that she was safe, that they both were, but especially Sophie. She was right. It *would* have broken him if she'd paid that price for his freedom. He was still upset and would be for a long time. It had been too close a call with both their lives. But he was relieved, as well. *So relieved.* Newsome hadn't violated her, hadn't hurt Sophie in that most horrific way.

"I didn't want to be angry—and I wasn't with you. I wouldn't have been, even if you had—had bartered yourself. But I don't know if I could have borne it, knowing you suffered so—for me. I understand why you went to see Newsome, but—"

"Along with a certain prison that shall never be mentioned again, I believe that we should also never mention a certain viscount again. Through the grace of God, he is dead. He cannot hurt us or anyone else anymore. He is not worth another second of our thoughts."

Graham nodded his agreement, though he knew it would be a long time before he would be free of the thoughts about Newsome charging through his mind, haunting him. "We were blessed with a great deal of God's grace today."

Sophie's fingers swirled patterns across his shirt. "Many. Some I still don't understand. What happened at Rothschilds?"

"It was a setup," Graham said. "William and I were never alone from the moment I entered his carriage. Newsome insisted on sending armed men with William. The man at Rothschilds was in on it too. He said you'd not be returned to me until I'd signed the plantation over to—the viscount. Then, once I had, he called for William and me to be arrested, saying that I'd escaped prison and that William was my accomplice."

"As if anyone could escape that dungeon," Sophie huffed.

"Aye, well a few have over the centuries, but I was not to be one of them. I was also not going back and certainly not going to allow them to put William in there as well." Graham suppressed a shudder, thinking of that frigid underground cell. He'd never forget it, any more than he'd ever forget his father's cruelties or the sounds of his mother's and sister's cries. What a blow to his cheek felt like, or how it felt to nurse his own wounds in the darkness of a closet and to go days without food the first time he'd tried to stop his father.

The weeks at Newgate had left a mark, several of them—scars—that were a part of who he was now, for better or worse.

"William and I intended to run or fight—probably both—once we'd left the bank and before they could force us into any vehicle. Your sister—another fine actress in your family—arrived just as we were leaving, and she caused a distraction that bought us a few precious seconds. Lady Palmer called to us from her carriage right outside and whisked us away."

"But how did you know where to find me?" Sophie rolled slightly and raised her head, resting her chin on his chest so she could look at him as he continued his tale.

"A stroke of good fortune, or rather another of God's graces," Graham said. "We drove around the other side of the building, and there, coming out of Rothschilds, was the very man who had bade me to sign the deed and then proclaimed William and me to be criminals. He held a packet that looked very much like the one containing the deed, and he stepped into a cab and was off. I bade our driver follow him at a distance, and he led us right to you."

"He wasn't with you when I came out," Sophie said. "What did you do to him? What other trouble is William in?"

"None, from Rothschilds at least. When the man alighted from his coach and we arrived a minute later to confront him, he was suddenly most cooperative, handing over the deed and even apologizing to me. It was about that time that your mother appeared, carrying on and near hysteria that New— *the viscount* was hurting you."

"What hurt me the most was hearing that you were on your way back to prison. I didn't know how I'd possibly get you out again, and that panic and desperation gave me the strength to act, to try to get away from the viscount."

"You did get away. We both did." Graham stroked gentle fingers down the side of her face. He was still half afraid that if he closed his eyes she would disappear.

"I'll feel much better when we are away from the shore and underway." Sophie snuggled against his side, her head resting on his shoulder.

"As will I," Graham said. "I've felt but a step ahead of death all day." He'd cheated it, but it wasn't done with him yet, and worse, he feared the Reaper might just snatch Sophie up and take her instead.

But no. She was here. In his arms. *Safe.* Or as safe as could be for now. But he would feel better when there was an ocean between them and England. Or when they were at least a few miles from shore.

"When do we leave, do you suppose?"

"I've no idea." He'd made it a point not to speak with the captain or crew or anyone else on board. They'd kept their heads down and gone straight to their quarters, as arranged by Sophie's mother. "It may be a few hours yet. We should rest. Neither of us had much sleep last night."

"True." Sophie sighed. They lay silently a few minutes, the gentle bobbing of the ship as effective as any lullaby for a bairn.

By degrees he felt his body began to relax. The taut

muscles unclenched, the senses that had all been on alert gradually shut down. *Sleep.* Real sleep, finally. Good sleep with his wife next to him and a bed—if not as warm and comfortable as the one at home, at least a vast improvement over what he'd been attempting sleep in these past weeks.

Sophie untucked his shirt and slid her hand beneath. *Heaven.* To feel her hand upon him. After her visit in the prison, he'd relived the moments of her removing his shirt, bathing him, and dressing him again over and over in his mind. It had not been a sensual act, but one of pure love, and it had hauled him from despair and buoyed his spirits over the following days.

Now her fingers splayed across his chest, then drifted lower. A different kind of touch than that day. One he welcomed, though—

Graham drew in a sharp breath as her hand brushed the top of his trousers. "I cannot sleep with you touching me like that."

Sophie lifted her head to look at him, and a slow smile bloomed. "Perhaps not, but I promise you'll sleep better after I'm done."

Seventeen

OLIVIA PULLED THE pillow over her head and rolled away from the wall separating her cabin from Sophie's and the duke's. *Unbelievable.*

The Sophie she'd grown up with would never have behaved thus, even if she thought no one else could hear her. She would never have fallen in love with a duke—with any man—but would have marched on, resolute in her ideals and ambition. This Sophie was a stranger—passionate about a nobleman instead of noble causes. Her sister, surprisingly, astonishingly, had turned out to be a lot like Torie.

Olivia squeezed her eyes shut and tried to no avail to block out the low murmurs and sounds of affection coming from the other side of the wall. Had Torie and Jonathan even been that bad? Perhaps, but at least they'd always been discreet. The way Sophie was carrying on, you'd think she hadn't seen her husband in weeks. *Or nearly lost him forever.*

A corner of Olivia's heart softened, empathy overtaking revulsion. Sophie *had* almost lost her duke. It had been that close. Olivia supposed that if she had a great love and had almost lost him, she might not care who overheard their reunion either.

She felt glad for her sister, in spite of the sounds of intimacy keeping her awake. Seeing Sophie like this was—

encouraging. If bookish Sophie could end up finding a great love, then perhaps there was hope, after all, for Olivia herself.

Even without balls to attend and suitors to vie over my hand.

Yet Olivia felt certain she would cry when she felt the first pull away from the dock. Yes, she wanted to see Jonathan, to keep her promise. She'd thought of little else these past months in hiding. Staying free for him had been her purpose, the thing to focus on so she didn't focus on all that she'd lost, the Season and life that had been snatched from her almost before she'd begun to live.

But now that the moment was here, the time to part with England—perhaps forever—at hand . . .

She pulled the pillow from covering her head and instead buried her face in it, catching the first sob as it came. Would she ever walk in Hyde Park on a gentleman's arm? Would she ever enjoy the luxuries of her room at their townhome again? Would she ever dance at a ball and have a card filled with gentlemen's names dangling from her wrist?

With whom would she laugh and flirt? Surely not Jonathan. If they were to make a match, he needed a woman to nurse his broken heart, not a flighty girl wishing to capture the attention of the most handsome man in the room.

Torie had found romance with him, but that felt like a lifetime ago. *I was but thirteen when they married.* He was older now, a widower, a man having travailed through much sorrow and hardship and having crossed an ocean to escape it.

Could I love him? Will he accept me? And care for me at least a little?

She knew the answer to the first question already. Part of her had loved him since the summer she and Sophie had spent with Torie and Jonathan. He'd taken them both under his wing, acting as any older brother might and teaching them all sorts of unladylike skills. Sophie had reveled in it. *And I . . .* Olivia had watched Torie and Jonathan with a childlike jealousy. What the two of them shared—it was unique. Special. Sacred.

Her parents had nothing of the sort in their marriage. She'd never seen another couple who did, but then she hadn't been allowed out in Society much at that age. Even now, having enjoyed a brief taste of London's social scene, attending balls and parties and musicales, she could tell—what Torie and Jonathan had shared was special.

Why? What made their love so great? Olivia suspected that Sophie and the duke shared a similar affection. *Certainly passion.* Which nullified Olivia's theory that Torie and Jonathan's love had been so true because he was from a different class, where marrying for love mattered more than marrying for money or status. Had Sophie and her duke married for love? Or had that come later? If so, what had Sophie done to encourage those feelings?

Tomorrow. And the next day and the next if necessary. Every day until their ship landed in America, if need be, Olivia vowed to observe Sophie and her husband, to learn what she could. She would ask Sophie for advice as well. Perhaps it was as simple as something Sophie had read in a book.

The sound of crying that wasn't her own reached Olivia's ears. Brushing her own tears away, she sat up and looked over at her mother's bunk. *Asleep.* The steady rise and fall of the blanket, and her mother's still face, confirmed it.

"All is well now. He cannot hurt us anymore. Nor will your father." The duke's soothing voice carried through the thin wall, comforting Olivia as well, though from the sound of Sophie's sobbing, she was not as easily calmed.

Sophie never used to cry. Another change in her sister to catalog. Olivia wasn't certain if being in love was good for Sophie or not. But that she was committed to, her very heart and soul entwined with, the duke's, was becoming more apparent by the minute.

Thank goodness my ruse worked. Her part in today's rescue had seemed exciting and fun. Marching into Rothschilds at the precise moment necessary—thanks to the dowager and her looking glass, which had spied the duke through the window—had been so simple. They had known he was inside already, as Olivia had walked into the bank after them and seen him ushered into a room by two unfriendly looking men.

After reporting this information to the dowager, Olivia had armed herself with all of Father's documents that Mother had gathered and intended to burn or throw into the sea. Instead, Olivia had scattered them all over the lobby at Rothschilds and had not bothered to stay to retrieve even one of them. She supposed that was as good as having them in ashes or at the bottom of the Thames. It might even be better, had some miscreant snatched up a deed or promissory note and decided to make good use of it.

Father had always accused her of being given to hysterics, so she had played that part well today and had thoroughly enjoyed sending his papers and personal documents flying everywhere across that foyer. The scream she'd emitted a second later, when one of the men guarding the duke had trod upon those papers, had been all too easy to summon and had been a genuine release of the pent up emotion she'd contained the past several months. Anger, frustration, sorrow, loneliness, fear, the unfairness—all of it came tumbling out of her in a wail that had caused every head in the lobby to turn in her direction.

The duke believed her a good actress, but she hadn't been acting. When she'd started beating on the man in front of her, that hadn't been pretended either. It was her father and that loathsome viscount who deserved it, but the man working for them had been a good substitute. Pity she'd had her gloves on and hadn't been able to use her nails to claw at him as well.

She'd run out after him, then to the waiting cab that had taken her to the dowager's house, where she'd waited a tense few hours for word and for the dowager to return to escort her to the ship.

All had turned out well. Sophie had her happily ever after. And now . . . *I must find mine.*

Jonathan. Olivia searched her memory for his face, though it was difficult to conjure without her sister's by his side. Their sweet Torie was gone. Jonathan's sweet Torie. Did he know of the promise Torie had extracted from her youngest sister? Olivia doubted it and worried and wondered about the reception they would get upon arriving at his home in New York. She would go alone the first time, she'd decided. Seeing her would likely be shock enough for him. Olivia needn't bring the whole entourage to see him all at once.

Did he hate them? Would seeing her remind him of Torie and hurt him even more? *How long, and what will it take for him to fall in love with me?* Was such a thing even possible? Six months from now would she be lying with her husband as passionately as Sophie and her duke did now?

The sounds from the other side of the wall had finally subsided. Olivia sat up and looked over at her mother again, still sleeping in the other bed. Today had been especially hard on her. She'd nearly lost Sophie, and after already losing one daughter . . . Olivia could only imagine how difficult it must have been for her mother to hear Sophie's screams and be unable to get to her.

A mother's love knows no bounds. Does a sister's? She'd given Torie her word, and she intended to fulfill it. The prospect was even enticing—intriguing. Jonathan was a fine man, in looks, manner, and spirit. Or he had been, before Father's wrath destroyed everything dear to him.

How was Jonathan changed now? Was that teasing light in his brown eyes forever gone? Or might she bring back some of that sparkle? *Might he someday look at me the way he used to look at Torie?* The way Sophie's duke looked at her?

That is all I ask, Torie. Just let him love me at least a little bit as much as he loved you. That wasn't too much to hope for, was it? Not when she was giving up her Season and balls, callers and courtship, bouquets of flowers and rides in Hyde Park. She'd read everything she could about upstate New York, and it didn't seem there was much in the way of operas or musicales, ballrooms, or banquets where they were going. *Just a simple life, far from home and all those things I love.*

But if once in a while Jonathan could look at her like he used to look at Torie, that would be enough. It would have to be.

Eighteen

THE GENTLE ROLLING of the ship nudged Sophie toward the center of the narrow bed. Half asleep, she reached for Graham and to brace herself, but her hand met only the cool, stiff sheet. Her eyes flew open, and she sat up, panic flaring for the few seconds it took to recognize her surroundings. They were on the *Columbia*. It was moving. Graham *had* been here.

Her current state of undress confirmed that she hadn't imagined his presence and their earlier activities. *Where is he now?*

Sophie groped about the bed until she found her discarded clothing at the end. She pulled the shift over her head and stood on the cold floor, bracing herself against the wall as the room rose, then fell again. Her stomach followed suit. This voyage wasn't going to improve her sickness. *Perhaps the fresh air will.* Discovering Graham's whereabouts definitely would.

Sophie threw her cloak over her shift, stuffed her stockingless feet into her shoes, and left their room. The setting three-quarter moon illuminated the deck and the sea beyond. She stepped farther away from the bank of cabins and up onto the main deck, then turned a slow circle, taking in her surroundings and searching for her husband.

Distant pinpricks of light to the east indicated that they

had at last left London behind. *Good.* If she never saw the city again, that would please her greatly. She did wish they might return to Caerlanwood and felt a pang of sorrow at leaving it behind for who knew how long. But she could not deny the thrill of being on a vessel bound for America. She had always wanted to travel, to see the world, and now she was going to see some of it at last.

But it would be infinitely better to see it with Graham. *Where is he?*

Sophie started toward the bow, nodding to the few men on duty as she passed, her eyes darting to and fro, searching for her husband. He had to be here somewhere. *Unless—* Had someone discovered he was wanted and taken him in the night, locking him in a shipboard prison? *Impossible.* She would have heard. They would have had to drag him over her to get him out of the bunk. Besides, he wasn't traveling as himself, or even a nobleman. Their simple clothing and humble cabin matched their middle-class roles as Mr. and Mrs. Martin, shopkeepers.

"Where is the shopkeeper keeping himself?" Sophie mumbled, as she started down the opposite side of the deck, heading for the stern this time. She'd nearly reached it when she found Graham, seated atop a crate, staring toward what had been the faint lights of London only a few minutes before but what was now only empty sea.

Sophie came up beside him and took one of his cold hands in her own. "You're freezing. How long have you been out here?"

"A while." His voice was quiet, somber. But not sad—or at least she didn't think it was.

Sophie released his hand, then held her arm up, stretching a side of her cloak around him. "Bring a blanket next time, at least. We didn't save you only to have you freeze to death." Beneath the shared cloak, she snuggled up to his side.

"I've been colder."

His solemn expression told her he was thinking of Newgate, but she didn't ask, didn't utter the forbidden name.

"There's no need to be cold now. You are to be warm and dry and fed, and *at my side* throughout this voyage and beyond."

He turned to her at the touch of reprimand in her voice. "I'm sorry if I worried you. I've no plans to go overboard or anything else."

"Good." Why was he out here, then? *More nightmares?* If so, were they those from his childhood that had plagued him before, or were these new horrors, summoned by his time in that dungeon?

"Look." Graham nodded his head toward the horizon, beginning to pink with morning light. "I wanted to see the sunrise. In that cell there were no sunrises or sunsets. It became difficult, if not impossible, to keep track of the days, as meals were delivered sporadically, and I slept so much— especially at the beginning."

Sophie turned from the colors rising over the water to look at Graham, a sense of wonder, of appreciation rising in his expression along with the sun.

"Others had tried to scratch out their days there, and I tried as well, with a bit of loose rock, onto the wood of the door. But it didn't help to count them. I felt myself going mad just the same, and a reminder of how long I'd been there, all the time I'd missed with you and the children, only added to my anger and melancholy. I would have done better had they set me to hard labor somewhere. At least then my hands wouldn't have been idle, and my body would have been exhausted at day's end.

"And I would have known day. I would have felt the sun, no matter how distant, on my face. I had no hope of going free, not with New—with the viscount against me, so I began to pray that instead of hanging me they'd send to me Australia, to the penal colony there. I imagined you at Caerlanwood when you received the news, and I had faith that you—determined and strong woman that you are—would find a way to join me eventually. My heart broke at the thought of never seeing Caerlanwood again—"

"You *will* see it again," Sophie insisted. "We will. All of us. This is temporary exile."

Graham took her hand and brought it to his lips, pressing a lingering kiss there. "If I do not, I can live with that. But to lose the children, and especially you . . . it was that I could not bear the thought of."

"Now you have Ayla and Matthew, me, and the sunrise." Sophie wrapped her arm around him as they stared out at the distant orb and the pinks and oranges shining from it, skimming across the water, practically to their feet.

Graham leaned his head toward hers. "I have everything."

Nineteen

A WEEK INTO their voyage had given Graham both his sea legs and some of his strength back. Fare on the ship wasn't as grand or plentiful as it had been at home, but it was far better than what he'd had at the prison. He ate as heartily as he could, often finishing Sophie's meals, sick as she was from the bairn growing inside of her.

Our child. They'd finally had time to talk of the future, of the child that would be joining them in late spring. The news seemed to have brought some joy, some relief, to Sophie's mother, but the lady still wasn't herself—according to both Sophie and her sister, and what little Graham had observed of her prior to their voyage.

He believed he knew what ailed her, and today he intended to find out if he was correct, and if so, what he might do to help.

After watching the sunrise alone—today as with most days, as Sophie felt too ill in the mornings to join him—Graham returned to their cabin to check on her. She still slept, but sounds of movement from her mother's cabin told him that at least one occupant was awake. Graham knocked softly, and a minute later Lady Claybourne answered. She was dressed for the day but had not done up her hair yet, a hardship for her, he had come to understand, as she was used to having a lady's maid to help with the task.

"Good morning—Your Grace." She whispered the last, after a furtive glance in either direction, making sure they were alone.

He smiled. "Mr. Martin will do for now, Mrs. Cox. And in the future, when we have solid ground beneath our feet again, Graham would be preferable. I'm given to understand, by your daughter Olivia, that where we are going in America, titles are neither useful nor appreciated."

Lady Claybourne returned his smile, though hers was fleeting. "Olivia is still abed, if you're seeking her. She's still keeping hours of the Season, though she has not kept to any social calendar of late nights for several months."

"It is you I wish to speak with." He did want to talk to Olivia as well, about her silence around him and why he frequently found her staring at him and Sophie, but that could wait. Lady Claybourne's melancholy seemed a more urgent matter. Graham stepped back and extended a hand in invitation. "Would you walk with me this morning? The sea is calm, the rocking minimal at present."

"Of course. Give me a minute, please."

Graham nodded his agreement and turned away as the door again closed. He waited perhaps five minutes instead of one before Lady Claybourne reappeared, her hair no longer down but pulled back behind her in a low, loose chignon. The style—less starched and polished than before, especially with her simpler clothing—was becoming on her.

"You look fine this morning, Mrs. Cox." He offered her his elbow, and she placed her hand gently upon it.

"Thank you, sir. I feel a bit better than in days past."

"Our news has cheered you?" He knew it had—had witnessed the first true smile from her when he and Sophie had told her of their forthcoming child.

"I am happy about it, happy for you both. A child is a

great blessing, and this one is going to have exceptional parents."

"And a doting grandmother," Graham added.

"That too." Lady Claybourne's expression clouded again, and Graham could practically feel the weight burdening her as they strolled the deck.

"I am not sure I am worthy of the title," she admitted quietly.

Graham led them to a spot at the rail far from anyone else. Lady Claybourne dropped her hand from his arm, and he turned to face her. "Because you were unable to stop your husband from the events that contributed to Victoria's death? Or is it because you *did* stop your husband and Viscount Newsome from destroying Sophie and perhaps Olivia as well?"

Her eyes widened at his bluntness. "*Both*," she admitted. "I have failed as a mother in so many ways. How can I be any sort of grandmother?"

"Because—" Graham took her hand and met her gaze, waiting until her attention was wholly focused on him. "You are to *be* a grandmother *specifically* because of the brave mother that you are. Were it not for you, Sophie would be with the viscount on a ship bound for Saint Kitts, both she and our unborn child in grave danger, and I would be dead."

Lady Claybourne shook her head. "I'm the one who suggested she should go to the viscount. It was because of me that she was in danger in the first place."

"You don't think Sophie would have gone on her own, without your support?" He didn't wait for an answer. "I know she would have, and the consequences could have been much more dire, had you and the dowager not stepped up—at great personal risk—to help." He released her hand. "I owe you my life, and for that I am most grateful."

Love UNDYING

"You are most welcome, but in freeing you and Sophie, I . . . I—" She looked away, the color draining from her face as she released a soul-weary sigh.

"You took a life," Graham said quietly.

Her eyes snapped back to his.

Graham nodded slowly. "I know. Lord Fitzgerald guessed too—and thought no worse of you for it. Indeed, we are both in your debt."

Lady Claybourne swallowed, and tears filled her eyes. Graham withdrew his handkerchief and handed it to her. "There are times when the world forces us to make cruel choices. No matter what we do, it will seem wrong—there will be a cost either way. In my estimation, the cost in this circumstance was well worth it. As it was the day I put a bullet through Oliver Higgins's heart."

Lady Claybourne suppressed a shiver, and Graham wondered if he'd said too much, if his bluntness and honesty frightened her.

"That feels—different," she said. "He was whipping a child."

"No different." Graham shook his head. "The viscount was armed, and Sophie had no defenses. He would have done terrible things to *your* child. Just because she's grown doesn't mean you love her less, or that you've no need to look out for her best interest or to aid her as needed. You were protecting Sophie, protecting Olivia as well. I admire you greatly for the courage to act as you did, for the foresight and planning it must have taken. The risk."

Lady Claybourne's head bobbed slightly in acknowledgment before she turned from him to look out at the Atlantic.

"How can I help you be relieved of this burden?" Graham asked. "You've had to shoulder much these past months, the past years, and Sophie and I wish to see you happy—or as much as you can be, given the loss of Victoria and who your husband is."

"I would like to be happy too. I'm not sure that is possible. But seeing Sophie thus—" She turned to him. "It is I who am in your debt, for answering my letter last spring, for coming to help, for keeping her safe—and more. So much more than I could have hoped for. I can see how very much you love her."

"You gave me the greatest gift in your daughter," Graham said, his throat constricting. "I was tangled up with the viscount and your husband long before I met Sophie, so don't think for a minute that my helping her was what landed me in prison. They would have come for me eventually one way or another—for being a threat to their livelihoods with my work toward abolition.

"Even had the outcome not been as favorable, I would have gone to my grave having experienced more happiness in the past few months than during the entirety of my lifetime. Sophie is the very best thing that has ever happened to me. So you see, I am indebted to you twice and, therefore, must endeavor to relieve you of your burden of guilt."

"It is a burden," Lady Claybourne said wearily. "I knew what I was doing, knew what the end result would be, and yet when I saw it, saw the viscount's body slumped on the ground, I was—unprepared for it."

"Tell me," Graham coaxed. "Tell me all of it, if you will. You'll feel better for it, and I can shoulder at least some of that burden."

She took a deep breath, then released it. "The viscount liked to drink. I still remember the way his eyes lit up the first time he visited our cellar. Every time he visited after that, he wanted my husband to open one of our finest bottles. After Sophie left and I sent Olivia into hiding, my husband gave the viscount two of our oldest and finest vintages—as a matter of apology for the inconvenience of temporarily losing Sophie."

"She was not his to lose," Graham muttered.

Lady Claybourne nodded. "Yes, but it became apparent that neither the viscount nor my husband was going to let the matter go—they were going to hunt until they found one or both of the girls. My husband very much still wanted the merger, and it was a matter of pride for the viscount. Sophie was safe enough with you, for the time being, anyway, but there were several close calls with Olivia. I knew I couldn't hide her forever. I needed another solution."

Graham was fairly certain he knew what that solution had been, but he remained silent, listening as Lady Claybourne unburdened herself.

"After one particularly horrific evening, during which the viscount assaulted one of our youngest maids, I felt I could stand by no more. I wanted that vile man out of our house and out of our lives—permanently."

"Both understandable and justified," Graham said, his tone coaxing her to continue.

Lady Claybourne glanced up and down the deck, as if to ascertain that they were still alone. Her voice lowered. "With the help of a servant—a young man who was fond of the maid the viscount assaulted—I acquired some arsenic. Then, whenever my husband was out of town—away following leads on Olivia—I started sending bottles of our best wine, laced with arsenic, to the viscount. I practiced imitating my husband's handwriting until I had a good likeness, and I sent forged notes with each bottle, so the viscount would believe the wine was a gift from Lord Claybourne."

Arsenic. Colorless, odorless, tasteless. The perfect poison. Had he known about it when he was a boy, he would have found a way to give some to his father.

He hadn't, and had not had any other means to protect his mother and sister. But Lady Claybourne had found the means and, as Graham had suspected, had acted courageously to protect her girls.

The bump to the viscount's head that day when they had found him in the warehouse hadn't appeared severe, not enough to kill a man, though heart failure was. But Lady Claybourne's expression as she'd looked at him and then glanced at the nearby bottle, had made Graham suspicious.

"Lord Claybourne never noticed any of his best wines were missing during all those months?"

"Once. Only recently, thank heavens. I'd taken to replacing the bottles I took with others, knowing he wasn't likely to notice, as those I took were vintages he was intent on saving for some time. He noticed one missing about a month ago, and then he discovered several of the others that had been replaced. He was livid."

"What happened?" Graham tensed, expecting to hear how she'd been struck or worse.

"He dismissed one of our newer footmen, one with access to the storeroom. He'd been found with a bottle in his room, tucked behind his bed, and though it wasn't even one of our bottles, and he proclaimed his innocence, my husband did not believe him. He was ready to send the man to prison, to have his hand cut off, or worse. I helped him get away before he could be arrested.

"I was never even questioned. And Lord Claybourne dared not mention the matter to the viscount, who already thought him the fool for having two daughters vanish without a trace."

"You were brave to continue your plan after such a close call."

"What choice did I have? I knew I could not hide Olivia forever, and I'd hoped . . ." Lady Claybourne shook her head. "I believed, that if Lord Newsome went away, if he died, my husband's flaws might recede. He might perhaps be at least tolerable once more. But I fear my hope was in vain. Sophie has told me of his abominable behavior in Scotland. If ever he felt anything for our daughters or me, it seems those feelings are no longer."

"I am sorry for that," Graham said, unsure what he ought to say or might say that would comfort her. "Many women are condemned to loveless marriages for the sake of a convenient match. My own mother was one and suffered greatly at my father's hand."

Lady Claybourne finally pulled her gaze from the water to look at him. The lines of her face softened with compassion. "I am sorry. Sophie has told me a little of your upbringing, of the abuses you endured."

"It was my mother who experienced the brunt of it," Graham said. "I know a great deal of guilt because of that. I would like to spare you a similar burden. Had I been able to stop my father—even by methods of violence—and thereby spare my mother, I would have acted thus. And I believe I would have been justified, as you are in your actions toward the viscount."

Lady Claybourne sighed. "That remains to be seen, most likely until I face our Maker."

"Was it not He who entrusted to you three daughters?"

"Girls whom I fear I have largely failed."

"Nonsense," Graham said. "I didn't know Victoria, but Sophie and Olivia are wonderful women—strong and smart and capable. They didn't get that from their father."

"No." Lady Claybourne's mouth twisted in a half smile. "They did not. Though perhaps because of him they developed those traits, as a matter of survival."

Graham returned her smile, then sobered once more. "You acted out of love, to protect them. You were a David slaying a Goliath who was intent on hurting your children. It was the right thing to do."

"Yet your mother did no such thing, did not poison the man hurting her and her children."

"I wish that she had," Graham said vehemently. "She and my sister might still be with us, and I would not have almost missed the opportunity to marry Sophie, because I was so burdened by and afraid of carrying on my father's legacy of abuse."

Lady Claybourne's eyes were sorrowful as she looked at him. "We are a burdened pair, you and I."

"It is a weight I will carry the rest of my life," Graham agreed. "My failure to protect my mother and sister resulted in the loss of their lives. But you—you did *not* fail." He touched Lady Claybourne's arm, then gently turned her toward him. "Imagine for a minute that you did not poison the viscount. What would have been the outcome?"

"I don't care to think on it." Lady Claybourne pursed her lips.

"You must," Graham insisted. "I would be dead. Sophie would be in the viscount's possession, probably in one of those cages, and bound for a life of the worst kind of slavery on Saint Kitts. How would you feel right now, were it only you and Olivia on this vessel? If Sophie, too, was lost to you forever and enduring the horrific?"

Lady Claybourne's eyes filled with tears. "I could not bear it. To have lost Sophie, too, and to that monster."

Graham nodded. "But you *can* bear this, the choice you really had little choice but to make. And when, someday, you face our Maker, you ought to be able to speak to Him with a clear conscience, for you were protecting the children he blessed you with. You did the best you could, and, like David, you slew an awful giant and saved them."

Tears slipped down her face. "I could see no other option. He was never going to leave her alone." Her voice quavered. "And I'd already lost one daughter."

Graham placed his hand over hers. "You did the right thing. Your actions saved many lives, even above mine and Sophie's."

"Then why do I have nightmares about what I've done?"

He gave her a sad smile. "Because you are a good person. You have a conscience."

"Are you saying you don't? That you've never been bothered by your actions?"

He considered her question. "Not until recently, when I believed they might cost me my life with Sophie. Before I met her I did not care about many things, including my actions toward those who had wronged me or others. I existed in a haze of anger with a strong desire for revenge. Sophie helped me see that there is a much stronger, much better, power in this world."

"Love." Lady Claybourne smiled. "You are both fortunate to have found it. I will be forever grateful to you, as well, for answering my letter and saving her."

Twenty

"You cannot move that piece that way," Graham said to Matthew for perhaps the tenth time in as many minutes.

Such patience, Olivia marveled, watching him from the corner of her eye as she sketched the scene. Attempting to teach a three-year-old to play chess seemed utter madness—or a losing proposition, at the least. But there were few diversions for the children on the ship, so, of necessity Sophie and Graham had become creative. *But not Maime.* Though the woman shared her cabin with the children, her days were hers to do with as she pleased. She was neither servant nor slave to Graham, but a free woman traveling with the family because she wished to.

It was Sophie and Graham who saw to the children's needs from sunup until bedtime. *So strange.* Olivia did not believe they were merely playing the part of a lower-class family while onboard. Their relationship with the children said otherwise, said that these loving, nurturing relationships were normal and the way life had been for the past several months in Scotland.

True, Sophie had begun her life at the duke's Scottish estate as a governess, but when they married surely she could have hired another in her stead. But it did not appear that she wished to, nor did it appear that the duke minded his time with the children either.

When a chess set had been located, Graham had promised to teach them to play. This morning was Matthew's turn while Sophie sat with Ayla a short distance away, attempting to teach her to read, using the only book she'd brought with her.

From her observations, Olivia didn't think those lessons were going much better.

"Watch again." Graham moved the pawn toward the middle of the board, away from Matthew.

Matthew rose on his knees to peer over the game. "Your pieces go that way. Why not mine?"

"Because I am playing on the opposite side. I cannot move mine backward or toward me either."

"You'll get me then!" the little boy exclaimed, drawing his pawn toward him anyway, clutching it tightly, as if to protect it.

"And then you'll be able to get one of my pieces after I get yours." Graham held his hand out until Matthew surrendered the pawn. Graham placed it back on the board, then moved the pieces, showing Matthew how he could capture a pawn as well.

Olivia did her best to record the moment understanding dawned on the child's face. She sketched for several minutes, half listening to their conversation as her pencil illustrated the scene. When she felt she'd captured it sufficiently, she stopped and studied it closely.

The duke did not appear the same handsome, imposing figure who had commanded the entire room at her father's townhome last spring. There had been a power emanating from him the night he announced that he and Sophie were to marry. The air had felt charged with it, and Olivia had found him dashing and romantic and a little frightening. She'd felt jealous of Sophie having made such a match without even trying. But here, playing chess with a three-year-old, the duke seemed a different creature altogether—relaxed and casual, nothing commanding or fierce about him.

He was still too gaunt, still undernourished from his weeks in Newgate. The clothing her mother had procured for him prior to their sailing hung on him, making him look even more the part of a poor relation. The dark circles beneath his eyes had cleared, though, and when he smiled at Matthew and ruffled the boy's hair as he praised him, a bit of the dashing figure Olivia remembered reappeared. Sophie seemed to see it in him all the time, given the looks the two of them exchanged almost constantly.

She was looking at him now, adoration and love shining in her eyes as she stared over the top of Ayla's head at the man she'd chosen to marry.

Chosen. Sophie had *chosen* to marry him. She had not been forced to it at all. How that had come about was still entirely perplexing to Olivia. Prior to last summer, her sister had practically taken a vow of celibacy. She wanted nothing to do with any man—ever. And now . . .

The sounds that traveled through the wall each night when Sophie snuggled into bed with her husband indicated her full and complete change of heart as perhaps nothing else did. Except possibly the looks the two of them exchanged constantly. Graham was watching Sophie now, a smile pulling his mouth upward and appreciation lighting his eyes.

What is there to appreciate? Sophie was dressed as poorly as he, in some cast-off dress Mother had garnered from a servant. The style hadn't been in fashion for several years, and the fabric was faded and worn. Sophie's hair hung down her back in a simple, sloppy braid that she did herself almost every morning, and her cheeks were rosy and freckled from the sun and the wind and her refusal to wear a hat most days. By the *ton*'s standards she was no great beauty, yet her husband appeared to think otherwise. Why had he fallen in love with her?

What will it take for Jonathan to fall in love with me? Olivia closed her eyes and tilted her face up toward the warmth of the sun, allowing her hat to slide back, if only for a moment. Her skin was fair and unmarred, and she intended to keep it that way. And while she might be dressed as a pauper for this voyage, the trunk in her cabin—and half of her mother's as well—was filled with her finest gowns, shoes, jewelry, perfumes, bonnets, and gloves.

With her darker hair and pale complexion, she could be a great beauty when dressed for the part. Right now she probably looked as raggamuffin as her sister. But when it came time to call on Jonathan, she would look her best. Sophie had looked her best the night of that fateful dinner party, which must have caught the duke's attention. His admiration. Attraction had been at play. The ever-important *attraction* that mamas in the *ton* primed their daughters to create from the youngest age.

Olivia lowered her face and secured her hat once more. The wind was calm today, making the temperature feel warmer, especially in the sun. But the doldrums also meant it would take longer for them to reach New York. She was impatient with waiting, more so than the children. Though it wasn't exactly excitement she felt at the prospect of reaching New York and finally seeing Jonathan again. It wasn't nervousness either, but something of a mix between the two. She was eager to get on with her life, to be doing something other than the waiting she'd been doing for so many months now. At least now she wasn't in hiding, though she couldn't be herself on this voyage.

Other passengers of their social class who might have interested her and been amusing to pass the time with were off limits. She and her mother, Sophie, Graham, the children, and Maime, all had to stay in the lower-class areas—not the steerage below ship, thankfully, but neither were they allowed to mingle with those passengers of the upper crust.

Our class. Or it had been. They dared not chance being recognized by anyone during their voyage, and Mother had warned her that they would have to be cautious and careful with their funds if they were to sustain themselves for a long while in America. The gowns in her trunk were going to have to last. The frivolities of her youth, along with her hopes and dreams, were gone. Everything was going to be different in America. Everything already was different, and Olivia wasn't certain she liked it at all.

Twenty-one

"Do I have something in my teeth?" Graham directed his question at Olivia, instead of Sophie, though she was seated right beside him.

"What? No." Olivia shook her head and turned away, but not before he noted the blush creeping across her cheeks.

Caught staring. It was time he discovered what was going on with his sister-in-law. They were over halfway through their voyage now—plenty of time for her to have become comfortable around him, especially given the close quarters they all shared. He had a feeling he was falling short somehow, but he didn't know how he was to remedy that when she hardly ever spoke to him. It might be that he simply wasn't living up to the standards Jonathan had set as her first brother-in-law, but it was time he—they—knew what was troubling her. Sophie had noticed her sister's odd behavior as well.

"Livie, will you join us, please." As if she'd read his thoughts, Sophie beckoned to her sister.

Olivia closed the book she'd been pretending to read—Graham hadn't seen her turn a page in ten minutes—and crossed the narrow strip of deck to their bench. Sophie scooted closer to him, then patted the bench on her other side, indicating that Olivia was to sit there.

She slid into place but did not look at either of them.

Sophie wrapped an arm around her sister and gave her a sideways hug. "What's wrong, Livie? You've been staring at Graham and me all morning, like we've broken out in the plague or something."

"If I've done something to offend you, I'd like to know," Graham added. "Or, it may just be that my presence offends you, and you've been plotting a way to throw me overboard and free your sister from marriage to such a dastardly fellow."

"Not likely, when I am at least partly responsible for your reunion and safe arrival on this ship." Olivia gave a slight shake of her head and rolled her eyes.

"True enough," Graham said. "What it is, then? Were you as candid your sister, I would have known weeks ago. She's never been one to shrink from telling me my faults."

Sophie bumped her shoulder into his as she frowned at him. "Many that they are."

He grinned. "I warned you before we married—even tried to tell you I'd be a poor bargain."

"You did?" Olivia looked at him, then shifted her attention to Sophie. "He told you not to marry him?"

"More than once." Sophie reached for Graham's hand. "But I knew I could handle him. He tried, but he couldn't scare me off."

Olivia's wide-eyed gaze flitted back and forth between the two of them. "I've been watching you because I've been trying to figure out what it is between you—why your relationship works and why you fell in love with one another."

Sophie smiled. "You should have just asked."

Olivia shook her head. "I thought I'd learn more from observing. That was about the only thing I could do these past months, and I've become quite good at it. I couldn't speak with anyone or dance or dine or play games or attend a musicale. But in each house that I stayed, I learned where I might hide so I could observe others doing those things. From behind curtains or cupboard doors I could listen and watch, and I learned a great deal that way."

"My sister-in-law is a spy." Graham grinned. "That could be a useful gift. Though I'd say your methods need improving. On board this ship, at least, you haven't been discreet at all."

Olivia's cheeks reddened again. "I was careless. Though not as careless as the two of you are at night! From my bunk I hear everything you say and do."

Sophie was the one blushing now, but Graham merely squeezed her hand. "I love your sister, and I won't apologize for that. Though I do apologize if my loving her—our loving each other—has disturbed your sleep."

"You have no idea how disturbed," Olivia said with a huff as she turned away.

Sophie laughed. "I'm sorry, Livie. Truly. We shall endeavor to be less—affectionate. Though I suppose the harm has been done."

"No harm in our actions, only loving," Graham corrected. "Something for you to be prepared for if you're thinking to marry Jonathan."

Livie gave a tiny gasp of outrage and stared at Graham. "I never said that."

"You might as well have," Sophie said gently. "That is why we are on a ship bound for New York, is it not?"

"We're going to America because it isn't safe in England—or Scotland—for either of us at present, with Father making deals to barter us away. Ships often sail to New York Harbor."

"And Boston, Philadelphia, Baltimore, and New Orleans," Sophie said. "Though New York is the most common port," she acknowledged.

Graham smiled down at her, not at all surprised that she knew of those places. Most likely she could recite their current populations and the topography of each as well. The lure of furthering her education, including lessons in geography, was how he had first persuaded her to come with him to his home, not to marry but to be a governess. His jealousy of her teacher had cut those lessons short, but he still intended to keep his promise someday. And while he wasn't exactly pleased to be sailing to America, he was pleased for her, that she was able to travel as she'd hoped and dreamed.

"You do intend to search for Jonathan when we arrive, do you not?" Sophie asked, her free hand covering Olivia's. "There's no shame in it. He is a good man, and I seem to recall that you were half in love with him long ago."

Olivia snorted. "I was thirteen when they married. I didn't know what love was."

"Do you now?" Sophie queried.

Olivia shrugged. "I—" She met Sophie's gaze, then glanced briefly at Graham. "I don't believe that I do. That is why I have been watching the two of you. I've been trying to understand how love works, how it happened for you." She looked at Graham. "I can tell you love my sister. But *why*?"

"Why, indeed?" Graham laughed.

Sophie scowled at him and withdrew her hands from both his and Olivia's.

"I'm serious," Olivia said, a slight whine of desperation to her voice. "Mother and Father certainly don't love each other. And I was young when Jonathan and Torie married. I truly don't understand how love happens. I was taught how to dance and how to flirt, how to behave properly when it comes to being courted by a man, but I have no idea how to actually get one to fall in love with me. How did you do it, Sophie, when you were the person I thought least likely ever to marry?"

"She wasn't trying to get me to fall in love with her, that's how," Graham said. "There was no scheming or planning.

Sophie was just being herself." That was mostly true, though he recalled some scheming and planning once Elizabeth had joined the cause of getting them married.

"And you *liked* that?" Olivia's incredulous tone drew another scowl from Sophie.

"I did." Graham nodded emphatically. "Your sister was like a breath of fresh air after being trapped amid the pollution of London. She wasn't, *isn't,* like any other woman I've ever known."

"He had no idea what to do with me," Sophie teased.

"I had plenty of ideas," Graham said, sending Sophie a look that prompted a sound of disgust from Olivia.

"I think the first thing I noticed and loved about Sophie was her spirit and pluck. She wasn't afraid to stand up to me. She had no use for conventions, but a strong will to do as she pleased." He pulled Sophie close and kissed her temple. "She has great intelligence, and she uses it for good."

"You like her because she's stubborn and always has her head in a book?" Olivia's brow furrowed.

"I *love* her," Graham corrected, looking into his wife's eyes, "because she is brave and courageous. She knows what she wants and aims to get it—no matter the obstacles in her way. She can be fierce but is also kind, and being with her makes me a better man."

"I am none of those things," Olivia said, mournfully.

"I disagree." Sophie reached for her sister's hand again. "You *are* stubborn. All three of us girls are—were." Her smile slipped a little. "You *are* brave, hiding all those months, staying a step ahead of Father and the viscount, and then barging into that bank to save Graham. And you are faithful, sailing to another continent to find Jonathan because of a promise you made Torie long ago."

"What promise is this?" Graham asked. He'd heard nothing of it.

Olivia looked out at the ocean. "When Torie was first expecting their child she was terribly sick. I was visiting her on a day she was particularly ill, and she made me promise that if something happened to her, if she died, I would take care of Jonathan."

"Ah." Graham nodded. "Your pursuit makes much more sense now. That was quite the vow for your sister to extract from you."

"She didn't demand it," Olivia said. "She asked it of me, and I gave her my word freely."

"She didn't ask me, because she knew I'd say no," Sophie said honestly. "She knew I never wished to marry—even a man as good as Jonathan."

"So she asked Olivia instead. Hmm." Graham rubbed his chin, considering. "You were very young, and I do not think she'd hold it against you if you didn't keep that promise."

"It really wasn't fair of her to ask," Sophie said.

"I know," Olivia said. "I've thought about that, but I cannot be angry with her. She must have known, must have had some premonition she was going to die, and she loved Jonathan enough that she didn't want him to be alone."

"And she knew that you already loved him a little," Sophie added softly.

Olivia nodded, then gave a heavy sigh of admission. "I do love him a little. Or I think I do, at least."

"You love his memory," Sophie corrected. "But Jonathan may be a very changed man now. Terrible grief, losing his wife and child and the livelihood he had worked years for, having to flee to America, those are all scars he has had to bear, and they very well may have changed him into a different man from the one we once knew."

"I do worry about that," Olivia confessed. "And that he will want nothing to do with us, with *me*. I don't want to add to his pain by reminding him of what he has lost."

"Then you must show him what he has to gain," Graham said. "Don't worry about flirting or dancing or even manners. Just be your true self. If he does not care for you then, it is his loss—and you will have fulfilled your promise, you will have tried."

Olivia nodded. "Thank you both for listening to me. I'm sorry if I've made you uncomfortable these past weeks."

"I did wonder what had become of my talkative younger sister," Sophie said. "You are changed too, Livie, deprived as you have been of all that brought you joy in life."

"I have not had nearly as pleasant a time of it as you, though nor as difficult as your past weeks have been."

"That is the cost of love," Sophie said, her innate wisdom coming forth again. "It carries you to the highest peaks, but you may also know the lowest valleys. To truly love someone is to give them your heart and know that someday it very well may end up broken when you part." She tilted her head back to look up at Graham.

He brushed a hand across her cheek but looked past her to Olivia. "I daresay Jonathan has known both. It will be up to you to show him that love is worth the risk again."

Part Two

"Friendship is a single soul dwelling in two bodies."
—Aristotle

Twenty-two

"'MERICA! I SEE it. I see it!" Matthew jumped up again, attempting to keep his head above the ship's rail.

Graham reached down and scooped him into his arms. "So you do."

He stood beside Sophie, whose hand Ayla clutched on the other side. With the afternoon sun shining down on them, they made the perfect family picture. Olivia wished she hadn't packed her sketchbook already, committing the scene to memory to be drawn later.

"We really are going to another continent." Sophie raised up on her toes, though she was already well above the rail. "I can hardly believe it." She squeezed Ayla's hand, and the two grinned at each other.

Olivia had no trouble believing it. *Finally.* The day she'd dreamed of for months was here. Or almost here. The true day she'd imagined over and over in her mind was her reunion with Jonathan. She knew which dress she'd be wearing and how she'd style her hair. He would be astonished to see her, utterly taken by surprise. He would tell her how grown up she'd become . . .

"It is good to see land again after so many days of endless blue," Mother said, linking her arm through Olivia's.

Their twenty-six-day crossing had not been overly long,

but for Olivia every day had felt tedious. Her birthday had come and gone during that time, with little to mark it, save the promise from her mother of a celebration next year. She was nineteen now. Her only Season had been hardly one at all before she was shut away. She'd never had any real suitors, hadn't danced in months or had tea with friends. She might never do those things again.

But Jonathan. She'd clung to her promise for so long now it was hard to believe the time for action was nearly here.

The ship drew ever closer, and there began to be talk among the passengers at the rail about who would disembark first. Would there be smaller boats to tender them, or would there be a dock and a gangway? She would have to be patient a little longer. Those passengers who had paid more for better lodgings would surely be allowed off first.

Only a short while more. Soon she could burn this dress and resume wearing those made specifically for her. She'd wanted to wear one this morning, but Graham had advised against it, saying that it would make her an easy target for thieves.

"Better they think we're paupers a while longer," he'd insisted, "and have no idea the value of what rests inside your trunks."

So the burgundy traveling gown she'd wished to don had gone back into the trunk to wait with the others, all the fabrics and designs the latest from Paris—or they had been six months ago. No doubt fashions had changed again already. But if she was fortunate, America would be a bit behind, and she would still be the height of fashion here. Certainly in upstate New York, at least. She hoped the countryside would be as beautiful as that in England and the house parties as amusing.

Jonathan was probably not a regular at events such as that, but he might accompany her.

Their ship entered the bay, and Olivia's mind slid from what life in the American countryside would be like to the approaching shoreline.

New York. A bustling city of over 200,000, if Sophie was correct. *She probably is.* Sophie had a mind like an encyclopedia, filled with facts and knowledge about everything and every place.

"This area of the city is called Manhattan," Sophie said, spouting that encyclopedia whether or not anyone wished it.

"So many ships," Maime noted, her voice a mixture of fear and awe.

"New York abolished slavery," Olivia reminded her. "But it still won't hurt to be cautious and stay close to us."

"Aye," Graham murmured, his voice low. "America has a worse problem with slavery than we do. It's threatening to divide the new nation already."

"Maybe with you here, it won't come to that." Sophie glanced up at him with an expression that was half pride and half concern.

"Maybe," Graham said, his tone non-committal.

Sophie's attention returned to the landscape. "I believe that's known as Battery Park." She pointed to the southern tip of the strip of land jutting out to greet them. "The fort there was built in anticipation of the War of 1812, but it was never used."

"But it's still there," Graham noted. "A reminder to the British, should they decide to come poking around again."

"Tall buildings," Matthew exclaimed.

"So many people," his sister murmured.

She wasn't wrong. Olivia frowned. *How am I ever to find Jonathan among so many?*

"He isn't in the city," Mother said, as if she'd overheard Olivia's thoughts.

Maybe she had spoken them out loud. Olivia turned to her mother. "What if—" *He doesn't want me.* What if, in the years since Victoria's passing, Jonathan had married someone else? *Then what?* She would be thousands of miles from home and everything familiar, all in the name of keeping a promise she never should have made. *What will I do?*

"One problem at a time." Mother patted Olivia's hand. "We've just crossed an ocean of them and left so many behind. You're on the same continent as Jonathan now—or nearly so—and we'll meet whatever happens here with the same courage that brought us this far."

Twenty-three

Upstate New York
December 1831

ELIAS HENRIE HELD the reins loosely in his mittened hands as he guided the sleigh over the fresh snow. It had been falling for the better part of the day, dumping several inches on top of the foot they'd already had in the past week. In the last hour the blizzard-like conditions had finally eased and then dwindled to peaceful flurries spiraling slowly to earth in the amber hue of dusk.

It's a beautiful evening, Anne. When I get home we'll bundle up, sit on the porch a spell, and enjoy it.

And they would have. *If* he'd been going home. If Anne's body wasn't buried at the churchyard beneath all this snow and six feet of earth. If her soul wasn't in heaven waiting for him.

He feared it was going to be a long wait. He'd beaten the smallpox that had claimed her, and he needed to keep beating whatever life threw at him—for their daughter. Thirteen-month-old Evie needed him.

He found something to smile about as he anticipated her little arms reaching out to him as soon as he got home—or to his cousin's home, at least. Jonathan had been more than generous, allowing him to stay these many months, nearly a full year now. *I need to leave, to return to my own place.* But he hadn't found the courage to face it, to walk through the house he had built, where he and Anne had planned to spend their lives. Two years hadn't been enough, but it had also been too much. Anne's memory was etched into every corner of the house, every piece of furniture, every dish, every curtain and quilt. He wasn't certain how he was supposed to live there without her, or if he even wanted to try. With the village springing up, it wouldn't be hard to sell the property, though it wasn't a huge parcel for farming. As a doctor he hadn't needed or wanted a lot of land to care for. Just enough for a few animals and Anne's garden. *Enough for Anne.* She'd grown up on a farm and hadn't wanted a home in town.

But the house in the village that he'd looked at today seemed like the best solution for moving on. He didn't have time to care for animals or a large garden, and he didn't have the heart to contend with the memories their dream home held. *In town I'll be closer to many of the patients I see.* And closer to Evie, if he could find someone in town to watch her when he did have to see a patient farther away.

It wasn't ideal, but it was probably the best he could do.

The road curved, leaving the new settlement of Seneca Falls behind. Elias urged the horses to move a bit faster. He wanted as much time with Evie as possible before she went to bed. She was his reason for living, the one constant that kept him going, the only spot of joy in his life—even during this Christmas season of brotherhood and love.

He was so grateful to still have his little girl, thankful that God had spared her life—and his—even if he didn't always feel that way. *I* am *grateful.* He reminded himself of that several times each day. Loneliness was a constant and difficult companion.

Another lonely figure appeared on the road ahead of him,

and Elias blinked several times, uncertain of what he was seeing. *Who would be all the way out here at this time of the day?* It would be full dark soon, and there weren't any homes, other than Jonathan's, out this way.

Bundled against the weather, the slight figure trudged slowly through the drifts, taking one laborious step after another. A lone child, perhaps, kept late after school for some infraction of behavior, and who had now lost his way? But Seneca Falls didn't have a school yet, did it? Aside from the tavern and the new church—a place to sin on Saturday night and a place to repent Sunday morning—Jonathan's store and the livery were the only other buildings, that weren't houses, in the village. It was that new. So who was out here, all alone, on a day not even he'd wanted to venture out?

If the five-year-old Davis twins hadn't raced each other this morning, jumping from the loft in their cabin at the same time, one striking his head on the stone fireplace and the other landing on his arm, then Elias would have spent the day at home. But a frantic father had summoned him mid-morning, so he'd packed his medical bag and gone out to stitch a wound and set an arm.

A good thing, too, for it put him on this road at this precise time, to help the weary traveler he was about to come upon.

As he drew closer, Elias saw that it was no child, but a woman, struggling on alone. Who on earth was she? And where did she think she was going? She must have taken several wrong turns to be all the way out here. He slowed the sleigh as he approached.

"Hello there," he called. "May I offer you a ride somewhere?"

The woman turned to him, blue eyes barely visible above the scarf wrapped multiple times around her face. Her hair, brows, and lashes were white with snow, and even from here he could see she was shaking with cold.

With trembling hands, she tugged the scarf down long enough to speak. "I am—looking for the home—of Jonathan Henrie." Her teeth chattered. "Can you—tell me if—I am headed in—the right—direction?" She pulled the scarf back up, but not before Elias noted her red cheeks and nose.

How long has she been out here?

"Jonathan is my cousin. I'm headed there now myself. I'd be pleased to offer you a ride."

"No, thank you," she mumbled through the cloth, not bothering to lower the scarf again, and started off once more, each step an enormous effort, as the snow was practically to her knees.

A blessing in disguise. The exertion required was probably the only thing keeping her from freezing to death.

Elias urged the horses forward, drove the sleigh a few feet past her, then stopped again. He jumped down, facing the woman as she approached.

She paused, a flicker of fear widening those blue eyes.

He hastened to reassure her; he couldn't leave her out here on her own. "I'm staying with Jonathan at present. His place is another three miles up this road, too far to make it on foot before dark. The bears around here hibernate in winter, but the wolves and cougars don't. It isn't safe for you to be out here alone. Please, will you allow me to give you a ride? If you're a friend of Jonathan's, he would be most displeased if I left you out here alone." Even if she wasn't a friend, Jonathan would be displeased. Appalled, as would any decent man.

She pulled down the scarf again. "Name?"

The single word seemed a great effort for her, and it was all he could do not to step forward, pick her up, and deposit her in the sleigh. The lower half of her skirts and cloak were soaked, her fancy gown peeking out beneath no match for this kind of weather.

"Elias Henrie." He stuck out a mittened hand, but her gloved one did not take it.

"I've just come from Seneca Falls, where we are putting the finishing touches on Jonathan's store set to open later this month."

"He has—a store—again?" She attempted a smile. "You are *Elias*?" His name must have registered and matched whatever she knew, as she practically sagged with relief. "You're—the cousin who helped—him move here—from England?" She tugged the scarf back up, but it did little to hide her chattering teeth.

"Yes. That was a while ago." *How does she know that?* "Will you come with me, then? Before you freeze to death, or a predator hunts us both for his supper?" There would be time enough later to learn how she knew of him and who she was—after she was warm and safe.

She nodded, and he stepped forward, taking her arm and helping her into the sleigh. As she lifted her skirt and stepped up, he glimpsed the toe of her soaked boots.

Elias came around the other side and climbed in, then took a minute to tuck the heavy robes around her. He would be all right without them for the last few miles.

Mrs. Davis had heated rocks in her fireplace to keep him warm on the drive home, and he debated what to do with those now. Their warmth might be good for the woman's feet right now and prevent frostbite, especially as her body was likely to cool further and her circulation slow now that her exertions had ceased. However, if she already had frostbite—a possibility, given the state of her shoes—then warming her feet too quickly might worsen the damage.

He decided to arrange a few of the rocks around her feet

and hope it was the right decision. "Don't get your shoes too close to these." He leaned across and set one on the floor of the sleigh on her other side. "The heat wouldn't be good for your feet with how cold they must be right now."

She nodded without looking at him.

Elias unwound his own scarf and wrapped it around one of the rocks until the warmth seeping through was considerably lessened. He held it out to her. "Hold this in your hands. It will help warm them as well. Your fingers must be half-frozen."

"Thank you." She grasped the rock, or tried to. Her hands didn't appear to be working very well. *Not a good sign.*

He glanced at what he could see of her before starting off again, worried that he'd met up with her too late. Her fine cloak, muff, and gloves might be all right for walking around New York City or London—given her accent, he'd wager the latter was where she'd come from—but they were no match for winters here. He'd been only partially jesting when he'd said her fingers might be half-frozen. *And her feet...*

He'd removed more than a toe or two from frostbitten patients and would not wish that on anyone, particularly an innocent woman.

Is she innocent? He still had no idea who she was or what she was doing here. Elias clicked his tongue, and the horses started moving again, no additional prodding necessary. They were as eager as he for home, for their warm stalls and pails of oats.

They drove in silence for several minutes, Elias giving the woman time to catch her breath and warm up a bit before he broached conversation. But when he glanced over and saw her head nodding with sleep, he dared not wait any longer. "Might you share your name as well? And how it is you know my cousin."

With apparent great effort, she lifted her head by degrees.

She pushed down the scarf, but just barely, then turned slightly toward him. "Miss Olivia Claybourne." She swallowed and brought a hand to her throat, as if speaking had pained her.

"When was the last time you had a drink?"

"Pardon?" Her eyes widened again.

"Of water." He reached beneath his seat and pulled out the pouch he always carried with him. He had some jerky as well, if she was hungry, but he doubted she could eat that right now. He held the pouch out to her.

She looked at it a long moment, revulsion—evident in the wrinkling of her nose— warring with need as she licked her dry lips, then finally took it. Several, painful seconds passed as she fumbled with the lid before finally freeing it. Elias slowed the team so she had a better chance of drinking without spilling the water down her front. She lifted it to her lips and began to drink. Her shaking hands made that difficult, so Elias leaned over, holding the pouch steady. The scene made an incongruent picture. *Elegant lady drinking from a buckskin pouch in the wilds of upstate New York.* He'd wager she was far more accustomed to teacups.

After several seconds she stopped, then refastened the lid. "Thank you." She held the pouch out to him. He would have bade her to keep it as long as she liked but felt it more important that her fingers be wrapped around the warm rock.

"You're welcome, Miss Olivia Claybourne," Elias said, smiling at her. The way she hugged the edge of the seat spoke volumes about her unease and mistrust. *Then why be out here all alone?*

"I am Jonathan's sister-in-law—or I used to be. His wife, my sister, died. But I suppose you know that already."

Elias didn't. *Jonathan lost a wife? He was married before?* It would seem he would have mentioned this grief. *Especially considering my own of recent months.* Elias nodded, both encouraging Miss Claybourne to go on and pretending he knew of what she was speaking. If he admitted otherwise, she might not believe he was Jonathan's cousin, might not wish to ride with him, after all.

She sighed heavily, and her gloved hands clenched around the wrapped stone in her lap. "You must also have heard that it was our father's fault."

Her teeth were chattering less, and she was making coherent speech. Both good signs that he hadn't come upon her too late.

"I am not certain I knew of that," Elias said carefully.

"I don't mean to say that he killed her directly, but he may as well have. He denied her a doctor after making it impossible for Jonathan to provide one himself."

Coherent speech, but confused? Miss Claybourne wasn't making a lot of sense right now, and that concerned him.

Her shoulders hunched as if carrying a great burden. "I didn't stop my father, did not defy him when I should have. None of us did." She looked down at her lap. Her words were coming easier now as she warmed up a bit, but Elias was more baffled than ever.

"It may be that Jonathan does not want to see me or wish for a reminder of what he has lost. I would not blame him." She looked up at Elias as if seeking his opinion on the matter.

There was something about her story that was starting to sound familiar. *And something about her eyes.*

"You are uncertain if Jonathan will receive you, yet you've come all this way to see him anyway?"

She nodded. "I promised Torie that if something happened to her, I would look after him. It has taken me a great deal of time to find him so I might keep that promise."

Torie? Could she mean— "How far have you come, exactly?" Elias asked, trying to fit together the puzzle pieces he had while determining which ones were still missing.

Love UNDYING

"I set off this morning from Waterloo. I had no idea it would take me so long to get here. It was only supposed to be a distance of four miles to Seneca Falls."

She'd come on foot—in this weather—all the way from Waterloo! Elias studied her again. Miss Claybourne had to be made of stronger stuff than her fancy clothing indicated.

"I assumed—wrongly—that Jonathan lived in the village. The postal address I'd found indicated that. I knocked on doors in town until someone was able to direct me to this road. The snow made walking difficult and slow, and I was beginning to fear I'd taken a wrong turn and would never find him. I was contemplating turning around and retracing my steps when you found me." Her mouth twisted in a look of chagrin. "Thank you for stopping." She held up the scarf-wrapped stone. "For everything."

He nodded. "Where did you come from before you were in Waterloo? I gather you haven't been there for long?"

She shook her head. "Just two days. That was the closest lodging we could find to Seneca Falls."

We. Who else was with her? Probably not a spouse, given her errand to look after her deceased sister's husband.

"Before that we came from New York City, and before that, England."

"You've learned your first lesson already. Don't venture out alone—or at all, if possible—on days like this. New England winters can be brutal."

"I'll remember," she promised. "I'm afraid I wasn't very patient. Not after it has taken me so long to find Jonathan." She gave Elias a rueful smile. "And I did want to speak to him alone, before the others come."

Her eyes are the same. The hope he read in them pierced Elias as the pieces snapped into place in his mind. *She cares for Jonathan.* Elias felt ill for her as he realized what was coming.

"*Others?*" Maybe he was wrong about her starry-eyed gaze. Maybe she had a husband and wasn't interested in—

"My mother, my sister, and her husband. And the two children they have guardianship over. And Maime. She's a former slave who works for Graham now."

"Quite the entourage," Elias murmured, beginning to worry how Jonathan was going to take this intrusion. When he'd first arrived in America, it had been with a strong conviction of leaving all behind in England, including and especially the family who had wronged him, though not apparently in the way his sister-in-law believed. "How is it that you all decided to come?"

She sighed again. "It was supposed to just be me, with a chaperone or companion, but my mother needed to get away from my father. Then Sophie's husband was arrested, and it became prudent for all of us to leave." She looked at Elias again. "Do you think Jonathan will mind—much?"

Yes. And he's not the only one. "I think he will be very surprised," Elias said honestly. Other words hovered on his lips—questions about what crime her sister's husband had committed to get himself arrested. And he ought to tell Miss Claybourne what awaited her.

It's not my place. She'll realize soon enough.

"That's why I came alone today. I thought it best to visit by myself first. It may be that he won't even want to see me, given what our father did."

What her brother-in-law, the one she'd brought with her, had done to get arrested recently seemed the more pressing issue, as he was *here*. Elias wondered if he ought to take Miss Claybourne back to town instead of bringing trouble to Jonathan's doorstep.

"Tell me of your brother-in-law, the one who was arrested."

"Graham is the seventh Duke of Warwick. He was tried for murder and found guilty, but Sophie, Mother, and I helped to get him out of Newgate."

"He's a murderer—and you broke him out of prison?" Elias shook his head and wondered yet again if Miss Claybourne's mind wasn't a bit addled.

"We didn't break him out, and he's not really a murderer. He did kill two men, but it was self-defense, or defense of another—something like that. I wasn't in the courtroom because I was still hiding from my father and the viscount." She visibly shivered, then wrapped her arms around herself.

Warding off some terrible memory, along with the cold? "Who is the viscount?" Some other relation she'd dragged across the sea with her?

"A terrible man, but he's dead now. He had a heart attack while trying to kidnap Sophie."

Elias held the reins in one hand and lifted his other to rub his temples. He'd picked up a lunatic. He should have known that before she ever opened her mouth. No person in their right mind would have tried to walk from Waterloo in weather like this. But now that he had her, what was he supposed to do? There had to be at least a little truth to her story. She had spoken of Jonathan.

Who just might murder me *for bringing trouble to his doorstep.* Was he putting them in danger? What of Evie? If this Miss Claybourne was going to be at the house, perhaps he and Evie should find another place to lodge. The idea of sleeping under the same roof with a woman not in her right mind didn't sit well.

Elias asked a few more well-placed questions and thought he mostly understood what had transpired between the two families by the time they pulled up to the house.

Beside him, Miss Claybourne straightened in her seat

and leaned forward, eagerly taking in every detail of the well-ordered yard and sturdy two-story home similar to his own. He'd helped Jonathan build it.

This evening the windows were already shuttered, but smoke curled from the chimney, and a path had been shoveled to the front door, where a wreath of fresh holly hung. *A woman's touch.* Would Miss Claybourne take note?

"Whoa." Elias tugged on the reins and pulled the team to a halt in front of the house instead of heading to the barn as was his usual habit. He jumped down and walked around the sleigh to help Miss Claybourne. She accepted his hand, squeezing tightly as she climbed down and took a couple of hobbling steps in her soaked boots.

Whether she was in her right mind or not, he was going to have to look at her toes, and soon.

She paused before continuing to the door and looked up at him, her eyes filled with uncertainty. "Has Jonathan remarried?"

"He—has not," Elias answered truthfully, though it felt like a lie.

A relieved smile broke out over her face. With her pink cheeks and nose, she seemed almost childlike. But Elias guessed that beneath that youthful façade was a woman's heart that was about to be broken. *And healed at the same moment?* She might be relieved, and even happy as well, he hoped.

"Thank you." Without a second glance back at him, she limped toward the door, then knocked on it. Elias stood by the side of the sleigh, knowing he should take the horses to the barn but unable to make himself go just yet.

The front door opened, swinging inward a second before Jonathan appeared, an empty wood box in his arms. "Afternoon, Elias."

Miss Claybourne cleared her throat. "Hello, Jonathan. It's me. Olivia."

Jonathan stopped, lowered the box, and came closer. "Little Livie?" His mouth hung open as he looked her up and down.

She nodded. "Not so little anymore, and I found you at last." She burst into tears.

Jonathan dropped the box, then stepped forward and awkwardly pulled her into a hug, his gaze sweeping the yard as he did, as if looking for someone else. His eyes met Elias's.

"She's alone." *For now.*

A look that wasn't quite relief eased a bit of the tension that had appeared on Jonathan's brow. He stepped back and held Miss Claybourne at arms' length. He studied her again, then reached forward to snatch the hat from her head. "You've grown up, you say?"

"I have." She smiled through her tears, as if immensely pleased with Jonathan's having taken notice.

Elias fought an absurd urge to rush forward and shield her from Jonathan, from what was coming.

"Elias? Is that you holding the door open and causing a draft?" Victoria's voice held a teasing reprimand. She appeared behind Jonathan, Evie balanced on her hip.

Elias's gaze—usually focused on nothing but his daughter whenever they were together—remained on Miss Claybourne, who gasped at the same time as her sister.

He did rush forward then, intent on whisking Evie to safety before she ended up in the middle of an overly emotional reunion.

"Torie?" The color drained from Olivia's cheeks, and she took a step back instead of forward.

"*Livie?*" Victoria looked from Jonathan to her sister as Elias scooped Evie from her arms.

Olivia reached a shaking hand out, as if afraid to touch the apparition in front of her. "You're—you're *alive?*"

Twenty-four

"OH, LIVIE!" VICTORIA ran forward and pulled her into a hug. "I thought I'd never see you again."

"I'll put up the horses," Jonathan said, squeezing past them.

Torie pulled back and sent him a look. "Coward."

"Maybe." Jonathan ducked his head. "But Elias is just home and wants to be with Evie. I'll be back, and then we can all talk."

Yes, we can. Olivia's head swam. She felt like she might pass out and be sick all at once. She clasped Torie's arms and looked at her sister's face. It was the same, yet changed. Softer, fuller than it had been before, but there was no mistaking the features that closely mirrored her own and Sophie's.

"Talk later," Mr. Henrie said, his hand at Olivia's back, though his words were directed at Torie. "We need to get your sister inside and out of those wet clothes quickly. She's been out in the cold all day."

Victoria pulled Olivia into the house, and Mr. Henrie followed, still holding the baby. *Whose baby?* Had Torie *and* her child both lived? *Why would she lie to us like this?* Olivia knew the answer before her mind had even finished the question. *Father.* To get away from him, Victoria and Jonathan would have done anything. *As Mother, Sophie, and I have just done.*

And yet Jonathan had just welcomed her. *Jonathan.* With a jolt, the implications crashed into her. Jonathan didn't need caring for. He didn't need a wife. He still had Torie. *He doesn't need me.*

Olivia's knees threatened to buckle as she looked around the cozy room, seeing nothing and feeling suddenly lost, as if she were at a great crossroads, instead of in her sister's sitting room, with no idea where to go or what to do now.

"I'll find you some clothes," Torie said and headed for a doorway on the other side of the room.

A hand at Olivia's elbow guided her forward. "Are you all right, Miss Claybourne?" Mr. Henrie gazed at her, his brow furrowed in concern. He helped her to the nearest chair, then set the child he had been holding beside him and reached for Olivia's foot.

She tucked her feet beneath the chair, out of his reach. "What are you doing?"

"Helping you get those wet boots off." He leaned forward and gently pulled one foot from beneath the chair.

"I can do that."

His brows rose as he turned her foot slightly and began untying the side laces. "How about you work on taking off those gloves, and I'll see to your shoes."

"It isn't proper." New tears formed on the heels of those she'd just shed. She already felt humiliated, having crossed an ocean to care for a man who didn't need her. She would only make matters worse by allowing his cousin to see her feet.

Torie came back into the room, a pink cotton dress draped over her arm. "It's entirely proper. Elias is a doctor. If he wants to see your feet it's because he's concerned about an injury."

Olivia shook her head. "There's no injury. My feet are fine." Better now, thanks to the warm rocks he'd put around them in the sleigh.

"I'm worried about frostbite. You were outside a long time in these woefully inadequate shoes." He tugged the first from her foot, which Olivia promptly tucked beneath the chair again.

"Please." Mr. Henrie looked up at her but did not reach for her other foot. "Allow me to help you, if I may."

"Papa," the little girl beside him babbled as she leaned into him.

She's his *daughter.* Which meant he must be married. Did that make him looking at her feet worse, or better? Olivia mustered a smile for the little girl then reluctantly held her other foot out to him. "I don't wish to delay your time with your daughter. It looks as if she has been waiting for you all day."

"Thank you," he said, smiling as if she'd just handed him a wrapped package instead of a foot inside a wet, ruined boot.

Olivia nodded, held back her tears, and tried to find some dignity in the situation.

Torie's hand on her shoulder felt comforting. "You have grown up, and I am *so happy* to see you." Her voice quavered, as if she, too, were struggling with a myriad of overwhelming emotions.

Olivia reached her hand up and covered Torie's. "As am I to see you, sister."

THE DRESS AND underthings that Torie had helped her to change into felt stiff and unfamiliar against Olivia's skin. She shivered as she left the bedroom and hobbled toward the fire.

"It's best if you don't get quite so close to that yet."

She turned to see Mr. Henrie, *Doctor* Henrie, standing beside the sofa. He had removed his coat, and his shirtsleeves were rolled to the elbow, as if he were preparing to do some outdoor task.

"Why not? The fire is warm, and I am cold."

He came closer to her. "It has been found that in cases of prolonged exposure to cold, such as you experienced today, warming up too quickly can actually cause more damage to your extremities—namely your hands and feet." He reached for her hand, and reluctantly Olivia held it out to him.

He took it in his own and guided her a few steps from the hearth, then bent over, not with a kiss as a gentleman would have done, but with an expression of deepest concern. He ran his own fingers over each of hers, an altogether peculiar feeling that made her want to pull away. He looked closely at her nails, then turned her hand over and pressed several points on her palm and the pads of her fingers. At last he looked up with a smile. "The coloring is good. I am very hopeful there is no lasting damage."

"Thank you, Doctor." She tried to withdraw her hand, but he still held it.

"Elias," he said, with a gentle squeeze before releasing her. "You must call me that, as we are practically family now."

Olivia nodded uncomfortably. *Elias.* A brazen request from a man she'd only met this afternoon.

He reached for her other hand, then performed similar ministrations. "Will you allow me to help your circulation return to your feet now?"

"Must you?" She sounded like a pleading child and hated herself for it. She was nineteen now, a grown woman. A woman who had come all the way to America prepared to marry and care for a man.

"It would be best." Elias's smile was gentle and his tone not mocking in the least as he led her to the sofa. "You might wish to lie down for this. It isn't going to be pleasant."

"*What* isn't?" Olivia sat, rather than lay down as he had suggested. Torie had gone into the kitchen to prepare supper—*she knows how to cook!*—and taken his daughter with her, so it was just the two of them here, alone. Olivia was not about to lie down anywhere and told him so. Instead she sat primly, her hands clasped in her lap.

Shaking his head, he reached for them. "Your fingers look good, but you should take care, nonetheless. Entwining your hands thus won't encourage blood flow. Instead, keep them separate, and move them frequently." He released her hands, and Olivia placed each separately on her lap, feeling ridiculous and awkward.

Elias knelt on the floor in front of her. "May I?" he asked, before touching one of her feet.

Olivia held in a sigh and nodded. She barely felt his hand against her bare heel, but a second later burning agony tore through her foot. She jerked away and looked down to see his other hand full of snow he had, evidently, been pressing on the top of her foot.

"What are you doing?" She rubbed one foot atop the other, trying to stop the stinging.

"Your feet have been without feeling for so long that it is going to be painful as they warm. Rubbing snow on them will help them to do so gradually. I promise it is better than, say, putting them in a pan of warm water. This will also help protect the tissue."

Olivia folded her arms across her middle and frowned, then realized she must look like a child again, especially with her hair taken down, still damp and drying, and wearing a simple dress and with bare feet. She closed her eyes, feeling tired and so very discouraged, but she held her foot out to him again.

Elias scooped up a handful of snow and began rubbing

the top once more. Olivia clenched her teeth and closed her eyes as tears leaked from them, wishing herself thousands of miles away, back to England and all that was familiar.

I cannot return, she told herself sternly. *I can be happy here with Mother and Sophie and Torie.* She'd loved Torie and mourned her. It was just that . . . *Jonathan.* She brought a hand to her head, feeling a pain there and in her heart, to accompany the fire in her feet.

"Are you almost finished?"

"I'm afraid not," Elias said apologetically.

Olivia flinched as he started on the side of her foot, rubbing life back into her frozen appendage. "Who would—have thought—snow—could—hurt so much?" She pressed her lips together to keep from crying out and gripped the edge of the sofa.

"It sometimes helps to think of something else," Elias suggested.

What was left for her to think of? Every plan, every hope she'd held for her future had just vanished, as if they had never been there at all. Which left her with nothing. *I have nothing. I am nothing.*

Except for pain. So much pain.

"Breathe, Miss Claybourne," Elias said and stopped his torture momentarily.

Olivia released a breath she hadn't realized she'd been holding, then sucked in another when he placed her other foot on his towel-covered lap and began all over again.

Olivia brought her hands to her head and leaned forward, wanting to scream—as much about her confused and altered circumstances as about pain.

"Your head aches as well?" Elias gave her a look that said he guessed at least a part of what she was feeling.

What had she told him during her ramblings on the way

here? How much of herself, of her purpose for coming, had she shared, and would Elias Henrie share that with Torie and Jonathan? *Please, no.* It was going to be difficult enough to explain herself. She didn't need them thinking about what had actually driven her to come all this way.

"It was brave of you to walk almost all the way here by yourself."

"And foolish," Olivia muttered through her hands.

"That too." There was no reprimand to his words, only a slight teasing. "Impressive, nonetheless. I would wager that Miss Olivia Claybourne is more resilient than she looks."

Olivia groaned, not wanting to think about her appearance. She'd spent weeks imagining just how she would look when she first saw Jonathan again, and her current, bedraggled state was about as opposite to that as she could come. Not that it mattered now.

She winced and sucked in a breath as a particularly stabbing pain shot from her foot upward.

"I'm sorry," Elias said quietly.

His movements gentled—no more snow rubbing against her skin—as he carefully probed each toe.

She peeked at him through her fingers, noting the unruly cowlick at the front of his brown hair as he bent over her feet. She couldn't believe she was allowing a man to touch her like this. It was indecent, embarrassing—

Warm hands covered hers, gently pulling them from her face. "All done. I've seen grown men cry more when going through the same. You *are* brave, Miss Claybourne."

"Olivia," she said, offering him use of her given name as he had offered his. It felt personal, but so much less so than his hands on her feet. What was one more impropriety, at this point?

"Will I live?" she said, attempting to muster a smile but failing badly.

"Definitely." He released her hands and settled back, still kneeling. "Both long and well, but you may have trouble walking for a few days. Your feet are covered with blisters, and I am concerned about one of your toes." He lifted her foot so she might better see it. He pointed to the smallest toe on her left foot. "The color is not changed since I rubbed it with the snow. Which means the circulation isn't returning as it should."

"Can you do anything else?" Olivia asked, unable to hide her alarm.

"I don't want to damage your skin. It is a delicate balance between trying to restore what is on the inside without doing harm to that which is on the outside. For now, we need to watch it carefully. The good news is that I believe your other toes and your feet are going to be fine." He picked up a pair of socks that Olivia had not noticed before. They were brown and bulky.

Ugly.

"It would be best for your feet if you did not wear shoes for a while, or even tight stockings of any sort. You may borrow these. They are thick and should keep your feet warm."

Men's socks? Could her day get any worse, any more humiliating?

He slipped them on her feet, then collected the pan of melting snow and stood. "You did well, Olivia. I am proud of you."

What was there to be proud of? Her foolish decision to walk miles in a snowstorm, in search of a man who was already married? Olivia bit back the negative thought and instead expressed her gratitude. "Thank you for helping me. Had you not stopped and offered your assistance today, my toes and I would not be so fortunate."

"I am grateful that I happened to be upon the road at that time." He turned to go.

"Elias," Olivia began, and he turned back. "Could you please—" She glanced toward the kitchen, then lowered her voice. "I would appreciate it if you would not say anything to Torie or Jonathan about what I said to you on the way here. My reasons for coming."

Compassion shone in Elias's brown eyes. "Of course not. I am sorry I did not warn you what, or rather who, was awaiting you. I did not think it my place, and I know it is not my place to say any of what you shared with me today in confidence. It is yours to tell, if you wish."

She didn't.

Twenty-five

"TEA AND BISCUITS." Torie came into the room, carrying a tray. "Almost like home. Except that the tea in America isn't as good, and my biscuits are rather hard." She frowned. "I'm still learning."

Olivia gaped at her sister. "You mean to say that you *made* the biscuits?" *And the tea?* And she'd carried the tray in like a common servant. But somehow Olivia had known, the second she'd crossed their threshold, that there were no servants to be found in this house. Not with Jonathan carrying the wood box and going out to see to the horses. In England, Victoria and Jonathan had employed a few servants, at least until Father had ruined their finances.

"I did make them, though keep your expectations low. I've mastered bread and several other things quite well, but English biscuits continue to vex me." Torie poured a cup of tea and handed it to her.

"It won't taste the same as you're used to, but it's warm."

"Thank you." Olivia lifted the cup to her mouth and sipped. Torie was right. It was weaker than that at home, but it still felt good to be sitting in front of a fire with a teacup in her hand.

Torie settled into a rocking chair with a basket of yarn and knitting needles beside it.

Torie's? When had she learned to knit? Where had she learned to keep a home herself, even a small one like this?

Olivia turned solemn eyes on her sister. "What happened to you, and your baby? Will you tell me everything, please?"

"Yes. Of course." Torie nodded. "I owe you at least that much, and I want you to understand that we thought we had no other choice."

Olivia tucked her feet up beside her on the sofa under the blanket Elias had brought to her. A few minutes earlier he had taken his daughter upstairs, presumably so that Olivia and Torie could have privacy to talk. Jonathan had not yet returned from the barn. Olivia wondered where the doctor's wife was, and if she was staying here too, and why? Maybe they had come for Christmas or to help Jonathan open his store. *That must be it.* Hadn't Elias said something to that effect when he had first offered her a ride?

Torie smoothed the wrinkles from her dress and looked down at her lap. "Our baby was stillborn. She lies in a cold grave in England. That I shall never be able to visit, and that no one else is likely to pains me greatly."

"Mother visits." Or, she had until they'd come here. "I've gone with her, too, as has Sophie. The grave is marked with your name as well, and Mother brings flowers and speaks to you. She apologizes for failing you. She hasn't been the same since . . . since she thought you died."

"It is I who needs to apologize, to all of you." Torie stood and pulled her chair closer to the sofa and Olivia. "I did nearly die, and I was so ill and sick at heart after the birth. Jonathan was beside himself as well, and so angry with Father."

"He ought to have been angry at all of us," Olivia said, bearing her portion of the guilt.

Torie shook her head. "He didn't blame any of you, especially you, as young as you were. He knew how Father controlled that household. Jonathan feared he would control ours for the rest of our lives as well. He'd destroyed so much of our livelihood and much of Jonathan's hard work and good name in the process. Jonathan had been writing to his cousin in America for some time, and the day our daughter died, Jonathan decided he had had enough—that our persecution had gone too far, that maybe the next time I was with child, it *would* cost me my life because he again wouldn't be able to procure a doctor because of Father's malicious intent to ruin us."

"So Jonathan said that you died as well?"

Torie nodded. "He told everyone—including our closest neighbors. He was a man filled with grief, so his initial refusal to allow anyone in to see my body was understandable. He built a casket and told everyone he was going to bury his wife and daughter together. He told anyone who asked that he didn't want others to see me as I was—tortured from the hours of childbirth and having bled to death."

Olivia suppressed a shudder at the image that conjured in her mind.

"Jonathan did show our neighbor the baby before he placed her in the casket—along with some stones to make it seem as if I was inside as well. He and a few friends buried it in the kirkyard of the small church where we had married. By then, I was already on a ship to America."

"By *yourself*?"

Torie nodded. "I was still very weak and ill, and Jonathan was not at all certain that I would survive the journey, but he feared what would happen if we stayed even more. You have to understand the lengths Father had gone to already."

"I know of them. His methods have not improved since you left. Sophie had to run away to Scotland to get away from him, and I have been in hiding for over half of the year." At

Torie's open-mouthed expression, Olivia added, "I'll tell you all of it, but first the rest of your tale."

"I barely made it to America. I was sick the entire voyage and rarely left my bed. Elias and his wife were there to greet me in New York, and they took me home and nursed me back to health. About a month later Jonathan arrived, after spending a few weeks playing the part of a man destroyed by grief—not at all difficult when he'd lost his first child and he had no idea if he would ever see his wife again. He wanted Father to believe that I was dead and that Jonathan was a ruined man in every sense possible, having lost everything. Then, he vanished."

Torie gave a sad sigh. "Jonathan made me promise that I would never reach out to any of you. It was too dangerous. Father might discover our whereabouts, and who knew what he'd do next?"

"I understand." Olivia gave her a sad smile. "I promise that I have not brought him to your doorstep. He has not known my whereabouts for months, and I sailed under an alias."

Torie held the plate of biscuits out to Olivia, then took one for herself. She bit into it, her brow furrowed as she chewed the crunchy treat.

"How *did* you find us?" she asked quietly.

"Persistence, mostly. After you—after we believed you dead and then Jonathan disappeared—I returned to your neighborhood a few times, inquiring after Jonathan. It wasn't easy to do so without Mother or, especially, Father finding out. I had to be very careful. During my brief visits, I spoke with your neighbors, believing that someone must know something of where Jonathan had gone. Then one day one said something that gave me an idea."

"What did she say?" Torie bit her lip, anxious lines crinkling her forehead.

"*He* told me that he didn't believe Jonathan was anywhere in London or even England. He'd talked once of taking his family and going far, far away. And now that he'd no family, this neighbor supposed that it was likely Jonathan had done just that."

"But how would you know that he'd gone to America and that we were here, in New York?"

"I didn't—yet. But I remembered something from the summer Sophie and I stayed with you. One evening Jonathan had read a letter to us from his cousin in America. It was a most colorful letter, filled with humorous anecdotes and some unusual tales. This cousin had also mentioned buying some property in New York. When I remembered that letter and that Jonathan had a cousin in America, I set out to see if I could find Jonathan's name on any of the ship's logs."

Torie leaned back in the rocker. "That seems an impossible task."

"Oh, it was difficult." Olivia sipped her tea and took a second biscuit. "I stopped haunting your old neighborhood in favor of sending a trusted servant to scour as many ship's passenger logs as he could find. Not all captains were amenable to sharing their records, and what if Jonathan had sailed on one that never returned to our port? I spent months of my pin money paying the servant before he returned with the news that he'd seen Jonathan's name on a manifest. I had to see it for myself, so I returned with the servant to the docks. I nearly cried when I read *Jonathan Henrie, Merchant* on the eighth line of the log for the *Amethyst*. Because he sailed under his own name I was able to find him—to find *you,*" Olivia added with a smile, her eyes tearing suddenly. Instead of nibbling her biscuit, she placed her hand over her mouth, attempting to hold in the emotional dam that felt it was about to burst. *Torie is* alive. *I am in America with her.* It all felt surreal, as if any minute she might awaken and find it had all been a dream.

"This servant who helped you, is it likely he might share what he knows with Father?" Torie's look of concern had only grown.

"No." Olivia shook her head emphatically, trying to reassure her sister. "It was Lucy's husband Adam. He doesn't even work for us anymore. They both left last spring."

"Good." Torie moved the rocker back and forth quickly, as if matching the thoughts that were no doubt rushing through her mind. "Did you sail alone as well? Or did anyone come with you?"

"Mother, and Sophie." *And a few others.* Olivia would explain later.

"They're both *here?*" Torie half rose from her chair and looked toward the door.

"In Waterloo," Olivia corrected, tugging her sister back down. She wanted Torie to herself for a little while, at least. "I came on my own today. They would have insisted on waiting until the weather cleared. I wasn't that patient."

"You never were."

They both laughed.

"Sophie always had her head in a book—if she wasn't out and about, galloping on a horse somewhere or walking in a meadow of flowers. And you were just impulsive."

"It's a good thing too," Olivia said, defending herself. "Or I wouldn't be sitting here with you right now."

"True." Torie leaned forward and placed her hand over Olivia's. Her smile dimmed. "Why *are* you here, Livie? If you thought I was dead?"

Olivia shrugged. Perhaps Torie would believe this another whim of hers, another impulsive decision. "It seemed the best place to go to get away from Father."

Torie scowled. "It was the *only* place we felt might be far enough from him. But now that you've found us . . ." She bit her lip. "You're *certain* he won't follow? That he doesn't know where you've gone?"

"Yes. Mother will tell you all that she did to ensure he would never find us. She is very clever. She helped Sophie too. She is married now," Olivia blurted. "Her husband came with us as well."

"What?" Torie's brow furrowed. "Sophie vowed to never marry. Unless—did Father force her to it?"

"Not exactly. He betrothed her to an abhorrent viscount, so she ran away and married a duke instead."

Voices sounded outside the door.

"I'll explain it all when Jonathan returns. It sounds like he's almost back."

"Who is with him?" Torie stood again. "No one else lives around here, and it's too late for visitors."

At the sound of a distinctly female voice and a shriek of happiness, Torie ran to the door and flung it open. Sophie ran straight into her arms.

They stood there, clinging to each other, alternately sobbing and laughing while Jonathan and Graham watched from the doorway.

An old familiar pang of envy flared inside Olivia. Torie and Sophie had always been close, while she'd been the one too young to join them on most of their adventures. Why had she believed that any of that would have changed? Sophie had been kind to her on their voyage, but most of her time had been spent with her husband or the children she now claimed as her own. Olivia hadn't minded—too much. But this, being excluded again—

Torie hadn't held her and laughed and cried like this. Had Sophie arrived first, would she have been questioned as Olivia had just been? Or would Torie have simply been overjoyed to see her, as she was right now?

"Livie, come here." Sophie pulled back to beckon her over. Olivia stuck out a socked foot. "I don't have my shoes on."

"As if that is something that should stop you?" Sophie smiled through her tears. Looping her arm through Torie's, Sophie propelled them across the room as Olivia stood.

Sophie stopped in front of her, eyes wet with tears. "*You* did this, Livie. If not for you, we would have believed Torie gone from us forever, we never would have known the truth, never would have seen her again, but now—" Fresh tears sprang from her eyes as she wrapped an arm around each sister and pulled them close in a hug. "Thank you."

With those arms wrapped tight around her, and her sisters' heads bent close to hers, Olivia felt like she could breathe again for the first time since setting foot inside this house. Her dream of a life with Jonathan was gone, but she *had* done some good. And maybe she was grown up enough now to be included with her sisters.

"Mother will be so happy," Sophie said. "You've no idea how she's grieved you, Torie, and how she's blamed herself."

"Where is she?" Torie asked.

"In Waterloo with Maime and the children. It was too late and too cold when we set out to find Livie." Sophie gave her a slight frown. "You shouldn't have gone off on your own like that, but I'm glad you did." Her wide smile erased any scolding she might have given. "I just wish we could tell Mother tonight." She glanced over her shoulder at Graham and Jonathan, standing just inside the door, removing their coats.

"Absolutely not," Jonathan said. "It's starting to be a real blizzard out there. Every one of you is staying right here."

Olivia grinned at her sisters and felt suddenly glad that Sophie was with them too. It had been forever—since that summer she and Sophie had stayed with Torie and Jonathan— that the three of them had spent any real time together.

"Build up the fire then," Torie called, at last breaking their circle as she straightened to her full height, "while my sisters and I prepare a feast of celebration."

Twenty-six

THERE WAS ONLY one other time Elias could remember Jonathan and Victoria's table being so full and their home so brimming with gratitude and happiness. He put that evening, when Anne had still been alive, out of his mind and tried to enjoy this one and the joy overflowing from each of the reunited sisters.

For the entirety of the time that he had known Victoria, there had always been an underlying aura of sadness about her. She wasn't a complainer, and her smiles were plentiful, but he'd always sensed a deep sorrow within her, much as others probably sensed similar feelings within him now. He had assumed, wrongly perhaps, that her sorrow came from the loss of her baby. But watching Victoria now, laughing and reminiscing with her sisters about their childhood, Elias could no longer see it. No doubt a piece of her heart would always long for her stillborn daughter, but reuniting with her sisters seemed to have restored Victoria to a woman he'd never seen before.

But Jonathan most certainly had. Elias wondered if this wasn't the Victoria his cousin had first fallen in love with—one more adventurous and mirthful than the American Victoria, who had arrived ill and frail but had healed quickly and then thrown herself wholeheartedly into learning how to care for her husband and home and worked tirelessly at both.

"Do you remember the scolding we received after we started that fire in the garden?" Victoria asked, her eyes dancing with merriment.

"You mean the scolding *I* received," Sophie spluttered. "You were nowhere to be found when the gardener caught me! And he'd no imagination or appreciation for our efforts to reenact that scene from *Gulliver's Travels.*"

"He'd probably never read it," Olivia pointed out. "Most people don't consume books the way you do."

Sophie turned to her husband, explaining, "Torie and I had spent days building a tiny palace of sticks and leaves. It was almost a shame to set it afire, but we were pretending the scene from the book."

"Playing Gulliver," Graham asked, his eyes twinkling. "And intending to use his, rather crude, method to put out the fire?"

"*That* I should have liked to witness," Jonathan muttered, though his expression was amused as well.

"Of course not." Victoria drew herself up properly and removed her elbow from the table, as if just now recalling her strict upbringing. "The cook's son often played with us. *He* was to be Gulliver and use his, uh—abilities—to put out the fire. But we didn't get that far before we were caught."

Laughter roared from the men, Elias included, at that tidbit of information. The idea of two little girls setting fire to a stick palace they had built in the garden, with the sole intent of having a boy pee on it to extinguish the flames, was too amusing. He might have thought the story made up but for Sophie's next words.

"I didn't believe it could be done." She raised her chin a bit. "I still doubt it."

"A challenge, brothers!" Jonathan slammed his cup on the table amid more laughter.

Only Olivia was not laughing but confessed, "I admit to feeling fortunate that I was still stuck in the nursery during that escapade."

"Be grateful you were," Victoria said, nodding her head sagely. "Sophie's plots involved much mischief. She was forever coercing me into one scrape or another."

Sophie gave an indignant snort. "I recall you being a willing participant, if not the instigator at times."

Graham rested his arm around the back of his wife's chair. "I fear not much has changed." He leaned down and kissed her soundly, silencing her protest.

Victoria's smile widened as she watched the exchange. "Sophie always insisted that she would never marry, but I am well pleased to see that she has met her match in you, Your Grace."

"Graham," he corrected with a slight shake of his head. "I never wished for my father's title, and I would give it away if I could. Here, there is certainly no place for it."

"As you wish." Victoria's smile was warm.

She likes him already, Elias mused and felt much the same toward all in the company who had joined them today. He'd been especially relieved as he'd taken the measure of the duke, Sophie's husband who'd been accused of murder. Though Jonathan and Victoria hadn't heard that story yet, Elias felt confident that Graham was no threat, but a good, honest man—one who had also suffered because of the girls' father.

But they had all escaped him. And tonight the room was brighter, the mood merrier than usual. Evie seemed to feel the same, bouncing in her high chair and waving her hands about and laughing when the others did.

It is nice, so many of us gathered here. For once Elias didn't feel like the third wheel to Jonathan and Victoria's relationship. Though they had insisted many times that he was welcome to stay as long as he wished, he had felt more keenly of late that it was time he and Evie moved on. That if it was just Jonathan and Victoria here, alone together as they ought to be, then they might have a better chance at conceiving another child and growing their family, as Elias knew they both wished to do.

"While we are on the topic of names," Victoria continued as she looked first at Sophie and then at Olivia. "I no longer go by Torie. During the Revolution, a *Tory* was considered a loyalist to the British—not a pretty thing to be at that time, or even now. Were you to call me that in the presence of others outside our family . . . well, it wouldn't be good, especially as we came from England so recently. There are still those who fear the British will try again someday to reclaim this new nation."

"They might believe her to be a spy." Jonathan winked at her.

"As if I've time for that with this place to run." Victoria rolled her eyes.

"I no longer wish to be called Livie, either," Olivia announced. "It was fine when we were children, but now that we're all grown up I prefer Olivia."

Sophie frowned. "Very well. I shall endeavor to call you both by your proper names, but I do not wish to hear Soph*ia* from anyone in this room."

"Unless we are scolding you for some misdeed?" Victoria teased.

"Is that the secret to getting her to behave herself?" Graham asked. "I had best take to calling you Sophia more often. Perhaps it will yield better results."

The table erupted into laughter again—all but Sophie, who scowled as if exasperated.

"Sophia was always too sophisticated a name for me. Too

polished and ladylike. If I recall—" she looked pointedly at her husband, "you first fell in love with me because I was *not* so very polished or ladylike. I was different."

"True enough," Graham said, the merriment in his eyes yielding to something more serious, an intimate reflection that had Elias looking away, unable to bear such exchanges between couples, painful reminders that they were of what he had once had and lost.

"Our courtship was not at all the usual sort," Graham said, by way of explanation to the others at the table. "Sophie was often at her best when her shoes were off and she was wading in a cold spring. Or when she was wearing a dress she'd made herself from canvas and that was covered with grass stains from rolling down hills. And especially . . ." Graham's look was faraway. "Especially when she was covered in sand, literally head to foot, and explaining that she was late to dinner because she'd been building the Taj Mahal or some such thing on the beach at night."

Victoria nodded. "That sounds rather like my sister."

"I hope she never changes." Graham's voice had turned husky, reminding Elias that the couple were still newlyweds, and that he had once, not so long ago, looked at Anne with that same adoration.

As if uncomfortable with the atmosphere as well, Olivia rose from the table. "I believe I saw a pie in the kitchen. I'll bring it in."

She vacated the chair beside Elias and hobbled from the room, and suddenly their numbers were at odds again—two couples, plus himself. Evie, for all that he loved her, did not quite fill the void. He stood as well and started reaching for dishes, as had become his habit in the months he'd lived here. *Help. Whenever and however I can.*

Because going home to his own house, facing life alone without Anne, was unthinkable.

OLIVIA LOOKED UP from her attempts at slicing the pie to see Elias standing in the kitchen doorway, his arms laden with dishes. He set them near the sink, then turned to her.

"Would you like some help?"

"Yes, thank you. I can't seem to slice this evenly." She handed him the knife before she could do more damage to what had, before she'd touched it, been a lovely pie. "You've already spent your afternoon helping me. You must think me the most incapable female who ever lived."

"I think you are very much like your sister when she first arrived here." Elias grimaced as he looked at the pie. "Next time, instead of trying to cut individual pieces, slice it in half and then fourths and then eighths." He showed her, doing his best to follow the cuts she'd already made, though that wasn't entirely possible.

"Very logical. I should have realized—"

"Have you ever sliced or served a pie before?"

At Olivia's shake of her head, he added, "Then don't feel badly. I'm guessing you've spent more time in the kitchen tonight than possibly ever before in your entire life."

"Guilty as accused." Olivia held up her hands. "My mother taught me about selecting menus and how and where to seat guests. There was never any instruction on how to prepare the meal."

"Welcome to America, land of opportunity—to make your own supper."

"Does no one employ servants here?"

"Like anywhere else, those who can afford it do. Plates are over there." He inclined his head toward a shelf on the opposite wall.

Olivia picked up the stack of blue china plates, smaller

than those they'd used at supper but with the same pattern—each with a sailing ship in the middle and a picture of the New York Harbor along the sides and a great eagle at the top perched over *E. Pluribus Unum.* "Out of many one."

"You're capable—you can read Latin."

"Such a useful skill in the kitchen." Olivia shook her head. "I don't understand how Victoria has learned to do so many things. I am rather in awe of it all, of her and of this house she keeps. We were raised not even knowing how to make a pot of tea."

"Necessity is the mother of invention," Elias quipped. "Victoria had little choice in the matter if she and Jonathan wished to survive. They came here practically penniless, and he set to work at once to change their fortunes. Victoria did the same. They stayed with us for the first several months, and Anne taught her how to do everything, from making soap to doing the wash, milking a cow, and making butter and bread to put it on. Victoria adapted and threw herself into her new life most admirably."

Elias carefully removed the first slice from the pie tin and placed it onto the plate Olivia held out.

"I am glad to see their fortunes have changed somewhat." Olivia ran her finger along the edge of the plate. "That Victoria has some fine things in her home as well."

"The dishes were a gift from Anne and me when they moved into this house. Most couples around here have a celebration when they marry, and they're gifted quilts and spoons and the like—things needed to set up house. Jonathan and Victoria didn't have that and had left everything from their former life behind. We were happy to help them get started."

"They were fortunate to have you." Olivia set the first plate on the table and handed him another.

"I am the fortunate one," Elias said. "Blessed greatly by their friendship. Jonathan is more like a brother than a cousin, and Victoria very much like a sister."

He did not elaborate more, and Olivia did not ask him the questions that had been running through her mind all evening. What had happened to his wife, to Anne? Had she died in childbirth, as Victoria nearly had? There had been no time, not a moment of privacy to question Victoria on the matter, but that Elias was living here with his daughter seemed answer enough.

"In America there is a healthy middle class," Elias said, returning to their former subject. "There is still poverty too, of course, but I believe less so than the stark differences in class that are found in England. The middle class here is made up of those who are not considered wealthy but who provide well for themselves. They own and farm their own land, they own livestock and have fine homes. Not as fine as those in England, perhaps, but sufficient for their needs and with many of the comforts of life."

Like this home. He had described it perfectly. There was nothing grand about the simple, two-story house, but it was warm and comfortable. *Peaceful and happy.* Two things their fine home in London had rarely been.

She held another plate out to Elias.

"If we top each piece with cream, the damage won't be as noticeable. If you'll finish here, I'll go out back to the ice box for the cream." He held the pie server out to her. Olivia took it from him, though she half-suspected he was handing it off to her as an opportunity for her to practice the most menial of kitchen tasks.

"I shall endeavor not to drop any on the floor."

"I can't promise not to eat it even if you do. Victoria's apple pie is that delicious." He turned from her and headed out the side door after propping it open with a rock.

Olivia shivered in the draft coming through the partially open door but focused on maneuvering the pie knife beneath one of the cut wedges, as she'd seen him do. She managed to plate it without further damage. By the time Elias returned with a covered crock, all seven slices were served.

"Excellent." He smiled, then proceeded to scoop a generous dollop of cream onto the top of six of the pieces. When he'd finished they almost looked pretty again.

Almost.

"They'll be too busy enjoying the taste of apples and cinnamon to notice anything amiss," he assured her. He picked up three of the plates, and Olivia took three others, leaving only the slice that didn't have cream.

"Is the one without cream for your daughter? I think I can carry it too."

"That's why you served seven?" Elias's eyes, already kind, seemed to soften even more as he looked at her.

"I know what it is like to be left out," Olivia said. "And didn't want to forget her."

"That was thoughtful. Evie doesn't eat that much. She can share mine." He stepped aside so Olivia could go ahead of him.

She hobbled past, her feet still refusing to work properly, and her arm bumped against his as her skirt brushed his trousers. "I'm so sorry." She leaned away, nearly missing the odd expressions crossing his face—the first revelatory and then, immediately after, stricken.

Slashed with pain. If she were to sketch him in this instant, that is how she would have described the emotion so clearly written in the lines of his face and the downturn of his mouth.

"Elias?"

His sorrowful eyes met hers.

They stood like that for only a second or two, but long

enough for her to feel a jarring awareness. *Jonathan's cousin. An American country doctor. Widower?* None of those attributes were anything close to those she had ever admired in, or desired from, a man. So why, as she turned away again and stepped past him, did she feel as if his pain had just awakened her soul?

Twenty-seven

OLIVIA SLIPPED BACK into her chair at the table—no one rose to pull it out for her—and tried not to think about Elias, busy tending to his daughter. Whatever Olivia imagined had just happened between them was nothing more than an effect of her overwrought mind. After all, she could have died out there today. Elias had saved her, and so—distraught and confused as she was at her changed plans regarding Jonathan—her mind had conjured . . . a replacement? Another man in need of someone to care for him?

Absurd.

She took a bite of pie. It was delicious, the apples soft, the syrup sweet, and the crust light and flaky. *Victoria* made *this*.

She'd made everything else they had eaten this night as well, and while it had been simple fare, soup and fresh bread and butter, it had been filling and delicious.

Olivia studied her eldest sister across the table, marveling at the adaptations she'd had to make and that she appeared both content and happy with her life here.

Something I could never be. Freed from her promise, there was no reason for her to stay now. *Other than Mother, Victoria, and Sophie.* She enjoyed Jonathan's and Graham's company as well, and she'd become friends with Maime and the children on their voyage. Being with each of them these past weeks had been easy and pleasant. Her family was here now. But if she returned to England . . . *I might have the opportunity to marry well and have a family of my own someday.*

In England she wouldn't have to worry about slicing pie or baking biscuits. She wouldn't have to wash clothes or make bread or do any of the numerous things that Victoria had learned to do and did every week.

I could attend parties and balls. I could be courted properly and marry someone with both money and a title.

As Sophie had. She and Graham weren't likely to stay here forever. They wished to return to Scotland, and that wasn't so very far from England that she would never see them.

"What are you so deep in thought about, little sister?" Jonathan asked.

Olivia flinched inwardly and would have sworn that beside her Elias tensed, as if he, too, had taken offense at the title. Jonathan had dropped *Livie*, but the *little* still stung. *No matter.* He could consider her a child for the rest of his life, if he wished. "I was thinking about home, about England."

"That is no longer *our* home," Jonathan said, a slight warning in his tone, as if even mention of the place was forbidden at their table.

"It is still mine," Olivia retorted, her chin raised in challenge. "I miss it already, though we've only been parted for a month."

"Do you intend to return?" Victoria asked, her voice rising with concern.

Olivia nodded. "Eventually. When it is safe. Perhaps I'll sail with Sophie and Graham when they take their leave."

"You intend to return as well?" The hurt in Victoria's voice was unmistakable as she looked at Sophie.

"My home is there," Graham said quietly. "In Scotland.

My mother's ancestral estate. My father nearly ruined it, and I've given my word to the people living there that I will help restore the prosperity and good fortune that once graced our land. Any of you would be welcome to join us there."

"We are content here," Jonathan stated in a tone that brooked no argument. "Lord Claybourne so fully ruined my good name and my livelihood in England that I could not even persuade a doctor to come to my aid when Victoria's life hung in the balance. I've no desire to ever set foot there again."

The previous good humor that had filled the room was now replaced by an underlying tension, and Victoria looked as if she might cry.

Olivia wrung her hands beneath the table, wishing she had not spoken so boldly or selfishly.

"Your feelings are understandable," Graham said quietly, his words directed to Jonathan at the head of the table. "My reputation is likely beyond repair in England as well, and Lord Claybourne was part of a plot that nearly ended with my neck in a noose. If not for Sophie, Olivia, and their mother, I would not be here now."

His words drew the attention of everyone at the table—everyone but Olivia and, perhaps, Sophie, who, like her, probably did not wish to relive those miserable days and hours. But the others sat with rapt attention as Graham related the story, starting at the night Newsome and Father had invaded his home. Graham told of being wounded and taken to Newgate. When it came time for him to recount all that had happened during the trial, his words grew slower, his voice gruff, and his arm tightened around Sophie as he spoke of her valiant efforts to free him.

He concluded his tale with Olivia's timely entrance at the bank and her charade that distracted and detained his pursuers long enough for him and William to escape to Lady Palmer's waiting carriage.

When he'd finished speaking, a different feeling pervaded the room and the group gathered around the table, all with their pie only half eaten, given that they had been entirely focused on Graham's story.

"I'm so glad you've come, so glad you were able to escape those horrible men—our father included." Victoria reached across the table to grasp Sophie's hand. "It seems your mind has grown into something that can get someone out of trouble as much as it used to get us into it." She turned to Olivia. "And you, dear sister, truly saved the day, barging straight into that building and those men as you did. I wish I could have seen it."

"And heard it." Graham placed his hands over his ears and grimaced. "Olivia might have pursued a career with the opera, given her lung capacity. I've never heard a woman scream like that, and I hope to never again." He sent her a genuine smile of gratitude as the others at the table laughed and the mood lightened somewhat.

Only Jonathan still seemed contemplative and solemn. "As you have invited us to your home in Scotland, consider yourselves welcome here as well. We are brothers now, united by marriage to our strong and beautiful wives and by our experiences surviving their father's attacks. Though I admit to feeling worried when I first saw Olivia, I am grateful to have Victoria's family—excepting her father—returned to us. You are welcome to stay here as long as you would like."

Where? How could they possibly all live here? For any length of time?

The dining room was really little more than a space for the table—full with six of them seated here—between the wall separating the kitchen from the rest of the house and the sitting room, which one entered directly from the front door. There was no vestibule for receiving guests, and there weren't even enough seats in the sitting room for all of them gathered here tonight.

The whole of the first floor of the house would have fit into the drawing room of their London townhome, with room to spare.

But this feels nicer. Olivia couldn't deny that Victoria's home felt cozy, warm, and welcoming, though it lacked any finery. The walls were plain, neither paper nor portraits covering any of them. The furniture was simple, the rugs homespun. There were no vases or art, no adornments of any sort. It was a practical home in every sense, but the people filling it warmed the space with their laughter. *Real laughter. Real happiness.* Unlike the mostly false tittering and the rigid conversations where one had to mind her every word, in London.

Yet she missed those still. They were all she knew. Even in their formality, even with the rules and expectations and knowing her every move had been watched and scrutinized, Olivia had felt more at home in those settings than she did here. That was the society she had been bred for, not this one.

"To freedom from Father," Victoria said, raising her glass.

The others followed, Olivia clinking hers against Elias's.

"*Very* capable," he whispered, giving her a look filled with admiration. "Who cares if you can slice a pie, when you stopped a villain and helped save an innocent man?"

Everyone drank to that solemn cheer, then Elias raised his glass for another. "To America, its freedoms, and those who are newly arrived here. May it come to feel like home, in the absence of your own."

Olivia raised her glass to his once more but did not meet his gaze as she told herself that his words did not mean anything. The last thing she wished was to encourage his interest in any way.

I will not end up here. I will *return to England someday.*

The thought made her both happy and sad. Eventually she would have to leave her mother and sisters. *If I choose England . . . I will be alone.* At least until she married. She could have her family or the life she knew and loved. But never again would it be both.

Twenty-eight

ELIAS STACKED THE dishes on the drainboard as laughter and chatter carried through the wall from the other room.

All is as it should be. He and Evie were on dish duty, while the others gathered around the fire to learn more about what had happened to each sister in the years they had been separated.

He set a pot in the sink and primed the pump until the water began to flow from the well beneath the ground. While the pot filled, he added wood to the stove and retrieved the soap from the shelf where he had set it last night, after washing the supper dishes. Behind him, sitting in her high chair that he'd brought into the kitchen, Evie slobbered on a biscuit and impatiently banged her little tin cup on the tray.

"We'll be done soon," Elias promised, though given the stacks of plates and bowls and pots needing to be washed, it wasn't going to be soon enough. Victoria had told him to leave them, that she and her sisters would clean everything up later, but Elias had insisted he would keep to their agreement. After all that she did for him, caring for Evie each day, the least he could do was wash a few dishes each night. *Or a few dozen.*

The pot finished filling, and Elias quickly swapped it out for a second one, then set the first on the stove to heat. He stopped in front of Evie for a quick game of peek-a-boo, the guaranteed way to make her giggle.

He started by covering his face with his hands and then opening them, then progressed to ducking around her chair and finally crouching on the floor and popping up in front of her.

Evie was laughing hard, and he was kneeling on the floor in front of her when he looked up to find Olivia, arms laden with the remaining dishes from the table, staring down at him.

"Peek-a-boo," he exclaimed, popping up in front of Evie. She squealed with delight and kicked her chubby legs.

"It's one of her favorite games," Elias explained, as if that wouldn't be obvious to anyone watching. He turned from them and went to the sink, just in time to pull the pump handle up and stop the flow of water before the pot overflowed. Carefully he carried it to the stove and placed it beside the first pot.

"What are you making?" Olivia asked. She still stood there, arms full of the china Victoria so treasured.

Elias hurried forward to take the dishes from her. "Nothing. Just heating water to wash the dishes."

"Oh." Her face colored slightly, and he regretted embarrassing her. Once Victoria had been as ignorant as Olivia about all things related to a kitchen.

He added the dishes to the already large pile on the drainboard. Apparently adding three extra people for supper added three times the dishes as well.

"Thank you for bringing those in," he called over his shoulder.

He heard nothing for several seconds as he gathered dishtowels and all else he needed. Then a timid—

"Would you like help?"

Elias turned to her, the *yes* on the edge of his tongue having little to do with the number of plates needing to be washed. Olivia Claybourne intrigued him when precious little, save Evie and caring for his patients, did these days. But to encourage her attention would be wrong. She'd been hurt enough today already. The best thing for her would be to bide her time here, before she could return to London and marry a proper lord, wealthy enough to keep her in fine clothes like those she'd been wearing earlier.

"Thank you, but no. You should be in there catching up with your sisters." He turned away, but not before noting her expression that was part relief and part disappointment.

Behind him the door closed softly, leaving him and Evie alone once again. *As it should be. As it will be the rest of my life?*

A long life, if he had any say in it, and who really did? He could be involved in a carriage accident tomorrow. Or catch an illness from one of his patients. But he did all he could to ensure he'd be around for Evie.

He pulled her chair closer to the sink now, so she could watch him. He'd made a game of counting the dishes with her as they came out of the rinse water. And if she became too impatient, he would allow her to play with the spoons.

A long life. A long, lonely *life.* Thirty-two wasn't exactly young anymore, but neither was he old. He'd married later than most because he'd been attending medical school and barely able to support himself. Then he'd started his practice and found Anne. But now the years ahead without her stretched before him like a bleak, unending road.

There might be beautiful vistas along the way—a sunset like they'd had tonight, or a patch of wildflowers in spring, the bright colors of autumn, the first snowfall of winter. There would be moments of joy too. Already he'd experienced Evie's first words and first steps. There would be her first day of school, the first book she read, her first doll and first fancy dress, her first dance. He would find joy in all those moments and more, but still the road stretched long and lonely. Dreary because he would travel it alone.

It doesn't have to be alone. He'd known that from the very beginning, when, mere weeks after Anne's passing, a well-meaning woman at church had offered him her daughter as a replacement wife. But there was no replacing Anne and the love he'd felt for her. He'd politely declined the offer and others that had been hinted at in the months since. He had no plans to marry again. No woman had caught his attention or even vaguely interested him.

Until today.

Elias removed the pots from the stove, set them in the sink, and got to work scrubbing away remnants of the most pleasant meal he'd enjoyed in months. It had been more than the food, fine though that was. It had been the company, the camaraderie he'd felt around that table, though technically he'd been the outsider among them.

He hadn't felt that way though. For a few minutes at least, he'd belonged. *One of six. Three men, three women. Three couples.*

A trick of his mind, certainly. He was a widower, and the last female he should take notice of was Olivia Claybourne. For many reasons.

She's too young. He had no idea how old she was, but he doubted she'd reached twenty yet. *She's too English.* She'd all but said she couldn't wait to return to England and would probably catch the next ship across the Atlantic were it safe to do so.

She's not suited to any sort of life here. By her own admission she didn't even know how to slice a pie. She possessed none of the skills necessary to care for a home and family.

She's observant and thinks of others. Twice she noticed Evie and considered her needs.

She's honorable. She crossed an ocean to keep a promise.

She's strong and determined. She walked over five miles through a snowstorm, in a strange land.

She's brave. She endured having her frozen feet scrubbed better than some men I've seen.

The skills Olivia lacked could be learned. But attributes like compassion, loyalty, and fortitude could not. One either possessed them, or one didn't. After only a few hours in her presence, Elias could already see that, much like Victoria, Olivia's character was admirable.

"If I'm a wise man, I'll leave the admiring to someone else," he told Evie.

OLIVIA STRUGGLED TO keep her eyes open as the firelight danced before them, and at last she felt almost warmed through. The chill from her hours spent walking through the snow had lingered, even after she'd changed her wet clothes for dry ones, but her proximity to the fire, seated in Victoria's rocking chair, was finally warming her.

A hot bath would truly warm me. But with no bathing room or tub in sight and no servants to prepare such a luxury, she didn't suppose that was a request she could make. *Just one of the many extravagances I miss.*

Graham and Sophie sat close together on the sofa, much as they had throughout the voyage, as if they were still afraid to be separated after the ordeal each had faced without the other. Victoria pressed close on Sophie's other side. They were holding hands, still reminiscing about childhood adventures Olivia had had no part in. Jonathan sat in the chair opposite her, his expression more relaxed than it had been previously, though Olivia suspected their presence still worried him.

If I returned to England perhaps that would placate Father. He would be furious, of course, and she would bear the brunt of that wrath and have to lie about where she had been all these months. But he need never know what had become of his wife and other daughters.

But then . . . Newsome might be dead, but there were any other number of horrible men her father might insist she marry. The dream she'd always looked forward to, a Season in London during which she might dance and dine and choose for herself whom she wished to be courted by, had probably been doomed from the start.

She could not return. At least not yet, and perhaps never. *But what am I to do here?*

The most immediate answer was to fall asleep in front of the fire, blocking out the view of her sisters and their husbands, cozy together with little thought for her. But she wouldn't allow sleep to claim her yet. A bath she might have to forgo, but a glass of water she did not. Since her sojourn outdoors today, she'd been unable to quench her thirst. How strange that being surrounded by all that snow should render her so parched.

At home she would have used the bell pull in whatever room she happened to be in and asked a servant to bring her a glass of water. Or, more likely, the servants, anticipating the needs of those they served, would have seen that a pitcher and glass were already waiting in her room.

But there were no bell pulls or servants here. She could ask Victoria to get her a drink, but that would only point out her own ineptness all the more. She thought of the pump in the kitchen and all that glorious water spilling into the pot Elias had been preparing for washing dishes. Her mouth felt even dryer, the memory mocking her need. She should have just asked him for a glass then, but she'd still felt flustered by whatever it was that had happened between them earlier, while preparing to serve the pie. And now . . . *I shall have to go to the kitchen myself.* It was enough that she considered coping with her thirst.

Foolish. Why should she fear being alone with him for a minute or two? That was all it would take to locate a glass and fill it. And nothing had happened between them earlier. She had imagined the look he'd given her. Nothing more.

He'd paid her little attention when she'd ventured in before, with the stack of dishes. Olivia smiled as the image of him playing with his daughter replayed in her mind. Though she could not recall her own years of early childhood, she felt positive that her father had never played with her. He'd barely acknowledged any of his daughters—until they were older and might be of use to him. The love Elias felt for his daughter, however, had been evident in his actions, focused solely on her and meant to bring her joy.

Olivia swallowed, forcing the hurt that had surfaced back down her parched throat. If she rifled through every one of her memories with her father, there would be none where he had done the same, considering her happiness and working to bring her joy. *I was a thing for him to use. Nothing more.*

She could not return to England and become that again. If, for no other reason, than that it might further the evil he propagated on Saint Kitts. Both Graham and Maime had opened her eyes to the wicked realities occurring on the island and elsewhere—all because of men like her father. *I can be no part of that.*

And now she had no part here. No purpose. Except to exist until she figured out what she was to do with herself, and that existence required water. Enough of being the coward. She would fetch a glass herself.

Olivia stood and walked toward the kitchen, padding silently in Elias's oversized wool socks.

"Where are you going Liv—Olivia?" Victoria asked.

Love UNDYING

"I'm thirsty, and no servants were appearing to read my mind and bring me a glass of water." Olivia offered her sister a wry smile.

"Ah." Victoria nodded. "None will, I'm afraid. But perhaps you'll find, as I have, that being able, and doing for oneself instead of having to rely upon others for everything, including your most basic needs, is quite freeing."

Olivia shrugged. "Perhaps." Right now it just seemed like a great deal of work. She crossed through the dining area—it could hardly be called a room—and entered the kitchen again.

Elias stood at the sink with his back to her, washing dishes and singing to Evie while she clanged two spoons together.

"Baa-baa, black sheep, have you any wool? Yes sir, yes, sir three bags full. One for the master and one for the dame. And one for the little boy who lives down the lane."

His rich baritone stopped her. *The doctor can sing.* The tune was familiar, but the words were different from those she had learned as a child in her lessons.

When he finished the verse and took to humming, she sang along. "*Ah! Vous dirai-je, maman.*"

Elias turned around. "The lady speaks French as well."

"*Mais bien sur. Et toi?*"

In answer he continued the song with the lyrics she was familiar with. "*Ce qui cause mon tourment? Papa veut que je raisonne comme une grand personne.*"

What is causing my torment? Papa wants me to reason like a big person. "*Moi je dis que les bonbons valent mieux que la raison,*" Olivia finished, absurdly pleased that he knew the song. Such a trivial thing, but it felt like a little piece of the familiar. *Of home.*

"And *do* you feel sweets are worth more than reason?" Elias pulled another dish out of the rinse water and set it on the drainboard.

"Of course." Olivia bent down to retrieve a spoon Evie had dropped. She handed it to the little girl with a smile. "Sweets, sweet moments... They are the best of life and should be both indulged in and savored. There will be plenty of time to reason later. Though only with me if I am able to have a glass of water now. I fear I am still recovering from my overlong walk today."

"No doubt you are." Elias looked at her with concern, then retrieved a clean mug from the row of those waiting to be dried. He held it beneath the pump with one hand while his other moved the handle.

The clear stream filling the cup looked better than anything she'd ever had to drink before. He handed her the full mug, and Olivia brought it to her lips and drank the whole thing.

Elias took it from her and refilled it again. "Drink another. It's what your body needs after its ordeal outdoors today."

"Yes, Doctor." Olivia took the second glass from him and drank more slowly this time and only half before setting it aside. The discomfort around him that she had worried over only minutes ago seemed to have dissipated, so she picked up a cloth and then a plate to wipe dry.

"You didn't tell me you had experience drying dishes," Elias said. "I might have taken you up on your offer to help earlier."

"No experience, but it does seem obvious that they shouldn't be put away wet. And as I feel a bit the odd one out among my sisters and their husbands, I offer my limited services." Olivia finished wiping the plate and set it on the shelf she and Sophie had taken them from earlier.

"I assume your tutors taught you both French and Latin?" Elias asked.

"*Oui.* Though I've had little cause to speak either for some time. I did not expect to here."

"We aren't all as backwoods as the English would have one believe. I was educated as well. America has fine universities, and many families educate both their sons and daughters."

"At university?" Olivia asked, her interest piqued not for herself but for Sophie.

He shook his head. "No, unfortunately. Though I feel many young ladies, like yourself, would both excel and benefit from it. But many have tutors who instruct them quite thoroughly—in subjects beyond embroidery and pouring tea. Have you ever been to France?"

"No. I always dreamed of going to Paris, to the dressmakers there. I'd hoped to go for my trousseau before I married, but..."

"Are you betrothed? Did you leave a fiancé behind—in favor of fulfilling the promise to your sister?"

"No." Olivia returned another plate to the shelf. "I didn't even have a full Season." She'd barely had time to begin to take note of which gentlemen were available in the marriage mart before Mother had whisked her out of London and into hiding. She sighed. "But I *am* safe here, and my sisters and mother and I are all together. That is what matters." The words, meant to convince herself as much or more than him, sounded morose. "I don't mean to pout. It has been a long, difficult day, and I am tired is all. Tomorrow will be better."

"I tell myself that every night," he said solemnly.

"And is it true?" Olivia stopped drying the pot she'd picked up and studied his expression.

"Sometimes," Elias said. He looked over at Evie, beginning to nod sleepily in her chair. "There is always something to be grateful for. When I remember that, the day is usually better."

Twenty-nine

"YOU SHOULD RETURN to the other room and join your sisters. I'll finish in here." Elias reached for the towel in Olivia's hands.

She held it away from him and shook her head. "Evie is practically asleep. Put her to bed, and I'll finish."

Elias glanced at Evie, looking back and forth between the two of them, her eyes droopy as she fought sleep. He ought to put her to bed, but it didn't seem right leaving Olivia here to finish. "This is my responsibility. Not yours. You should be in there with your sisters."

Olivia placed a hand on her hip, then reached around him to grab another plate to dry. "America certainly is different. In England you'd never find a man washing dishes. Even among servants."

Elias shrugged. "Well, this man does. Because he is immensely grateful to your sister. I shall remain in her debt no matter how many dishes I wash. Victoria cares for Evie much of the time, when I am gone seeing patients at all hours. Caring for a child and feeding another man is a lot of extra work. I can repay her in part by washing the dishes each night so she does not have to. And so *you* do not feel obligated to this night." He inclined his head toward the door. "Go."

"Not when your daughter so clearly needs your attention," Olivia said. She sidled past him and added the last plate to the stack on the shelves. "If you will not get her out of that uncomfortable chair, at least allow me to."

"Have you cared for many young children?" Elias asked, again puzzled at her concern.

"No," Olivia threw over her shoulder as she turned her back to him and proceeded to extricate Evie from the chair. "But I have spent my life as the youngest and forever waiting child. I'll take Evie to Victoria, who no doubt is an expert."

Elias shook his head. "Don't do that. Allow Victoria to have an evening off. She and Jonathan rarely get any time to themselves or to enjoy another couple's company—without Evie or me there as well."

"They don't seem to mind." Olivia lifted Evie in her arms, wrapping them securely around her as Evie laid her head against Olivia's shoulder.

Was it the similarity in the sisters' looks that had Evie so comfortable with Olivia already? Or maybe Evie was simply too tired to care who held her. It *was* past her bedtime.

"*I* mind," Elias said, more gruffly than he'd intended. If he was being honest with himself, he objected to Olivia holding Evie as well. It was one thing for Victoria, who was practically his sister, to care for Evie. But until this moment, he'd never allowed another woman to do the same. On Sundays at church, he held Evie the entire time, never passing her off to others. Anywhere he took Evie, she never left his arms. She was his baby, Anne's, and no one else's.

"Since you insist on finishing in here and don't want me to disturb Victoria, would you like me to rock Evie until you're through?"

"I'll take her." He watched as Olivia read his expression and understanding dawned.

"I'm sorry. I didn't mean to interfere." She held Evie, asleep already, out to him.

Elias took his daughter and held her close, his eyes shut briefly against the hurt he'd just seen in Olivia's.

"She's all I have left," he said, as if that would explain his strange behavior. He knew it wouldn't, knew it hadn't, when he looked at Olivia again.

"I'm sorry," she repeated, then hobbled past him to stand at the sink. The candle positioned on the shelf above gave a last flicker and went out, casting the room in near darkness. Elias wanted to tell her where she might find another, but a more persuasive part of him demanded that he flee. He did, exiting the kitchen and leaving Olivia alone to ponder what had just gone wrong.

OLIVIA SCRUBBED THE bottom of the large pot—the last thing to be washed—but couldn't figure out how to get the remaining soup off of the bottom. Everything else had been cleaned—it hadn't been as terrible as she'd imagined—but apparently she'd saved the worst for last, and though she had watched his process as Elias washed and rinsed, no amount of scrubbing seemed likely to free the vegetables stubbornly stuck to the bottom.

"I can't even do the simplest task!" Exasperated, Olivia pulled her hands from the water and frowned at their wrinkled condition. She pressed down on either side of the sink and leaned forward over it, wanting again to scream. Was there no end to the frustrations in her life?

She'd wanted to leave the kitchen clean, to prove to Elias she wasn't completely inept, as he'd obviously believed she was—at caring for a child, at least. She might have gone about that all wrong, as she had misjudged her ability to walk in the weather today. She didn't have the faintest idea how to cook a biscuit or anything else, but she'd believed she could at least wash the few remaining dishes.

She stuck her hands in the tepid water again, determined to succeed. *Maybe hot water would help.*

That was probably it. The wash and rinse water had long since cooled.

But where to dump them out? And how to light the stove to heat fresh water? After watching Elias, she thought she could make the pump work, but little good that would do if she didn't have the means to heat the water.

One day here, and I'm a disaster.

What would Sophie do? Find a book on lighting stoves or keeping house, probably. The thought made Olivia smile and glance around the kitchen just in case. No books to be found. But Sophie wouldn't let a little thing like this defeat her.

Neither will I.

Olivia heaved the pot of rinse water out of the sink and lugged it toward the side door. She set it on the ground and opened the door, then held it open with her stockinged foot. Wind howled and snow blew into the kitchen, but she persisted, hoisting the pan and tossing the water in it out onto the snow. She repeated her actions with the wash water, then secured the door and returned both empty pots to the sink.

The toes of her borrowed socks were soaked, but it seemed a little price to pay for success.

She moved the pump up and down as she'd seen Elias do, then stepped back and clasped her hands together when water started flowing. *Not so difficult. I can do this.*

She left the water filling the pot and went to the stove. Its many handles and doors were confusing. She hadn't seen Elias do anything with it, other than put the pans of water on top. *Maybe it's still hot?*

Olivia lowered her hand to hover over the cook surface.

Warm, but not hot. Probably not enough to heat a large pan of water. There had to be a way to increase the temperature again. She'd add wood stacked in the box near the stove. But where was she supposed to add it? Which door?

She grabbed the handle closest to her, then yelped, pulling her hand back quickly but not fast enough to prevent the angry burn striping her palm.

Tears sprang to her eyes and slid down her face. One fell on her outstretched palm making it sting even worse.

Foolish. Stupid. Olivia bit her lip to keep from crying out and waved her burned hand, as if that somehow might help. But it only seemed to increase the pain.

Cold. She needed a way to make it stop burning. She whirled around the kitchen, her eyes landing on the door. *Snow.*

Olivia used her uninjured hand to yank open the door, then stepped outside. Using the same hand, she scooped up a handful of snow to carry back inside and administer carefully to the burn. She turned back toward the kitchen as the door slammed in her face. She leaned into it, pushing, but it didn't budge. With her good hand full of snow, she couldn't grab the handle. She dumped the snow back on the ground, then grasped the handle, but it held fast. *Locked? From inside?* Too late she remembered that Elias had propped the door open with a rock when he'd gone out earlier.

Her tears came faster, and she wrapped her arms around her as she shivered, her feet soaked now and the snow swirling around her. She doubted anyone would hear her if she banged on the door.

Why had she ever come here? Staying hidden in the English countryside or in London townhomes indefinitely would have been better. *Without Jonathan to care for—*

As if I would have been able to do that! What had

possessed her to believe that she could take care of him? He didn't need someone to entertain his guests or attend the theater with, or to look pretty on his arm. He needed a cook and a laundress, a dishwasher, a gardener, and a seamstress. She would have been a disaster of enormous proportion. *I am a disaster.*

Cradling her injured hand against her, Olivia turned from the door and began trudging through the knee-deep snow, around the side of the house toward the front.

Instead of reading books all those months she'd been in hiding, she ought to have been spending time with the servants, learning how to do basic things like make a meal or mend a shirt. That was the kind of caring a man in America needed. And she was completely unprepared to do any of it. Elias had realized that, of course. Little wonder he had practically snatched his daughter from her arms.

Head ducked against the wind and snow pelting her, Olivia hugged the side of the house until she reached the corner and stumbled across the front yard. Her feet burned with cold, and the lower half of her borrowed dress was soaked by the time she found the trail that had been shoveled between the front door and the barn. She paused, hugging herself, freezing as she weighed her options.

Warmth awaited her on the other side of the house door, but a hefty dose of humiliation was sure to accompany it. She hung her head, imagining what her sisters and their husbands might say when they saw her and her burned hand. If she were fortunate, perhaps Elias would already be upstairs with Evie for the night.

The barn was a good distance away, but there was a clear path to it, enough light from the moon to see her way there, and it would be warmer inside too. She'd never slept in a barn—that sounded more like something Sophie would do.

The thought of sleeping beside a horse or a cow wasn't appealing, but how much worse could it be than appearing at the front door in the state she was in now? Maybe she could borrow a horse in the morning and ride to Waterloo before anyone awoke.

And maybe Elias would have to rescue me again as he did today.

The memory of his warning about mountain lions and wolves set her stockinged feet moving quickly toward the front door. She lifted her uninjured hand, frozen now like the rest of her, and pounded, then stood shivering, awaiting her fate.

After what was probably only a minute, but felt more like ten, the door opened. Elias stood there, his mouth agape as he took in the sight of her.

"Hello, again," Olivia managed with a grimace as he reached forward and pulled her into the warmth of the house.

Thirty

"WHAT IN THE world?" Victoria exclaimed, rising from the sofa as Elias ushered Olivia toward the fire. "Why were you outside?"

"I was locked out," Olivia mumbled, her teeth chattering as they had done when he had found her on the road earlier today.

"Why did you go out there in the first place?" Victoria demanded. Sophie had joined her, and they took Elias's place, flanking their sister on either side as they helped her move toward the fire. "Sit," Victoria demanded, pointing to the rocking chair.

Anne's rocking chair. The one he hadn't wanted to see Olivia rocking Evie in earlier. Elias wondered now if his selfishness had caused whatever chain of events had led to Olivia's being outside in the blizzard.

"What happened?" Sophie asked, gentler than Victoria as she knelt and began peeling Elias's soaked socks from Olivia's feet. As she had earlier today, Olivia tried to pull back, attempting to tuck her feet out of sight.

"I'll get another pair," Elias said, heading for the stairs, hoping he could sneak into his room without waking Evie.

"I burned myself on the stove and went outside to get some snow to put on the burn."

Elias paused on the third stair, then turned and retraced his steps. He stopped before Olivia, appreciative when her sisters parted to let him through. He crouched in front of her. "Show me your hand."

She sighed, then untucked it and held it out. Sophie and Victoria gasped at the angry red lines crossing her palm.

"I couldn't get the soup pot clean. I thought if I had more hot water that would help, but the stovetop wasn't hot anymore. I wanted to add more wood but didn't realize the handle was hot."

"Snow was a good idea," Elias said.

"I'll get some," Graham offered, heading toward the front door.

"Take a bowl from the kitchen to scoop it," Victoria called.

Graham nodded and disappeared through the kitchen door, then gave a shout of surprise. "Sophie! Come help!"

Olivia's face paled, and she half rose from the chair before Elias's hand on her shoulder kept her in place.

"The water—oh no! The pump was refilling the pot when I stepped outside."

Jonathan jumped up, running after Victoria and Sophie as they headed toward the kitchen.

Olivia groaned and leaned forward, face buried in her good hand. "I should take the next ship back to England before I ruin anything else."

"Nonsense."

Elias finished removing her wet stockings, then took each of her feet in his hands and rubbed some warmth back into them.

Her hand was going to hurt for several days, and it would blister. But other than a scar, he didn't think there would be permanent damage. But her toes, or one of them at least, still worried him.

"I shouldn't have left you alone in the kitchen," he said, feeling responsible for her misery.

Olivia sniffed, and a tear dripped off her cheek onto her sleeve. "I wanted to show you that I'm not completely inept. But apparently I am. I'm sorry if I alarmed you earlier when I picked up Evie. I don't blame you for not trusting me with her."

Not trusting—that's what she thought? And she had been trying to prove to him that she was capable? Why?

"Trust had nothing to do with it." Elias gently lifted her chin, his guilt multiplying at the misery pooling in her blue eyes. "Since Anne died, I've never allowed any other woman—aside from Victoria—to hold Evie. And when you offered to rock her . . ." He closed his eyes, grappling with a wave of grief as it crashed into him.

He never knew when they would hit or what would trigger one, thrusting him backward into the hollow of despair he was constantly climbing out of.

Elias gripped the arms of the rocker, the very chair he had built for Anne when she was expecting Evie. It had taken him months, this gift of love. Anne had been thrilled with it, imperfections and all. And he had been overwhelmed with love for his wife and daughter when, the day after Evie's birth, Anne had walked from the bed and settled into her chair. He'd placed tiny Evie in her arms, and Anne had rocked the baby and sung to her. If he closed his eyes, he could still see her sitting there, could still hear her voice.

The chair and Evie's cradle were the only pieces of furniture he'd brought with him from the house after Anne died. He knew Victoria used the rocker but never when he was home. He didn't mind seeing others sitting in it, but the thought of someone else rocking his baby girl in front of him . . . A trivial thing perhaps, and something he ought to get over, but he wasn't ready for that, for anything that might taint that sweet memory.

Anne had spent less than a week using that chair before she became ill, before she'd begged him to send Evie away so the baby wouldn't get sick. He'd heeded her request, taking their daughter to Victoria.

Then he'd returned to care for Anne until she had died and he'd become so sick himself that he could hardly get out of bed.

"Elias?" Olivia's voice was soft. The tears on her face had dried, and she was looking at him with grave concern. "Are you all right? I didn't mean to upset you. I won't pick up Evie again or offer to rock her."

No. That didn't seem right. That wasn't what he wanted. He'd been touched by Olivia's genuine concern and caring, her thoughtfulness and observation. She might not be skilled in the kitchen, but Olivia had a nurturing nature, instinctual and kind. She didn't need anyone telling her what to do for a child; somehow she just knew. *She'll make a good mother someday.*

When she married some lord in England.

Elias frowned, and she drew back, as if frightened she had offended him.

"I'm sorry." He reached for her uninjured hand, touching it gently. "It wasn't that I didn't trust you or that I was upset with you. It's just this chair, and a memory I have—one of my few with Anne and Evie together. Anne rocked Evie in this chair, only for a few days, before Anne came down with smallpox. Her sister had come from New York City to stay with us, to help after the birth. She didn't know she was sick, that she was bringing death to our doorstep. She succumbed first, and Anne died a couple of weeks later. We sent Evie to stay with Victoria and Jonathan as soon as we realized Anne and her sister were sick. Anne never had much time with Evie. And this chair, those few times she rocked her, hold some of the only memories I have."

Olivia clasped his hand in return. "I'm so sorry, Elias. I didn't know—any more than I knew how to add wood to that stove."

"I realize that." He gave her a half smile. "You've had quite the first day."

She sighed. "Perhaps it should be my last, before I cause any real harm." She glanced toward the kitchen and the raised voices and noises coming from there. "If I haven't already."

"You haven't," he assured her. "I could tell you stories about Victoria's mishaps that would make this incident mild."

Olivia smiled. "I think I should like to hear those tales." She yawned. "But not tonight."

"Another time, then." Elias released her hand to study the burn on the other. "We still need to get some snow on that. I'll be right back."

He left her there and ran out to the yard, scooping a handful from the drifts piling up against the house. This snow was heavy and wet, and he shuddered to think of her out in it, even for a few minutes.

Thank heaven I found her today.

He returned to Olivia's side and used his fingers to pinch a tiny amount of snow onto her palm. She stiffened and sucked in a breath. "That hurts worse."

"It will help it get better," he promised. "Though it's going to sting for a while."

She nodded. "I know. My penance. I should never have come here. I couldn't have begun to care for—" Her voice lowered, and she looked down at her lap. "Jonathan."

"Perhaps not right now, not yet," Elias acknowledged. "But I'm sure, like Victoria, you could have learned. And I find it admirable that you came. I heard what you told Victoria today, all that it took to find him, to find them. And I couldn't help but think that it might have been nice if Anne had had another sister and made her promise to look after me."

Thirty-one

JONATHAN ROLLED HIS eyes as a shout of laughter came from the bedroom on the other side of the wall. "The girls all stayed together in one bed like this a few nights during the summer Sophie and Olivia stayed with us." He shook his head. "No one got any sleep."

"Just so long as they don't wake Evie." Elias looked down at his sleeping daughter, snuggled in his arms. She'd been stirring when he went upstairs to get another pair of his thick stockings for Olivia, but he hadn't minded. He'd carried Evie back downstairs, realizing he was the one who needed the comfort of rocking her far more than she did. "Olivia has to be exhausted after walking all day in the cold and snow," he added. He'd been grateful to see her sisters take her under their wing and usher her into Victoria and Jonathan's bedroom, after Victoria had announced that the women would be taking over the bedroom for tonight. "I can't imagine they'll stay up too much longer."

Jonathan and Graham exchanged a look.

"One would think," Jonathan said. "But you don't know the Claybourne sisters as well as we do."

Graham nodded. "Wills of iron and endless vivacity, those women. You don't ever want to be on the wrong side of that—especially if one of them has a gun." He stretched his legs out before the fire, then looked at Jonathan. "I owe you for that, for teaching Sophie how to shoot. It likely saved her life—and possibly mine as well."

"Aim for the heart or the head to kill, the hand or the plums to wound and stop."

Elias choked. "You taught two young girls that?"

"He did," Graham confirmed. "Imagine my surprise when Sophie shared that tidbit with me—wisdom that someone named *Jonathan* had imparted to her."

Elias smiled. "Cause for concern, I gather?"

Graham nodded. "And jealousy. She wasn't even my wife yet, and some other man had taught her—"

"How to defend herself. Nothing more." Jonathan raised his hands. "All innocent, I assure you. Besides. You know Sophie. Anything I told her was something she'd probably already read in a book."

"Too true." Graham smiled. "She's a rare woman, and how I do love her."

Elias stood. If the conversation was going to continue in this vein—their love for their wives—it was time he went to bed. He had enough trouble falling asleep on a normal night, when the conversation beforehand wasn't about love or *plums*.

After a year alone, thoughts of either weren't welcome. "I'll bid you gentlemen goodnight." He tucked Evie's blanket up around her so it wouldn't drag on the floor.

"Goodnight," Graham and Jonathan echoed.

"You should take the other room upstairs, across from Elias's," Jonathan said to Graham. "I'll sleep on the sofa."

"Thank you," Graham said. "But I prefer to be down here, closer to Sophie. Neither of us has quite recovered from our forced separation. The sofa will do fine for me tonight."

Elias headed up the stairs alone, contemplating Graham's words. *Does any man ever recover from forced separation from his wife?*

Graham stretched out on the sofa, or as much as he could, anyway. His feet pressed against one end while his shoulders and head angled up on a pillow at the opposite. It didn't promise to be a very good night's sleep.

He hoped his hunch—that Sophie might join him sometime in the night—was correct. For all that they had spent the day together, they hadn't *been* together much. Earlier it had been traveling in a storm that made talking difficult, and since their arrival she'd been preoccupied with her sisters.

As she should be. He was happy for her, though a little concerned that Sophie might never wish to return to Caerlanwood now. And how could he ask her to, when her family was here? Yearning for Scotland and for Sophie swirled through his mind until a fitful sleep claimed him.

Graham woke to find Sophie bent over him, tucking a blanket up to his chin. He grabbed her hand. "Stay? Please?"

"That was my intent."

Her quiet words calmed his troubled thoughts and somehow set everything right inside of him. Sophie was his anchor in any storm. He needed only to be with her. He *always* wanted to be with her. The answer to his dilemma came swiftly. It was sudden and simple. Wherever she was, he wanted to be there too. He could still keep his promise to those living on his ancestral lands. Others would just have to oversee them. He would miss his homeland, would miss Scotland dearly, but he could live without that. He could not live without Sophie.

He pulled her down beside him, scooting in to make room for her. She slid against his length, facing him, and Graham wrapped an arm around her, holding her tightly. She laid her head on his chest, over his heart, and gave a sigh of contentment.

"That's better. Sleeping with my sisters used to be fun—and it was for a while tonight. But this is where I belong."

"Aye, it is." He gave a grunt of agreement that elicited a laugh.

"Careful," he said, "or you'll wake the household. And I don't feel like sharing you right now."

"Nor I you," Sophie said.

Graham wondered if, like him, she was recalling another time they had snuggled on a sofa—not quite as intimately as they were now—but with results that had set events in motion that had led to their marriage. *And the overwhelming joy I feel with her.* "Do you remember—"

"Yes." Her head bobbed against his shirt. "I was never the one who claimed to forget that kiss."

"I was an idiot," Graham confessed.

"You were," she agreed, causing him to chuckle this time.

"It was a lie, you know." Every second of that kiss—their first—was seared into both his mind and heart for eternity. "I'll *never* forget it." His arm tightened around her.

"Nor will I." Sophie tipped her head back to look up at him. The dwindling firelight reminded him of that night too, the flames highlighting the gold in her hair. Tonight, it was neither wet nor tangled, as it had been that night they'd been caught in a spring storm. But she was wearing only a shift again—they hadn't taken the time to pack clothing when they'd started on their search for Olivia. The garment slipped from one shoulder, as it had that night in the gatekeeper's cottage, but now it was his privilege to rest his hand there, to touch her as she liked. *As we both do.*

Sophie squirmed as if trying to get comfortable. "Not too many more months, and we won't be able to lie like this."

Graham's hand left her shoulder and slid to her stomach, still flat beneath her shift, with no sign yet of the bairn growing inside of her. He sensed the child though and marveled at its creation, the miracle of it, of what he and Sophie had brought forth together. Someday, not too many months hence, he would hold this life they had created.

"You're feeling better now?" he asked. Sophie hadn't been sick since they'd left the ship, but he asked just the same, ever concerned for her health. He was glad Maime was with them and would be able to help Sophie when her time came. And he'd been immensely relieved to learn that Victoria hadn't died in childbirth after all. It was a thought, a worry, that had been in the back of his mind since learning Sophie was carrying their child.

"Much better. The sickness is gone. Maime said that's as it should be, and I should feel fine for the next few months—until I begin to look and move like an elephant."

"*My* elephant," he teased, his arm squeezing her tight against him. "And I doubt you'll ever reach such proportions."

She shrugged. "We'll just have to see what size infant that Scottish blood of yours produces."

Graham yawned, sleep beckoning him again. He didn't want to give in, to go there yet. Not when holding Sophie close, touching her, whispering together was so pleasant. He'd needed this after today. It had been a good day, wonderful in many ways, but right now he needed her.

"Graham?"

He adored the sound of his name on her lips. "Hmm?"

"It was so good to see Victoria today. I . . . I felt so many things. So much joy and relief. But still sorrow and anger over the years we missed and the anguish I endured at what I thought was her death. I wasn't angry at her so much or even Jonathan. I understand why they did what they did, but I'm still furious it had to be that way, that our family has had to be torn apart like this."

"Now it's mending. You're together." He rubbed his hand up and down her arm, as if to soothe away her hurt. "Your sister is *alive*. It's—incredible." He couldn't help but think of his own sister today, especially in those first moments, when Sophie and Victoria had clung to each other, alternately sobbing and laughing. How would he and Katherine have reacted, had they experienced such a miracle? His heart throbbed a little even now, the pain of losing his only sibling never completely healed, never too far from his mind.

While sitting in that cell in Newgate, that had been the only thought to comfort him. If he was to leave this life soon, at least he had the possibility of seeing his mother and sister again. He'd no doubt their souls existed in heaven. Where his was to journey was another matter, but he had to believe that a merciful God, one who loved his children, would permit at least one last visit with them. One last time to tell them he loved them, that he was sorry he hadn't done more, hadn't protected them.

During his musings, Sophie moved so that she lay partially on top of him now, her arm braced across his chest as she leaned up, able to see his face. "I was so happy today, but amidst our reunion and that joy, I felt a stab of sorrow. I felt your pain as you watched us. And I wished so very badly that you might rejoice in Katherine again as I do in Victoria."

"I wish that as well." His voice was gruff, and he swallowed the emotion thick in his throat. "But I have *you*. Katherine led me to you. I believe that with all my heart."

Sophie smiled. "Someday, I will thank her." She laid her head over his heart again, filling Graham with another surge of overwhelming love for her.

God is merciful. He is good.

The sofa they were attempting to sleep on was not. Sophie wiggled against him, probably trying to get comfortable. He should send her back to the bed with her sisters. She'd sleep better there, but he didn't want to let her go. Not yet. *Not ever.*

"I miss our bed at Caerlanwood," he muttered, as the wood support of the sofa dug into his back.

"I miss everything about Caerlanwood," Sophie said. "But at night, just before I sleep, I imagine that we're there."

"Tell me," Graham said. On their voyage across the Atlantic he'd discovered what a good storyteller she was. Deprived of her usual stash of books, Sophie had made up stories for the children every night, and Graham had been as delighted with her imagination as Ayla and Matthew had been.

"It's summer again," Sophie said, obliging him. "The children are asleep. The house is quiet, save for Boyce, who is walking the halls as he's taken to doing at night, banging into furniture or some such thing, with every other step."

Graham's mouth lifted in a smile. "Aye, clumsy old coot. Loyal to a fault, he is, and thinking it his job to protect us, day or night." Graham's smile faded as he recalled the last time he'd seen his old butler, clad only in his nightshirt and wielding a skillet as a weapon. He *was* old. Much too old to be answering doors still and especially too long in years to be standing at Graham's side to defend Caerlanwood against intruders. Yet he'd done just that. *Will he still be alive to thank by the time I return?*

"We leave our room and tiptoe down the sturdy new staircase."

Graham gave a snort of disbelief. "This *is* a dream."

Sophie poked him. "Quiet. It's *my* story. Or do you not wish me to share it with you?"

He snapped his mouth shut.

"We leave the house by way of the kitchen—"

"Do we snatch some bannocks on the way out? You know how I get hungry at night. Especially after—"

"Graham Murray!" Sophie's whisper was stern. She leaned up to stare at him. "You are ruining the picture I'm trying to paint for you, for us."

He scrunched his brow, as if confused. "I thought you were telling a bedtime story."

She flung herself away as if exasperated and attempted to leave the sofa. He held her fast. "I'm sorry. It's—we haven't had enough of these moments lately. To talk, to laugh. Just the two of us." Their weeks aboard the ship had been a time of healing, physically and emotionally, from their many wounds. It wasn't the location he would have chosen for that, surrounded by so many people and living in crowded quarters. Ayla and Matthew had needed them too, and he and Sophie had devoted much of their time and efforts to helping the children overcome the trauma of the past months and to regain the security they'd only just begun to feel at Caerlanwood.

Since leaving the ship, they hadn't had a room or a night to themselves, crowded together as they'd been in whatever lodging they could obtain. "I promise I'll be quiet." He closed his eyes and inhaled deeply. "Paint your picture with words. Take me home to Caerlanwood."

Sophie waited several seconds, and he felt her stare still upon him. Finally she settled at his side and began again.

"*Carrying a basket of bannocks and a bottle of wine, lest you get hungry,* we cross the back garden and start down the steps to the sea gate. The moon is full, dark hasn't quite arrived yet, and we take no lanterns. But, truly, we wouldn't bother with lanterns even if we didn't have the moon this night; we know the way by heart."

"Mmm." He nodded, imagining Scotland's magical summer nights.

"It's windy tonight, and the tide is in, so we don't go all the way to the beach, but to our favorite place among the dunes. We've quilts there already, and we lie down together, the sand beneath our blanket cradling us, and the tall grasses sheltering us from the wind.

"Below, the waves crash onto the shore, one after the other, their melody not menacing but a comfort. We are alone, surrounded by sea and forest—the bridge forever washed away. The world cannot touch us. Time is ours to do with as we please. No one and nothing can take it from us."

Graham breathed in deeply, smelling the floral fragrance of Sophie's hair and imagining he could smell the sea as well, that he could hear the surf pounding on the rocks below, that he could feel the cool, moist air around them, while Sophie lay warm in his embrace. "I miss it," he murmured.

"Me too," Sophie said. "I thought I wanted to travel the world, and I admit to enjoying this adventure, but it turns out I just wanted to go to Scotland, to a town called Annan and to a remote estate on the other side of the forest beyond it."

"We can return someday—if you wish. But with your mother and sisters here now . . ."

Sophie leaned up again, her expression puzzled as she looked at him. "Caerlanwood is our *home*."

How his heart sang to hear her say that. But he stood by his earlier conviction. A place was just that, but this extraordinary woman God had blessed him with was so much more.

He tugged her down beside him, into his arms, where she belonged. "My home is wherever you are."

Thirty-two

HOLDING EVIE IN his arms, Elias danced about their room as the sun was barely rising. He was often the first in the house to awake—or rather, Evie was, reaching up from the trundle beside his bed to pat his cheeks.

Her sweet face and cooing "Papa" made it impossible to be grumpy, even if he was tired. This morning it was his own fault. He hadn't been out all night tending a patient but had spent hours tossing and turning, trying to wrestle his mind into submission and calm. For a long time it had refused, parading memories of Anne before him, from their first meeting, to their courtship and wedding, through all their days and nights of happiness after.

Torture. Anne, her love for him, those joy-filled moments were gone forever. And while he knew it was important to remember, if for no other reason than to tell Evie about her mother someday, part of him wished he might forget and live the ignorant life of a man never having known love.

Giving up on sleep sometime well after midnight, judging by the trek of the moon, he'd risen from bed, lit a candle, and retrieved the papers from his bureau—most were letters to Anne that would never be sent. Some were memories he'd recorded. Others were simply the ramblings of his mind. Releasing those to paper was often the only way he could sleep.

There was no desk in the small room, so Elias had sat on his bed, a medical book on his lap with the papers on top. He'd set the inkwell on the windowsill, telling himself to be sure to move it when he was done so it wouldn't freeze in the night. He'd dipped the quill in the ink, then carefully brought it to the paper and began to write.

December 18, 1831
Dear Anne,
I am missing you tonight more than ever. There are times when I think I shall be all right to carry on through this life alone. Then there are others when the solitary condition of my unaccompanied travail is laid bare before me, and I am reminded of how very much I have lost in your passing. I shall endeavor to explain why today was one of those days. It began with a miracle, in the form of a snow-covered waif traveling on her own through conditions no man should be about in. Her name is Olivia Claybourne...

He had written the details of their meeting, how he'd believed her insane at first, and then how he had realized that she was Victoria's sister. He'd written of Olivia's bravery during his scrubbing of her feet and the rather amusing—now that it was past—anecdote of her being locked out of the house and flooding the kitchen. By the time he had finished writing, the sky had been a deep purple hue instead of the black of night, and he'd fallen asleep at once.

"Only to be awoken by this one." Elias extended his arms above him and hoisted Evie high in the air. Her laughter rained down on him and gave him the strength to carry on another day.

Once they had dressed, he opened his door as quietly as possible and headed downstairs. Dancing only entertained Evie for so long, especially when she was hungry, and he had no desire to begin the day with a cranky child. *Today is going to be good.*

But longing for Anne slammed into him as Elias reached the bottom of the stairs and took in the parlor, where Graham and Sophie lay on the sofa, facing one another. *She must have joined him in the night.*

Graham's arm anchored her to him, and hers wrapped around him, as if she intended to hold on and never let go.

Don't let go. Ever.

Elias tiptoed past the sleeping couple and into the kitchen, where he set Evie in her chair while he started her breakfast. He opened the stove and emptied the ash box from yesterday's fire. He stoked the embers and added more wood and kindling until he'd coaxed the fire back to life. Then he gathered the ingredients for hasty pudding.

"Elias, you'll make me look bad in front of our guests." Victoria yawned as she entered the kitchen. She grabbed her apron from the hook and made a shooing motion with her hand. "Tend to your daughter. I'll see to breakfast."

"You were up late. We heard you all in there, talking and laughing half the night."

Victoria's smile lit her entire being. "It is such a miracle. When I first awoke this morning, I was afraid to open my eyes for fear it wasn't true."

"Afraid you'd just find *me* beside you?" Jonathan came up behind her and wrapped his arms around her waist.

Victoria tilted her head back to meet his gaze. "If I could choose one or the other—I already chose you."

His expression turned solemn. "I know. And I'm sorry I had to ask it of you. Watching you with your sisters yesterday helped me see the cost. I am grateful they've found us and that you can be with them again."

Olivia found you. Elias hoped she'd been given proper

credit. It was her sleuthing and persistence that had led them all here.

Jonathan kissed Victoria on the cheek, then headed for the door. "Don't hold breakfast for me. I'll eat when I get back. It snowed all through the night, and it's still going. I'm going to be awhile digging my way to the barn."

"I'll help," Elias offered, then glanced at Victoria. "If you can watch Evie while you cook?" He never wanted to assume Victoria was always available and willing to step in for him.

"Of course I can. Go." She shooed him away once more, then took down the biscuit tin and headed toward Evie.

"You spoil her," Elias said. He would have made Evie wait to eat a proper breakfast first.

"That's my intention." Victoria held a biscuit out to Evie, who was already reaching for it. "Love and spoil her as much as possible."

THE SOFA WAS occupied by Sophie and Victoria, the latter busily knitting, when Elias, Jonathan, and Graham at last returned from shoveling their way to the barn and caring for the animals. Graham had joined them shortly after they'd started and had proven himself far more useful than the average duke.

When Jonathan had commented on this, Graham had replied that he was a Scotsman first, a duke second—if he had to be one at all.

It bodes well for him to survive here. Elias observed Graham's practical clothing and boots. Sophie was dressed similarly, in simple attire. Only Olivia had come clad in impractical finery.

Olivia. Where was she this morning? Evie played on the floor in front of Victoria and Sophie, but Olivia was nowhere to be seen.

"Where is your other sister?" Elias asked casually as he hung up his coat.

"Still abed," Sophie answered. "She has always been one to sleep in."

"Olivia had a long, exhausting day yesterday," Elias said, feeling the need to defend her. "It was evening when I came upon her, and she had been out in the cold for over ten hours. Has anyone been in to check on her recently?"

Both women shook their heads.

"Then if one of you will accompany me, I should like to. I'm still concerned about one of her toes having frostbite, and I should check her burn as well."

"Are you certain you wish to wake the sleeping bear?" Sophie asked, though she was already rising.

"I'll risk it, and I promise to be brief."

They crossed the room to the door opposite the kitchen. Sophie knocked.

"Olivia? May I come in?" When there was no answer, she pushed the door open slowly and walked into the dark room. "Olivia, Elias would like to check your burn and your toes."

A moan that was neither disagreement nor agreement came from the center of the bed.

Elias hung back, lingering in the doorway. A large stone fireplace, matching the one on the opposite side in the sitting room, took up almost one entire wall. The bed stood across from it, with a curtained window on one side and a bureau and pegs for clothing on the other. Like the rest of the house, it was cozy and practical.

Nothing to compare to the opulence she's come from. Olivia probably felt that she'd been made to sleep in servants' quarters, and that Victoria had become little more than a servant.

Sophie marched across the room and pulled back the

curtains that Anne had helped Victoria make during one of her first sewing lessons.

"It's stunning outside. You must wake and see it," Sophie insisted.

That was true enough. Another foot of snow had fallen in the night and lay sparkling and pristine atop everything, from the bare trees to the fence surrounding the garden and the half barrels that would hold Victoria's flowers come spring.

Another groan came from the bed. "I don't ever want to see snow again."

Sophie laughed. "Then we shall have to blindfold you until at least April."

"Go away," Olivia ordered, her voice scratchy. "But first, bring me a drink of water."

Elias took this as his cue and left the room to fetch the requested drink. Liquids and nourishment would be especially important today, to restore what Olivia's body had been deprived of yesterday during her hours of exertion without food or water.

He returned with both a glass and a pitcher of water to find Olivia sitting up in bed, the blankets pulled nearly to her chin, her hair draped over her shoulder in a long braid.

"Good morning," he said cheerily.

"Good morning." She did not sound as if she found much about it good at all.

He handed her the glass and waited as she drank the entire contents.

"Thank you."

He filled it again and set both glass and pitcher on the bedside table. "May I look at your hand this morning?"

Olivia held it out, and he carefully unwrapped the bandages. The angry welt still puckered her palm, but he could see the miraculous healing properties of the skin already starting to take place. "I would advise leaving the bandage off as much as you are able today. You want to protect the wound, of course, but exposure to the air is good for it as well."

Olivia frowned as she looked at her hand. "Will it scar badly?"

"Time will tell," Elias said, somewhat evasively. "The skin that is blistered will fall off, and new skin will replace it. And as it is in your palm, it's doubtful to be noticed by many."

Olivia nodded.

"And now—your toes? I would like to see how they are faring this morning."

She grimaced and drew the blanket up tighter with her free hand. "Is that absolutely necessary?"

"No. But it could help you keep all of them."

"If you are concerned about a little scarring on your hand, I would think you'd be more interested in keeping all of your toes." Sophie came to sit on the opposite side of the bed. "Let Elias help you if he can."

Olivia sighed but thrust her left foot out from beneath the covers. "This is—"

"Highly improper?" Elias suggested, grinning as he knelt beside the bed to better examine her foot.

"Scandalous?" Sophie teased. "Cause for ruin?"

"Don't say that," Olivia warned, her tone serious. "As if I don't have enough stacked against me already."

Elias wished they had not teased her. Olivia's world had been turned upside down yesterday, and, all things considered, she had handled it—on the surface, at least—rather well. He wished he felt better about what he saw now and doubted she would accept the loss of a toe as gracefully as she had the loss of her purpose in coming here.

He wasn't ready to act yet, but if there was no improvement by tomorrow . . .

"Will it always be that color?" Olivia's brow furrowed as she peered at her foot.

"No. It will either return to normal, as I would have hoped it to already, or the toe—or part of it—will need to be removed." He prayed it wasn't the latter, but he well knew that prayers were not always answered as he wished them to be.

His words hung like a weight in the air.

Then a timid, "I see," from Olivia. "When will you know?"

He looked up from her foot to meet her gaze. "If it has not improved by tomorrow morning, it would be best to take care of it then, before additional tissue in your foot is affected."

She turned her head away, staring out the window. "I would like to rest a little more, please."

"I advise it," Elias said and stood, then left the room.

Thirty-three

EVEN AFTER YESTERDAY, Olivia had never seen so much snow, had never imagined a world of white like that which was piled up outside of Victoria and Jonathan's home. Certainly nowhere in England that she had lived had storms like this. While not as thick as it had been last night when she'd been locked outside, white flakes continued drifting to earth all morning, detaining them here even longer.

She wanted nothing so much as to have her foot heal on its own so she could leave and be alone with her mother, where she could cry out all her frustration and disappointment. *I can't do that. Even when we are together again.* Her mother was going to be overwhelmed enough when she learned that Victoria was alive. There would be no time for Olivia to cry on her shoulder, much less any sympathy if she did.

This is the happiest of mistakes. Olivia heard her mother's voice already, echoing the sentiment Sophie had expressed last night when the three sisters had talked late into the night and Olivia had confessed her reason for coming. Victoria, recalling what she had asked of Olivia so long ago, had been overcome with both guilt and gratitude at the lengths Olivia had gone to, trying to keep her promise.

If I lose a toe, it will not be happy. Since Elias's visit this morning, she'd been trying not to panic. In leaving her homeland, she already felt as if she'd fallen off a sea cliff. She'd taken a risk, leaving everything to run to the edge, but she hadn't meant to fling herself off so completely.

Were it Sophie in her place, she would likely consider the whole thing a grand adventure and be having the time of her life. After listening to the tale of her journey to Scotland and all her adventures there, Olivia felt even more in awe of Sophie. Victoria was no less inspiring with all she did, cooking, sewing, washing and all else required to run her humble home. Both of Olivia's sisters seemed content with their lot. Happy, even.

Why am I so different from them? Olivia wished she could feel the same, but everything around her that had ever felt familiar, secure, or at least promising was gone. Her future was a vast unknown as big as the American wilderness, and it frightened her.

Graham and Sophie had hoped to leave this morning, worried as they were about Ayla and Matthew. But when the weather had made it clear that travel wasn't possible, they had both settled in cheerfully to wait out the storm.

At noon, when it still hadn't stopped, Victoria popped corn on the stove, and they all gathered in the sitting room, clustered around the fire as they enjoyed the tasty treat and continued sharing stories of their lives over the past few years. Only Olivia did not have much to share. She remained mostly silent, seated on one edge of the sofa, wiggling her toes often and praying the circulation would return to all.

Elias, too, was quiet during the storytelling, as he rocked a dozing Evie in his arms. Olivia wondered if he was thinking of his Anne and missing her. How could he not be with her sisters and their husbands, cozy together before him? She tried to imagine that kind of pain but could not, never having loved before. It was easy to read in Elias, a shadow always lingering, casting darkness over even the happy moments.

Loss. Perhaps better than any other, that one word summed up how she felt. And his had to be greatly magnified. *How does he deal with the pain? The sorrow.* She guessed at least a little of what he must be feeling and resolved to turn the conversation elsewhere, away from stories of courtship and marriage.

"Let's play a game," she suggested at the next break in the conversation. Everyone turned to look at her.

"What did you have in mind?" Sophie asked.

Olivia considered. Nothing with any forfeit attached to losing. Nothing that paired them off. Nothing too challenging that would make her look the fool, when at least Jonathan already thought her childish. "How about rhyming?"

Victoria nodded. "You go first."

Olivia turned to Sophie, seated to her right on the sofa. "What do you think of all this *snow?*"

"It has a very lovely *glow*," Sophie replied, then turned to Graham. "Did you like our journey across the *sea?*"

"It was a fine adventure, because you were right beside *me*." Graham and Sophie exchanged a look that Olivia thought should be reserved for private moments.

She glanced at Elias and caught the discomfort in his expression. *This is not helping.*

"Jonathan, when do you think we'll be able to leave in the *sleigh?*"

"Not anytime *today.*"

The rhyming continued a full round without anyone getting out, but then Jonathan caught Victoria with his sentence, "In spring I hope to purchase a *buggy.*"

"You do?" She gaped at him. "Why? They're so expensive."

"So my wife can have protection from the sun and drive around Seneca Falls in style—up and down the entire street of the village—assuming the store does well, that is. And you're *out,* my dear." His grin reminded Olivia of the old, teasing Jonathan. The one she had known as a girl and fallen half in love with.

"In the summer the weather here is quite *muggy,*" Elias said, amidst Victoria's protests that she had been tricked.

"Just for that, you had better really buy me a buggy—the finest, fanciest to be had." Victoria folded her arms and scooted farther away from Jonathan.

"I recognize that look," Graham said, earning him an elbow from Sophie.

"If the weather in summer is muggy and it's so cold here in the winter, why do you stay?" Olivia asked, breaking into the game before Elias had issued the next rhyme.

"Spring and autumn," Elias, Victoria, and Jonathan all answered at once.

"Especially autumn," Victoria gushed. "You've never seen such colors."

I hope I do not. Olivia kept the thought to herself, recalling how upset Victoria had become at supper when the subject of returning to England had been brought up.

"Is the burn on your hand starting to *mend?*" Elias asked, giving her another easy rhyme.

At this rate, the game would go on all day. She needed to make things more difficult. "Yes, thanks to my new *friend.*"

She turned toward Sophie, but not before catching Elias's smile at her rhyme.

"Sophie, why are you so very *changed?*"

"Because I met a man who was most *estranged,*" she replied without a second's hesitation.

"Nice try," Victoria said, sending Olivia a sympathetic gaze. "Sophie always wins this game. It's all those books she reads. Her mind is crammed with words some of us don't even know."

"I wonder how Paden is tending the garden in our *absence*," Sophie said to Graham.

"It is impossible to know from this *distance*."

"Not a rhyme," Victoria said. "You're out too."

"I disagree," Graham said. "Absence, distance. That's as close a rhyme as you'll get."

She shook her head. "E N C E and A N C E do not sound exactly the same. Absti*nence* would have been a rhyme."

"You mean a *crime*," Jonathan chimed in, a playful smirk directed at Victoria. "No man is going to use that word."

Olivia leaned back on the sofa with a sigh of exasperation. Did all married couples act thus, or just her sisters and their husbands? She glanced at Elias, who merely offered a shrug, as if she had voiced her question out loud.

"I tried," Olivia said, her words drowned out beneath the rhymes and barbs and insinuations flying back and forth on the other side of her. She was left out again, but so was Elias. It really was nice to have a friend.

Thirty-four

OLIVIA LAY ON Victoria's bed, eyes squeezed shut against the inevitable, the horror that was about to occur. Last night Elias had looked at her toe once more and ruefully pronounced that it had not improved. This morning he said it was unwise to postpone the procedure that promised to bring agony and would leave her foot forever marred.

"Will I be able to dance again?" she asked, opening her eyes and staring at the ceiling. The thought of never being able to waltz around a ballroom sent the tears already blurring her vision cascading down her cheeks.

"I believe you *will* dance again," Elias said soberly. "I will remove as little as possible and do my very best."

Sophie and Victoria sat on either side of her, and she clasped their hands. They were there to offer comfort and to hold her down if need be.

I won't shame myself by giving in to hysterics. Elias had said she was brave. She could be again. *Please, God. Help me be brave.*

"Are you ready?" Elias asked.

No. How did one ever feel ready to have a toe cut off? No infusion of courage had come from her desperate prayers. But Olivia nodded, then lifted her head to look at him. "I trust you." She found it true as she lay back and closed her eyes. Elias was as kind and gentle a doctor as she could hope for. *And my friend.*

He removed her sock. Olivia tensed for the first cut of the scalpel she'd seen laid out beside him.

But he only held her foot and didn't move.

What is he waiting for? She wanted this over with.

"Praise God," Elias whispered.

Olivia opened her eyes and looked at him.

He smiled at her. "Much of the discoloration is gone, and the tissue looks healthy all around the base of your toe and on top. It is—a miracle. There is no other explanation. I will still need to cut away some of the flesh on the outside—that which had the greatest exposure to the cold—but I believe the toe itself can be saved."

"Thank you." Tears of relief followed those already falling.

"It was not my doing, but a higher power. I have never seen anything like this. Dead tissue does not recover. But yours ... You will most definitely dance again."

An hour later Olivia lay on the sofa, her bandaged foot throbbing, her tears dried, and her body limp and spent from the tension and pain.

"You're certain you don't mind my leaving?" Victoria placed a hand on Elias's sleeve as she stood in the doorway, her cloak in hand.

"Not in the least," he said. "Go. See your mother. I don't wish to be parted from a patient so soon after a procedure."

I won't have a chaperone. Olivia didn't bother protesting. Victoria's mind was already made up. *As would mine be, had I not seen Mother in so long.* Hopefully no one would learn that she and Elias had spent an afternoon alone together at the house. Evie would be here too, of course, but that hardly counted.

"We'll be back as soon as we can," Victoria promised. "After we drop off everyone's belongings at your house."

"*Their* house," Elias corrected. "Mine no more. I am relieved to have someone who wants it."

Victoria left, hurrying after the others already outside, and he shut the door behind her. Olivia closed her eyes, feigning sleep when he came over to check on her. She was too exhausted to talk, and she really did wish to sleep, to dream of other places and happier times. Elias watched her a minute, then took Evie and left the room.

ELIAS SENSED OLIVIA'S presence behind him before she said anything. Instead of turning to greet her, he waited for her to approach. He continued talking to Evie while he stirred the mixture in the pot on the stove, melting the chocolate into the milk and cream that Jonathan had brought in from the barn this morning. Elias had hoped the aroma might cheer Olivia, hoped the treat might sweeten the bitterness of this morning. He had been able to save her toe, but the process of removing the dead tissue had been excruciating for both of them— Olivia from the pain and him from the regret he felt at having caused her suffering, no matter that it was in the name of helping her.

"Is that—" She paused, as if not daring to suggest that something as delicious as chocolate might be found in America.

"Hot chocolate," Elias confirmed, finally turning to her, noting her bandaged foot held in the air as she leaned against the table for support.

He left the stove and hurried to pull a bench out for her, then helped her to sit. "My family's secret recipe. Handed down from our Dutch ancestors who first came to America in the early 1700s."

"I thought my imagination was playing tricks on me." Olivia inhaled deeply. "It smells divine."

"Wait until you taste it," he promised and continued stirring the last of the chocolate block into the liquid.

"For now I'm content to sit here and bask in the sweet scent. The memories this recalls." She closed her eyes and gave a sigh of pleasure.

Elias took a few seconds to study her, to look at her as he'd not been permitted before, given all the activity and worry of the past two days. This morning her brown hair was still bound in a braid that draped over her left shoulder. Victoria's pink calico—her nicest dress, though Olivia likely didn't realize that—looked pretty on her, matching the blush of pink on her fair complexion. Long, dark eyelashes and a pert nose, one he'd seen turned up or scrunched in displeasure a time or two in the last couple of days, completed the picture of a lady displaced. Her aristocratic features did not match the homespun dress and especially his wool socks. She made a lovely picture, nonetheless. He hoped she'd figure out her place here and be happy, but perhaps she was right and England was the better choice for her.

When the chocolate was melted and swirled throughout, Elias added a dash of cinnamon and a generous spoonful of honey. He mixed both in thoroughly, then lifted the wooden spoon from the pot, blew on it briefly, and brought it to his lips. The warm chocolate touched his tongue and slid down his throat. *Good.* But not quite up to his mother's standards. Whenever he made this recipe, he liked to think of her watching over him, giving her approval or disapproval depending on the outcome, which *was* always a little different each time.

Evie reached her hands out in anticipation, wanting him

to share. Elias placed a drop on her tongue and grinned at her squeal of delight. He added another scoop of honey into the pot and stirred once more.

"An exact recipe, I see," Olivia teased.

"Most precise," Elias said. "And secret! I did not realize you were watching me." He moved in front of Olivia, blocking her view of the pot.

"I don't think you have to worry, as I cannot even light a stove."

"Would you like to learn?" Elias returned to his previous position, allowing her to see his creation once more.

"I believe I would," she said. "That seems to be a useful skill if a lady wishes to eat in this country."

"Indeed it is, and the stove at my old house is the same as this one. If you learn to use it today, you can impress your family with your skills tomorrow." He took a mug from the shelf, pulled the dipper from the water pail, and used it to scoop hot cocoa into the mug. He pushed it toward Olivia. "It's hot. Mind your hand."

Olivia looked at the steaming mug. "I'll let it cool a bit first. I don't need a burned tongue as well."

Elias filled a second mug for himself and Evie to share. He moved the pot to the back of the stove, then pulled the bench out from beneath the table and sat on the end nearest Evie. He took a biscuit from the tin on the table, dipped it in the cooling chocolate, and handed it to Evie, who immediately attempted to shove the entire thing into her mouth.

"It might be better if you broke it into small pieces," Olivia suggested. "Victoria was right. Her biscuits are harder than those at home."

"Good idea—if I can get it away from her long enough to do that." His attempt to tug the treat from her mouth was instantly met by a loud screech.

Olivia took another biscuit from the tin and quickly broke it into pieces, then leaned forward and placed them on Evie's tray. The little girl looked at them for several seconds before ejecting the larger biscuit from her mouth and reaching for a handful of the smaller pieces. As she did, Elias smuggled the larger one beneath the table.

"That was rather brilliant. I thought you said you'd no experience tending young children."

"I don't have much. Shelby—our lady's maid—has a little boy. Sophie and I took turns watching him sometimes while Shelby did our hair. He loved to play hide-and-seek in our room, particularly among the dresses in our wardrobe. We always pretended we could never find him." She smiled at the memory.

"Evie is a little young for hide and seek."

"Obviously," Olivia said. "Not to mention there are no armoires full of dresses to hide within in this house."

Elias had a sudden vision of an older, dark-haired Evie peeking out from the doors of a large armoire filled with elegant dresses. She was grinning and happy, calling for her mama to come and find her. He blinked, then shook his head to clear the image. Evie had no mother to call for. She was too young to know the difference, to understand what she was missing right now. But someday . . . someday she would want a mother and likely need one. He'd become adept at many things most fathers had no notion about, but even he knew— especially as a doctor—that there would come a time his daughter would need a woman to confide in and talk to. Someone who would guide her from childhood into womanhood.

Could that woman be Victoria? Would she be enough for Evie? Or would Victoria be too busy with her own family by then to concern herself as much with Evie's needs?

"Oh my. This is heavenly." Olivia's eyes closed again, and she sighed with pleasure at her first taste of his chocolate. "I believe if you were to make this for each of your patients, almost all would be cured posthaste." She held out her bandaged hand and foot. "Just now the pain has subsided considerably, because all of my senses are directed to this deliciousness."

"I should have given you some this morning while working on your toe."

"You should have," Olivia said, her voice slightly scolding.

"If only I'd had a pot at the ready." Elias felt vastly relieved at her teasing instead of tears. He believed her foot would heal quickly now, but until this moment he had worried about her spirit. Elias sipped from his own mug, savoring the flavors and her compliment.

OLIVIA PUSHED AND pulled the dough in her hands, copying Elias's movements on the other side of the table. After they'd spent the morning playing with Evie, Elias had put his daughter down for a nap, and for the past hour he'd taught Olivia everything from how to load the stove with wood and light it, to how to boil water for tea—or washing dishes—and then how to make dough for bread. As surreal as the winter storm and accumulation of snow had been, this felt even more so. But to her great surprise, she'd found her lessons fascinating. Or perhaps it was just the enigma of the man teaching them.

"Are all men in America like this—both capable of and willing to do what in England is considered a female servant's work?"

"The short answer is no. Many men haven't any idea of what to do in a kitchen—myself included until it became a necessity. I'm sorry to say that when Anne was alive I did very little to help her in the house. I chopped wood and the like—men's chores, as one might say—but she did all the cooking and wash and cleaning. She gathered the eggs from our chickens and milked our cow as well. A doctor is frequently called away both day and night, and so at times she did everything that was required to keep our home going."

Olivia heard the regret and pain in his voice and wished she could alleviate at least some of it. "Though I've known you but two days, I have to think that Anne felt blessed to have you as her husband and that you made her very happy." Olivia glanced around the kitchen. "I've yet to see Jonathan doing much in here, yet my sister loves him dearly and is most content as his wife."

"That she is," Elias agreed with an easy smile.

"You came to live with them soon after . . . Anne passed away?"

He nodded. "They were and are the truest friends one might ever have."

"They would say the same of you." Olivia took the rolling pin he offered and began rolling her dough into a rectangle like his, taking care not to put too much pressure on her bandaged palm—the result of which was a rather lopsided shape.

"What one sows, one also reaps. Anne taught Victoria how to make bread, and then Victoria taught me." Elias took the sifter and added more flour to the table. "Be sure to flour the entire area your rectangle will cover, or the dough will stick and you'll end up with a mess."

"You speak from experience?" Olivia leaned forward, pushing the dough beneath the wood roller as best she could from a sitting position. Her foot was too sore to stand for any length of time. She'd never done anything like this, and it felt very much like playing, like something she would have done as a child. *If I hadn't been confined to the nursery for French, music, art, and etiquette lessons for hours each day.*

Once her dough had been flattened into a rectangle—sort of; Elias's looked far better—he showed her how to roll it up, fold the ends under, and place it in the greased pan.

"Never forget to grease your pan. Something I also know from experience."

She laughed. "Thank you for having *so many* experiences so I hopefully do not have to."

"Anytime."

Their exchanged smiles across the table eased the remaining sting and ache in her heart she'd felt since this morning. Though she hadn't lost a toe, the procedure had been traumatic. She'd had enough incidents requiring a doctor over the last few days to last a lifetime.

She wiped her hands on Victoria's borrowed apron as Elias put their pans on the back of the stove to warm and rise.

He returned to the table and scraped the flour into a pile near the corner. "We'll use this to brown the meat for our stew tonight. But first—peeling vegetables."

"Somehow that doesn't sound like as much fun as making bread was."

"It's not." Elias picked up a basket near the side door. "Victoria brought these in from the root cellar this morning."

Olivia peeked inside at the dirt-crusted potatoes and carrots. Her nose wrinkled with distaste. "Looks delicious. I can't wait."

"Wait until you see what the beef looks like before we cook it," Elias promised.

He lugged the basket over to the sink and began priming the pump. "First we wash; then we peel."

For the next half hour, Olivia had a less-enjoyable lesson on washing and preparing vegetables. It was decided that she would not do the peeling, as her hand was still tender from the burn. But Elias made certain she was clear on the process—the blade moves away from you, never toward you.

She was able to help with chopping, and when they were finally done with the chore, they had a large pot of raw vegetables covered with water.

"That still doesn't look very appetizing."

"It will," Elias promised.

Cutting up the raw meat was far worse than preparing the vegetables had been. Olivia had never seen meat before it was cooked, and watching Elias remove the fat and gristle made her stomach queasy.

"Beef is a delicacy," he said. "It's not something we eat often, but one of our neighbors butchered a cow last year, and we were able to buy a portion. Victoria saves it for special occasions—like hosting your family tonight. Most of the time any meat we have is from wild game Jonathan hunts."

"You don't go with him?" Olivia asked.

Elias shook his head. "I'm rarely around this much. The storm has likely kept too many folks from going out, but it probably won't be long before someone needs me again. I contribute to Jonathan and Victoria's household by giving them a portion of my income—I often get paid in kind—and I help out where I can." He gestured to the apron covering his shirt.

Elias showed her how to brown the beef and had Olivia turn it in the pan on the stove, so she would learn how to tell if it was done. Then they added that to the pot, along with a multitude of herbs and spices she was certain never to remember.

Elias put the lid on. "My ancestors would put this Dutch oven right over the fire. We're a little more modern now and can set it on the stove in the kitchen."

"Thank goodness," Olivia said, meaning it. "This is difficult enough. I can't imagine trying to cook over a fire." Truthfully, she still couldn't imagine trying to cook at all, yet here she was.

"I promised Jonathan I'd see to the chores outside for him," Elias said, once they'd cleaned the kitchen and put everything back where it belonged. "Will you listen for Evie while I'm outside? She should sleep a while longer, but her naps aren't always consistent. Do you think you could make it upstairs if she cries? You wouldn't have to bring her down but could just sit with her until I'm back."

"Of course." Olivia hobbled into the sitting room as Elias bundled up and headed outside. She sat in the chair nearest the fire. She wouldn't mind a nap, too, after the exertion of her hands-on lessons. She leaned her head back and closed her eyes briefly. It seemed like only a moment before Evie's cries woke her.

Hanging onto the rail, she hopped up the stairs. It felt strange going into Elias's room, but then what hadn't been strange lately? What she'd once considered clear-cut boundaries of propriety were being broken on a daily, if not hourly, basis.

She sat beside Evie on her trundle bed, and the little girl wrapped her arms around her neck and snuggled close, laying her head against Olivia's shoulder.

Olivia tightened her arms around Evie, holding her closer, enjoying the unexpected cuddle. She shouldn't be here. It felt wrong to be sitting beside the bed Elias slept in and looking at the bureau where a portrait of a woman who had to be Anne stared at her. Olivia met that stare for only a second, but long enough to appreciate the woman's beauty and the kindness in her eyes, and to feel a pang of genuine sorrow for Elias. *How hard his life is.* And yet, how good he was. Never bitter, never complaining. She could learn a thing or two from him—aside from how to make bread.

"The bread!" Her exclamation startled Evie, who pulled back to look at Olivia.

"It's all right," Olivia said, patting Evie's back to soothe her. "We just need to see if it's risen enough to bake." *I was supposed to watch it while your father was outside.* Holding Evie with care, Olivia scooted down the stairs, then held Evie's hand and led her into the kitchen. She carefully peeled the cheesecloth back from the pans. The dough—*her* dough, and Elias's too—had more than doubled in size and rose in perfect domes above the pans. "Look at that," she marveled to Evie. "Isn't it amazing."

She set Evie in her chair, brought her some water, and held the cup for her while she sipped. Then Olivia spread a spoonful of cold peas on Evie's tray and hobbled over to tend to the bread. The black beast of a stove stared at her, and pain throbbed through Olivia's hand, reminding her what the stove was capable of—and more.

Using a cloth, she lifted the handle of the main door and pulled it open. Heat surged from the chamber within, the orange glow of it red hot and frightening. Olivia took two steps back, then remembered her purpose and took a piece of wood from the box and carefully added it to the fire. She shut the door again with a relieved sigh.

But she wasn't finished yet. Elias had told her that the bread needed to go into the oven as soon as it was risen—or it would fall. Another lesson he had apparently learned the hard way. Olivia didn't want to repeat it, so using the same cloth to protect her hand, she lifted the handle of the little door to the side of the larger one. She opened it and peered in at the space perfectly suited for two bread pans, front to back.

With utmost care she slid hers in first and then Elias's, then shut the door carefully.

"Well done."

Olivia turned to find Elias standing in the doorway clapping for her. "Now the most important part—"

"Don't forget it's in there," Olivia repeated with him.

He nodded. "Check it often. Stir the stew as well, so the bottom doesn't burn now that you've built up the fire a bit."

"Aren't you going to be here to help with that?" Olivia asked, suddenly wary as she looked at him, with coat, mittens, and hat still on.

"Maggie Taylor's boy is in the yard. He ran all the way out here to tell me his six-year-old sister is fevering and hasn't been able to keep anything down for two days. Maggie's a widow with four children, and they're often ill. They don't have much nourishment there, I'm afraid." Elias's eyes strayed to the pot on the stove.

He wants to leave me here alone? "You want to take that to them?" Olivia asked, trying not to think of all the work they'd put into it and what everyone would have to eat instead when they arrived this afternoon.

Elias nodded. "Some of it. George out in the yard is thin as a rail. I'm not sure how he had the strength to come all this way."

"I'm sorry the bread isn't ready yet," Olivia said, looking around the kitchen for something else she could send with him. Her eyes landed on the biscuit tin. She reached for it and held it out. "Take these too. The children might like them."

"They will." Elias stepped forward to collect the tin, and mud pooled on the floor beneath him. "Sorry." He glanced down at his feet. "It's a muddy mess out there in the barn."

"I'll—clean it after you leave." With what, she wasn't certain. "What do you want to put the stew in? Will they have a way to finish cooking it there?"

"Mary has a Dutch oven. Most people have at least that,

no matter how poor. Though she doesn't have a stove like this." Together he and Olivia worked to transfer a portion of the stew to an empty crock. Elias covered that with a cloth tied around the top with a string, then picked up the biscuit tin and headed toward the door. Evie held her hands out to him as he passed by her chair.

"It's all right," Olivia said, stopping to comfort her. "He'll be back."

"I'm not sure if it's me or the biscuits she's reaching for," Elias said with a wry smile as he leaned down to kiss the top of Evie's head. His gaze left his daughter and met Olivia's. "Will you be all right here? It's a lot to ask of you—tending Evie and the bread and what's left of our supper all when you can hardly walk. I wouldn't ask it of you, but—"

"Go," Olivia said, thinking of the little girl who was sick.

Elias hesitated, as if he was suddenly uncertain himself.

She's all I have left. Olivia remembered—he had never entrusted Evie to another's care besides Victoria. "The others should be back soon," she said. "I promise to be very careful with her."

Elias lingered a moment longer, kissed Evie once more, then nodded. "Thank you. I trust you, Olivia." He headed out of the kitchen, leaving more muddy footprints.

Olivia sighed as she looked at them. It had been a day for trusting—and work. *English ladies have no idea what they are missing.*

Thirty-five

"I *AM* CAPABLE," Olivia repeated for at least the twentieth time in the four hours since Elias had left. The bread cooling on the table in the kitchen proved that. The stew simmering on the stove was proof as well. The pile of muddy rags she'd used to clean the floor was no doubt evidence to the contrary—*how does one clean a floor?*—as was Evie's current state of undress.

Olivia watched the little girl from the corner of her eye as she searched Elias's room for additional baby clothes. Evie had wet through two outfits and soiled another since her father had left. Olivia was beginning to understand what he'd meant when he said that Victoria had a lot of extra work because of him and Evie. So much mess for one so small. Olivia had done her best to clean her up, even going so far as to heat water and give Evie a bath in the small washtub she'd found. This had proved a wonderful idea and kept the child entertained, splashing in the water for the better part of an hour.

But now . . . *Clothes.* There had to be something else she could wear. Feeling like she was breaking every rule of privacy and propriety, Olivia opened the top drawer of the dresser in Elias's room. Men's underthings—or she supposed that's what they were—lay in neat piles, beginning with handkerchiefs on the right and moving to— She slammed the drawer shut and opened the next.

Trousers.

The third. *Shirts.*

The last. A treasure trove of miniature clothes in pink and white and blue and yellow. Baby clothes. More than Evie probably needed. Olivia glanced at the little girl again, ensuring she was still safely playing on the bed, entertaining herself by putting a gentleman's top hat on and off her head.

Olivia knelt on the floor and began removing the garments, one at a time, admiring the delicate stitching and beautiful details. She might not know her way around a kitchen, but she knew fine clothing when she saw it. No expense had been spared on these clothes. Sweaters of the softest yarn with matching booties and hats, dresses with tiny, puffed sleeves and edged with ribbon, pantaloons with frilly layers. Lined vests and knee pants for little boys. *Anne wouldn't have known whether or not her baby was a boy or a girl.*

Evie would look adorable in these. Yet the past two days she'd worn only the simplest gowns of plain muslin.

Not tonight, Olivia vowed. She picked out a cozy sweater of pale green and a dress embroidered with green and pink flowers to go beneath. Matching stockings and bloomers completed the ensemble.

Wrestling Evie into all that took more than a few minutes, but as Olivia fastened the buttons on the sweater, even Evie seemed entranced by what she wore, her chin down as she studied the flowers and her fingers tried to grasp them.

"I wish I had a looking glass so you could see yourself." Olivia rose from the floor and brushed off her own, borrowed dress. She scooped Evie into her arms and left the room, then scooted downstairs again, sorely missing the use of her foot and hoping it healed as quickly as Elias predicted.

The light in the sitting room wasn't as visible as in Elias's south-facing bedroom. She needed to light candles soon and add more wood to the fire. *No end to the things a woman has to do to keep a house going.* Her appreciation for their bevy of servants at home was growing by the minute.

She found the candles in the kitchen and brought several into the sitting room. With Evie settled safely in her chair and well away from the stove, Olivia used it to light the candles, one by one, tipping each briefly into the low flames until they caught. When she'd lit two each for the table, the kitchen, and the sitting room, Olivia set them in their places, then added more wood to the fire and checked the soup and the stove once again. She'd had the idea to add more vegetables this afternoon and had managed to scrub and peel and chop them without incident, even with her injured hand. She hoped they'd had time enough to cook through and become soft. And hopefully Elias or her family would be here soon. The thought of being here alone at night was rather frightening.

She sat facing Evie on the sofa, entertaining her with a button looped onto a length of yarn while they waited. Every time Olivia got it spinning well, Evie giggled with delight and tried to catch the button.

At last she heard sleigh bells in the yard. *Finally.* Olivia gathered up Evie and unlatched the door, and a minute later Victoria came into the house, Mother right behind her, and the others behind them. Olivia felt an odd pang of regret that it wasn't Elias who had returned, even as her eyes teared with relief. She'd spent the whole of the afternoon alone, or nearly so—Evie wasn't much for conversation yet. And after months of being alone before their voyage, the sight of her growing, noisy family filled her with joy. *How can I leave them? Yet, how can I stay?* She felt so exhausted from the day's work, and the thought of repeating those same chores and more, day after day, was overwhelming.

"Olivia, darling, I'm so glad you're all right. I was so worried." Her mother threw her arms around her and pulled her close, squishing Evie between them.

"I'm sorry." Olivia's apology was muffled by her mother's thick cloak. If not for Evie she would have sagged into that embrace, eager to be held by her mother and to have all her worries and confusion eased merely by her presence.

"All is forgiven," her mother said as she drew back. "After all, *you* led us here. This must be Evie."

Evie grinned at hearing her name.

"She be a beautiful child." Maime touched one of Evie's curls, more prominent since her bath.

Matthew wiggled his way between the adults to stare at Evie and then offer her his most disarming smile.

"Her curls are no match for yours though," Sophie said, ruffling his hair. Matthew leaned into her, his arm tangling in her skirts, while Ayla stood shyly at Sophie's other side. Sophie wrapped an arm around her. "Come by the fire and get warm." She ushered the children forward with motherly gestures and affection.

They are blessed to have her. It was the same sentiment Olivia had felt several times during their voyage, whenever she observed Sophie and the children, but it seemed all the more poignant tonight, as she sat on the sofa again and held Evie. *Sophie is their mother now.* But little Evie had none and would never know hers. Victoria, for all that she took care of Evie, would never be her mother. *Will Evie* ever *have another?*

"Where is Elias?" Victoria asked as she removed her cloak.

"He was called away several hours ago. Maggie Taylor's six-year-old is ill." *I am capable.* Olivia straightened. "But there is stew and bread in the kitchen. The table is set, and all is ready for dinner."

"It smells good," Maime said, giving Olivia an encouraging smile.

It really did. A fact that had surprised Olivia, given how the ingredients had begun. "Elias and I prepared it this morning before he left."

"*Elias?*" Mother asked. "You call him by his given name?"

"We're in America," Sophie said. "People don't worry about formalities here."

"Apparently not," Mother said, her expression more curious than pained as she crossed the room to stand with the others near the fire.

"Do you want me to take Evie?" Victoria asked.

Olivia shook her head. "And leave me to serve dinner? No, thank you."

Victoria smiled. "Smart girl. Was your day tiring?"

"Very." Olivia returned her smile, feeling a camaraderie that hadn't been there before. "I don't know how you do it."

"There have been days—many of them—when I didn't think I could. I have to admit that today was a nice reprieve from the ordinary." Her brow furrowed. "What is Evie wearing?"

"Clothes I found in the bottom drawer in Elias's room. I didn't have anything else dry to put her in. But aren't they beautiful? There's a whole drawer of lovely things like this."

Victoria stepped forward and leaned over the back of the sofa to look closer. She touched the hem of Evie's dress, studying the stitching. "Anne made this. I remember her working on it. I'd forgotten about all these clothes. She sewed and sewed for her baby. She couldn't wait to be a mother."

The door opened again. "Hello." Elias's gaze went straight to the sofa and his daughter. Relief lit his face.

Olivia tensed. What if seeing these clothes upset him or reminded him of Anne, of losing her? *I should have found something else for Evie to wear.* She ought to have realized the clothes were special, that they were in the bottom drawer and unused for a reason.

"Welcome back," Victoria said. "I understand we have you to thank for dinner tonight."

"Olivia too." Elias stomped the snow from his boots, reminding her of the mess he'd made in the kitchen earlier and her poor attempts to clean it up.

"Papa." Evie held out her hands, and Olivia helped her down from the sofa so she could toddle over to her father.

He came forward, arms held out. Elias picked her up. "Don't you look . . ." His voice faded as he took in her clothing for the first time.

"I couldn't find anything else for her to wear," Olivia began. "I'm sorry I looked in your room and that I—"

A shake of Elias's head silenced her. He shifted Evie to one side and ran his free hand down the front of her sweater. "Shell buttons." He touched the tiny, polished surface of one. "Only the best for our baby. Anne sent away for these. They came all the way from Ocracoke Island. She had fabric from New York and Boston, yarn from Virginia, dyes from Maine. She sewed every evening for *months*, clothes in every size for an infant all the way up to a four- or five-year-old."

"Almost like she knew she wouldn't be around to—" Victoria broke off.

"To see her child properly clothed." Elias hung his head. "I haven't used any of the things she made—until now."

"I'm sorry," Olivia said again. "It wasn't my place. I—"

"It was Anne's place. But as she's not here, it should have been mine," Elias said. "To see Evie dressed as fine as Anne wanted. Were she here, she'd have words for me on the matter, no doubt." A corner of his mouth lifted in a wry grin. He studied his daughter and her clothing once more. "She looks sweet. Just the way Anne imagined her."

"Evie is sweet, no matter what she's dressed in," Victoria said.

Olivia felt her mother beside her. "Elias, this is my mother, Lady Lilian Claybourne. Mother, this is Doctor Elias Henrie."

"It's a pleasure to meet you." Mother held out her hand, and Elias kissed the back of it briefly.

"The pleasure is mine," he said. "I'm very happy for Victoria. For all of you." He looked around the room.

"Thank you for the generous use of your home," Mother gushed. "We stopped there on our way this evening, and how grateful we all are to have a roof over our heads that is more than a couple of cramped rooms. And to be so near to Victoria . . . I can't thank you enough. I have our payment for the first three months with me and can—"

"I am grateful someone can use the house," Elias said. "It's yours for as long as you would like it, and we can talk about payments later."

"Thank you," Mother said again before turning abruptly to Olivia. "I hear you taught my daughter how to make bread. I believe we have some children—and adults—who are rather famished and would like to try some."

"As would I," Elias said. He stepped aside and held his hand out, indicating that she should precede him to the table.

Victoria looped her arm through Mother's and led her to her seat. "No servants to tend to you here."

"It's just as well," Mother said.

Sophie, Maime, and the children followed. Olivia remained on the sofa, tired from her day and knowing they all could not fit around the table.

To her surprise Elias joined her, collapsing as if he were even more exhausted than she.

"How is the little girl?" Olivia asked.

"Somewhat better, though not out of the woods yet. I'll be returning to her house tomorrow morning. Thank you for making it possible for me to go today."

"It was the least I could do after you didn't chop off my toe and made me hot chocolate."

Elias gave a bark of laughter that had heads at the table turning toward them. "Three days ago I would not have pegged you for a woman with such a sense of humor."

Olivia shrugged. "Perhaps my tongue was frozen too."

He grinned. "In that case, I am glad that it has thawed. And I am glad to have made your acquaintance, though it was not under the best of circumstances. But look at our circumstances this evening." He swept his arm in an arc toward the kitchen and then around to the fireplace. "The house is warm, and you kept the fire going. The bread and stew smell delicious. Evie is safe and clean and dressed better than she ever has been. You will do just fine here in America, if you decide to stay."

Thirty-six

ELIAS SLIPPED OUT the partially opened, double-side doors of the Grangers' large barn, turned dance hall for the Christmas Eve festivities. The cool air was a welcome break from the crowd and heat inside, and he found himself grateful that Lady Claybourne had asked him to go after Olivia. He'd wanted to go in search of her anyway and had been debating the wisdom of such a move when Lady Claybourne had sidled up to him and made her discreet request.

He tried to keep his movements inconspicuous now, choosing to step on the frozen drive rather than on crunchy patches of snow. He didn't think Olivia had gone outside with anyone, but in the minute or two he'd lost track of her, he supposed that was possible. He had no desire to interrupt a courtship, if that's what was transpiring out here.

He rounded the corner of the barn, and relief eased the tightness in his chest. Olivia stood alone at the fence, staring out at the dark beyond with a look of pure longing, as if the simple wood rails truly had her penned inside.

He hadn't seen her much in the past week and a half, since her family had moved into his old house. He still didn't want to be at the house but had stopped by once, to check Olivia's toe, and had been relieved to see it healing nicely. The blistered skin on her hand had peeled, and new skin was growing in its place as well. It appeared no lasting harm had come from her first, difficult days here. Elias had also been pleased to learn she'd had no more mishaps and had become the designated one to light the stove. Though Maime was doing most of the cooking.

Lady Claybourne had paid him a generous sum for rent the next three months, and Graham had insisted he would pay after that, as he expected to have arranged access to his accounts by then. The money had allowed Elias to complete the purchase of the home in town that would serve as both his residence and office, and between seeing patients he'd been slowly moving his belongings from Jonathan's house. He would miss Jonathan and Victoria's company—and help—but it was time he moved on.

Jonathan's store had opened three days ago, and everyone had been consumed with the last-minute preparations. The extra family around to help had certainly been fortuitous. He'd heard that Olivia was working there, at least for now, while Victoria stayed home with Evie. Soon he'd be buying his eggs and all else that he could at the store, and Elias told himself that the contact with Jonathan and Victoria, and now their extended family, would be enough that he would still feel their camaraderie and support.

But right now, it looked as if Olivia might be in need of some of both. He wondered how she'd been faring. Neither Jonathan nor Victoria had specifically mentioned her, though Victoria was over at the house with her sisters and mother now more often than not.

"Tired of dancing? Is your toe bothering you?" he asked, hands in his pockets and his steps no longer quiet, as he drew closer to Olivia. She ought to be tired. For the past two hours, he'd watched as she'd danced with just about every single man in the county—from those a couple of years younger to those far too old. A few had claimed her hand more than once and thus stated their intent. A new, beautiful, *available* female in these parts would not retain that status for long. If he were a betting man, a safe wager would be that, if she stayed here, Olivia Claybourne would be a married woman by this time next year. *If not much sooner.*

The thought further dimmed his already depressed mood. Christmas was hard without Anne. He didn't want to think about Olivia settling for some farmer and giving up her dreams of a grander life.

"My toes, all of them, are a little sore in these shoes, and I *am* tired. Though it's not the dancing. At home our balls went much later than this."

At the forlorn note in her voice he came closer, striding past Olivia to settle on her other side. He angled his back against the fence, partially facing her and also putting himself between her and any danger that might be lurking in the yard. Her mother had likely sent him after her as a precaution against any man who might try to take advantage of her, but there were greater dangers than that out here in the wilds of upstate New York.

He took her bait easily, knowing it would lead to a discussion that swept his mind far from his own woes. Olivia was young and somewhat self-centered, but that suited him fine when it came to distracting him from his own melancholy thoughts. Hers were no less valid—important as they were to her and looming large in her life, at present.

"What are you tired of?" Possibly being surrounded by her sisters so happy and in love with their husbands? He could relate. While he didn't begrudge any of them their joy, seeing it so often sometimes felt like rubbing salt on the raw, gaping wound in his heart.

"I'm tired of being lonely. And sad. I miss my friends and

London. I miss home." There was no whine to her voice, only sadness.

Maybe he could help her by reminding her of good times she'd had. It was a trick he often employed himself, the only way he could fall asleep most nights—reliving a memory with Anne. "What would you do during the Christmas season in London?"

"We attended plays or musicales. Someone usually hosted a Christmas ball—I'd only been able to attend those for the past two years, but, oh, they were grand." She turned toward him, the hint of a smile appearing. "Last year, the Westfields hosted one at their country estate. The party lasted for *three* days. Their house was resplendent—evergreen boughs on the railings and kissing balls of mistletoe hung over the doorways, and they had a giant tree in the parlor. They'd traveled to the continent the previous year, and that was a tradition they'd been introduced to. The tree was lit with candles and was simply the most gorgeous sight you can imagine."

"Sounds like a good way to burn a house down," he murmured.

Olivia shook her head as her lips turned down in a pout. "That's what my father said. Nothing caught fire, and the whole house smelled and looked amazing. The musicians played until well past midnight, and all the ladies had the loveliest gowns. I had a new one as well . . ." Her voice trailed off as she brushed her fingers against the extravagant silk of her skirt. "This one, actually." She turned to him, uncertainty and hurt and embarrassment flickering in the depths of her eyes. "Sophie and Victoria were right. I shouldn't have worn this tonight. It's too much for dances here. All my gowns are. I tried to get them each to wear one too, but they wouldn't. Sophie was never one for fancy clothes, but Victoria used to be . . ." Her voice trailed off, and Elias could see her thoughts had returned to the past once more.

He shrugged, attempting nonchalance. "You have nice gowns. You might as well wear them. It doesn't make sense not to. Thanks to you, Evie dresses quite well these days too."

Earlier this evening, he'd had to look away when Olivia had first entered the dance, her wide skirts taking up most of the double doorway. In the half-second he'd viewed her, his eyes had drunk in the sight like a thirsty man in the desert with a pail of water before him. That mass of dark curls, her sparkling eyes, a simple jeweled ribbon resting above her throat, followed by bare shoulders, puffed sleeves, and slender arms, also bare above her gloves. That slim waist, where he'd once placed his hands to lift her into his sleigh. If he wasn't careful he'd be tempted to put his hands there again, no better than the desperate man snatching the pail and tipping it to his mouth to drink greedily.

He was too old for Olivia, too somber, too poor—or at least by the standards she was used to. *Too married.* That Anne wasn't physically here with him hadn't altered that status. He was still hers, still faithful, and he intended to remain so.

But he was still a man—one starved for affection—and earlier tonight, if he hadn't looked away, he'd been afraid he'd be caught gawking. Olivia was beautiful, but never more so than in this creation of green and gold. He took his fill of looking at it—at *her*—reasoning that she needed some genuine admiration. "It's a beautiful dress. Made even prettier by the woman wearing it."

She flashed him a grateful smile, then looked away with a soft, murmured, "Thank you, Elias."

A groan rose in him at hearing his name on her lips. "What else did you do to celebrate in England?" he asked, clearing his throat, trying to mask the huskiness in his voice.

"We hosted parties. Our friends came, and we played parlor games and drank wassail. We gathered around the piano and sang carols together. It was all so—"

"Ho-hey!" A chorus of shouts interrupted, and the barn doors flew open as one of the Ryder boys staggered into the night, then leaned over the hedge and threw up. Loud, raucous laughter followed, coming from the three figures silhouetted in the light spilling from the barn.

"So cultured?" Elias suggested with a disgusted shake of his head. Any holiday around here—any day, really—was cause for the Ryders to indulge in too much drink. He'd been summoned to their farm on more than one occasion to stitch a wound that had come about during their hours of drunkenness.

Olivia pursed her lips and gave a small shudder of revulsion. "I thought I smelled alcohol on his breath when we danced."

"I don't recommend dancing with him, or any of his brothers, again," Elias said and stepped closer, lest they look over and think Olivia was out here alone.

"I most certainly won't." Her pert nose wrinkled in disgust.

They watched in silence as the brothers punched and poked at one another before finally returning to the dance, including the one who'd vomited. Pity the next woman who danced with him.

"I'm sorry that you miss your home," Elias said, understanding at least some of her longing.

"It's not only missing it," Olivia said quietly. "It's knowing I can never go back."

"Never is a very long time." *Never will I hold Anne in my arms again on this earth.* "I thought you planned to return to England as soon as it was safe for you to do so."

"Maybe it won't be never, but I may be an old woman by the time I can. So long as my father is alive, it isn't safe for me to return."

"Well, I hope you can—someday. At least hold onto that possibility. It's more than some of us have."

She turned to him, her eyes wide with realization and pity he didn't want. "I'm sorry." She reached a gloved hand out, placing it on his arm. "How selfish of me to be complaining of missing ballrooms and the theatre when you've lost something—someone—so much more important."

Elias shrugged. "All losses hurt."

She nodded, swallowed, and withdrew her touch, looking away, but not before he caught the glimmer of tears. "I'm so sorry. For both of us."

Her tears moved him, especially that any might be for him. He hated to see a woman cry. From Graham he'd learned that Sophie rarely did. Victoria didn't often get overly emotional either. It seemed Olivia was the crier in their family, a sensitive soul who felt things keenly and then wore those emotions on her proverbial sleeve.

Elias turned up the collar of his jacket, beginning to feel the cold. Olivia had to be near frozen in that gown. Every time she spoke her breath came out in little puffs of white. He considered offering her his coat, if only so they could stay outside a little longer.

From inside, the strains of a waltz reached their ears as the violinists started up again.

"You haven't danced with me," she said suddenly, turning a questioning gaze on him. "You haven't danced at all tonight."

He was surprised that she'd noticed, particularly as her attention had been commandeered by so many other men this evening. "I don't want to give anyone the wrong idea."

Her brow quirked, demanding explanation.

He cleared his throat before attempting to clarify. "If I dance, some people—some ambitious mothers or women—might think I'm in the market for a wife again."

"America is not so dissimilar to London." She gave him a mischievous grin. "Ambitious mamas are most feared by eligible men during the London Season."

He wondered which men her own mother would have singled out for Olivia's attention, were she still in London. A dashing duke, as Sophie had married, or a lesser, but still titled aristocrat with enough wealth to keep Olivia in elegant gowns and jewels for the rest of her life? "Most folks in these parts tend to pair off quickly and see these types of activities as an opportunity to find someone to court. We haven't the social season your London has. The only seasons are for planting, growing, harvesting, and resting—and even that rest is ripe with chores to be done and tasks to accomplish in preparation for the coming spring. Many are prosperous here, but it's because of the labor of their own hands."

"Better than the labor of slaves," she remarked quietly.

"Much better," Elias agreed, glad to have veered the topic away from his lack of dancing.

"But all that labor leaves little time for courting. Is that what you're saying?" she asked.

He nodded. "So parties like this take on more importance. The men you danced with more than once tonight will most certainly come calling on you."

She frowned. "That was not my intention. I do not wish to be courted by any of them."

"Make that clear up front when they call on you," he advised. "Perhaps tell them that you are here only for a short while and intend to return to London."

"Would that I might," she said, then shivered.

Elias shrugged out of his dress coat and draped it around her shoulders. "Time to return to the party." He held his arm out to her.

Olivia placed her hand on it. They took a few steps; then

she paused. "I have a better idea. Dance with me out here, where no one will see us." She tugged him sideways, behind the front wall of the barn, where they might hear the music but remain unseen. She dropped her hand from his arm, turned, and faced him, giving a slight curtsy.

Elias froze, his heart thundering suddenly, though nothing had changed from the minutes they'd been casually talking. *But dancing . . .* He hadn't danced with anyone since Anne. It didn't seem right. He wasn't ready.

Olivia reached for his hands, took them, and placed one at her waist while keeping the other clasped in her own. "One, two, three," she counted, and then they were off, his feet moving obediently with memory.

"Tell me about Anne," Olivia said, meeting his gaze and holding it. "Tell me about dancing with her. When was the first time you danced? How did you meet?"

"I—" Elias swallowed. He rarely spoke of Anne to anyone. It was too painful, but Olivia wasn't asking about Anne's death. She was asking about her life, their love—a memory like those he lost himself in each night to fall asleep. He could do that, could trick his mind for a minute or two here, now.

"We met in summer. I hadn't been a doctor very long, and her mother was ill." He closed his eyes briefly, and Anne's home appeared before him, as clearly as if it was, once again, that day he'd ridden up the lane. He heard her laughter and that of her younger siblings as she pushed them in the swing out front. He remembered his first glimpse of her as he passed on his way to the house.

The story spilled from him—their meeting, their first dance, their courtship. Happy words, joyous memories that were easy to share as he held her hand and waltzed around the frozen yard. *Frozen yard?*

Not Anne's hand. Elias crashed into the present and

realized that he and Olivia were no longer turning to the music. A livelier reel was playing now, but they stood unmoving as if in the last stance of the waltz, his hand still at her waist, one of hers at his shoulder, their other hands clasped between them, but no longer raised in the manner of dancing, as she watched him and listened.

Elias shook his head as if to clear it of the bittersweet memories and noticed Olivia shiver again. "You're freezing, and here I am rambling on."

"I liked your rambling. Thank you for sharing that with me. It helps me understand you better."

He nodded, released her hand, and stepped back, fully waking from the trance she'd somehow lulled him into. He hated to leave the yard, yet somehow even as he did he felt a bit better than he had earlier, his heartache a little less raw, his soul lighter. "Thank you for listening."

She smiled up at him and accepted his arm as he held it out again and turned them toward the doors. "Anytime," she said. "That's what friends are for."

December 24, 1831
Dear Anne,

A year ago you had just left me, and I thought I would shortly follow. For the past twelve months I've fought the feeling of wanting my time on this earth to be done too. I still miss you terribly and love you. But tonight I danced with Olivia. We spoke of you. And for the first time in over a year, I wanted to stay.

Part Three

"*Curas amet, qui nunquam amavit, Qauique amavit, crasmet.*
Let those love who never loved before,
Let those who always loved, now love the more."

Latin epigram, author unknown

Thirty-seven

ELIAS AWOKE IN his upstairs room at Jonathan's house. Tomorrow he and Evie were moving to Seneca Falls. All was ready there now. He would have moved in sooner, if not for Victoria's request that he stay for Christmas.

This change was hard on her too. Evie was practically like her own child. But the timing was right, with the store opening and her sisters and mother here now. It was time Victoria and Jonathan lived their own life and that he and Evie lived theirs.

He glanced down at his daughter, for once sleeping longer than he, snuggled deep into the quilts and curled on her side in the trundle bed. In another hour or two, she would be enjoying her second Christmas, though it was their first together.

Last year he'd been too sick still to be with her. Anne was dead and buried—he'd been too ill to attend her graveside—and though the threat of death had passed for him, Elias didn't want to be anywhere near his daughter until he had fully recovered and showed no trace of the disease that had taken his wife and sister-in-law.

He'd been fortunate to contain it to their home; it hadn't spread throughout their little community. He was especially grateful that Jonathan and Victoria hadn't fallen ill. They'd taken a huge risk the night he'd brought Evie to them and begged them to care for her until Anne was well.

Victoria had taken the two-week-old baby without hesitation, but Elias hadn't missed the flash of fear in Jonathan's eyes before he'd given a slow nod of consent. Elias could well imagine his cousin's thoughts. Victoria had already lost one child. If she came to care for Evie and something happened . . . Or worse, Jonathan had nearly lost Victoria, and to put her at risk of a sickness that might claim her life—

Yet he'd done just that, accepting Evie into their home when Anne had smallpox.

Since then Elias had often wondered many things. Would Jonathan have done it if he didn't feel he owed a debt to Elias and Anne, who had taken both him and Victoria into their home for months and had nursed Victoria back to health?

Would it have been better for both Jonathan and Victoria if I had died too? Would it have been better for Evie? She would have had a mother then, and Jonathan and Victoria would have had a child, without putting Victoria through another perilous pregnancy and birth.

After Anne died, Elias had told God to take him too. He didn't want to live without her. But there was no telling God what you wanted or didn't want. There was only faith that he was ultimately in charge and would succor a man through his trials. Elias had lain sick for weeks, his body neither improving nor worsening. He'd existed in some half state, severely weakened, barely eating, asleep most of the time as he awaited the day he would no longer wake.

He would have gone on this way, would have died whether God willed it or not, but for a dream in which Anne stood before him and scolded him, of all things.

Do you not love our child? Would you have her grow up without a mother and *a father?*

She'll have both. Jonathan and Victoria—

—are not her parents. You are. *If you let me down, Elias, I'll return to haunt you.*

Aren't you haunting me already? Elias had rubbed sleep from his eyes and stared harder at his wife, standing a few feet away. Her expression had softened. She shook her head, the auburn curls he loved thick and full again, free today and falling well past her shoulders. Her skin was clear once more, free of the lesions that had plagued her to the very moment of death.

I'm saying goodbye.

No. I can't do this alone. Elias struggled to sit up, to reach for her.

I know. Anne didn't reach back, didn't come any closer. Her smile seemed wistful but also radiant. Peaceful. *Love her for me. Love them.*

He had blinked, and Anne was gone. Truly gone. Forever. He'd known it before, but that truth settled deep in his bones and in the very core of his heart that day. He had wept. For hours, or possibly the entire day. But when his tears at last were spent, he'd climbed out of bed, crawled into the kitchen, and eaten the food Jonathan had left by the door three days ago. The next day, Elias had washed. First himself, taking care of his skin, which was still healing, and then slowly, over the coming days, everything else in the house. He'd shaved, trimmed his hair, and scrubbed everything in sight until his fingers were raw. He'd eaten, he'd slept, he'd cleaned, he'd read his Bible for comfort. And gradually, he'd returned to life.

When a knock had sounded on his door ten days later, he had answered it, had collected his medical bag, and had gone out into the night to help where he could. The next morning, he'd gone to Victoria and Jonathan's house and held his little girl for the first time in two months. And then he'd stayed, returning to the house only to pack the necessities—Anne's rocking chair and clothing for himself and Evie, some of which he hadn't had the courage to look at again until two weeks ago.

Elias rolled onto his back now, put his hands behind his head, and inhaled deeply, tensing for the inevitable pain that existed within him now. Inhale—*Anne's gone.* Exhale—*I'm still here. Alone.*

That pain had lessened a bit over the past two weeks, and he attributed it to the busyness of his move, the unprecedented number of house calls he'd made due to an influenza outbreak, and the arrival of Victoria's family, particularly Olivia. In her he had found an unexpected friend.

In many ways she was young and immature, but in others... she was attuned to his sorrow, the weight he carried with him, as no one else, not even Jonathan and Victoria had been.

Olivia wasn't afraid to ask him about Anne or to dress his daughter in clothes Anne had made. Olivia was often impulsive, acting on her instincts without always thinking things through, and that could get her into trouble. Yet there was something to be admired about her risk-taking nature.

Last night, when they'd returned to the Christmas Eve party, she'd pulled him onto the dance floor before he could protest. He'd had little choice but to dance a reel with her, all the while noting the speculation of numerous women around the room.

When the dance had finished, he'd felt most cross with Olivia, who'd been laughing and smiling during the entire set, attracting the attention of everyone in the room in her fancy gown and the graceful way she moved through the steps.

"Do you realize what you've just done to me?" he'd practically growled in her ear, as he led her off the floor.

"I do," she'd said, her smile wide and confident as she looked up at him. "I've just claimed you as mine. Every woman here now believes that you're courting me, so they aren't likely to bother you anytime soon. You're free to go out in public without worry now." As if for extra measure, Olivia had batted her eyelashes and bestowed a look upon him that was steeped in adoration. "You're welcome."

"I—you." He'd closed his mouth and stared at her. His mind—long past the rituals and games of courting—scrambled to follow her logic. He'd steered her toward the refreshment table, noting the looks that were being given to him by the other women they passed.

Disappointment. Speculation. Envy.

Snatches of whispered conversations reached his ears.

"You should have been more persistent."

"He only likes her because she's Victoria's sister."

"See, Mama, the doctor is already taken."

They'd reached the table, and Elias had picked up a glass of punch and handed it to Olivia.

"You're right," he whispered. "That was rather brilliant."

She'd rolled her eyes. "London ballroom basics—remedial level."

He'd chuckled and leaned close. "What would advanced tactics look like?"

Her eyes had widened, then narrowed. "Are you flirting with me, Mr. Henrie?"

He shrugged as he considered. "I honestly don't know."

Olivia's laughter had rung through the air then—through him, a balm that wrapped around his heart. It still hurt to breathe, to live, to exist. But he had an ally now, a friend, and that had lightened his burden at least a little.

Evie stirred in her bed now, and a few seconds later her eyes opened and her arms stretched high above her.

"Good morning. Merry Christmas." Elias sat up and reached for her. She snuggled into his embrace, still partially asleep, and he enjoyed one of his favorite times of day, when she allowed him to hold her. She'd become so busy the last month, since she'd started walking, always wanting to be on the go and getting into something. He hoped his plan for the house in town, containing her in a nursery of sorts where he could easily watch her, was going to work. To that end, she'd be getting an abundance of playthings today, far more than her stocking could hold.

He'd enjoyed making and buying things for her. He was eager to give Jonathan and Victoria their presents as well. But he wished he'd had time to get something for the others—for Victoria's family, and especially for Olivia.

Still holding Evie, Elias rose from the bed, pushed the trundle in with his foot, and crossed the room to look out the window. Fresh snow had fallen in the night and blanketed the yard and the forest beyond it. Leafless trees and evergreens alike had their branches coated, creating a dazzling world of white.

Winter here is beautiful too. He remembered Olivia's question about why they stayed if the winters were so harsh and the summers muggy. He wished he could help her to find the beauty here and to feel at least some of the joy she'd left behind in England.

Elias held Evie close as he looked out at the pristine winter landscape. He knew better than many that it wasn't always easy to find that joy, particularly when missing someone or something so keenly. *If only I could bring a little bit of England here . . .* His gaze lifted to the pine forest bordering the edge of Jonathan's field, and a slow smile grew on his face.

He gave Evie a joyful squeeze, then turned away from the window. "I believe a little sleigh ride before breakfast is in order."

OLIVIA HELD HER arms out to Matthew and helped him down from Jonathan's wagon-turned-sleigh. Jonathan had come for them mid-morning, bringing Olivia and the children back in the wagon with him, while Sophie, Graham, and Maime rode in the sleigh Mother had purchased. Olivia had hoped Elias would be driving the wagon but tried to curb her disappointment when he was not. It was Christmas Day, and of course he would want to spend it with his daughter.

As she made her way to Victoria, standing in the open doorway and holding Evie, Olivia felt more discouraged. It might be that Elias wasn't home at all, but out caring for one of his many patients.

Victoria's smile seemed extra bright as she pulled Olivia close for a hug. "Happy Christmas, sister."

"It is happy, isn't it," Sophie said as she wrapped her arms around both of them.

"My girls. All together again," their mother said, and they opened their circle to include her.

Evie's shriek at being squished between them ended their greeting. Victoria stepped aside, and they all filed into the house.

Olivia stopped just inside, her eyes wide and a hand to her mouth as she stared at the evergreen tree taking up a good portion of the sitting room. She turned back to Victoria. "It's beautiful. When did you—"

"*I* didn't," Victoria said. "It was all Elias's doing."

He stepped out from behind the tree, an unlit candle in one hand and a spool of wire in the other. "Merry Christmas!"

"Papa." Evie reached her hands out to him. Victoria set her on the floor, and she toddled across the room toward her father.

Olivia followed. She stopped a few feet from Elias and breathed in the fresh pine scent. "Thank you, Elias! I *love* it."

He grinned. "I wanted you to see that some things can still be the same here." He handed her the candle, then bent to pick up Evie. "Want to help?"

"Yes." Olivia nodded enthusiastically.

"Put that one here," Elias instructed, pointing to a circlet of wire already waiting within the tree's branches. "I'm trying to space them evenly, so tonight the whole tree will be lit."

"Just so long as it's not my *house* that's lit," Jonathan said as he came inside. He shook his head. "Elias, you're usually known for your common sense and good judgment, but this time..."

"This time I believe he's exhibited both keen intellect *and* perception," Mother said, her smile nearly as wide as Olivia's.

Thirty-eight

SOPHIE LEANED INTO Graham, enjoying the feeling of his arms around her, his hands resting over the place where their child was growing. The day spent together, cozy and close in this little house, had been everything a Christmas should be. There had been presents and pastries, games and song, love and laughter. And now, as the sun set on the day, Elias and Olivia had lit candles on the evergreen that was taking up much of the crowded room. The candlelight danced and sparkled against the green branches to great effect.

"I think we shall require a tree in the house every year at Christmas after this," Sophie said.

"It is magnificent," Graham agreed. "Imagine how big a tree we could put in the hall at Caerlanwood."

"Enormous." Sophie thought of the cavernous space and tall ceilings. "How would we get it into the house?"

"I'll task Paden with figuring that out as soon as we get home."

Sophie laughed as Graham explained to the others, "Paden is our gardener. He's at least eighty years old and mostly blind."

"I should like to see your garden," Victoria said.

"No. You would not." Maime clucked her tongue. "What the old man do to those poor plants..."

"Caerlanwood's garden is *unique*," Sophie said. "The first

time I saw it, I didn't know what to think. Honestly, it was a little disturbing. Half of the bushes were practically bald, and the other half were like the overgrown jungles I'd only read about."

"You never said anything." Graham poked her side, as if to tickle her.

"I didn't want to hurt your feelings," Sophie confessed. "Plus, you have the ocean as your neighbor, so it didn't much matter what your garden looked like. And Paden's influence doesn't carry to the rest of the grounds, thankfully."

"Thank goodness for that," Graham agreed, sounding only partially mollified.

Sophie wrapped her arms over his. "I adore Caerlanwood. You know that. The oddities about it only make me love it more."

"I think I should like to see this Caerlanwood," Olivia said.

"Me too," their mother agreed.

"We'll plan the next Christmas in Scotland, then," Graham said cheerily. "Or perhaps the one after or even one a year or two beyond—whenever it is safe for all of us to be there." The enthusiasm in his voice dimmed. "Someday." He hugged Sophie tighter. "It would be our pleasure to have you all there with us."

"I would like that," Victoria said quietly.

Jonathan didn't say anything but stared contemplatively into the fire.

Sophie glanced around the room at her mother, Maime, Victoria, and Olivia all squished together on the sofa. Jonathan sat in the chair near the fire while Elias rocked a tired, but resisting-sleep Evie, her eyes glassy as she stared at the candles twinkling on the tree. Ayla and Matthew were curled up on either side of her and Graham on the floor. Sophie savored the moment, appreciating everything about it and having all those she loved close. A year from now it might not be the same. She and Graham and the children and Maime might be in Scotland again—a happy thought, though she would be sad to leave her mother and sisters.

Olivia might come with us. Or she might not, Sophie mused, as she noted that Elias's attention wasn't fixed on the tree as everyone else's was, but on her sister, as it had been much of the day. *A good thing, or not?* She wanted Olivia to be as happy as she and Victoria were in their marriages. To make a love match and to have the life she wanted. For Olivia that probably meant marrying a member of the gentry and living in London.

It wasn't that Olivia was spoiled—or too much so, at least—but that as the youngest the lifestyle of the ton had been thrust upon her all the more, especially as Sophie and Victoria had resisted it.

Mother had doted upon her youngest daughter, encouraging her love of fine and fancy things, teaching her that to act the part of a lady, to *be* a lady and to marry well, was important above all else and tantamount to a happy, successful life.

These were the same lessons that Sophie and Victoria had been given, but Olivia had taken them to heart. She'd wanted to please their mother, and to live the life that had been so carefully outlined for her.

She wouldn't be able to do that here. She wouldn't thrive as Victoria was, happy at Jonathan's side, both working hard every day to provide basic necessities and build a life together.

Olivia deserved someone who could love her completely, and not someone who had already been married and still obviously loved his deceased wife. Olivia needed someone young and full of life, someone who would take her to the theatre and to balls, who would bring her flowers and jewels and dote on her as the center of his universe.

Elias brought her a tree.

The thought stopped Sophie, and she glanced once more at Olivia, her countenance the picture of peace and contentment—far more than it had been at the start of their voyage or even two weeks ago—as she leaned her head against Mother's shoulder and gazed at the candlelit tree.

Maybe I am wrong. It wouldn't be the first time. Sophie considered the possibility of her sister and Elias together, recalling that her previous beliefs about love and marriage had been incorrect in a number of ways. Thankfully, so had Graham's.

Sophie let her concerns about Olivia's happiness drift to the back of her mind as she snuggled deeper into Graham's embrace, grateful for his solid chest behind her, supporting her, and mostly for his love that filled her life with purpose and joy.

Beside her Matthew's head bobbed, then snapped back up. He was fighting sleep as well.

"I have a new story tonight," Sophie said. "Or a poem, actually. But it feels like a story, and it's about Christmas."

Matthew sat up at this. There wasn't much he loved more than their evening ritual of reading together.

Graham handed Sophie the book and papers she'd brought with her. "Maybe you should sit nearer the tree—for better light to read by."

She couldn't tell if he was teasing. "I'll be all right here," she said. "I've already read it a few times and almost feel I could recite at least part without even looking." She smoothed the papers in her lap. "I bought this at the bookstore in New York City and have been saving it for Christmas. It's called *A Visit from Saint Nicholas*, or *The Night Before Christmas*."

"That was last night," Ayla said, then ducked her head as if embarrassed to have spoken.

Sophie gave her a warm smile. "You're right, and I would have read this last night, but most of us were at the dance."

"I wasn't," Matthew grumbled.

"No," Graham agreed. "You were being spoiled by Maime, eating her johnnycakes."

"'Twas the night before Christmas," Sophie began, "when all through the house, not a creature was stirring, not even a mouse." She read on, telling the story in verse of Jolly Old Saint Nicholas, who slid down chimneys on Christmas Eve and left presents. Both Ayla and Matthew leaned closer, absorbed in the tale.

The fire burned low, the tree glowed bright with its candles, and love and happiness seemed to fill every inch of the room. Sophie remembered feeling the same way a few months ago, as she'd stood on the grounds of Caerlanwood, taking in the colors of autumn and the life and the splendor of all she and Graham had there. In that moment it had seemed her life couldn't be any more perfect.

And then it hadn't been. Evil had come to their peaceful home, Graham had been taken, and everything had fallen apart. *No. That isn't true.* Their love had been tried, their very lives threatened, and she still recognized that the outcome might have been so very different. It would have been tragic, but that would not have changed anything about her love for those in this room, and especially for Graham. No matter what the future might bring, what they might encounter, their love was undying.

She glanced at Elias again, his face contemplative as he rocked his daughter and stared into the fire. His love for his deceased wife was the same. Death had no claim on that. She was glad of that, for him, for all of those who would someday be parted.

Elias's gaze slid to Olivia again, his expression unreadable.

But might there be room and love enough in his heart for another?

Thirty-nine

ELIAS KNEW THE exact moment that Olivia and her family entered the church. The simultaneous hush of the older parishioners combined with the whisperings of the younger, particularly those near Olivia's age, told him it was so.

Evie wiggled in his arms, already impatient with the services, though they had yet to begin. He struggled to contain her while wrestling within himself to remain facing forward instead of turning around for a glimpse of Olivia.

What was she wearing today? Another gown he'd never seen before? *One as pretty on her as the dress she'd worn to the dance?* She seemed to have brought dozens of gowns with her from England. Yet she wasn't vain about that. He had never seen any behavior from her that indicated she felt she was above anyone else. If anything, she was bewildered and struggling here, trying to find her place in an environment vastly different from that she'd been raised in. *And turning the heads of every young buck for miles around while doing it.*

Elias noted that several of them were not bothering to restrain *their* desires for another look at Olivia. *Why should they?* Were he younger and in search of a bride . . .

Elias stopped the thought before it could burrow any further into his mind. Just because Olivia had *pretended* interest in him at the Christmas dance, and just because the two of them had enjoyed decorating the tree together and had talked frequently and with ease throughout the whole of Christmas day, did not mean that they would ever be anything other than friends.

If she were amenable, would I even want to be more? Could I?

Elias shifted Evie in his arms, so that she was pressed close to him facing the back of the church, her head on his shoulder. *At least she can enjoy the view.*

Was that what *he* wished? To be able to admire Olivia's beauty? To flirt with the impossible? *It is impossible, isn't it?* On two fronts—that she would ever consider him a serious suitor, and that he would ever encourage such. Because . . . *Anne.*

Elias sighed inwardly, displeased with this new conflict within him. In addition to sorrow and loneliness, he now felt yearning. *For something that can never be. For someone other than Anne.* It troubled him. He shouldn't feel this way.

He'd already had his turn falling in love and being married.

It was Olivia's time for that now. *Not mine.* Even if he'd felt ready to entertain marrying again—and he did not—he wasn't what vivacious, beautiful, impulsive Olivia needed. If anything, he was the opposite.

OLIVIA SMOOTHED THE front of her simplest winter gown, a deep navy blue with a nipped waist, gigot sleeves that fitted at her wrists with delicate buttons, and a skirt that was only modestly wide and fell just past her ankles with no ruffle or adornment of any kind. At home she had rarely taken the dress from her wardrobe, finding it too plain for any sort of company. But here, on their first Sunday attending church in

Seneca Falls, she worried it was still too extravagant compared with what the other women would be wearing.

Sophie and Victoria were no help, in their simple dresses. Only their mother wore something comparable, though she insisted that the puffed sleeves so in fashion did her figure no favors and had always instructed her dressmaker to keep them at a fashionable minimum.

Head held high, and trying to hide her nerves, Olivia walked up the aisle beside Maime and her mother. Sophie and Graham walked ahead, with Ayla and Matthew at their sides. Though most of them had attended the Christmas Eve dance as newcomers the week before, going to church seemed even harder. Perhaps it was because not many had greeted them on Christmas Eve. Victoria had introduced them to as many people as she knew, but only a few had seemed to reach out in genuine friendship, and none of those had been near Olivia's age. Sophie had probably been correct in advising her not to wear such an elegant dress. But it had been Christmas and that dress the only tie she had to Christmases past.

Until Elias's tree.

The infusion of warmth that she'd felt at his unexpected Christmas-morning surprise surged through her again, reminding her that she had made one friend here, even if he wasn't the usual sort she would have had in England. She longed for other girls her age— *women*—to befriend her. How wonderful it would be to have others to visit with over tea or to walk in the park with. Except that no one here had much time for visiting, and there were no parks.

But I have Elias. The warmth of that knowledge wrapped around her. Surprisingly, she'd found in him someone she could talk to and laugh with. He listened to her, and she enjoyed listening to him, even if he was speaking of his beloved Anne.

Love UNDYING

On Christmas Eve, she had sensed that he needed to speak of her, that no one ever asked him to anymore. So Olivia had asked, had listened to a sweet love story with a tragic ending. And when Elias had finished, she had wanted nothing so much as to take him in her arms and hold him tight.

Since that wouldn't have been proper, she did the next best thing she could think of. She'd danced and flirted with him, so the other women there would believe that he was courting her and would hopefully leave him alone. In peace. To linger in his memories of Anne as long as he pleased. *Just as I am lingering in memories of home.*

But home was not here, not in this simple plank building, so new that it still smelled of fresh-milled pine. They found seats on a hard pew near the middle, Olivia on the end, having let the others, all her elders excepting the children, take a seat first as was polite. Though she felt even more exposed, there on the end, to those watching them.

And it felt as if *everyone* was.

The minister was making his rounds, greeting parishioners, and as they waited for him to reach their pew, Olivia searched for Elias and Evie among those already here. She spotted him seated on the side, a few rows ahead, holding Evie. Jonathan and Victoria were there too.

"Ahem." Beside her someone cleared his throat.

She looked up to see the minister standing there already. He must have skipped several other rows to come to greet them.

Olivia smiled at him. "Good morning."

He did not return her smile. "Those three." He pointed a long, bony finger toward Maime first and then to Ayla and Matthew. "Are not allowed in here."

Olivia sat frozen, unsure what to do, but Maime was already rising from her seat.

No! That isn't right. Why shouldn't Maime be allowed here too? She was part of their family now and had become their literal lifeline, teaching them all everything they needed to survive here, from how to wash clothing to how to cook. And before that, she'd bravely stood up for Graham in a court of white, prejudiced men. She'd looked out for Ayla and Matthew after their mother died. *Someone needs to stand up for her.*

Olivia popped up, blocking the way before Maime could leave. She looked the minister in the eye and spoke loudly. "We shall all leave then. If this were a *real* house of God, *all* would be welcome. The Bible I read does not say that we are to love those whose skin matches our own. It says that we are to *love one another.* But perhaps, here in America, land of the *free,* that is interpreted differently."

Olivia reached behind her and grasped Maime's hand as they made their way from the church. She didn't look back to see if the others followed but knew they would. Graham had to be furious, given his feelings on slavery and equality. It seemed that though New York had abolished the one, its people were far from pursuing the other.

She marched down the steps and didn't stop until she'd reached the sleigh. Only then did she realize she was shaking.

"You ought not to have done that," Maime said, but there was no reproach in her voice. "I'm not worth the trouble you bring upon yourself here."

"Yes," Olivia said, "you are. And so are Ayla and Matthew." Tears blurred her vision as Sophie came up to her and enfolded her in a hug. "I think perhaps I should have had *you* represent Graham in court. That was brilliant."

Olivia shook her head. "What the minister said was *so* wrong."

"Aye," Graham agreed. "Even here, or especially here, all

men are not truly free. Thank you for your words, Olivia. I could not have said them better myself."

"I'm not sure you would have *said* them," Sophie teased, "but laid the man flat, possibly."

Graham pretended offense, but some of the tension drained from his expression. "I am a reformed man."

"As am I. No longer a member of the Seneca Falls church."

Olivia turned to see Elias striding toward them, Evie still in his arms.

"What are you doing? Your business, your patients—"

"Are still going to require a doctor, regardless of my church-going status, which has altered as of this morning." Elias inclined his head toward the building behind them. "His sermons were boring, anyway."

Sophie and Graham laughed. Only Mother remained silent, a look of deepest concern etched into the lines of her face.

Graham began helping everyone into the sleigh. Olivia lingered beside Elias, reluctant to part from him so quickly but also wanting to be far from the church.

He stepped closer. "There was another reason I had to leave," he whispered, so only she could hear.

"Oh?" She turned to him, their faces close now.

"After your grand efforts at the dance, I could not allow people to think I don't stand with the woman I'm courting." He grinned. "Ballroom basics step one."

Olivia held her hands over her heart, as it soared at his words. Their courtship was only pretend, but still, he had left to show his support for her. "I believe that's at least a level two."

Sophie leaned over the side of the sleigh. "Elias, would you like to join us for the afternoon? Then we can all go together to Jonathan and Victoria's later."

Hesitation shone in his eyes, and Olivia tried not to feel

hurt. She placed a hand on his sleeve. "It's all right. You don't have to."

"I want to," he said. "It's just—difficult to be in that house again."

"It must hold many memories, good and bad," she said. "That would be hard." She forced a smile, though she was disappointed. "We shall see you tonight, then." She patted Evie's arm briefly, and the little girl leaned forward, reaching out to her.

"Oh," Olivia exclaimed as she caught her.

"I believe Evie is telling me she would like us to join you," Elias said, his expression tender as he looked at the two of them together.

"Are you certain?" Olivia asked. "I do not wish to make the day difficult for you—even more than it has already been." She looked beyond him to the church.

He nodded. "Yes. It's time I stop letting the past, or my fear of revisiting it, rule my life and, especially, Evie's." He held out his arm. "Would you like to ride with us?"

Olivia shifted Evie to one side, then placed a hand on Elias's arm. "I would like that very much."

January 1, 1832

Dear Anne,

Happy New Year, My Darling. My faith bids me imagine that you are happy there in heaven, dancing with the angels in a field of wildflowers. That is often how I remember you, out among the flowers when I first came to see your mother. You were as pretty as any, and as radiant as the sunshine. May you ever be so now.

Yours always,
Elias

Love Undying

January 1, 1832
Dear Olivia,

Your words at church this morning stirred my soul in a way it has not been moved for quite some time. When first you stood and faced Minister Fredericks, my instinct was to jump up and intervene before your impulsiveness landed you in more trouble. But then you opened your mouth and spoke with such eloquence and conviction. You spoke truth, though I fear it a truth many in this country are not yet ready to hear. My admiration for you grew in leaps and bounds. I've rarely been so proud, and I could not help but follow you out of the chapel. I am beginning to fear that I cannot help but follow you anywhere. I wish I knew if you had any desire at all to be accompanied by me.

Yours,
Elias

Forty

AFTER THE BRIEF lift of spirits Elias had experienced during the holidays, January dragged on bleak and cold. He'd not anticipated that his loneliness would worsen to the degree it had with his move to the village. His proximity to others should have made his contacts more frequent, and it did—in some ways, but not in any that were helpful.

The sign he'd hung out front by the gate *had* attracted patients. He'd sutured a cut late on a Saturday night, when a patron of the tavern had wound up in a drunken fight and had a bottle smashed over his head.

He'd relocated a small boy's shoulder after the youngster had tumbled headfirst over the side of a wagon when it hit one of the many holes in the dirt street. Elias had been very grateful, then, for his proximity and that the child hadn't had to suffer a long ride out to Jonathan's house to get the help he needed.

This morning it was Miss Melody Larsen and her mother who rang the bell over his door as they entered, the latter complaining of frequent headaches while the former's smile showed so many teeth as to remind him of a picture he'd once viewed of a chimpanzee. Elias ushered Mrs. Larsen toward the room he'd set up for examinations.

Melody settled into the lone sitting room chair that the previous owner had left behind for him. Getting additional furniture, for both the office portion of the house and the space in back and upstairs that he and Evie lived in, was on his list of tasks to accomplish in the coming weeks.

"I'll just wait out here," Miss Larsen said, her smile bright.

Too bright. What's she up to? Both mother and daughter were two of the biggest gossips for miles. If there was news to be had—good or bad, true or false—they would spread it. Elias hoped Mrs. Larsen truly did have a headache and that there was no alternative reason for their visit.

He pushed the worry to the back of his mind as he pulled out his stethoscope and began questioning her about the onset and frequency of her pain. Evie played quietly in the adjoining room, where he could keep an eye on her over the half-door he'd installed. As soon as he'd heard the bell, he'd settled Evie in with the set of cloth balls she'd received from Victoria for Christmas. Victoria had sewn them for her from scraps of fabric, then stuffed them with batting, hoping Evie would enjoy those as much as she'd enjoyed getting into Victoria's balls of yarn.

"Take a deep breath in, then release it slowly," Elias instructed, as he held the stethoscope to Mrs. Larsen's back.

"It isn't my back that's hurting," she said before complying with his request.

"I'm listening to your lungs," he explained. "If there is any sign of congestion that could indicate—"

"My lungs are fine, " she snapped.

"They are," he agreed and stepped away. *Pleasant sort of woman.* He glanced up and noticed that the chair in the front room was empty. He hadn't heard the bell, and there was nowhere else for Miss Larsen to sit, no artwork on the walls to stand and study while she waited.

Where is she? Elias crossed the room and replaced the stethoscope in his bag, at the same time verifying that the front room was empty. Was Miss Larsen snooping in his house?

"Oh, my head. It's hurting now," her mother moaned. She brought a hand to her head, pushing on her right temple.

Elias returned to examining her and tried not to worry. If Miss Larsen was nosing about his house, she was sure to find absolutely nothing. His patient files were all in this room, and he was confident that there was nothing else she might find interesting to report on or gossip about. The house was tidy, the beds made. Evie had her own room here, with a pretty quilt Victoria had made for her on the bed and all of the clothes Anne had sewn for her put neatly away in the bureau.

The bell over the door rang again. "Good morning, Elias."

Olivia. His mood improved instantly. She appeared in the doorway, her smile bright as well, though it did not bother him as Miss Larsen's had.

This morning Olivia wore a gown he hadn't seen before—not surprising, as she seemed to have brought trunkfuls over with her from England. It was cream, with a pattern of roses, a fitted bodice, and a skirt so wide he wasn't certain how she'd made it through the door. Ringlets framed either side of her face, and a ribbon with a jewel in the shape of a rosebud rested at the base of her throat. Her cheeks were pink with cold—*where is her cloak?*—and she carried a basket in her hands. The very atmosphere of the house felt cheered by her appearance.

"Good morning," Olivia repeated, this time directing the greeting and her smile toward Mrs. Larsen.

When the woman did not respond or say anything at all, merely pursing her lips in a look of disapproval, Olivia returned her attention to Elias and, seeming unfazed by the interaction or lack thereof, touched her fingers to her lips, blew him a kiss, then turned away.

Mrs. Larsen gasped. "Well, I never—"

Elias had opened his mouth to explain—*what,* he wasn't sure—when Evie gave a shriek of delight. Olivia appeared in the hall behind him. She reached over the half door and scooped up Evie, who gurgled with excitement at being freed from her makeshift nursery.

"Show Papa your new trick," Olivia said, touching her fingers to her mouth again. Evie copied her, smacked her lips, and then waved her hand toward Elias.

He breathed an inward sigh of relief. *Olivia wasn't flirting at all.* At the same time he felt oddly disappointed, though grateful Mrs. Larsen would not have that particularly juicy bit of gossip to spread.

Or had that been Olivia's intention all along? *Ballroom techniques level three?*

"I'll take Evie to the kitchen," Olivia said. "I've brought some biscuits for her."

"Thank you," Elias called as Olivia and Evie walked toward the back of the house. With difficulty he returned his focus to Mrs. Larsen. "When you lie down does your pain increase?"

Mrs. Larsen narrowed her eyes at him in such a severe fashion that he thought he might understand the root of her headaches.

"Is it your habit, Doctor, to have single women gallivanting through your house at any time?"

Elias pretended to consider her question. "Not *women*, no. Miss Claybourne, who is practically family—" *let her figure out what I mean by that—* "yes. As you can see, she has an affection for my daughter. And for baking. Miss Claybourne brings us treats. We greatly enjoy her company." He worried he'd said too much and endangered Olivia's reputation, but she *had* come here alone. What else was he to have said?

With a great puff of air, Mrs. Larsen hoisted herself from the examination table. "Thank you for nothing, Doctor Henrie."

"Pardon?" He crossed his arms as he stood between her

and the doorway. "We have not concluded our visit, so how can you say—"

"Oh, yes we have. *Melody!*"

Elias cringed and only just managed not to bring his hands up to his ringing ears. It was a wonder *Miss* Larsen was not suffering from headaches as well, if her mother frequently bellowed like that.

He took a packet of feverfew and handed it to Mrs. Larsen as she left. "Simmer this for a tea. If that doesn't help with your headaches, come back. It may be that they're sinus-related."

Olivia, still holding Evie, with Melody right behind, met them in the sitting room, which Elias decided was too small for that many females at once.

"Look who I found upstairs," Olivia said, her smile as sweet as it had ever been. "She must have become confused and lost her way."

With a sneer of displeasure, contrary to the overly cheerful greeting she'd given upon her arrival, Melody swept past him. She followed her mother out the door, and Elias caught it before it could slam behind them.

Hands behind his back, he faced Olivia. "A *kiss*? Truly?"

She shrugged and did not appear the least regretful or repentant. "I did teach Evie that trick at Sunday dinner last week. I remembered this morning that we hadn't shown you yet."

"You know the Larsens are the biggest gossips for miles around. That is not an exaggeration."

"I know, but I saw them come in and had to do *something*. Everyone knows Mrs. Larsen is out to steal you for her daughter."

He hadn't known that, but now that he did he would be sure to avoid the women. "How is it you happened to be nearby today?"

"I'm helping at the store," Olivia explained as she set a

squirming Evie down and pulled back the cloth from the basket she'd brought with her. "Victoria isn't feeling well and sent word this morning asking for my help. The store is a nice change of pace from the house, where there is very little to do that isn't *work*." Olivia removed a biscuit from the basket and crouched beside Evie, holding the treat out to her. "I think you'll like these. They're sweeter *and* softer than Victoria's."

"Did you make them?" Elias snatched one for himself, then accepted the basket when she handed it to him. He wondered if he ought to call on his cousin later and check on Victoria. *Any* sickness worried him, as he never knew when something that seemed innocuous might turn out to be deadly.

"I did make these. All by myself." Olivia smiled. "Maime is an excellent cook and an excellent teacher—as were you. I make bread every morning now." She stood and faced him.

"I'm impressed," Elias said as he bit into the biscuit that was indeed softer and sweeter than any Victoria had ever made.

"It was either do the baking or feed the chickens and collect their eggs or learn to *milk a cow*." Olivia's lips turned down in an overexaggerated grimace. She shuddered.

Elias held back a smile as he imagined her displaying that same expression when those other chores had been suggested to her.

"Baking is infinitely better," she continued. "I positively *detest* chickens. Jonathan told me they mostly stay in their coop during winter, but they always come out when I'm around. They peck at me when I try to take their eggs, and they make such a mess of—you know." She waved her hand in the air, as if that would explain the indelicate matter of chicken waste. "*Everywhere*." She sighed. "Thankfully Matthew and Ayla like them, and that is their responsibility now. As for the cow—" She grimaced. "Have you ever *felt* a cow udder?"

Elias laughed. "Many times." *Unfortunately.* He was not fond of caring for chickens or milking cows either, but he didn't think it wise to tell her. The realities of life were that both animals were vital to feeding a family. And everyone in hers was going to have to do their part if they were going to survive here. That her mother and Graham had the means to buy the animals was a blessing in itself. Though Olivia probably didn't see it that way.

"Helping at the store is somewhat better?" Elias asked, hoping she was not the only one there today and that Jonathan was neither losing customers nor being robbed as they spoke.

"It is. I rather enjoy helping customers and especially like helping women select fabrics. Though I do wish Jonathan would consider stocking a wider variety." Olivia parted the front curtains to check the Larsens' progress. "I'll leave as soon as they are out of sight."

Elias propped his shoulder against the wall and leaned into it, enjoying the unexpected pleasure of Olivia's company and the way Evie was waving her biscuit in the air and running about the room from one end to the other. "I would ask you to stay longer, but I imagine you are already concerned about your reputation, being alone in this house without a chaperone and having the two village busybodies headed out to tell the tale."

"Let them," Olivia said, her lack of concern not at all like herself.

Elias frowned, certain her position on guarding her reputation could not have reversed so drastically in the past month.

"I may not be here much longer anyway, so what do I care what people say about me?"

"Where are you planning to go?" The improved mood he'd felt with her arrival plummeted. He did not see Olivia often. Aside from this morning, Sunday dinners at Victoria and Jonathan's had been the only times in January they had visited, and then they were always in the presence of her family, so visiting with Olivia for any length of time or with much privacy was difficult. But the thought of never seeing her, of her being gone for good, saddened him.

It should not. He held no claim over her, nor she over him. They were not truly courting. The idea was so absurd, he wondered that anyone should believe it. What would a young, vivacious woman like Olivia see in him?

Nothing.

It doesn't matter.

I am not in the market for a wife. He'd told Graham that last week when they had been readying the teams in the barn and the subject had come up. Graham had chuckled and shared that he had said those exact words to Sophie the night they met.

"I am going back to the store—for now." Olivia waved at him as she turned to go.

"Have you made plans to return to England?" he asked quickly, before she could leave.

Her face fell, and she shook her head. "It is neither safe nor possible right now."

"Has some fellow professed his love and you intend to elope?"

"No."

"Then where—"

She frowned, then looked up and met his gaze boldly. "The only man I have taken interest in here has not professed any feelings of affection toward me."

"*Who* have you taken interest in?"

Olivia stared at him another few seconds, then sighed and turned away. "Forget I said anything. I'll let you know if I make any plans to leave." She hurried past him out the door and across the street to Jonathan's store.

Elias watched until she'd gone inside, only just checking his desire to follow and insist that she tell him which of the gentlemen around here had caught her fancy. *Someone she met working at the store?* Was that why Olivia had seemed so happy of late? She did seem to have adjusted to life in Seneca Falls rather more quickly than he had imagined she would. He had hoped, had begun to wish, that possibly six months from now she might actually consent to him courting her. *Why would she consent to that? I am nothing like the gentlemen who would have courted her in England.*

Elias closed the door, the bell above jingling merrily, mocking the return of his melancholy mood.

January 16, 1832
Dear Anne,
I remain uncertain if the move to town was wise. While I am enjoying the opportunity to spend more time with Evie throughout the day, I worry that she misses staying with Victoria and Jonathan as much as I do, though she still sees them frequently, as they continue to help out when I am called away. In your absence, their home was somewhat of a replacement for ours, and I cannot deny that I miss their company—though it was never a replacement for yours.

I suppose that what I am trying to say is that I am struggling, as much as ever, with your loss. Town is lonelier, particularly at night, when I have only the scratchings of my quill upon paper and our imagined conversations to keep me company. I miss you, Anne. I will always miss you and always love you. Even if, at some distant future day, I decide that I cannot or need not carry on alone.

Yours,
Elias
January 16, 1832
Dear Olivia,

Love Undying

So much can change in one year's time. Twelve months ago I was in the deepest well of grief, certain that my life as I had known it, sweet and good and filled with love, was over, with those virtues never to be experienced again.

Twelve months ago you were just beginning your Season in London, and though I was not alble to witness you there, I can imagine the happiness on your face and how lovely you must have been twirling around ballrooms, catching the eyes of the gentlemen there, and oblivious to the sorrows and trials that awaited you.

What, but the will of God, could have possibly introduced two such different souls and made them balm for the other? I hope I have been some small comfort to you, for you have been a great comfort to me. More than that, you have awakened me to the possibility that I might one day love again.

It is too soon, I know, to profess such sentiment, or to even think on it with regard to you, and yet I do. I am. And I don't know what to do about it, about you, for it seems unfair to even consider the possibility of one such as yourself being burdened with one such as I. It is with that thought, that knowledge that we are so ill-suited for one another, that I endeavor to keep to our friendship and nothing more. And when the time comes that you have found the love of your life, I shall be cheering you on, joyous for your good fortune and wishing you every happiness. Even while I believe that it will only detract from mine.

Yours,
Elias

Forty-one

ELIAS LEFT THE road and turned up the drive toward his old home. *Olivia's home now.* Or so he thought of it, though six others lived here as well. Visiting was still difficult, and he didn't come often. For many reasons, it was simply easier to stay away.

The afternoon sun temporarily blinded him, and as he squinted against it, he imagined that he saw Anne kneeling in her garden, among her beloved spring flowers.

His horse plodded on without Elias's guidance as he sat transfixed, staring at the rows of brilliantly blooming daffodils and the woman toiling among them. Logic fled, and his heart pounded as he watched Anne's familiar, sure movements. He drew closer, and she stood and brushed the dirt from her gloved hands.

She turned toward him, and brown hair—not auburn—peeked out from beneath her hat.

Not Anne. Olivia. But standing there with the sun behind her, she seemed a near likeness.

Elias's palms were suddenly clammy on the reins. Heat, followed abruptly by a distinct shiver of cold, swept through him, along with the strangest sensation that he had just seen his wife, or that she *had* somehow been here with him, at least. The hairs on the back of his neck and his arms rose, not in fear but with a tingling awareness.

Does Anne's ghost haunt this place? The dream he'd had in the weeks after her death, the one where she had threatened to haunt him if he didn't love and care for Evie, came back to him. *I am loving her. I'm doing my best.*

But he was acutely aware that his best was nowhere near what Anne's would have been.

Olivia pulled the hat from her head and waved it at him. "Elias! It's good to see you." Holding up her skirt, she started across the lawn toward him.

Elias's heart tripped with anticipation instead of the sorrow he ought to have felt at what had just happened and the reminder of his loss.

He'd told himself he needed to come here today to check on Sophie. She'd had influenza, and with her pregnancy he had reason to be concerned. Though she *had* seemed almost fully recovered at dinner on Sunday, and was probably even more so now. *I didn't really need to come.* But he had wanted to stop by, for this very possibility. *To see Olivia.* It had been another long, lonely week between Sundays—she hadn't worked at the store as much lately, so he had not seen her as often—and he had deemed it worth the risk of painful memories if it meant he could enjoy her company for a few minutes.

Elias dismounted. "Is everyone here well?" Had she waved him down and called out to him because someone was sick?

Olivia stopped in front of him, her cheeks rosy with color, and her hair in a loose braid, with windswept strands flying about. She wore a plain cotton dress, with an apron covering most of it. He'd never seen her attired so simply. *Or looking more beautiful.*

"We are all quite healthy, Sophie included, though Graham is still insisting that she rest. The way he dotes upon her is rather ridiculous."

"As if she is his entire world?" Elias suggested, understanding completely what Olivia likely could not. *Not yet.* How long would it be before she understood that level of devotion?

Since that day several weeks ago, when she had hinted that there was a man who had piqued her interest, Elias had attempted to discern who it might be. He had seen her conversing a time or two with different gentlemen in town, but thus far had not been able to detect a courtship with any.

"Isn't it a fine day?" Olivia threw her arms out and tipped her face up to the sun. "Warm at last and blooming with life. I am beginning to understand why you and Victoria and Jonathan all insisted that spring in New York made the long winter worth it. The blossoms, the green grass, the flowers—everything is beautiful."

"We may yet have some additional winter weather," Elias cautioned. *Ever the rain cloud to her sunshine.* "At times, March and even April can be quite wet and cold here." He removed his bag from the back of his horse.

Olivia stepped forward and tucked her arm through his. "Well, *today* is perfect and meant to be appreciated and enjoyed." They strolled toward the house.

"I see you have discovered the daffodils." Elias stared again at the yellow and white flowers that had burst from the earth all along the front of the house. *Had they bloomed last spring?* He couldn't recall—possibly because he had avoided coming to the house for much of the year, and in his absence the yard had become overgrown and neglected.

"I was happy to find them growing among the weeds," Olivia said. "I've been tending to them, clearing out the flower bed so they can grow and be seen."

"I can tell," Elias said, noting how much better the yard looked. "Anne planted those," he said with surprising ease. "For a second when I came up the drive, you looked like her, kneeling there in the garden."

Olivia slowed her steps then stopped altogether and faced him. "I'm sorry. I didn't mean to—"

He pressed a finger to her lips, and she stilled. In contrast, his heart rate accelerated. He pulled his hand away, but it was too late—yearning flowed through him like blood through his veins.

What would it be like to kiss Olivia?

Her eyes locked on his, and he worried she could see right through him, into his mind and the errant thoughts dwelling there.

Elias broke their gaze, turning instead to stare at the daffodils once more. "I am thankful that you are taking care of the garden. It was important to Anne. She would want that."

"Then I am glad," Olivia said, her smile still subdued from a minute before. "I love flowers, and as there are no florist shops in Seneca Falls, I intend to grow my own. I've already sent away for some seeds."

"An excellent idea." Elias resumed walking, slower this time. He was in no hurry to reach the house and lose this connection.

"If we could only get you as excited about planting vegetables," Maime muttered as they made their way up the walk. Elias hadn't noticed her before, as she knelt in the shade of the house.

"Good afternoon," he said.

"It would be better if that girl hanging on your arm would get back to work. I'm too old to be doin' this myself."

"Indeed." Elias stopped then reached a hand down to Maime. "Why don't you take a rest, and Olivia and I will finish here." The few remaining rows shouldn't take that long, and since Sophie was apparently as healthy as he had suspected, he had the time to help here for a while. *Time with Olivia.* Elias helped Maime up then held onto her arm until she had her balance.

Maime expelled a breath. "Thank you."

"I am sorry that I cannot summon the same delight for beans and squash as I feel for flowers, but of course I'll help," Olivia said, a slight tinge of hurt and defense in her tone. "Clearing away the weeds from among the daffodils seemed more prudent, if we were to enjoy their beauty before they faded." She reached for a hoe leaning against the side of the house and began attacking the dirt and weeds where Maime had been working.

"Flowers not going to feed your family," Maime said, but there was more teasing than reproach in her tone.

Olivia sighed, paused her work, and leaned on the hoe. "How I dearly miss the days when food simply appeared on the table without my slightest thought as to where it came from or what it took to prepare it."

Maime laughed. "Those days be over, child."

"I know." Olivia hung her head and gave an overexaggerated sigh. "If I must plant and grow and harvest and then cook what is to be my supper, I should at least like to have flowers on the table to accompany it."

Elias patted her arm consolingly. "And so you shall, but for now let's banish these weeds so something else can grow."

Maime climbed the steps to the porch and settled herself on a chair, much to Elias's disappointment. He would have preferred having Olivia to himself. She had turned away from him, and was attacking the ground again. *Taking out her frustrations with her life here?* It was difficult to tell. A few minutes ago she had seemed perfectly content.

She was not raised to weed a garden. Elias looked around for another hoe or rake, intending to do the bulk of the work, so Olivia would not have to, but instead saw a carriage approaching the house.

"Olivia!" the driver called out as he came closer.

She turned from her work as Wallace Penington pulled to a stop. He jumped down and came toward them.

"Wally." Olivia smiled at him.

"We've just had word that a shipment is arriving a day early. Jonathan sent me to ask you to come in and mind the store so he and I can unload everything."

Olivia's smile widened. "Of course. Give me a few minutes to change." She handed Elias the hoe and hurried into the house without a backward glance.

Maime clucked her tongue. "How you like that?"

He didn't. *Wally?* That seemed awfully friendly, though he and Olivia did work together, Wallace being apprenticed to Jonathan. He was all of twenty-one. *Too young for Olivia.* But his family had money and acreage. If Olivia were to marry him, he could provide well for her.

Is that why she's set her cap for him? Is Wallace the man she alluded to?

"Good day to you, Doctor." Wallace doffed his hat then kept it off, swirling it in his hands as he waited for Olivia to reappear.

Elias turned away and began attacking the weeds with twice the vigor she had. Suddenly the three remaining rows seemed much longer. He shrugged out of his jacket and hung it over the railing then continued to work.

Ten minutes passed, and Olivia returned. She'd changed into a pale green dress that seemed to match the spring weather, and her hair had been tamed into a chignon with a few curls left to fall on either side of her face. A pretty bonnet with ribbon that matched her dress topped the ensemble.

From the corner of his eye, Elias noticed Wallace appreciating her appearance too.

"I'll help extra tomorrow," Olivia promised, giving Maime's hand a squeeze as she left the porch. She paused before Elias. "It was good to see you. I am glad you stopped by, even if only to check on Sophie." Olivia's smile seemed almost sad as she turned away.

Wallace placed his hat back on his head and held his arm out to Olivia. They strolled toward the waiting carriage, and Elias couldn't help but notice what a fine couple they made. He turned away to find Maime staring at him.

"You should have offered to take her into town."

"On my horse?" Elias shook his head. "Besides, I did come to check on Sophie."

"How you got yourself married the first time be a mystery." Maime nodded toward the departing carriage. "You want that girl, you got to go get her."

"I don't want—"

Maime wagged a finger at him as she rolled her eyes. She hoisted herself from the chair and headed toward the door. "I've been around too long to be lied to. A woman knows what a woman knows. But a man—sometimes he don't know nothing."

Forty-two

OLIVIA LEFT THE kitchen in time to see Elias hang up his coat and settle on Victoria's sitting room floor with Evie beside him. From his pocket, he withdrew a paper-wrapped parcel that jingled and rattled when he shook it. "Matthew, Ayla, I've brought something for you."

Matthew was at his side in an instant, while Ayla hung back.

Still mistrustful of white men. Olivia had observed this wariness and reluctance to engage from Ayla before, during the entirety of their voyage and in the weeks since, even with Elias and Jonathan, both of whom she'd spent considerable time around. The incident at church in January had not done her confidence any favors.

Olivia came up beside her. "Shall we see what Elias has brought?" She gave Ayla an encouraging smile, then crossed the room to sit on the sofa near him.

He handed the package to Matthew. "Unwrap it carefully. You don't want them to spill and get lost."

Matthew clutched the package and squatted low to the floor in his typical manner of play. Sophie said he'd spent hours in that position while playing in the sand at the beach; Olivia continued to be amazed at the ability. Should she try such a feat, no doubt she would fall backward in an incredible display of immodesty.

The string came off and fell to the floor. Matthew placed the packet beside it, and his little fingers peeled the folded paper back, revealing a ball and a set of shiny new jacks.

Matthew poked at them before raising his head, his eyes scrunched in a quizzical expression.

"They're called jacks," Elias said. "I'll show you how to play."

Evie was already on the move, toddling around him, her hands outstretched toward the new treasure. Elias glanced at Olivia. "Would you mind watching her?"

"Not at all." Olivia rose to intercept the toddler, though she really wanted to watch Elias instead. She hadn't seen him at all for nearly two weeks. *I wish he had come to call and brought me a present.* That he hadn't and had also ceased coming across the street to visit with her at the store, reaffirmed her uncertainty about his regard. Maybe during her first two months here he had simply been kind to her, as he was to Ayla and Matthew right now, and that was all. Perhaps she had read more into his words and actions. Bringing her a Christmas tree to remind her of England and following her out of church after her outburst were not necessarily romantic gestures. Maybe it was only her loneliness that had caused her to see them as such. She had been the one to initiate their pretended courtship, and while he had seemed to be in favor of that ruse at first, nothing had been done to further it— pretend or otherwise—in recent weeks.

If Elias was never to see her as more than a friend, then there was nothing for her here, no one in Seneca Falls whose feelings she wished to encourage and which feelings she might return.

Olivia snatched Evie a second before she could grab the paper containing the jacks.

She shrieked in protest and squirmed, but Olivia held

fast. She balanced Evie on her hip and turned her away from the game. "Let's go to the kitchen and find a piece of gingerbread."

By the time Victoria, Sophie, and Maime had dinner ready, Elias, Matthew, and Ayla were engrossed in their game, which had slowly migrated to the far side of the room with Matthew's erratic tossing of the ball. Jonathan and Graham came in from the barn, each with expressions that seemed too serious for men who'd simply been doing the evening chores.

What is wrong with everyone tonight?

"Supper's ready," Victoria announced as she set a bowl of steaming potatoes on the table.

"I'll play with the children while the rest of you eat first," Elias offered.

"Thank you, Elias," Victoria said. She wiped her hands on her apron and looked at Jonathan. "Someday we'll have a table that seats more than six."

"I'll help Elias," Olivia said, hoping this would give them at least a few minutes apart from everyone else in which they might talk. Her gaze swung to him, but he had his head down, focused once more on the game.

She returned to her seat on the sofa after picking up a ball of Victoria's yarn for Evie to unravel. Rewinding it later would be a small price to pay for the opportunity to have a semi-private conversation with Elias.

"I believe you've got it now," he said to the children, then rose from the floor and dusted off his trousers. "Olivia and I will watch while the two of you play." He crossed the room and sat on the opposite end of the sofa, about as far from her as he could be on the same piece of furniture.

"How was your week?" she asked. "Did you see many patients?" Had Melody Larsen and her mother returned, was what she really wanted to ask. *The nerve of that woman, being upstairs in his private rooms.* Olivia had caught Melody coming down the stairs, a smug expression on her face, as if she knew something that Olivia did not.

Perhaps she did. *It isn't as if* I've *been upstairs in Elias's house.*

"No more busy than usual. I treated a serious injury, though. Barrett Jones's son accidentally drove an axe through his foot. It wasn't pretty and required an extensive surgery to put it back together again." He shook his head. "Even now, I'm not certain he's going to be able to walk again normally."

Olivia suppressed a shudder, recalling her own, less-significant foot surgery, while at the same time marveling that Elias could mend a wound of that sort. "He is fortunate you were able to help him."

"Let us hope he feels that way once it has healed. I did my best, but . . ." Elias shrugged, then ran a hand over his face, and Olivia realized how exhausted he looked. Older too. She knew he was her elder by several years, but that had never seemed apparent, until tonight.

She set Evie on the sofa between them and leaned toward him. "Elias, what is wrong? Are *you* ill?" Who took care of the doctor when the doctor was sick?

"I am healthy enough. In body, at least."

Olivia pressed her lips together, waiting for him to say more, praying that he would. This was not the Elias she had come to know the past four months. Something had to be terribly wrong.

"I have not been sleeping well," he admitted, then leaned forward to toss a stray jack across the floor to the children. "It is—difficult to explain."

"I wish you would try." Olivia scooted herself and Evie closer to him, so that if he wished to say whatever was troubling him, he would not have to speak loudly. Though

Matthew was engrossed in the game, Ayla's gaze had strayed their direction a time or two.

Elias looked up at Olivia, and the despair in his expression nearly broke her heart.

"What is it? Please tell me. It may be that I can help somehow."

The corners of his mouth lifted in the briefest smile of appreciation. "I thought you could, and you did—for a time, but grief is a strange bedfellow. For weeks it may leave you alone to your rest, then suddenly it tears at you from the inside out, until you are so gutted you can hardly breathe." He leaned forward, head in his hands.

"*Elias.*" Olivia placed her hand on his shoulder. His words alarmed her.

"I win!" Matthew exclaimed and held up a fistful of jacks.

Ayla looked at him dubiously, her mouth twisted. She shook her head as Olivia caught her eye.

"Play again," Olivia encouraged. She picked up Evie and the tangle of yarn covering her, putting both in her lap so they could move to Elias's side. She touched him again briefly, unsure what else she should say or do. She'd never seen him like this—he was usually so confident and self-assured. *Positive, even amidst hardship.*

"Last week was Anne's birthday. She would have been twenty-six." Sorrow choked his words. "I took Evie out to see Anne's parents on their farm. It was hard, and part of me didn't want to go, but it was the right thing to do." He turned his face to look at Olivia, and she nodded, affirming his conclusion.

"Did something happen—"

"They wanted me to leave Evie with them. They think she'll have a better life there than she will being raised by me, and without a mother."

"That isn't true," Olivia said, indignant on his behalf. "She is *your* daughter, not theirs. I can understand why they might wish to raise her, having lost two of their daughters to smallpox, but she is yours. You are her father, and she needs *you*. Had my father shown me a tenth of the love you've given Evie already in her life, I would have been so grateful for that relationship."

Elias smiled sadly. "I appreciate that, but the truth is that they are at least partially right. I am gone a lot. As a doctor I have strange hours, and the solution of bringing Evie with me on house calls, day and night, isn't a good one. She deserves a home where someone is there to take care of her, where she always takes priority. As a doctor, sometimes that priority has to go to my patients. Is that fair to her?"

Olivia bit her lip, uncertain how to answer. There was a solution to his dilemma that seemed rather obvious to her, but she couldn't come out and tell him he ought to marry again. *Marry—me.* Now wasn't the time to allow herself to admit to or dwell on the idea that had been working its way around the back of her mind for a while now, since that day in church, when he had followed her, had sided with her against the minister and others in the congregation.

Weeks ago he'd told her he had no interest in marrying again. And hadn't her ruse at Christmas been all about keeping other interested women away? *Was it?* Olivia swallowed, uncomfortable with the revelation that it had, for her at least, been maybe a bit more.

"You aren't actually considering their suggestion to take Evie, are you?" Olivia's arms tightened around the little girl. The idea of Evie not being around, and not with Elias, was unfathomable.

He sat up, then heaved a weary sigh. "No."

"Good." That was a relief, at least.

"Evie—Evelyn. Did you know that is her real name?"

Olivia shook her head and smiled. "It's beautiful. Someday she may appreciate having a more grown-up name."

He gave a single nod. "Evie is my whole world. Selfish though that may make me, I cannot give her up."

Olivia tried to ignore the pinch her heart felt at that statement and the warning that began ringing through her. *Might I not be at least a bit of his world, as well?* "You haven't been sleeping because you feel guilty about raising Evie yourself?"

"Yes . . . And no." He turned his full attention to Olivia. "There is another solution."

Her hands slid down Evie's little shoulders and arms and came to a stop on either side, bracing her on the sofa. Her heartbeat escalated beneath his watchful gaze. "Yes?" It was an answer as much as a question. *Insanity?* Maybe it was that, too, because if he was about to ask her to marry him, to be his wife, to be Evie's mother, she would say yes. She would give up all possibility of ballrooms and the theatre, a life of ease and luxury, returning to England and all she held dear there. Because—*Elias.* He had done something to her, had changed her somehow in the short time she had been here. She felt different when she was around him, happier. *Cared for. Seen and understood.* She had tried, on Christmas Eve and since then, to really see him too. To listen, to notice his burdens, and to do anything she might to lighten them. Was that not love? The very thing she had observed in Graham and Sophie and Victoria and Jonathan? If her sisters could lead such different lives from that which was intended for them—and that which they had planned for themselves—and they could both be so utterly happy with their choices . . . *Can I not be as well?*

"I've made a decision," Elias said, breaking into her thoughts that had wandered too far, too fast—apparent by his next words. "It's about what is best for Evie, about giving her a home and surrounding her with as much love as possible. When I told Anne's parents that I would not leave her with them, they invited us to come and live with them. That way she and I can still be together, but she will be safe and taken care of when I have to be away."

"You're leaving?" The words barely squeaked out before Olivia's throat closed off, swollen with emotion that was not the giddy happiness she had anticipated. "Don't Anne's parents live far away?"

He nodded. "They're about twenty-five miles from here, on the other side of Waterloo. My practice used to be there, before I purchased the property here. It will take me a while to establish a practice there again, but doctors are always in need, and the population continues to grow."

"What about the population *here*? In Seneca Falls? What will those around here do for a doctor?" *What will* I *do?*

Olivia's head spun, and she felt like she might be sick. *Elias is leaving. Leaving!* The bright spot in her existence here wasn't just dimming—it was about to disappear completely. He was the entire reason she'd been trying so hard to learn all the things necessary to be competent here. She glanced down at her hands, still braced on either side of her, and noted her shorter nails and skin that wasn't as soft as it used to be. She worked every day now. *And for what?* For the opportunity someday to marry some farmer she didn't love?

Tears stung in her eyes and she started to blink them away, then decided that she did not care. Let Elias see that he had hurt her, that he was letting her and all of her family down.

I can't let him do this. Olivia raised her chin and looked at him. "You don't have to leave. I can watch Evie while you are away on calls. *I* will take care of her for you, and if—if you don't feel good about that—I know that Victoria and Sophie will help as well. We all love Evie." *And I could love you too, Elias.*

He shook his head. "That is a kind and generous offer, but your reputation is already in question. Having you show up at my house, all hours of the day and night—neither practical nor safe—would only confirm the rumors already going around. The Larsens, unfortunately, wasted no time spreading gossip about your visit."

Rumors. Gossip. The ugliest parts of the *ton* had followed her here. She was no stranger to those and knew the misery they could inflict, having lived through the backlash after Victoria's marriage to one not of their class. If there were now rumors spread in the village about her and Elias . . . *Little wonder he wants to leave.*

Olivia folded her arms around Evie as it hit her that not only would Elias be leaving, but Evie as well. *I will miss them both.* "When are you going?"

"Next month sometime. I've only just purchased the house in town, and I'll have to sell it now."

Olivia closed her eyes and tried to breathe. She wanted to run upstairs, slam the bedroom door, and throw herself onto the bed to cry. But she wasn't the same girl who used to do that. Not since she'd gone into hiding and there had been no one to listen to her tears or care about them, not since their journey here, since leaving her beloved London behind, not since realizing that Jonathan didn't need her.

And not now, realizing that Elias did not need her either, did not care for her as she cared for him.

How she hurt this time. Far more than at any other. *I really must love him.* And now, forevermore when she thought of him, it would be with even more empathy for his permanently broken heart.

Forty-three

SOPHIE CLIMBED BETWEEN the cool sheets and snuggled against the warmth of Graham's back. He rolled over and wrapped his arm around her, pulling her close.

"How is Ayla?"

"Sleeping again now. Poor girl. I don't think she's had such a bad nightmare since I first came to Caerlanwood. But I didn't mean to wake you too."

"It's all right." Graham sighed. "I couldn't sleep. Little wonder Ayla is troubled as well. She's not as safe here, and she knows it. I am worried."

"Tell me," Sophie said, her courage for whatever he might say bolstered by his strong arms around her. He'd grown stronger since their arrival in Seneca Falls, filling out again to his former build and more, between Maime's cooking and all the physical labor required of him here. Sophie had teased him about it just last week, even as she'd admired his muscled arms as he labored outside in rolled shirtsleeves.

"I think we have enough wood for two winters here. Do you know something about the weather that I don't? Are we going to have a monthlong, spring blizzard?"

"Chopping is—" Strike. "A good—" Strike. "Outlet." The log had splintered in two, each piece falling to either side of the block. Graham had swiped them from the ground and tossed them onto the ever-growing pile along the side of the house.

"An outlet for your many frustrations?" Sophie had finished.

They hadn't had time to speak of those frustrations because Matthew had come along then, running toward them at full speed, the rooster at his heels. Sophie had caught Matthew up in her arms while Graham waved the axe menacingly at the bird.

"I ken how to use this on a neck, ye wee beastie!"

His slip into Scottish brogue had told Sophie where his thoughts likely lay, though she'd not had the opportunity to ask him what those were. Until now.

"No one is here to interrupt us." She ran a hand along the plane of his chest, up to the scar near his shoulder, where the wound inflicted upon him last October had finally healed, thanks to Maime's ointment and knowledge.

"The children aren't safe here. There might not be slavery in New York, but there's plenty of prejudice. And too many of the other states—half of the union—is enthralled by it."

"I know," Sophie said grimly. She'd taken to buying *The New York Post* at Jonathan's store each week and reading it cover-to-cover. "I don't see how the country can continue to exist with men so opposed to one another."

"I can't see how it exists with such evil before God," Graham said. He rolled to face Sophie. His fingers brushed her cheek softly. "I meant what I said before, that *you* are my home. I can be happy wherever you are. But I fear for Ayla and Matthew here. At the least, they'll not be able to attend church or school with other children. They'll have no friends and perhaps many enemies simply by virtue of their skin color. And Maime cannot go about freely here as she did at Caerlanwood. She can make purchases at Jonathan's store, but that is to risk going into the village, where the minister and those like-minded as he live."

Sophie touched her finger to his lips. "I see all that too. You do not have to convince me to return to Scotland. But we can't, not yet."

"After our child is born." Graham's hand pressed against her growing stomach.

Sophie shook her head. "After it is safe for *you*. Together we can keep the children safe, but I need you with me. If they took you again . . ." She wrapped her arms around him and held tight, the terror of those recent times all too fresh in her mind. "Find a way to contact William. He'll know someone in England who can keep us apprised of my father's dealings and what is happening there with abolition."

"I will." Graham pressed his lips to her forehead, lingering there. "But I cannot wait to act. I need to be doing something now, something *here*, to help end this plague on mankind."

Sophie sat up and looked down at him. She recognized that tone, as well as the determination she saw shining in his eyes, even through the dark of the room. It both awed and frightened her. And reminded her of herself. "What do you have in mind?"

Graham sat up as well and took her hands in his as he faced her. "Jonathan told me that escaped slaves often come this route, on their way to Canada. They need help—places to shelter, food, warm clothing. And someone to guide them to their next place of safety. Jonathan and Victoria have helped some of them. That's why they didn't get up and follow us out of church when the minister said Maime, Ayla, and Matthew were unwelcome. Jonathan doesn't want anyone to suspect where their sympathies lie or that they might be involved in anything like that."

"They would suspect you, though, suspect *us*." Sophie

drew in a sharp breath. Graham had already nearly lost his life, fighting for abolition in England. This sounded even more dangerous. *More important. More noble.* It could make a difference to the one, which Graham had always been about. Above all else, he was a protector and longed to right the injustices of the world, especially to those unable to help themselves. How could she deny him this?

She took another breath, slower this time, drawing courage from the depth of her soul. She met his gaze. "What can I do to help?"

SHORTLY AFTER DAWN, Sophie gave up on getting any rest. Graham slumbered beside her, his heavy breathing evidence of his deep sleep.

So unfair. It was tempting to pinch him, since he'd been the cause of her restless night. But seeing the worry lines eased on his face, replaced by a peaceful expression there, stopped her. Wherever his mind was right now—at home in Scotland, she'd wager—she would let him be.

She slipped out of bed and onto the cold floor. She tiptoed across it to take her dress from the peg and to slip on her shoes. Once dressed, she walked down the hall past the room Olivia shared with their mother, when Mother was home. This week Mother was at Victoria's. She'd taken to trading off where she stayed every other week, so she could spend time with each of her girls.

Instead of rousing Olivia as she usually did, Sophie decided to let her sleep. There was no sense in both of them being up this early to start the stove and breakfast, though it was possible Olivia was already awake, as Elias would be coming by this morning, and she'd probably wish to see him. He was bringing Evie over to play with the children and be tended for the day while he made his rounds, seeing his extended circuit of patients and letting them know that he was moving.

Sophie's heart ached for Olivia, who had done her best to hide her feelings about Elias leaving, but whose heartache Sophie saw, nonetheless.

In the weeks since Christmas, Sophie had watched the awkward dance that was Olivia and Elias's developing relationship. All had been going well until the past Sunday, when he had announced that he and Evie would be going to live with his deceased wife's parents. The news had shocked all of them, but none more so than Olivia. Sophie had heard her crying that night and had stopped outside of her door, listening as their mother comforted her.

Olivia is young. She will find someone else, the one who is right for her.

Sophie descended the stairs and, yawning and bleary-eyed, entered the dark kitchen. Apparently Olivia did *not* wish to see Elias this morning. Sophie went straight to the window and parted the curtains, welcoming in the pink light of dawn. Every day felt a bit more as if winter's grip on the world was lessening. The sleigh runners had been put away until next winter now, mud had replaced the snow, and the impossibility of keeping the floors clean was vexing.

Sophie turned to the stove, eager for the heat it would provide the kitchen, but instead of opening the door to load and light it, she stared at a letter sitting squarely on top of it.

Her name was written across the front in Olivia's handwriting. She picked it up and turned it over. *No seal.* It either was not important or had been written in haste. Possibly both. Sophie unfolded the parchment, and a second note fell out, *Elias* written across the front of this one; it had been sealed. She set it aside and began to read her own letter, wondering why Olivia hadn't simply spoken with her.

Love Undying

Dear Sophie,

I've answered an advertisement for a nanny and am going to New York City to work in the household of a Mr. and Mrs. William Vancer.

As their nanny I'll be able to live in a home like that we grew up in, and it is my hope that when the Vancers discover me to be the daughter of an English baron, I shall be able to find my way into the upper society there and eventually find someone with whom to make a suitable match.

I thought, for a while, that I might be happy living a simpler life in Seneca Falls. You and Victoria showed me that is possible, and were I to be in a marriage as each of you are, with a husband who loves you deeply, I feel I could be. But there is no one here for me, and I am tired of waiting for my life to begin. As I cannot return to England, I am doing what I believe to be the next best thing. Mother disagrees. When I tried to broach the subject with her, she insisted I needed to stay with you and to give the situation more time. But there is only one man whom I believe I could love here, and he is unable to return my affections. I feel it best that I leave.

I will write to you when I am settled, and I hope you and the children will write to me as well. Please give all my love. I shall miss you and this time we've had together.

Yours,
Olivia

"Graham! Maime!" Still clutching the letter, Sophie ran from the kitchen. She charged up the stairs and into Olivia's room. She threw back the covers, revealing rolled blankets and pillows arranged to mimic the shape of a body.

Shock held her in its grasp a minute as Sophie stared at the bed that did not hold her sister. She brought a hand to her throat, fingers splayed as she cursed her own foolish example to Livie months ago.

"What is it? What is wrong?" Graham stumbled into the room, shoving an arm through his shirtsleeve as he came.

Sophie pointed to the bed. "Olivia has gone off on her own again, this time intending to make it all the way to New York City." Sophie held the letter out to him.

Graham scanned its contents as Maime entered the room. "What all this fuss be about?"

"Olivia is gone," Sophie and Graham answered at the same time.

"I'll saddle a horse and go after her," Graham said. "She can't have gone far."

Maime's hand on his arm stopped him before he could leave the room. "You sure you want to do that?" Her finger tapped the scar on his arm, a faint oval of teeth marks. "Don't you remember how you got these?"

"I had little choice then, as I do now," Graham said. "Ayla and Matthew needed to be protected, and to do that I had to take them from the island. Olivia needs protecting as well—from herself, to begin with. She won't be pleased to see me, but I doubt she'll bite."

"I wouldn't be so sure." Maime clucked her tongue. "You would not have this scar, but for your pride. Because *you* had to be the one to go in that jungle to fetch them kids, Maime offered." She pointed to herself. "But you say no. They your responsibility, and you gonna get them. But they don't know you, they don't know you gonna help them. And Ayla fight something fierce to protect her brother."

Sophie had never heard these particular details of Graham's trip to collect the children. But she didn't doubt Maime's wisdom. "What do you think we should do instead of sending Graham to find Olivia?"

Maime turned to Sophie, her eye roll and pinched expression of exasperation an indication of her feelings. "For a woman so in love with her man, how is it you don't recognize the same feelings on your sister's face?"

Olivia in love . . . Elias. The one she believed could not return her affections. "You want us to send Elias after Olivia."

"Uh-huh." Maime gave an exaggerated nod. "She listen to him, because she love him."

"But she believes he doesn't care for her," Sophie said.

"He care." Maime turned to go, waving her hands in the air as if to be done with the lot of them. "He care more than he know right now, but he'll realize. Oh yes, he will."

Forty-four

Dear Elias,

I promised to let you know of my plans, and the time has come. I am going to New York City to be a nanny for a Mr. And Mrs. William Vancer. They have two small children, a boy and a girl, and, as I have enjoyed my association with Ayla, Matthew, and Evie so much, I believe I shall be adept at this position (no chickens or cows involved).

I am also hopeful that when the Vancers discover that I am the daughter of an English baron, they will help me to integrate into New York's upper class, of which they are a part. It is as close to the life I know as I shall find in America, and I believe that my best opportunity for a good match lies this direction.

I admire you greatly, Elias. For a while I thought—well, it matters not what I thought. I know you to be the best of friends, and a good and honorable man. Your Anne was blessed to have had you as her husband, even if for only a short while.

I wish you and Evie every happiness. I will write when I am settled, and if you feel to send me a letter every now and again, I would be greatly pleased.

Yours,
Olivia

GONE—TO NEW York City? Elias's throat felt as frozen as his fingers were after the early-morning drive from town. "When did she leave?" He looked up from the letter in his hand at Graham, Sophie, and Maime, all watching him closely.

"Sometime during the night or very early this morning would be my guess," Graham said. "She was here last night, and she didn't take any of the horses, so she must have walked."

Elias swore, then apologized immediately. "I'm sorry, ladies. I did not mean—"

"Yes, you did," Maime said. "And rightly so. Fool girl, on her own out there. Does she think she gonna walk all the way to New York City?"

"No." The pit in his stomach grew deeper. "She's planning to take the stage. It's the first time in two weeks the roads have been good enough to travel. I saw it this morning on my way out of town." As he'd been leaving the livery with his team, the stagecoach driver had been there, asking the blacksmith how long it would take to reshoe a horse. *How long* does *it take? What time does the stage usually leave?*

Elias looked past the others at Evie, giggling as she held hands with Ayla and Matthew and danced in a circle in the middle of the parlor.

Anne and I danced in that spot too. Elias tensed, awaiting the inevitable pain that would wrap around him and hold him in its grip. There was always a moment of angst when he crossed the threshold of this house that had been theirs, the dread of memory lurking in every corner and one that might clamp onto him like a vise and render him helpless. He expected that now, closed his eyes and braced for it, but it didn't come. He still pictured Anne in his arms, swaying in that slow circle where the children played, but instead of bringing sorrow, the memory was almost sweet.

The swift pain that followed was different, new, hollow and throbbing in his chest. *Olivia is gone.*

"Will you go after her?" Sophie said, her hand on his arm jarring him from his lost and jumbled thoughts.

"She'll listen to you," Maime added.

Elias looked at Evie again.

Sophie's gaze followed his. "We'll take good care of her. I promise."

"If you don't want to go, I will," Graham said. "I was heading out when you arrived."

"No." Elias shook his head. "I'll go. I'll find Olivia. I did before. I can again."

ELIAS URGED HIS team faster. He felt colder now and more forlorn without Evie tucked beside him and with the wind picking up. He used his medical bag to hold the lap robe in place. His bag was heavier than usual, as he'd filled the bottom of it with the banknotes and coins his paying patients had given him over the past three months. His first stop this morning was supposed to have been Waterloo, just as soon as the bank opened for the day. Seneca Falls was still too small to have its own bank. It had been one thing to keep money at Jonathan's house, far from the village and where it was unlikely anyone might think to look for anything of value. But living in town, he didn't feel the same. It wasn't a good idea to have that much money in the house.

Not that it would be a problem for much longer, given their upcoming move. He thought of the patients he'd intended to see today and share that news with. Those visits were unlikely to happen now. Even if he caught the stage in time, he would need to bring Olivia home. *Please let me catch it in time.*

Elias snapped the reins, and his team lurched forward, heads tossed and no doubt surprised at such treatment from their usually gentle master. Panic drove him to push them more than they were accustomed to. The wheels seemed to move so much slower than the sleigh had, and he found himself wishing there was still a blanket of white covering the ground. His scarf came loose, and the wind stung his face. The two miles into town had never seemed so long before. When it finally came into view, he lifted his gaze to the far end of the street and the tavern that bordered the livery and newly opened blacksmith.

A short queue of passengers stood outside, awaiting their turn to board the vehicle parked there that would carry them east.

The tightness in his chest eased, and he said a silent prayer of thanks that the stage hadn't left yet. It had been a couple of weeks since it had made it this far, but with the rain finally easing a bit and the roads drying out, brave drivers were once again taking to the roads.

Brave drivers and *brave passengers. Foolish passengers.* Or one, at least, if she was among them. Did Olivia think it safe to travel alone? He slowed as he came into town and, as he passed the tavern, studied the faces of those in line. Olivia's wasn't one of them.

Then where— His confusion was short-lived as he glimpsed the flash of an elegant dress through the coach window. Excepting Olivia, no woman he knew of around here had clothing like that.

Elias drove his team to the livery yard, pulled them to a quick halt, grabbed his bag, and jumped down.

"I won't be going out this morning after all," he called apologetically to the groom on duty. Perhaps this afternoon, once he and Olivia had had a long talk.

"Not a problem, Doc. I'll see to your team. Have a pleasant day."

"Thank you." Elias waved a hand as he dashed toward the street.

He slowed as he approached the stage. He peered inside, confirming his suspicions. Olivia sat on the far side near the window, attempting to ignore the attentions of the man who had just seated himself next to her.

Elias weighed his options. He could ask her to stay, but what if she refused? If he insisted she get out, she would be both furious with him and humiliated, not to mention that he had no right to insist she do anything. But he couldn't just allow her to leave. It wasn't safe for a woman, especially a young, pretty, naive one like Olivia, to travel alone.

"How much?" the man ahead of him asked, slurring his words and swaying on his feet slightly. The coachman quoted him the fare, and the man dug in his pockets.

"Imabit short. Berightback." Staggering slightly, he headed into the tavern.

A male voice drifted from inside the coach. "Traveling by yourself today, darlin'? I'll be happy to act as your escort."

Elias peered in, trying to gain Olivia's attention, but she had her head turned away from him and her would-be escort.

"The stage is full now," the coachman said, moving in front of him, blocking the doorway. "Next one'll be leaving Thursday morning."

Three days from now! Olivia would be in New York City by then—if nothing happened to her before. "That looks like a seat to me," Elias said, nodding to the empty one on the other side of the man next to Olivia.

The coachman glanced toward the tavern, then back at Elias. "You got money now? We're already late getting out of here."

"How much?"

"Depends on where you're going."

"Your first stop," Elias said. He'd convince Olivia to get off there.

"That'll be Auburn. Two dollars twenty-five."

Elias counted out the money and handed it to the man, who then stepped aside so Elias could enter. He placed a foot on the step and leaned forward, peering into the coach.

Olivia was squished against the far side of the forward-facing seat, her face still turned toward the window, away from the man beside her who was still trying to engage her in conversation and was sitting far closer to her than necessary.

An instinctive surge of protectiveness took hold somewhere deep inside, and it was all Elias could do not to growl at the man. "Actually, she *isn't* traveling by herself." He stepped inside and moved toward Olivia, who turned to him with wide eyes.

"If you would be so kind as to move over, sir, so I might sit beside my fiancée."

The man's eyes narrowed as he took in Elias.

Sizing me up, no doubt. Elias ignored him, inserting himself on the seat between Olivia and the man, forcing him to scoot to the other side.

"I've made the arrangements for our bags, my dear," Elias said, smiling at her.

"Thank you." Her voice was soft and filled with awe, as if she didn't quite believe he was here, but aside from that she did nothing to reveal their ruse. Neither did she reveal any more of her mood—whether she was annoyed that he had joined her, or whether she was grateful he had saved her from unwanted attention.

Elias placed his medical bag between his feet and smiled at the three men across from him, none of whom he recognized. "Elias Henrie," he said, leaning forward and holding out his hand as the stage door closed.

"Nathaniel Barnes, and this is my partner, Sydney." The two shook Elias's hand in turn. "We've been out this way surveying for the railroad."

Some of the tension eased from Elias's body. Two men working for the railroad weren't likely to cause any trouble.

"It'll be forever before there's a line out here," the man seated beside them predicted. "James Parker." He shook Elias's hand as well but did not offer the reason for his trip.

"Nevertheless, the railroad *is* coming," Nathaniel said.

"I don't see why. Nothing out here but farms and little towns not worth much," the man who'd attempted to be cozy with Olivia said.

Elias bristled at the derogatory tone, liking him even less. But he was curious as to his purpose here. "I suppose that means you won't be bringing a new business to our village that's *not worth much*?"

"Nope. The only business worth pursuing in these parts is slave hunting." The man settled his hat low over his forehead, signaling the conversation was over.

Elias was glad, his dislike of the man having grown exponentially with his statement.

"Someday travel will be much more convenient than these crowded, bumpy coaches," Sydney said.

As if to prove his point about bumps, the coach encountered a rather large one—likely a hole in the road—almost as soon as they had set out.

Olivia's head tapped against the window, and she stiffened, bracing herself against further jostling.

"Lean against me, and try to get some sleep. You were up so early, dear." *Too early. Too alone on that long, dark road.* Elias took her hand in his own and squeezed gently. *We'll talk later.*

She surprised him by returning the gesture, then leaned

her head carefully against his side and closed her eyes, but not before he caught their sad expression and the telltale puffiness that told him she'd been crying.

Forty-five

THE HOUSES VISIBLE from the road increased in number, alerting Elias that they were almost to Auburn. He leaned his head back against the seat and inhaled slowly, trying to marshal his errant thoughts to the inevitable discussion that was soon to occur.

Olivia. The reason he was miles from home and accomplishing nothing today. She was also the reason for his current state of blissful torture. Sitting next to her this morning, their sides touching, her head on his shoulder, had opened what felt like a barrel of emotions he'd believed sealed forever. But the smell of her hair, the feeling of her gloved hand in his, the way she'd relaxed into his side had pried the lid right off, leaving him to deal with hours of inner turmoil.

How pleasant it was to sit beside her and hold her hand, to pretend that he was not alone in the world. How good it felt to know that she trusted him and cared for him—at least a little, as a friend. How right it felt to be her protector, even if there had been no real danger on this journey.

And how awful he was to feel these things for or about another woman, when Anne had been gone little more than a year. Even if it had been longer, if years had passed, it felt like a betrayal of his wedding vows, his promise to love and cherish her forever.

He still did love and cherish her. Not a day passed that he

didn't think of Anne or miss her terribly. Grief was his spouse now, that constant, hollow ache he was learning to live with. But did it have to remain his companion for the rest of his life? Had he died, and were Anne still here, he would not have wished that for her but would have wanted her to know years of joy and happiness and love.

Love her. Love them. The words of the dream in which Anne had appeared to him still haunted him. Had it been just a dream, the conjuring of his desperate and desolate mind? Or had it been something more? Had she somehow crossed the barriers between heaven and earth to tell him goodbye, and that it was all right if he moved on?

Even if she had, did he want that? Was he capable of loving another woman? He hadn't believed so—until recently. And even now, he wasn't sure. He didn't trust his judgment. How could he when the woman who'd awakened him to that possibility was only nineteen, little more than a girl herself?

Elias carefully pulled Olivia's folded letter from his pocket, held it close, and read it again.

I had thought . . .

What had she thought? That he really might court her? That they could be a good match?

Aside from their age difference of thirteen years—not unheard of in many marriages—he and Olivia came from such different backgrounds. They wanted different things from life. *Don't we?* He wasn't actually sure what Olivia wanted, but he intended to find out. If, as she had suggested in her letter, she wished to integrate herself into New York's upper class, he could do little for her. *And she will have little interest in anything I might offer.*

Might I offer? Would I be the biggest fool? She'd left, at least in part, to put herself in a better position to find a husband. Would she have done so, had he not made plans to leave first?

Elias glanced down at Olivia, sleeping beside him. How strange that he should be sitting in a coach beside her. *The lonely country doctor and the vibrant English beauty.* He was no beast, but neither was he Prince Charming. Olivia had her whole life ahead of her. She had dreams and hopes, and none of them included binding herself in matrimony to a man of limited means living in a small country hamlet.

But still, it felt good having her next to him right now. A drink for the thirsty man wandering long in the desert, a ray of light after so many months spent in darkness. But not a ray of hope, not a true quenching of his thirst. He'd had his time for those already, and it had passed. His purpose here was to see that she did not endanger *her* time of joy, which was still to come.

"WAKE UP, OLIVIA. We're in Auburn." Gentle pressure on her hand accompanied the softly spoken words.

Olivia forced her eyes open, then blinked a few times to clear them and orient herself. *The stagecoach, New York, my plans . . . Elias.*

She sat up quickly when she realized she'd been leaning against him. She hadn't intended to sleep, had only meant to close her eyes and gather her thoughts for a few minutes, but the coach wasn't very warm inside and the cold made her sleepier. Leaning against Elias had been both comforting and comfortable.

But now she felt embarrassed at such familiarity. She didn't know whether she was grateful for his presence or angry. Had he followed her? Or had he truly been planning a trip today? She doubted it, as he never wished to be parted from Evie for very long.

The three men sitting opposite them exited the coach, followed by the rather forward man who had first seated himself beside her. Elias put his bag on his lap and scooted away from her but, instead of leaving the carriage, turned back. "Are you awake now?"

Olivia nodded. "I had to rise so early this morning that I was quite exhausted. Thank you for lending me your shoulder."

"You *walked* to the village by yourself. In the dark, I assume?" Elias's brow furrowed, and his lips pressed together in a disapproving line. "I thought you realized the dangers—animals are frequently out at dawn, and you came close to losing a toe to frostbite the last time you were out in the cold."

"It wasn't snowing, and it isn't as if I have a carriage at my disposal," Olivia said, defensive at his disapproval.

"You could have asked me to drive you," Elias said, his tone pained.

"Would you have?" Her brows rose, challenging him to answer in the affirmative.

"If you wanted a ride into town, yes. If I had known you intended to board a stagecoach and travel by yourself—no." He turned away from her and climbed down from the carriage, then held his hand out. Olivia took it, but only briefly.

"Why not?" She demanded as they walked a few paces from the stage and the other passengers milling about, awaiting the coach that would carry them the next leg of their journey.

"Isn't it obvious, given the man who first took the seat beside you? It isn't safe for you to travel alone. I cannot imagine that you did so in England."

"As a matter of fact, I did." She raised her chin in challenge as they faced off. "I spent the last half of the past year traveling by myself, being shuttled in secret from place to place, always trying to stay a step ahead of my father."

"That is different," Elias said. "You weren't in a public

coach with four other men, four strangers you did not know." His voice rose, and some of the others on the platform looked their way.

Olivia held a finger to her lips. "If you insist on scolding me as if I were a child, at least have the courtesy to keep your voice down."

Elias leaned closer to her, his words quieter but no less intense. "If you wished to leave Seneca Falls, why not discuss it with your family and make a plan to see you safely to your destination?"

"I tried that," Olivia said. She walked stiffly toward the edge of the platform, attempting to put a bit of distance between them, though her legs were uncooperative after their hours of little movement. "I tried telling my mother that I needed to go somewhere else, to be someone, to *do* something—aside from watching my sisters be so happy and doing chores, which is all any of us seem to do all day, every day now."

Elias caught up to her and turned to face her once more. "What did your mother say?"

His genuine interest silenced her annoyance. *He only followed me because he cares.* "Mother said that I had not given this place—Seneca Falls—enough of a chance yet. That I needed to wait it through until at least summer. I needed to experience a different season and what other opportunities might come my way."

"I can see how that answer might be frustrating."

Olivia nodded. "It was. Especially when I had found the perfect place already, through an advertisement in the *New York Post*, with the Vancer family. The circles they move in, the parties they attend—it will all be similar to that which I am used to. Everything, from my clothing to my English rules of etiquette, will fit in better there."

"Will they?" Elias's expression grew more solemn. "Do you suppose that as their nanny you will be invited to attend the theatre or balls with them?"

"No—not at first. But when they learn who I am and where I've come from and see that—"

Elias shook his head. "That's not how the upper class works, even in New York City. You, of all people, should realize this. If you arrive as a nanny, you will remain a nanny. There will be no social climbing, no fairy tale where they discover that the girl dressed in simple clothing is really a princess."

"I'm not traveling in simple clothing, as you can see." She indicated her purple skirt with its ruffles and frills.

"And how do you think the staff below stairs is going to look at you and accept you if you turn up wearing a gown like that?" He shook his head. "They won't. They'll shun you and say that you're putting on airs and thinking you're better than they." Elias set his bag down, removed his hat, and ran a hand through his hair. He pivoted away from her, pacing a few steps before turning back. "If you truly wish to be a nanny in New York—fine. I'll see you safely there. But only if you understand how it will really be for you. You will be *a nanny*. A position only slightly elevated above a household servant. You won't take meals with the family or be invited to their parties. You won't enjoy any of the privileges that they do as members of the upper class and likely will be restricted to certain rooms of the house, most of which are below stairs. The probability of that ever changing is so miniscule that I would hate to see you pin your hopes on it. If you feel you're out of place now, I fear that will only multiply in a household where you are surrounded by the opulence you're accustomed to but can enjoy none of it. Is that truly what you wish?" Hat clutched in his hand, Elias held her gaze, awaiting her answer.

Olivia fought a rush of tears. She had thought about these

very things, the possibility that she was making a mistake and that nothing would ever turn out as she had dreamed. But this was her best opportunity. Her only chance to try to connect with a world here that was similar to what she had known. Her only chance to find someone who could make her happy, who would love and understand her. If she remained in Seneca Falls, the best she could hope for was a home and a life like Victoria's. *But without the love Victoria has that makes it all worth it.*

Elias would have made it all worth it.

"I know I'm taking a risk," she said, her voice shaky and her throat thick with sorrow. "It may be that after a few months I return, having failed at my goal. But if I don't try I'll never know." She placed her hand gently over Elias's. "If I stay in Seneca Falls now, I'm guaranteed to never have what I want."

"What *do* you want, Olivia?" Elias asked, his voice gruff, his expression pained, as if her words had hurt him.

Olivia gathered her cloak tighter around her against the chill. "I want to stop waiting for my life to begin. It feels like I've been doing that my *entire* life. As a little girl, I was forever waiting to be old enough to join Victoria and Sophie. They had dancing lessons while I sat on the side of the ballroom. They were performing at musicales while I was still stuck practicing scales. They took horseback riding lessons while I watched from the window. I was always too young for their adventures. But Mother promised me that I would grow up, and all would be equal. I would have my turn at every wonderful and lovely experience.

"Then Sophie and I had to postpone our Seasons. Father said that it was necessary to put time between our coming out and the scandal of Victoria's marriage. Sophie didn't care at all that our Seasons were postponed. She would have been just as happy never to have one. But *I* minded. She finally had hers, a year late. Then last year it was my turn—only to have it cut short when she fled to Scotland with Graham and I had to go into hiding so as not to be matched with a horrid man to further my father's business dealings. I spent five months being quiet and alone and lonely.

"Then I came here to keep a promise, only to find out I wasn't needed. And now I'm just drifting—no purpose, no prospects." She turned away so he wouldn't see her angry tears.

"For what?" he urged. "Do you want to marry someone wealthy? So you can have a houseful of servants and a life of parties and balls?"

She shook her head. "No. But if I did would that be so terrible? That is what I grew up expecting, what I was led to believe was my future." Why were they arguing over this? *Were* they arguing? Why did he even care what she wanted?

Olivia took a deep breath and tried to rein her thoughts into something explainable. "I want to feel as if I *am* living, and not waiting for my life to begin. I do want to marry—someone who loves me. In my mind that love has always involved ballrooms and fancy gowns, bouquets of flowers and drives in the park. I wanted it all—but mostly someone who truly cared for me, faults and all. A knight in shining armor who would ride up on a white horse and sweep me off my feet and carry me away to his castle."

"Coach to Ithaca!" a voice called, jarring them both.

Elias shook his head. "I don't think you're going to find that in New York City. You might live in a house that feels like a castle, but as a member of the staff the only men you'll be eligible to marry are those who clean up after the horses, not those who ride them."

The tears that had been hovering in her eyes fell in earnest now. "Thank you for that eloquent vote of confidence. My coach is here. If you'll excuse me."

He grabbed her arm before she could turn away. "You're *still* going?"

She nodded. "I am. It promises to be an adventure, at least." With her free hand, she brushed away her tears.

"Not a pleasant one," Elias muttered. He released her arm but followed her toward the stage. When they reached the coach, Olivia produced her ticket, then climbed aboard.

"How much for the fare to Ithaca?" Elias asked behind her.

"Stage is full," the man who'd checked her ticket said. He shut the door of the coach, then slapped the side as Olivia took her seat—the last.

A flare of panic and a beat of triumph struck her heart simultaneously. *I am on my own.* She looked out the window as they began rolling forward.

Time slowed as Elias's gaze met hers, his shock and dismay apparent in his shimmering eyes. His face had gone pale, and he took a step toward the moving coach, his hand outstretched.

"Olivia."

Forty-six

NIGHT HAD FALLEN by the time they reached Ithaca. The road had been slightly better on this leg of their journey, though the ride was far less pleasant than she'd had this morning.

Sitting near the door she'd felt a constant draft coming in through the crevice between wall and door, and she felt frozen through, in spite of staying wrapped tight in her cloak throughout the entire journey.

That hadn't been the worst part, however. The passenger across from her—not beside her, thankfully—smelled as if he hadn't bathed in months. The tears in her eyes when she'd boarded had quickly turned to a burning in her eyes and nose as she'd fought the awful stench.

I probably smell now too.

She was to overnight here, though there had been a coach that traveled through the night which she might have taken. When planning her route, she had decided that it would not be safe for her to be traveling in a coach at night, assuming America had highwaymen as England did. Despite what Elias thought, she had been careful and prudent in planning.

As soon as the stage stopped and the door was opened, Olivia was out of her seat, fearing the man across from her would try to exit first and she would be subjected to his stench even closer to her person.

She stepped out onto the street and away from the coach, then took a minute to get her bearings. The men filing out behind her all headed toward a building across the street. Olivia waited for her bag to be taken down, then started after them and was relieved a few minutes later when the sign for the Green Tree Tavern became visible.

Until she had crossed the ocean to America, she had never stayed in a tavern before—never imagined that she would. But Sophie and Graham had seemed most comfortable with the idea, and they had all stayed in several taverns on their way from New York City to Seneca Falls—this very one included.

She knew exactly what to do. Pay, order dinner to be delivered, and go straight to her room and lock the door. Graham had taught her how to wedge a chair beneath the knob as well, as an added precaution against unwanted visitors.

Olivia hurried her steps to keep pace with the others who had also been in her coach. The man ahead of her held the door to the inn open, and she thanked him as she entered.

The warm air inside enveloped her, and her mood improved at once. She smiled as she waited her turn to request a room and added another item to her list. *Water for a bath.* She shifted her heavy bag from one arm to the other. Bringing her trunk hadn't been practical, so she'd stuffed as many clothes as she could into the satchel that had held the whole of Sophie's possessions on their voyage over. *I'll send for my trunk later. After I am settled.*

Her conversation with Elias trailed through her mind, as it had during the long drive all afternoon, though she'd continuously tried putting it out of her thoughts. What if he was right and the other staff didn't like her, and the Vancers did not care that she was the daughter of a baron? What if their children were horrible, and not sweet and amusing as Evie,

Matthew, and Ayla? *What if I have made the most dreadful mistake?*

She was over fifty miles from home now and—

Home? She was *hundreds* of miles from home. *Thousands.* Sophie had told her the distance was well over three thousand miles from London to New York.

Seneca Falls is not my home. But it had started to feel like it, odd though it was to live in a farmhouse and share a room with her mother. To begin each day in the kitchen starting a fire and making bread. *Is Maime angry with me because she had to do it today, in addition to all of her other tasks?*

It was also odd to have the social event of her week be Sunday dinner at her sister's house, where they all couldn't fit around the table and had to take turns eating.

It was enjoyable, though. In a way she'd never imagined before. *Pleasant.* Especially the time spent with Elias, sitting at the table discussing everything and nothing. Laughing together like the oldest of friends.

We are the oddest *of friends.* The country doctor and the lady fresh from England. That they'd found anything in common was a wonder. *But we did. Elias is a good friend.* Or he had been. Likely, he was furious with her now. She prayed he had been able to catch a stagecoach back to Seneca Falls. He wouldn't want to be away from Evie overnight.

"I'm sorry," Olivia whispered, wishing she could tell him in person. She would write a letter tonight, and another again when she reached New York City, letting him know that she was safe and apologizing for anything she had said and done to hurt him. He had hurt her, too, but not intentionally. Moving to Anne's parents' home had been about what was best for Evie, and he was the best sort of father to put her first. *He would have been the best sort of husband too.*

If his heart hadn't still been broken, his love for Anne all-encompassing.

The man in front of Olivia turned abruptly, a scowl on his face. "They're full up." He stalked past her and out the door into the cold night.

Olivia stepped up to the counter, but before she could speak the man on the other side shook his head and apologized.

"I'm sorry, miss. We've no rooms left tonight."

"None?" The dismay in her voice shook her as much as his words had. There was no one here to solve this problem for her, no Graham or Sophie to rely on. What was she to do? Where was she to go?

"Are there other inns nearby?" she heard herself ask and was grateful for whatever part of her mind had resisted full panic and thought of that.

The clerk studied her. "None I'd recommend for you, but you might try the Clinton House. It's a piece away. You'll need to hire a ride. And a room there will cost you a pretty penny, but you look like you can afford it, and you'll be safe."

"The Clinton. Thank you." Olivia nodded, then turned from the counter and retraced her steps in a haze of despair and fear. *Clinton House.* She need only find it, and all would be well. The added cost of more upscale lodging did not bother her. She had all of the money she'd brought with her to America plus what she had earned working at the store the past few months.

Outside, the cold seemed even worse than before, seeping through her cloak as if she wasn't even wearing one. Staying close to the building, she peered up and down the street, searching for any vehicle that looked like it might be a public conveyance. From Sophie she had learned to be certain, before she entered one, that it actually was for hire.

I doubt I would be so fortunate as to find a kind and handsome duke in mine.

Not seeing anything promising to the left, Olivia shifted her gaze to the right and saw not a coach but a rider on horseback approaching swiftly. She pressed back against the tavern, the cold stone biting into her back as horse and rider headed straight toward her. At the last possible second, the rider pulled back, reining the animal to a halt in front of her.

"Olivia!"

Her eyes widened as she looked up. "*Elias?*" Tears of relief sprang to her eyes as she took in the sight of him seated atop a tall, magnificent horse. He swung his leg over to her side and dismounted, and it was all she could do not to run into his arms.

"You're *here*." There was no mistaking the relief in her voice, but she didn't care. He'd come after her; he had *followed* her. Through some miracle, some fate, some heroic action of his, he was here in front of her, and she wasn't alone, and she never wanted to be again.

What an utter fool she'd been. Instead of running away to New York City, she ought to have stayed and fought for him, ought to have told him outright how she felt and that she wanted him to stay. He was right. A nanny *wasn't* the position she wanted.

In two strides he was in front of her and then pulling her into his arms. He held her close, her cheek pressed to the heart she could hear thundering beneath his coat.

"Thank goodness you're all right." He held her away from him. "You are, aren't you?"

She nodded and smiled through the tears that were already falling. *Why do I always have to cry in front of him?* "Much better now that you're here."

"Why are you outside? Did someone in there try to—"

She shook her head. "I was inside, but there are no more rooms to let. I came out to see if I could find a conveyance to take me to the Clinton House. It is supposed to be a reputable place to stay—or so the tavern keeper led me to believe."

"It's more than reputable." Elias stepped back and grasped the reins of the horse that had been obediently waiting behind him.

Olivia looked closer at the animal and then Elias and realized for the first time that they both were breathing heavily and the horse's coat beaded with sweat and foam. Elias's hair stood up wildly, and his hat was nowhere to be seen, though his medical bag had been secured behind the saddle.

"You *rode* here—all the way from Auburn?" They'd covered over thirty miles since then. It had taken all afternoon, and if the inside of the coach had been bitter cold, she could not imagine what it had been like out in the wind on horseback.

"There wasn't any other way to get here, and you were alone."

A sob burst from her throat, and she threw herself into his arms again. "I'm so sorry. So very, very sorry."

He held her, his hands comforting as they moved up and down her back. "It's all right. You're safe now. All is well."

She pulled back and looked up at him. "It isn't, though. You aren't home with Evie."

"With Matthew and Ayla there to entertain her, she probably doesn't even notice that I'm gone." His attempt to sound as if the distance between himself and his daughter was not of concern didn't quite work.

Olivia brushed the tears from her eyes and smiled at him. "I can't believe you came all this way for me. That you *rode* all this way in the cold."

"It was not only for you," Elias said.

Olivia furrowed her brow as she looked up at him. "Did Sophie ask you to come?"

"No—I mean yes, but that's not why I did." As if he'd read the change in her demeanor, he took her arm, steering them both closer to the horse and the street, but out of the way of anyone passing by on the sidewalk. "I came because I was worried about you—I stand by my opinion that it isn't safe for a woman to travel alone—and I came for *me*. Because the thought of not seeing you anymore wasn't one I wanted to live with. Because I'm half in love with you, Olivia, and I had to see if there was any way you might feel the same."

Forty-seven

OLIVIA SUCKED IN a breath, then brought a hand to her mouth as more tears slid down her face. She shed so many of them, Elias could never quite tell what they meant. If they were tears of regret—because he had followed her—or tears of pity or even anger, then he was about to make an even bigger fool of himself. But he'd started down this path, had purchased a horse and ridden over thirty miles today, so there was no sense stopping now.

"While I rode I had a lot of time to think about what you said earlier—about what you want," he clarified. "And about what I want. At first glance those things seem kind of opposite, but when I dug a little deeper, that isn't what I found at all."

Olivia shivered, and belatedly Elias realized this probably wasn't the best place to spill his heart. *If her toes freeze again—*

"Come on. There's a livery down the street." He held out his arm.

Her lips turned down, and her nose scrunched as well. A look he found particularly adorable.

"I need to take care of Fairfax. He served me well today."

"*Fairfax*? You dug deeper and realized you needed to *care for your horse*?"

He smiled at the way her mouth twisted in a disparaging expression. She'd perfected the art of giving a look of disdain;

it would have served her well as a member of the English aristocracy. It was unfortunate she'd likely never get to use it there. As she had noted before, it probably would not be safe for her to return for many years. Years he didn't want her to waste. Years he wanted her to be happy and not waiting for life to begin, not scraping and scrambling up through Society hoping that something good would happen when she arrived there.

"No. That's not what I found or meant. But I realized you're freezing, and my horse is exhausted and needs to be cared for. I'll explain more when we're somewhere warm."

Somewhere warm took longer than he had intended by the time he'd arranged for his newly acquired horse to be boarded and had paid for extra oats and grooming. He gave Fairfax a pat of appreciation after approving of the stall where he was to stay the night. "Thank you, my friend."

Elias turned to find Olivia seated on a bale of hay and watching him closely. It was another of those incongruous moments, with her fine skirts spread all around her over the hay and a stable as her backdrop. *A lady displaced* came to his mind again.

Help me find her place. And mine.

He was starting to doubt the wisdom of the many thoughts he'd had on his way here, but he'd already told Olivia at least a few of them, and he owed it to her, to himself, and even to the horse who'd worked so hard to get him here, to tell her the rest of it.

Elias looked up and down the row of stalls and saw that they were alone. The only noise came from Fairfax, happily munching his supper.

Elias pulled up another bale of hay and sat opposite Olivia. "Are you warmer now?"

She nodded.

"Good." He rubbed his palms across the top of his trousers, looked at her, and began.

"When you told me all those things today, about not being included in dance lessons and having your Season delayed, and having to hide from your own father, it seemed to me that the common thread in all of that was that not only were you left out or left behind, but you were left feeling unloved."

Olivia's eyes glistened, but she didn't say anything.

Elias took a deep breath and continued. "I think your mother and sisters do love you—quite a lot. But circumstances being what they are now, I can see how you feel left out again. I can also see how going to the city, being surrounded by people who are living a lifestyle similar to what you came from, is appealing. And where you believed you might have the best chance of meeting someone, a knight in shining armor to ride up on his white horse and sweep you off your feet.

"You might find that," he conceded. "But I don't want you to."

Olivia gave a tiny gasp and opened her mouth, but Elias continued before she could berate him.

"I don't want you to find your knight in New York City because *I* want to be him." He leaned forward and took her hands in his. "I did find a white horse for sale in Auburn, but I could see that it wasn't going to get me where I needed to go. It was pretty, a fine show horse, but it lacked the stamina and strength to carry me all the way to Ithaca. That spotted one"— he inclined his head toward Fairfax's stall—"*was* strong enough, though. Not a thoroughbred but a purebred mixed with a wild pony. Not as pretty, maybe, not as fancy, but he's in it for the long haul. I knew I would be buying a horse that had both strength and endurance to get me here."

She tilted her head. "Are you comparing me to a horse?"

"No!" Elias brought a hand to his forehead and rubbed it briefly. He was worse at this than he'd thought. Anne had been a farm girl who didn't require fancy words or a lot of sentiment. But Olivia needed at least that, if he couldn't give her all the other things.

"*I'm* the horse. I have spots too. I'm a widower. I've loved a woman before, and part of me will always love her."

The tears shining in Olivia's eyes seemed to brighten.

"I have Evie—she's not a spot, but nevertheless I need someone who will love her and care for her as much as I do. I'm older, thirty-two to your nineteen. I'm a country doctor. I do well enough, but I'll never be wealthy. You'll probably never live in a castle or a mansion if you marry me. There won't be fancy balls or trips to the theatre—at least until we get one closer to Seneca Falls—but there would be love and laughter. Joy. Compassion. Friendship. I don't care for milking cows or collecting eggs either. I wouldn't ask you to do that. But life in Seneca Falls, in upstate New York, is still life as you've seen it. A lot of the time it would be hard. I would do my best so that as much of the time as possible, it is good too. I think we could be good together. Good for each other. We *have been* good for each other, since that first day we met." He squeezed her hands.

"I think I agreed to move to Anne's parents' home because that was safe. I wouldn't have to face and conquer the guilt I felt at caring for you—guilt because of Anne and guilt because I felt you deserved so much more. If I left, I didn't have to risk finding out that you did not feel the same about me."

Olivia nodded then swallowed, as if she were holding back a sob.

A good sign? Bad? He didn't know but plunged on. "Something has happened to me since the day we met, Olivia. My heart was as cold as your feet that day, hard and frozen, barely functioning. Then you started to thaw it. You made it remember how to beat, how to feel, how to love. When I watched that coach leave today with you in it, my heart broke again. I didn't realize it still could—that you had repaired it enough that it could hurt so much at your loss. It took less than a minute for me to decide I didn't want to live with that pain. I didn't want to lose you. That I was going to fight for you, to offer everything I had to give, my imperfections, my spotted horse, my all." Which didn't feel like much right now, not in comparison to her dreams. *Proposed to in a barn, with no ring or romance.* He wasn't even down on one knee.

"Kiss me, Elias." She held his gaze as she spoke the words, almost as if it was some sort of dare.

Kiss me? He'd just handed her his heart, and that was all she could say? The gap of their ages stretched between them once again. She was laughter; he was solemnity. But right now he wanted her to be serious too. He *needed* her to be. "I've just bared my soul to you, and you ask for a kiss?"

A light danced in her eyes, but it was neither teasing nor amused. "It's relevant. I promise." She continued to look at him expectantly.

Elias swallowed uneasily as discomfort began to creep up his neck. "Have you been kissed before?"

She nodded. "Once. It was stolen, though, so it hardly counts. *You* have my whole-hearted consent."

"Good. Though I should not like our first kiss to be in a barn."

"Why not? You've just proposed marriage to me in one."

Elias winced and glanced around at the stall doors, the dirt floor, the rough beams of the walls and roof surrounding them. "Perhaps I ought to have waited. But I have had the day to ponder my feelings, and I did not think I could hold them in any longer. I also feared that unless, or until, I spoke them there was a very real danger that you might disappear again."

Love UNDYING

Her expression softened. "I am not going anywhere. Not after the most beautiful declaration of love I have ever heard. All I am requesting is that you confirm your words with a kiss."

Sweat broke out on Elias's forehead. Maybe he ought to have spent some of his time today thinking about how he would go about kissing Olivia for the first time. *And the second and the third.* And all else that came with marriage. Physical intimacy had never been a problem for him before, but the greatest of pleasures. So why was the idea of it sending him into a panic now? "I have not kissed a woman in over a year. And I have never kissed another besides Anne."

Olivia nodded. "I know. That is why I am asking it of you. It will help me to believe your profession of feelings towards me. I believe that you mean the words you have spoken, but I also fear that you are not ready to marry again and perhaps may never be. This morning, as I boarded the stage that was to take me away from Seneca Falls and my family, *you* were the person I thought of missing. Your friendship has meant so much to me, Elias. You have been my lifeline here since you stopped for me and helped me into your sleigh. You saved my life and feet that day, and you saved me from despair and humiliation when I learned that the circumstances were not as I had believed and that my purpose in coming was no longer valid. In the short span of those three days we first spent together, you healed my hand and feet and my troubled heart concerning Jonathan and Victoria. You taught me how to do things so I could begin to physically survive, and you made me smile and even laugh. You gave me a reason to be here—to continue our friendship.

"This morning when I boarded that coach, I began crying, and while some of the tears were for my family, *most* were because I believed *you* had chosen to leave because you would never be able to move on from your beloved Anne.

"If what you have told me now is true, then I was wrong and I am happy for it. I will not pretend that it will be easy sharing you with her memory. You loved her first, you will always love her, and I can accept that. But I also want proof that you can love me as well—in every way. Not just as the friends that we have become, though I cherish that friendship, but as a husband loves his wife. And so I ask you to kiss me now, to show me that you are ready and there is enough room in that good heart of yours for me as your wife."

"I was wrong," Elias said. Then, seeing the shock on Olivia's face, he hurried to clarify. "The difference in our ages does not matter. For all your impulsiveness, you are wise beyond your years." He leaned near to her. "I can love you, Olivia. I *do*." He lifted his hands to cup her face. His thumb brushed the latest of her tears away. He angled his head and closed his eyes as his lips met hers. A soft kiss, slight . . . brief. *Sweet.*

He pulled back, lowered his hands, and looked at her as she opened her eyes.

"Again," she said pertly. "And longer this time, please."

Elias grinned. "That is how our marriage is to be, is it—you making demands upon me?"

Olivia returned his smile, her eyes sparkling, but no longer with tears. "I have not agreed to be your wife yet. You had best try that kiss again. I have seen my sisters and their husbands kiss, and it seems a great deal more complex and intimate than what I have just experienced. I am prepared to give up living in a fancy house and attending the theatre, but my standards remain high as to the quality of the kisses my husband will provide."

Elias's grin turned to a brief bark of laughter then clearing of his throat before he pressed his lips together and attempted to regain his serious composure. "Well then."

He stood and pulled her up to face him. He leaned close once more and brushed his lips lightly across her forehead, then her earlobe, her cheek, just to the side of her mouth.

Olivia's eyes had closed again, and he noted her quick intake of breath with every touch of his mouth. He wrapped his arms around her and pulled her even closer. He kissed her once more, as softly as before, but lingering this time, exploring the entirety of her sweet, soft lips. When she sighed, he deepened their kiss and the intensity of it, calling upon her to respond, to show him that he was loved as well.

Olivia took his cue. Her hands slid up the front of his shirt, over his shoulders and behind his neck. Elias groaned, as her fingers threaded through his hair. Still their kiss continued, their breathing labored, their searching and yearning and connection somewhat frantic. It seemed that, at only nineteen, Olivia was as starved as he for both love and affection.

At last they broke apart, their foreheads touching, eyes still closed—or his were, anyway—as he soaked in the miracle of the moment, of this wonderful and willing woman in his arms.

"Better?" he asked. It had been perfect for him. So perfect that he longed for a repeat.

"Yes." Olivia's breathing was still unsteady, and she swayed into him, as if she felt a bit faint. "Yes, I will marry you, and I expect to be kissed like that every day for the rest of my life."

"A bargain then." Euphoria enveloped him. Relief as well. He hadn't lost Olivia, and he hadn't lost himself, his soul, in loving her. Instead, it felt as if the final piece of his broken heart had been reattached, and now it beat stronger than ever. *Love her. Love them.*

I am. And the world was beautiful because of it.

Forty-eight

"HAD MY MOTHER known of this place, we would not have stayed at the tavern in town." Olivia's gaze was appreciative as she took in the Italian tile floor, the marble pillars, and the sparkling chandeliers.

"It has only been open for a short while," Elias informed her. "It is said to be the finest hotel between New York City and Buffalo."

"It is divine." Olivia's sigh was one of contentment that he had heard only recently—when they had kissed. *Truly kissed.* There would have to be much kissing to try to make up for all that she was giving up by marrying him. A challenge he felt more than up to. In the last half hour, the heaviness he'd been carrying for so long had seemed to dissipate. He felt young again. *Happy.* Filled with hope. *We are engaged to be married.*

He'd given her no ring—perhaps they would shop for one tomorrow. But their promises had been solemn, their professions of love real and binding. Standing in the lobby of the Clinton House, holding Olivia's hand, he felt as he had years ago, when entering medical school and standing on the precipice, looking out at all that was to be his life. It had felt so promising then and seemed even more so now. Love had made it so.

Olivia insisted upon paying for her own room, and he was

grateful. The stage wouldn't pass through town again for two days, and staying at the Clinton House that long—at all—was yet another extravagance he hadn't planned for. After purchasing Fairfax and now his own room, his funds were considerably lower than they had been this morning, and they still needed to eat for the next two days and purchase the fare back to Seneca Falls.

Elias pushed that worry and his concerns about Evie from his mind. All would work out.

After registering, Elias reached for Olivia's hand and took it in his again. She looked over with a surprised smile, as if this was all a little unbelievable to her too.

Mine. She can be mine. He'd no doubt his answering grin was that of a fool. *A fool in love.*

He led her up the sweeping stairs to their rooms, side by side. Elias unlocked her door for her and held it open. "Can you be ready for supper in about an hour?"

Olivia nodded.

"I'll knock on your door then," he said. When it had closed he went into his own room and barely resisted the idea of collapsing onto the bed and sleeping until tomorrow. He was exhausted. And still chilled from his ride. In the lobby he had requested that baths be brought up for them both, and he intended to send his suit down to see what could be done about it. At the least he needed to get the smell of horse off it.

And then, once all was in order with his appearance, he would lead Olivia down to dinner, over which they would discuss the details of their engagement and upcoming life together. But first, while he awaited the water for his bath, he would record his thoughts as he'd done almost all other days for the past year. Today, that seemed especially important. He withdrew a sheaf of paper from his bag.

Dear Anne,

It has been the strangest of days, and I regret to say that they have taken me far from home and Evie. But I have left her in good hands, with those that will soon be her family—aunt, uncle, and cousins—as I am to marry again.

It seems so odd to write that to you. I imagine you as I saw you last in my dream, telling me to love Evie, and then to love <u>them</u>. For many months your words troubled me, but I realize now that they were a gift, not only releasing me from a lifetime of loneliness, but encouraging me to leave it, and you, behind. I shall always love you, Anne. A part of me will always belong to you. But I have found that I have more love to give, and I crave it in return. Thank you for teaching me how to love, how to give of myself, how to be a husband and a father, and how to let go.

With undying gratitude and love,
Elias

ONLY THE THOUGHT of Elias's expression as he'd leaned in to kiss her could pry Olivia from the luxury of the warm bath. The scent of roses wafting around her, she finally stood and wrapped herself in a large, fluffy towel.

She felt both exhausted and exhilarated. It had been such a terribly long day. But she was in the most elegant building she had been in since leaving London, and Elias was here with her. *He followed me. He bought a horse and rode all day in the cold to ask me to marry him.* It wasn't exactly as she had imagined. Fairfax wasn't white, and Elias hadn't swept her into his arms and galloped off to his castle. But he had come to her rescue in her moment of despair, and the Clinton House was a pretty good substitute for a castle.

Olivia flopped back onto the comfortable bed, appreciating the soft mattress and the feather tick beneath her.

A knock sounded at her door. "Room service, Miss Claybourne. We have your dress."

Olivia donned her wrap, then stepped behind the door and opened it. A maid came in carrying the second nicest of the three dresses that Olivia had brought with her, freshly pressed and draped over her arm.

"Do you require assistance with your gown or with styling your hair?"

"Yes, please. To both," Olivia said. She hadn't enjoyed the luxury of a maid to help her with anything since they'd left England. She and Sophie and Mother all helped each other—or Sophie and Mother helped her, at least—with her gowns that were more difficult to get into and out of. But tonight, the night of her engagement, she wanted to look especially beautiful.

Thirty minutes later, Olivia opened her door to another knock. Elias stood in the hall, his expression uncertain, as if he hadn't really been assured of her opening the door for him.

He stared at her, really looked at her, much as he had out in the cold on Christmas Eve, when he had first told her she was beautiful. She'd treasured those words and carried them around in her heart the past weeks.

At the few balls she had attended before the abrupt end to her Season, other men had complimented her, but never had it held the meaning it did when those words came from Elias.

He is the beautiful one, in body and soul. He stood before her now, his suit pressed, and his brown hair combed perfectly, all except the unruly swoop in front that made him appear youthful. His eyes shone, bright with kindness and the love she now recognized. The corners of his mouth lifted in an easy smile.

"I'm not sure I want to take you downstairs. Every man in the building is going to have his eye on you in that gown."

Olivia blushed beneath such open praise. She pressed a hand to the bodice of the peach silk gown. "I'll only have eyes for one." She placed a hand on his arm, and they left the hall and descended the stairs to the dining room below.

It wasn't terribly crowded, being a Monday evening and later than usual for the supper hour. They ordered what promised to be the most sumptuous meal she'd had in months, then waited at the little table, staring at one another across the candlelit space.

"What are you thinking?" Olivia asked after a minute had passed in silence.

"I am wondering what both of your brothers-in-law are going to say when they find out that we are betrothed. I fear they, and your mother, may be less than pleased when they learn that we were alone together like this and are now engaged to be married. It may appear rather—suspicious." Elias lifted his glass and took a drink of the wine the waiter had brought a few minutes earlier.

"They won't be able to say *anything* if we are already married."

Elias choked on his drink and set his glass down quickly to retrieve his napkin.

"Are you all right?" Olivia asked innocently, or attempting innocence, at least. Perhaps she ought to have considered a less direct way to present that option.

"We *aren't* already married," Elias spluttered. He took another drink, presumably to clear the one that had gone down wrong.

"But we could be," Olivia suggested. "By this time tomorrow. We have to wait for the stagecoach until Wednesday anyway, which gives us the whole of the day tomorrow to marry."

"That would be taking your impetuousness to a new level." Elias shook his head. "Think of your mother and sisters. They will want to be with you to witness your wedding day. And a hasty wedding is not in alignment with the dreams you shared with me earlier. I imagine you have dreamed of a church with bells pealing, flowers in abundance, a lovely dress, and a gold ring. We have none of that here."

"We have each other," Olivia said simply, the words sinking deep into her soul. Nothing in America was as she had dreamed of for herself. But Elias loved her, and she loved him, and that mattered more than anything else ever had.

He reached across the table and took her hand in his. "I fear you would hate me later for it, that you would resent being cheated of your most special day, in standing before God and your family, speaking those sacred vows and then celebrating with those you love."

"How am I to stand before God in Seneca Falls? We cannot marry in the church that does not welcome half of my family—or likely all of it now, given the dressing down I gave the minister. Mother and Sophie and Victoria will understand. Victoria once threatened to elope with Jonathan. And Sophie practically did elope, running off with Graham to Scotland. Mother wants my happiness and will be relieved that I am committing to stay in Seneca Falls. If we marry now, you won't need to worry about someone to care for Evie when you are away seeing patients. I'll be there to care for her, and to care for you—so long as you can exist on bread alone." She grimaced. "I admit to having many things to learn still, but I would rather learn them *with you* than anyone else. Besides, if we base our wedding date on the suitability of my cooking skills, we may never marry."

Elias withdrew his hand and inhaled deeply, his expression still troubled, in spite of her sensible persuasions. She had spent the last hour pondering the possibility of returning to Seneca Falls already married. It *would* mean giving up more of her dreams, but many of those seemed shallow now, whereas the thought of being Elias's wife filled her with purpose and a renewed enthusiasm for life. The happily-ever-afters of her childhood imagination had changed, mellowed into the more realistic, and the more fulfilling. *More lasting and meaningful.* To love and to be loved by Elias . . . It made up for anything and everything she had lost or given up.

The waiter brought their food and refilled their glasses. Olivia sipped and ate, enjoying every bite of the delicious meal, from the warm, crusty bread, to the veal and vegetables, as she waited for Elias to say something. She had spent an hour thinking about the ramifications of marrying tomorrow; it was only fair that she allow him the same.

At last he spoke. "I had thought we might marry in June. As I mentioned on Christmas Eve, of necessity, courtships are often short where we live. Though, generally, not *this* short."

Olivia smiled. "It may be that the gossips will say that, intelligent man that you are, you snatched me up before any other could."

"Or they may whisper that you set your cap for me, from the moment of your arrival in Seneca Falls."

"Perhaps I did. What else was I to do, once you had both viewed and touched my feet?"

He laughed.

"To our cleverness in finding each other." She raised her glass.

Elias clinked his against it, then drained the contents. "It matters not to me what others will or will not say. Our characters will speak for themselves over time. I only worry about your regrets later. I do not want you to feel as if I've cheated you out of your special day or anything else."

"I appreciate that." Olivia leaned toward him. "I anticipate many special days in our future that will more than make up for those I had imagined. I *am* impulsive—call it fault or genius—but I do think about my actions. I just think about them more quickly than most. I have thought about little else since you professed your feelings to me this evening—and even before that. The night you told me you were to leave us, I had thought . . . that you were about to ask me to be your wife."

Surprise flickered again in Elias's eyes. "Had I, what would you have said?"

"*Yes*, of course." Olivia reached across the table and took his hands in hers. "Assuming you would have sealed your offer with a kiss." Her voice softened. "A hundred times yes. *I* fell half in love with you during the first three days of our acquaintance. It happened sometime between your gallant rescue and when you made me hot chocolate and then taught me to make bread. The morning you followed me out of church in a show of solidarity, I realized what a truly remarkable man you are and knew that, if you ever did decide to marry again, I wished to be the woman you chose. Though we were pretending courtship, I wished that it were real. As our feelings for each other are the same, I see no reason to delay our marriage."

"So logical," Elias mused. "All this practicality seems incongruous with the puffed sleeves of your gown and all the ribbon and embellishments adorning it. I pegged you for a romantic, Miss Claybourne, and now you tell me otherwise."

"Oh, I am a romantic," Olivia insisted, looking up at him through her lashes and giving him her most coquettish smile. "Marry me tomorrow, and I'll prove it."

Forty-nine

ELIAS SLID A note beneath Olivia's door and left the hotel early. He went to collect Fairfax, showing him additional appreciation this morning in the form of an apple he'd bought on the way to the livery. "Tomorrow we shall have another long ride, though it will not have to be accomplished so quickly."

The horse tossed his head as if acknowledging Elias's words. Elias almost regretted that he would be returning the magnificent animal tomorrow. He had paid the full amount for him—not knowing when or where he might catch up with Olivia and how long it might be before he returned the animal—and could keep him if he wished, but his agreement had also been that he might return the horse when traveling through Auburn again, and receive a good portion of his money back. As he had no room to house an additional horse—he already paid the livery in Seneca Falls handsomely to board his team—it did not make sense to keep the animal.

He paid the stablemaster for an additional day of boarding here and told him he would return with Fairfax in a few hours. Once mounted, Elias headed for the corner of Seneca and Geneva streets, and the Dutch Reformed Church that had opened its doors last year. Pastor Alexander Mason was a distant cousin—one Elias had never met, but he hoped their linked ancestry might beg him the greatest of favors today.

Elias had never seen the church, had only read of its being built in a short time span and of its named pastor in the paper months ago, so when he arrived in front of the imposing building with its white columns and portico, complete with cupola on top, he was pleasantly surprised. *An English baron's daughter could be married here.*

For as much as Olivia had insisted last night that it did not matter where they married, to Elias it did, because he believed that, deep down, it mattered to Olivia too. He had agreed to her idea that they marry today, only on certain conditions. One of which was that they be married in a proper church.

He secured Fairfax, then ascended the steps and tried the front doors. They were not locked but were solid and heavy. Anyone inside was sure to be alerted of his arrival. Elias stepped inside the building lit by sunlight streaming in through tall windows on either side. He made his way up the aisle, toward a man sitting near the front, an open book in his lap.

A half hour later, Elias was on his way again, his heart light and encouraged, though wishing Seneca Falls had a religious leader like Alexander Mason.

A short trot downtown led him to a jeweler and after that a florist. Elias left the latter and looked down at his suit, discouraged upon noticing its wear. He'd not purchased any clothing since Anne's passing. She had been the one to see to his wardrobe needs during their marriage, and it seemed those had been neglected somewhat since then. But there was no help for it now. *Olivia is marrying a poor man.* Or so it seemed today. He felt like one with his funds all but depleted by this trip. *She fell in love with me in my old clothes.* She wouldn't mind marrying him in them either, he hoped.

He returned Fairfax and was back at the hotel by eleven.

Ignoring the delicious aromas wafting from the dining room, Elias hurried upstairs, wanting to drop his parcels off before going to see Olivia. He opened the door to his room and stepped on a folded piece of paper bearing his name. He picked it up, unfolded it, and read it as the door behind him closed.

My Dearest Elias,

I trust you had success with your errands this morning, and all is ready for us to marry today. Should fortune not have smiled upon you in your quests, I am also content (well, not entirely, but I shall tell myself that I am) to remain your fiancée. I eagerly await your report.

While you were gone I accomplished a few errands of my own, the first being to purchase a new suit of clothes for you for our wedding day. While it is entirely possible that you may come near to starving with me as your wife, you shall, at the least, never lack for fine and fashionable clothing. Please do not take offense, darling. It is a wife's responsibility to care for her husband in this way, and as I hope to become your wife today this was something I wished to do for you.

I have also ordered a luncheon tray to be sent to your room, as it would be most unseemly for the groom to faint from hunger at his wedding. I love you, Elias, and I look forward to saying that every day for the rest of my life.

Yours with great affection,
Olivia

Elias wished Olivia were with him this minute. He would have kissed her. *I can do that much at least.* He had set physical parameters for their wedding night as part of their agreement to marry today, as well. He didn't want to give either of his two, soon-to-be brothers-in-law any reason to find fault with his decision, impulsive though it was. Marrying Olivia and returning to Seneca Falls without having consummated their marriage would hopefully prove that he really did love her and was not simply a man long-starved for affection who had taken advantage of a situation.

Though I am starved too. But his desires could be controlled longer, for Olivia's sake. For theirs in starting off their lives together right.

Deciding that he would stick to tradition, inasmuch as possible by not seeing the bride before the appointed hour for their wedding, Elias wrote a note to Olivia, telling her of the arrangements he had made, then slipped it beneath her door.

He returned to his room and devoured the luncheon that had just been delivered. That she had spent her morning thinking of him and anticipating his needs touched him deeply and made him love her all the more. When he had finished eating, he opened the large parcel from Taylor's Clothing Store that had been left on the bed. After removing the lid, he found a white, high-collared linen shirt, a navy waistcoat with a standing collar, navy wool breeches and matching tailcoat, and a scarf cravat and new gloves. Beside the gloves, a small box held a decorative cravat pin topped by horse and rider. A folded paper was secured beneath. Elias picked up the pin, removed the paper, and unfolded it.

A man does not need shining armor or a white horse to be all that a woman dreams of.

Elias twirled the pin in his hands. Never before had he wanted to be a knight or the hero of a story. But now . . . he wished he could make Olivia's every dream come true. *Someday.* He stared out the east-facing window and thought of a shimmering city across the Atlantic that he'd never seen but vowed that he would. Because she wished it . . . *Someday.*

AT ONE O'CLOCK, Olivia opened the door to her room to find Elias already there, hand outstretched as if he were about to knock. His arm slowly lowered as he looked at her. His other hand held a bouquet of flowers.

"Olivia." His voice sounded choked, and he gaped at her. "You brought that dress to be a nanny in?"

She laughed and shook her head. "No. I brought it hoping to have an opportunity to attend a ball. But today it will have to do for a wedding. What do you think?" She turned a slow circle in front of him, showing off the cream gown with its sheer overlay stitched with tiny pink flowers and green vines. The bodice was fitted, the skirt full, her shoulders bare, and the sleeves puffed. She'd never had the opportunity to wear this gown before she'd had to go into hiding, but she adored it and felt as beautiful as she believed a bride ought to for her wedding.

"It will more than do. Were you any more exquisite, I would not be able to hold off kissing you again until after we've wed."

"Who says you have to?" she teased, then reached behind her to retrieve her cloak for the drive to the church.

They descended the stairs together, her hand resting on the sleeve of his dark coat. "You look dashing," she said as they crossed the lobby. His cravat was smartly tied, with the pin topping it, and the trousers fit him better than the ones he had worn previously. He had probably lost weight over the last year, and perhaps even more since he had not had Victoria to cook for him.

I will have to remedy that. Which meant she was going to have to learn to cook—more than bread. *The running of the house will be up to me. There will be no servants.* That reality loomed large before her, as she thought of all that Victoria did each day. *But we are to live in town.* It would not be as much work as living on a small farm. *I can do it. For Elias.* She glanced at him, wondering if he had any apprehensions about her abilities as well.

They boarded the carriage he had arranged to take them to the church where they were to be married. Last night, when Elias had listed his conditions if they were to marry today, she had felt little hope they would all be accomplished and wondered if that had been his way of showing, indirectly, that he was not prepared to marry her so soon. After all, his proposal had been as surprising to him as it had been to her. He had not started off yesterday morning with the intention of proposing marriage.

The short drive ended in front of a stately white building, its tall columns and windows elegant.

"This is the church where your cousin presides?" She stepped out of the carriage and gazed up at the sparkling cupola on top.

Elias nodded. "I had a brief tour this morning. It is quite a wonder, especially considering the short time it took to build."

"A good portent for our marriage." Olivia took his arm again and held her wedding bouquet in her other hand. "Something magnificent *can* come about or be created in a short amount of time."

They ascended the steps and entered the building. Elias stopped just inside the doors, and as soon as they had closed, the organ up front began Handel's "Wedding Anthem for Princess Anne."

Olivia closed her eyes and savored the moment, the scent of roses, the music that reminded her of home, and Elias—kind, gentle, and loving—at her side. She opened her eyes to rays of sunshine slanting through the west-facing windows and felt as if God Himself was blessing their union.

Feeling the tears already brimming, she looked up at Elias. "Thank you. For all of this. For making it perfect for me."

His gaze, already tender, turned even more adoring. "I wish I could give you everything you've ever wanted. I won't always be able to make things perfect for you, Olivia. There will be much about our life that will not be, that will instead be difficult and challenging. Are you certain that is what you wish? I would not fault you if—"

She pressed a finger to his lips, or tried to, but it was more like a bouquet to his face, as her hand was full. She pulled the flowers away as his nose twitched with an almost sneeze.

"I don't need perfect all the time. *Some* of the time would be nice. I'll even take *occasionally*. Or not at all, if that is what is required. To have *you*."

"Those are some of the most eloquent wedding vows I've ever heard."

Olivia and Elias turned from facing one another to see the pastor standing before them.

"I could pronounce you husband and wife right now, given the loving commitments you've just spoken to each other, but if you would like to make some additional promises and invite God to be a part of your union, will you follow me to the front?"

Elias glanced at her. Olivia nodded.

"We would like that very much," he said as he squeezed her hand.

CANDLELIGHT FLICKERED FROM the nightstand as Elias lay back on the bed, hands behind his head as he considered the day's events. *I am a married man again.* Guilt about this still niggled him, but it was not an all-out assault as he had feared. Last night he'd made his peace with his decision to marry Olivia. It was either marry her or lose her, and the latter possibility, like a punch to the gut, had nearly knocked him out and then subsequently spurred him to action.

He was not normally a man of impulse or prone to act quickly, except when it came to saving lives and helping people. *It is my own life that I saved this time. Mine and Evie's.* He was married to a woman of action now, and he had no doubt that with Olivia's influence, his daughter would grow to be one as well. He rather liked that idea.

Thoughts of Evie faded as Olivia emerged from behind the dressing screen. Only a few minutes before he had helped her to unfasten her gown and then, rather stoically, he had left her to remove the gown and petticoats and corset on her own. *I am not going to touch her tonight.* The image of a thirsty man in a desert came to mind again. He was not going to be as that man, grabbing the water offered to him and gulping it down. He had shown Olivia every courtesy today and would continue to do so.

No matter how starved I am. But he drank in the sight of her in a simple white chemise, in some ways more modest than her dress had been, as her shoulders were covered. She'd unpinned her hair, and it spilled in rich, brown waves halfway down her back. As she stepped farther into the candlelight, he saw that he was mistaken about the chemise, as the thin fabric did little to hide what lay beneath.

Heaven help me. Elias sat up on the bed, then stood, pulling the blankets back. Olivia covered the remaining steps between herself and the bed in record time, then slid between the sheets and pulled them up almost to her chin.

Elias refrained from both chuckling in amusement and growling with displeasure at having the view he'd been enjoying taken away. *A starving man can look, can't he?*

Probably not, without playing with fire. *Think of Jonathan and Graham.* Elias wanted a long and happy relationship with his new, extended family, and holding off on marital relations until that family had both heard and accepted the news of his and Olivia's marriage seemed as good a way as any to begin. *If they can get over our elopement.*

Elias slid into bed without bothering to remove anything other than his shoes, jacket, and cravat.

Olivia turned toward him. "Men sleep in their clothes?" Her nose scrunched in the expression he so adored.

"This one does. Tonight. Keeps things simple." *Safe.*

"Oh." Her face relaxed. "Should I have kept my gown on?"

"Definitely not. As pretty as it is, there's enough fabric there to equal a whole other person, and this bed's not big enough for three." He rolled onto his side, facing Olivia.

Some of the covers fell away as she reached out to him, then tentatively placed her hand at his waist. "Is this permissible tonight? A sort of bedtime hug?"

In answer he brushed the back of his fingers along the

side of her face, then leaned in for a kiss, allowing his mouth to linger as long as he wished, savoring the sweetness of their connection, the warmth of their mingled breath, the thrill of anticipation surging through him. When at last he pulled back, Olivia's eyes were wide and glazed with passion. It pleased him greatly and made him want her even more.

"Bedtime hugging *and* kissing permitted and encouraged," Elias said.

Olivia's arm slid from his waist up to his shoulder and behind his neck. "In that case . . ." She initiated the kiss this time, following his moves of a minute before until they were both breathless.

Gently Elias moved her hand and placed it over his pounding heart. "Do you feel that? How fast it is? You're doing that to me."

"Mine is the same," she said in wonder and reached for his hand, as if to show him.

Elias held back. "Not a good idea tonight."

"Oh." She blushed and looked down.

He lifted her chin. "Perhaps tomorrow. It's not that I don't want to touch you." *You have no idea how much I want to.* "But—brothers-in-law."

"Have no place in our marriage bed." Olivia leaned over him, her lips silencing any feeble protest he might have made.

Elias groaned and deepened their kiss. She was going to kill him this way. He wouldn't need to worry about Jonathan or Graham doing him bodily harm, because he'd already be dead. When he thought he could bear no more without giving in to the need pulsing through him, Elias sat up and grasped her shoulders, holding her away from him.

"I love you, Olivia, and I promise to show you the extent of that love soon. As soon as I can—and live to do it again. But for now—tonight—" His breathing was ragged as his hand slid down to take hers. "Hold my hand, lie beside me. Let's simply savor not being alone anymore."

She didn't protest but lay beside him, clasping his hand, her shoulder touching his.

Such simple things. But how he cherished each one.

"Today has been perfect. I don't want it to end."

Perfect would have been if her family and Evie had been here too, but he understood what she meant. The church, the vows they'd spoken, how beautiful Olivia looked, the way they had strolled about the city afterward, hand in hand, the private supper they had shared in this room—all of it had been perfect. A day of happiness and fulfilled dreams, even if some were slightly different than they had originated. "You were a beautiful bride. I only wish your family could have been there with you."

"You were there. You are my family now. They will understand and be happy for us both." Olivia turned her head to look at him. "It isn't as if I married a stranger. You were practically family already. We've just made it official now."

"So we have." Elias pulled her toward him, then rested his chin on the top of her head as she snuggled into his embrace and laid her cheek against his chest, over his beating heart. "We should sleep now. We have to be up early to catch the stage."

"A pity, that." She fought a yawn. "But then, I suppose that a betrothal that lasted not quite a day before the wedding results in an equally short wedding trip."

"What do couples of your class in England do for their wedding trips?" Elias tried not to feel that his inadequacies as a husband were already surfacing.

"Often they travel to the continent." There was no trace of wistfulness in her tone. "Probably to escape the pushy mamas who, as soon as they have married their children off, begin demanding grandchildren of them."

"Your mother does not seem the type to do that."

"She isn't," Olivia said, then sighed. "She is not the type to do much lately. I worry about her, that this change—leaving all behind that she has known her entire life—is too much. She is happy having Victoria restored to her, and she will be happy that I have committed to staying, but I know at least a little part of her must be sad, as I was, being surrounded by so much happiness and love while having none myself."

Elias had made similar observations. In Lady Claybourne he had seen glimpses of the deep well of sorrow she carried within her, not dissimilar to the burden of loss and loneliness he had carried as well. "If she were free, do you think she might marry again?"

"I don't know. She has been hurt deeply by my father, and I believe it would be difficult for her to trust again."

Olivia's arm draped across his middle, and he closed his eyes in tortured bliss. Having her close, holding her like this, was gift enough. *We are married. There will be time enough.*

"Someday, if your mother is free, we must encourage her to find companionship and love. Especially if she has never known such blessings." He had known those and lost them, and now found them again. Loving Olivia felt even sweeter and stronger than that which he had experienced before. *Because I lost Anne, because of the dark valley of sorrow I traveled.* Loving Olivia felt like emerging into the sunlight after months of fog and gloom. He would not take that, or her, for granted, but would grasp every minute of happiness, every second they had together and hold on tight. *To our love. To our joy. To each other.*

Fifty-one

OLIVIA RUBBED HER thumb against the simple band on her finger beneath her glove. It felt odd there. She wasn't accustomed to wearing a ring, but it also felt right. She closed her eyes, reliving the moment yesterday when Elias had slipped the ring onto the third finger of her left hand as he had promised to cleave unto her and none else. Of all the vows they had spoken to each other, she felt the power of that one the most, knowing what it must have cost him to make it and how he had left his memories of the past, his Anne. *To love me now.*

The ring was silver, as he could not afford to buy a gold band after all else the unexpected trip had entailed. There were no jewels embedded in it, nor any mounted above, and yet the ring pleased Olivia immensely because it was a gift from Elias and a symbol of his commitment to her. *Strange how we don't often get what we want, but what we need.*

Victoria did not even have a wedding ring anymore. Hers had been sold in England to pay for their passage to America. She did not seem to mind this, or the loss of all of the other jewels she'd had when she and Jonathan had married. *Jonathan is her jewel, and she is his.* That they had each other after all they'd been through was the real treasure.

Sophie, who'd never wanted a marriage or a ring and generally eschewed all jewelry and frivolity, had the most exquisite wedding ring Olivia had ever seen—a ruby surrounded by diamonds on a band of gold. It was practically the only piece of jewelry Sophie ever wore, and her gowns were rarely befitting such a ring, yet she had told Olivia how much she loved it, and of the dramatic events that had occurred before Graham had given it to her with real intent.

It was not a comparison, not a contest among her sisters, but for the first time Olivia felt their equal. The always waiting phase of her life was over. She'd grown up at last and was finally going to live—not the life she had been raised for, but one better and more worthwhile.

As the stagecoach stopped at last in front of the tavern in Seneca Falls and she took Elias's hand, she felt like they were coming home.

He descended before her, then helped her down. He kept her left hand in his, while her right carried her wedding bouquet. It had been too pretty and too precious to leave behind. What better seeds to start her own flower garden with than those she could claim from her wedding bouquet, once it had dried?

Olivia stepped onto the boardwalk, and they emerged from the shadow of the coach into the twilight.

"Elias found her. Olivia's back!" A cry went up.

Olivia raised her head as her sisters and mother rushed forward, each throwing their arms around her and proclaiming their love.

"I'm sorry I didn't listen to your concerns more," Mother said. "The next time you want to go somewhere I promise to take you seriously and to go with you, if necessary. Just, please, don't go off on your own again."

"I love you," Sophie said. "And I'm sorry you've felt so out of place here and sad. We do want you with us, though, as a part of our family—here or in Scotland."

Victoria hugged her next. "I'm so glad you came back. We haven't had much time together after so long apart."

Jonathan and Graham did not hug her but seemed to be noting her proximity to Elias.

Olivia grinned, positively bursting to share their news.

"Papa!" Evie reached her arms out to Elias, and he took her, holding her tight.

Passersby glanced at the group, some with speculation, others with distaste. Though Maime, Ayla, and Matthew were not with them, no doubt many had not forgotten the words Olivia had spoken to their pastor in church.

Words I stand by.

"Why don't we all go to my house for a few minutes," Elias suggested.

Jonathan glanced at the sky. "It will be dark soon, and I want to get Victoria home before then."

"Olivia and I need to speak with each of you. We'll be brief," Elias promised.

Expressions, from curious to concerned, filtered across her family members' faces. Olivia merely smiled at them and remained at Elias's side as they all made the trek down the street to his house. *Our house.*

Graham unlatched the gate of the low, white picket fence and held it open for them as they filed through. Olivia studied the small square of plain ground that was to be their garden. She would do magnificent things with it, she decided.

Inside, the house was cold and nearly dark. Uncertain where any candles were, Olivia parted the front curtains to let in what light was left outside. Once everyone was inside, standing, filling the narrow room that was the waiting area for Elias's patients, he shifted Evie to one side and took Olivia's hand in his. They both faced her family.

"Olivia and I were married yesterday."

A few gasps met this announcement, along with stony silence from a few family members, namely her brothers-in-law.

Maybe Elias was right to be concerned. Olivia hadn't realized that Graham and Jonathan cared that much about her or her safety or her future, and it felt good to realize they did, even if their concern was misdirected at the moment.

"It was my idea." She spoke up before anyone else could. "Elias followed me in the stage to Auburn and tried to convince me to come back with him. I didn't listen and continued on to Ithaca, but there were no seats left for Elias."

"Then how—" Mother began.

"I bought a horse and rode there as fast as I could."

"He found me just as I'd been turned away from the tavern where we had stayed on our journey here. There were no rooms left, and it was dark and cold. I was about to go in search of other lodging when Elias rode up on a horse."

"That was not white." He glanced at Olivia, a teasing glint in his eye.

"In the interest of getting you all home before dark," he continued, "this is the synopsis version of the last seventy-two hours. When Olivia left on that stage, I realized I didn't want to lose her. When we were reunited Monday night I proposed. Olivia accepted, and then, over supper, she suggested we marry the next day."

"It isn't as if the church here would have allowed us inside or the minister would have consented to marry us—not that I would have wanted him to," Olivia said. "And there were no other coaches coming this direction until today. We had the whole of the day yesterday to ourselves, and since we had decided to marry, why wait?"

"My cousin married us yesterday afternoon in the church he presides over in Ithaca," Elias concluded.

"It was a perfect, lovely day." Olivia beamed at all of them.

Sophie came forward first, enfolding Olivia in her arms. "If you are happy, then I am happy for you. Elias is a good man, and I've known he cares for you for some time. I have watched that love we spoke of on our voyage growing between you."

"Thank you." Olivia wiped at a tear beginning to slide down her cheek. Sophie's acceptance and her words about observing their love meant much.

Her mother was next, expressing her delight that Olivia would be settled down with such a kind man. "You're safe now," she whispered in her ear. "Even if your father found us, he could not make you wed someone else."

Olivia glanced over her shoulder at Elias having what appeared to be an intense conversation with Jonathan and Graham. Victoria held Evie away from the trio. Olivia hurried over to them, intending to stop whatever protective bravado was happening before it became serious.

"Let me repeat, gentlemen, that marrying yesterday was *my* idea. Elias only agreed on several conditions—the first being that we were married in a church and spoke vows before God. The second and third were that I had a wedding ring—" She pulled off her glove and held out her hand, "and a bouquet." She inclined her head toward the flowers she had set on the windowsill. "The last condition was that we would wait to—" She stopped and felt a blush flooding her face.

"—to know each other as husband and wife?" Sophie finished.

Of course Sophie can speak of such things matter-of-factly. Olivia nodded. "Yes. That. It was not to be until after we had told all of you, and you had accepted our marriage."

Jonathan and Graham simultaneously blew out long breaths.

"Don't take this wrong, Olivia," Graham said. "We've

nothing against Elias, but as your brothers by marriage, and thus your protectors, it is our responsibility to look out for you, to keep you safe. Had I gone after you myself as was my inclination—"

"I would be in New York City right now." She lifted her chin to meet Graham's eye. "*No one* but Elias could have persuaded me to return. I love him. I never wanted to leave and never would have but for his announcement that he was moving away. It was then I felt there was no future here for me."

"You're not still intending to move, are you?" Jonathan asked, looking to Elias.

He shook his head. "I was a fool to consider it in the first place. It was the mistake of a man unsure of the affections of the woman he loves. But put yourself in my place—would you have believed you could be so fortunate to win a woman like Olivia?"

A corner of Graham's mouth lifted as he turned to Sophie. Jonathan and Victoria exchanged a long look as well.

"I was a merchant who fell in love with a baron's daughter," Jonathan said. "So far beneath her that for a long while I had no hope she would ever even know my name."

"Better merchant than murderer," Graham added. "My reputation made most women stay far away, and rightly so. Then Sophie stepped into my carriage and didn't leave when she had the opportunity. But yes, I think we can understand your doubt and hesitation."

"It appears Olivia's impulsiveness has led to yet another successful outcome." Mother's voice was steady as she spoke, strong and accepting, as was her smile.

The remaining tension in the room drained, and Elias pulled Olivia close and kissed her soundly in front of them all, to much applause, cheers, and whistling.

"Now, if you will all kindly *vacate our house*, my wife and I would like to enjoy our delayed wedding night."

Olivia felt her face rush through at least five shades of red. Where had her soft-spoken, self-restrained husband gone?

"Would you like us to take Evie until tomorrow?" Victoria asked.

"No." Olivia stepped from Elias's embrace and held her hands out to Evie. She leaned forward into her arms, and Olivia held her close. "We are a family now, Evie included."

Elias promised that they would see everyone at Sunday dinner, as usual, and her family made their hasty goodbyes.

When the last had left, Olivia closed the door behind them and leaned against it, her gaze zeroing in on Elias, standing at the window and now holding Evie, helping her to wave goodbye. "I cannot believe you said that to my family."

He grinned. "I was simply looking out for your best interest. We have a fire to light, a child to feed, not to mention finding something to eat for ourselves, and I imagine you would like a bath after our long day of travel. I feared that if I did not encourage your family to leave, it would be tomorrow before we found ourselves in bed together."

Olivia blushed again. "One might think that is all you have on your mind tonight." She pushed off the door and headed for the kitchen at the back of the house. Elias caught her arm as she walked past.

"It is all I have had on my mind *all* day."

IT WAS NEARLY eleven o'clock when Elias finished bathing and joined Olivia in bed. He half expected her to be asleep, but she sat up in bed, a candle beside her as she read from one of his medical textbooks.

"Thinking of becoming a doctor?" He slid into bed on the

opposite side, appreciating that Olivia had likely noted the side he usually slept on—based on the proximity of his belongings—and had chosen the other.

"No." She shut the book and looked up at him, her eyes widening at the sight of his bare chest. "Sophie—taught me that one might learn a great deal from medical books. Particularly those concerning anatomy."

"Books are good. But a real-life demonstration is always better." He took the volume from her and set it aside, her gaze following his every movement. "Was there anything in particular you—"

Pounding on the door below, accompanied by the bell he had installed that connected to the upstairs, interrupted. Elias gave Olivia what he hoped was an apologetic look. "I'm sorry. I have to answer that."

"I understand." There was no hurt in her voice, only disappointment, but she rose to help him into his shirt, her hands on his shoulders severely tempting him to ignore the continued pounding downstairs. He picked up his bag, then kissed her swiftly but with a promise of more to come. *Hopefully soon.*

He headed downstairs. Olivia followed, but only to the kitchen, where she might linger unseen by any in the front room.

Elias opened the door. Levi Jacobs stood there, a frantic expression on his usually haggard face. "I heard you was back in town. I woulda left a note for you yesterday but—"

But you cannot write or afford paper and pencil. "Is it Ruth?" Elias asked.

Levi nodded. "She's been laboring since yesterday. But the baby ain't comin'."

Elias grabbed his shoes from their place beside the door. "Let's go."

OLIVIA STOOD IN the cold kitchen long after she'd heard the door lock behind Elias. Finally she retreated up the stairs, peeked at Evie to make sure she still slept, then returned to the bed that was now cold as well. She climbed into it anyway, blew out the candle, and lay down, hugging Elias's pillow to her chest.

Such is the life of a country doctor's wife. He had warned her. *I agreed to this.* She held her hand up, staring at her wedding band in the glimmer of moonlight filtering through the curtains. *For better or for worse. In sickness and in health . . . When he is away and I am here.* Her purpose was to love him and care for him in any way possible, in any circumstance. *As he has done for me so many times already.*

She rolled onto her side and closed her eyes, feeling the soothing peace of contentment wash over her. *I will be the best wife.* She could hardly wait until tomorrow to begin.

Fifty-two

OLIVIA HAD EVIE and herself fed, bathed, and dressed, and bread baking in the oven when someone knocked at the front door. She had kept it locked this morning, not wishing anyone to be able to walk right in with Elias still away. He had been gone the whole of the night, and she had no idea when he would be home or where he was. But if he was not returned by the afternoon, she had resolved to take Evie and walk to the store. It might be that Jonathan knew where Levi and Ruth lived and when Elias might be expected back.

Checking to see that Evie was playing contentedly in the room beside Elias's office, Olivia peeked out the front window, then went to the door, half dreading and half eager to open it and set the woman on the other side in her place.

"May I help you?" she asked politely as she stared at Melody Larsen standing on the threshold, a paper in her hands.

A request from her mother for more herbs to help with her headaches?

"I am here to help *you*," Melody said, thrusting the paper toward her. Olivia took it but did not take her gaze from Melody.

"It's obvious you're trying to lure the doctor into marrying you. The way you flirt with him is shameless. That may be how it is done in England, but here women are less forward and more polite."

"Snooping around a man's house is polite?" Olivia crossed her arms as she continued staring at Melody.

"He'll never marry you," she said, ignoring Olivia's comment. "He still loves his wife. It says so in that letter he wrote to Anne. He's got a whole drawerful of letters he's written to her since she passed, all expressing his undying love."

"I know," Olivia said, hoping her bored expression covered the lie. "Was there anything else you wished to tell me?"

Melody nodded. "It's shameful the way you're here, in his house, the two of you alone. It's scandalous—*wicked*. The town won't stand for such behavior. We all know you're a heathen after what you said to the minister, but this is even worse."

Olivia started to close the door but rested her left hand upon it at Melody's eye level an extra few seconds, so she would be sure to see her ring. "Where I am from it is perfectly acceptable for a *wife* to be at home alone with her husband."

She closed the door, turned the lock, and walked quickly to Evie. She picked her up and brought her upstairs to their rooms, which were both more comfortably appointed and warmer. Without looking at it, Olivia set the letter on the top of Elias's dresser, only just realizing that her hands were shaking.

She's the wicked woman. Not me.

Olivia took Evie to her room to play, grateful for the sweet toddler and her antics that helped pass the time and mostly distracted her from the letter sitting on top of Elias's dresser. While Evie played, Olivia sorted through her clothing, taking the time to not only admire Anne's work but to study it closely. *These clothes won't last Evie forever. I will have to make her next ones.* She was going to need Victoria's help. *A lot of help.*

The rest of the morning passed slowly. Olivia retrieved

the bread when it was done baking and was temporarily cheered at her success using a different oven for the first time. She set the rounded loaves on the rack to cool while she fed Evie lunch. Afterward, she rocked Evie and sang to her, then continued rocking her long after Evie had fallen asleep. Her head against Olivia's shoulder was comforting, as was the idea that even when Elias was away she would never be completely alone.

When she at last laid Evie down, it was only to gather her gloves and bonnet, so they could go to the store to purchase something she might use to supplement their bread for dinner. Once in her bedroom, Olivia's gaze strayed to the bureau and the letter on top.

I shouldn't read it. It isn't for me. If Elias had wanted her to know that he wrote letters to Anne, he would have told her. *He probably will tell me.* It wasn't as if they'd had time to discuss many things.

Olivia crossed to the dresser and opened the top drawer, intending to put the letter inside and expecting to see only clothing as she had the last time she had looked in Elias's bureau, while searching for clothes for Evie.

This piece of furniture was different than that one had been. It was taller, with more drawers, and instead of clothes of any type, papers filled the top drawer. There were three stacks—one of blank paper, one topped with a letter filled with Elias's distinctive script, the same as that which had been on the letter he had slid beneath her hotel room door the day they married.

Dear Anne, it began. Olivia hurriedly slapped Melody's letter on top before she could read any further.

Her gaze drifted to the third, smaller stack as her hands began pushing the drawer in.

Dear Olivia.

She hesitated, then reached for the letter, folding it forward enough to see the one below. *Dear Olivia,* with an older date. She flipped through all of them. All were addressed to her. Beginning on the day she and Elias had met.

Her fingers hovered on the drawer edge, her curiosity burning. Would it really be so wrong to read letters written to her? *It's better I read those than the one Melody taunted me with.*

This argument won out, and Olivia took the stack and moved toward the window to read in the light. She began with the letter on the bottom, with the oldest date.

Dear Olivia,

How grateful I am to have found you trudging through the snow in search of Jonathan. I also find myself grateful that he was not, as you had been led to believe, in need of your care. Now my prayer is that your toes will not be in need of mine . . .

Dear Olivia,

Never have I dreaded a medical procedure more than I did the removal of your toe. In postponing it for an additional day, I was giving us both more time to prepare. The last thing I wished to do was to cause you pain, yet I was going to have to do just that. Dead tissue cannot be allowed to linger on a body without dire consequences. You had been so brave already. When we had prepared everything and you were laid out on the bed, eyes swimming with tears, with a sister on each side holding your hands, you raised your head long enough to tell me that you trusted me. I felt—I'm not sure what I felt in that moment, for it is indescribable. The weight of your trust? Humbled by your faith in me—certainly. And the deepest concern that I do right by you. You asked only that you be able to dance again, and I prayed that you would be able to, that I would not have to cut too much away beyond your toe. I'm not sure I've ever seen anything as beautiful as your foot when I removed your stocking. Overnight over ninety percent of the discoloration was gone, the skin pink and healthy. A miracle, for there is no other explanation. I wanted to shout for joy when I saw it. God is good! He has not always answered my prayers as I wish, but this one He did.

  You were stoic and brave and still and silent as I removed the only tissue that had not revived. Afterward, it was very good to hold your hand as we said a prayer of thanks together.

  Olivia wiped her eyes as she recalled that day—not the pain so much as Elias's kindness and tender concern. *He is the best doctor, filled with compassion and kindness.* How blessed she was to now have him as her husband. She set the letter aside and picked up the next.

  Dear Olivia,

  Having written to you regarding the miracle of your toe, I feel inclined to write more, though you are no longer considered one of my patients. I believe you are now my friend, a new and unexpected one for whom I am most grateful . . .

  Dear Olivia,

  How upset I was with you tonight, when you dragged me out to dance in front of everyone else. Our dance alone outside was perfect. I was still treasuring and pondering those moments in my heart and mind when your unexpected actions reversed the course of my feelings for you. Undoubtedly you are the most impulsive creature I have ever known. A little warning of your intent might have been nice, though in retrospect, I suppose that had you given it, I would have resisted your attempts. Instead I had a split-second decision—dance with you, or humiliate you in front of a roomful of people new to you. Though I was distraught at the idea of being on display and the ensuing problems that would result, I could not bring myself to act in a manner that would hurt you in any way.

And so we danced. It was apparent that you were far more experienced and graceful than any other in the room. You were a sight to behold as you whirled about in your green-and-gold gown. Every man in the room wanted you as his partner, and every woman in the room no doubt wished you had never come to Seneca Falls. Still, I resolved to take you to task for subjecting me to such public scrutiny and speculation as soon as the dance was concluded.

Imagine my surprise to discover that you had orchestrated the entire thing for my benefit—and it appeared to have worked just as you had predicted. In this instance, I admit to admiring your impulsiveness. But this time only, and I pray you will take more heed with your actions going forward.

Yours,
Elias

Olivia snorted. "That didn't happen, did it, dear husband." She smiled to herself, confident that Elias had no complaints about her latest acts of impulsiveness.

Dear Olivia,
You were right. A Christmas tree is a festive tradition. It brought me much happiness to bring you one today. Though I could not look at its splendor tonight, as yours eclipsed it . . .

Dear Olivia,
Your words at church this morning stirred my soul in a way it has not been moved for quite some time . . .

Dear Olivia . . .
Dear Olivia . . .
Dear Olivia . . .

She read letter after letter, many short, a few of them long, but all chronicling what she had not even realized to be their courtship. By the time she came to the last letter, her eyes were overflowing, requiring her to hold the paper at a distance so her tears would not fall onto it and ruin the ink.

Dear Olivia,
Today was a perfect day. You were a beautiful bride, and the words we spoke sealed the last of the cracks in my broken heart, many of which had already been repaired by you over the past three-and-a-half months. You are sleeping now, snuggled beside me in bed, and as I brush the hair back from your face and touch your soft skin, I can scarcely believe my good fortune, that God has blessed me so richly and you are indeed mine. That you chose me, an unlikely hero so different from those of your childhood dreams, is humbling. You already know many of my imperfections and will undoubtedly discover more in the coming days, but I promise to try, every day, to be the best husband I can to you. Our life may not be an easy one, but I vow to make it good, and to love you with my whole heart and being, with everything that I have and am.
Yours,
Elias

Olivia brushed at her cheeks as she set the last letter on top of the stack and put them all back in the drawer. She closed it and leaned against the bureau, no longer feeling any need to read what Elias had written to Anne. *All this time he was writing to me.* His words to her were such that she felt her heart might burst with love, both for that which she felt for him and what he had shown for her in his letters. She might have stayed in that very spot, arms wrapped tightly around herself and swaying in the cocoon of love spun by his prose, but for another knock from below and the jingling of the bell in the hall.

Wiping the last of the moisture from her cheeks, Olivia descended the stairs and went to the door. This time her visitor was welcome. Olivia opened the door and stepped forward, arms outstretched.

"Maime! I'm so glad to see you."

"Sure you are. You probably starving right about now. I figured I'd best bring you something before that man of yours reconsider his choice of a wife."

Olivia laughed, though there was some truth to the words. Her mouth watered as Maime marched inside, a large basket on her arm. "I brought you some freshly fried chicken, some vegetables and gravy, and a pie. I figured you got the bread covered all on your own." She lifted her chin, sniffing the air appreciatively.

"Yes," Olivia confirmed as she accepted the basket from Maime. "This will be amazing, though, and Elias will appreciate it so much. He's been gone all night and today, helping with a childbirth."

Maime snorted. "Men don't help with birthin'. They may think they do, but no man able to help with something he know nothing about, something his own body can't do."

Olivia didn't bother arguing. Maime was often right, though she suspected that Elias's medical schooling had included at least some training about helping a woman through childbirth.

"Can you stay?" Olivia asked. "This meal smells divine, but even more than your gift, I need your help. I need to learn how to cook—something." *Everything.*

"Told you, you ought to have paid more attention to old Maime this last while." She unfastened her cloak, handed it to Olivia, and began rolling up her sleeves. "Let's have a look at your kitchen and see what you got to work with."

Half an hour later, Olivia had a list of purchases she needed to make at the store and a few simple recipes to make with them. According to Maime, Elias had very few of the basic necessities for a functional kitchen.

"You will be living on bread alone if you don't get yourselves set up with a proper pantry," Maime predicted.

"I'll talk to him about it when he comes home," Olivia promised.

"Maybe you and Evie come out to see Maime each day, and we'll cook together while you learning."

The bell rang for the third time today, interrupting them.

"I best be going now," Maime said. "Jonathan say he give me a ride if I stop by the store."

"Thank you for coming," Olivia said. "Of all the people I know, Sophie included, I believe you must be the most knowledgeable."

"Child, I don't even read. But I thank you for the compliment." Maime patted her hand.

"You don't need to read if you can write the book," Olivia said as she made her way to the door. "You have practical knowledge about things that really matter." She opened the door to a young boy.

A street urchin, her past self in London would have said, would have turned her nose up at him and walked past. *How could I have been so shallow? So unfeeling?*

"Mistress Henrie?" he asked, looking up at her.

Olivia paused for a brief second, then nodded and smiled at the sound of her new title. *Melody must be spreading the word already.* "I'm afraid the doctor isn't home, but is there something else I can help you with?" In addition to looking half-starved, the boy appeared to be in dire need of a good washing. Olivia thought of both the tub in the kitchen and the loaves of bread cooling on the stove.

"I'm not here for the doctor. He's the one who sent me—wanted me to tell you that he'll be gone a piece more. My baby sister died, and my mama's not doing well. This birthin' about near killed her and it may yet, Pa says."

Olivia clasped her hands to her chest as she crouched down in front of the boy. "I'm so sorry." *A baby died. And this poor child's mother might too.* Elias would be devastated, as would this child and his entire family. It already appeared they were on the verge of—

"Why the doctor think your mama gonna die?" Maime asked behind her.

Olivia whirled around to face her. "*You* might be able to help this boy's mother. You healed Graham's shoulder, and I've heard Sophie say that she isn't afraid to have her baby because you'll be there."

"I've helped hundreds of women through their travail, but it may be that this boy's family don't want—"

"I don't care what they want. What they need is more important." Olivia turned to face the boy again. "Come inside. We'll go with you in a minute." Olivia rushed about, gathering things she'd need for Evie and refilling the basket Maime had unpacked, adding the two loaves of bread. She thrust that at Maime. "They'll need it worse than we do."

Fifteen minutes later they were all at the livery, Olivia giving instructions that the doctor's team was to be readied. When she drove them out onto the street a short while later, it was with Maime on one side of her, holding Evie and muttering prayers for their safety, and the boy, Michael, on the other, giving her instructions on how and where to drive.

His house was a long way out of town—long enough that Olivia began to feel more comfortable handling the team and long enough to second-guess her impulsive behavior. *What if Maime is right, and the family won't allow her to help?* But what if they would, and that made all the difference?

Elias is a good doctor. Competent. But Olivia suspected there was also truth to what Maime had said, about a man not knowing what to do like a woman could, at least with regard to childbirth.

When they arrived at the house that appeared as weary and worn-down as its occupants, Olivia handed the boy the reins and jumped down. She took Evie from Maime and hurried toward the door. There was no need to knock. The door was already swinging half open on its rusted hinges.

"Hello," Olivia called and walked inside, one arm holding Evie, while her other hand clutched Maime's as she pulled her in behind her.

The light was dim, the room filthy, but four sets of small eyes followed their movement.

"Elias," Olivia called.

"Back here." A few seconds later he appeared in the doorway, sleeves rolled up, his expression haggard, as if he had aged a dozen years since their wedding. "Olivia? What are you doing—"

"I brought Maime to help. She's attended hundreds of women during childbirth, and—"

"Come. Please." Elias held his hand out to Maime, and she followed him into the back room. Olivia's relief that she had done the right thing and Elias was not upset with her was replaced by temporary panic as four young children surrounded her, the youngest two pawing at her dress as if they'd never seen or felt fabric so fine.

They haven't.

"Dinner," Michael called, lugging the basket inside.

Olivia took it from him and told the children they needed to wash at the pump outside before they would be fed. She set Evie down at the table, located a few dishes—also needing to be washed—and set to work divvying up most of the food.

By the time the children trudged back inside, she had plates of chicken, gravy, and vegetables set out for each and was slicing bread with an extremely dull knife. There was no butter, jam, or honey to be found, but the children eagerly took the bread she handed them.

"Thank you, Mistress Henrie," Michael said.

Olivia nodded her acknowledgment—the best she could manage with the lump in her throat—as she crossed her arms over her chest and leaned against the drainboard, watching the children devour the food. They had been waiting their whole lives too—not for a turn at dancing lessons or to have a Season, but to have full bellies, and a sturdier roof over their heads. When she left tonight, they would still be waiting. *Will they be waiting for their mother to return to them too?*

Another two hours passed before Elias emerged from the bedroom. Dark circles ringed his eyes, and he walked slowly, as if exhausted. Maime was not with him, and all was quiet from the back of the house. Olivia looked up from her current task, braiding the hair of the youngest girl, while the other children sat at the table, playing an improvised game of jacks with rocks they had gathered from outside. Olivia finished the braid, tied a length of ribbon in it, then stood, scooping Evie into her arms. She settled her on one side and used her free hand to untie the filthy apron she'd found in the kitchen and borrowed as she'd swept and scrubbed the kitchen and the children.

"Where's our mama?" Michael asked. All five pairs of eyes turned to Elias.

He came closer to the table. "She is resting now. She is very tired, and it is going to be a while before she can be up and about again. But she is going to be all right."

"Just resting?" a boy slightly smaller than Michael asked. "She didn't go to heaven?"

"She didn't go to heaven," Elias confirmed, bestowing a tired smile on each of them. He looked around the room, his weary expression lightened when his gaze landed on Olivia and Evie. "You've been busy." He took in the children's faces, freshly scrubbed, and the girls' hair all neatly combed and braided. His gaze swung to Olivia's bonnet, ribbonless now, in the middle of the table, then back to Olivia.

She shrugged. "Sometimes a woman just needs something pretty—right, girls?" The two pig-tailed girls gave her toothless grins. Olivia returned their smiles and looked to Elias. "I'm fairly certain my husband will buy me a replacement ribbon."

"Indeed he will." Elias's smile was tired but pleased as he looked around the kitchen.

Olivia felt exhausted as well. She had never worked so hard in her life as she had the past two hours, feeding five children, caring for Evie, sweeping and mopping, washing dishes. And now brushing and braiding heads of hair that probably hadn't had any attention for weeks. "It looked like they could use some help. I saved you some supper, if you'd like."

"That sounds great." Elias ran a hand through his hair, causing several of the already-out-of-place pieces to stand on end.

Olivia wanted nothing so much as to smooth it down and then to wrap her arms around him and be held. *Soon?* It was nearing dusk already. They would have to travel home after dark.

"The basket with your food is outside in the carriage," Olivia said. "I was afraid if I left it in here it would disappear."

Elias hesitated and glanced at the children. "They need it more."

"The children have all been fed. I made up plates for Levi and Ruth and Maime, as well. You need to eat too." Olivia took his hand, leading him outside.

The air was chilly, but it felt good to be out of the overcrowded house. They stopped at the pump and washed in the frigid water, then Olivia took the basket from the carriage, and Elias sat on the trunk of a tree in the yard that looked as if it had been felled some time ago but never harvested or even moved.

Olivia sat beside him, keeping Evie on her lap and nearly asleep as she cuddled against Olivia. Elias pulled a chicken leg from the basket first. He bit into it, then gave a moan of delight and closed his eyes.

"Maime made it," Olivia said before he could get his hopes up too much. "But she's going to teach me. Though I won't be killing or plucking any chickens. Touching bare meat is my limit on disgusting cooking tasks."

"Fair enough." Elias finished eating the chicken and took the slice of bread Olivia handed him.

"I did bake that. This morning. Unfortunately, that is the last slice of the two loaves."

"This is delicious, and they needed it more." Elias finished the piece slowly, then walked to the pump for a drink. When he came back he took Olivia's hand in his.

"I'm sorry to have been gone our first night and day home."

"It's all right." She meant it, surprisingly. The Olivia who'd left England last November would not have been all right with any of the events of the day, but now . . . *That Olivia is gone.* And she rather liked the one who was emerging in her place.

Elias squeezed her hand, then brought it to his mouth and let his lips linger there before looking up at her. "If you've changed your mind, it isn't too late for an annulment."

"*What*?" Olivia tugged her hand from his.

Elias held his out, indicating the run-down yard before pointing to his shirt, smeared with blood, then reaching forward to wipe something from her face. "Dirt." He held his finger up, showing what he had removed. "This is not your dream. I'm not sure you could get any farther from it. So if you don't want to stay—"

Her mouth cut him off as she leaned close and kissed him, caressing the side of his face with her free hand. "I love you, Elias Henrie. And I *know* you love me. I . . . I read the letters you wrote to me." In a rush she explained about Melody's visit and how she had discovered the letters.

"I didn't read a single one of Anne's. I promise. Can you forgive me for reading those you wrote to me?"

"There is nothing to forgive." Elias leaned nearer until their foreheads were touching. "In medical school we were taught many things—how to identify illnesses, how to perform surgical procedures, proper medication dosages. But one professor taught us what I consider to be one of the most critical parts of being a doctor. He taught us about empathy, or putting ourselves in our patients' place and imagining what they must be feeling. This professor suggested that a way to do that was to write letters to our patients, particularly those whom we would be working with over a period of time. So at the beginning of my practice I started doing that. It has proved to be an excellent way in which to feel connected to those I serve. Then, after Anne died, I started writing letters to her, because I was hurting so badly that I felt writing letters to her might help me to feel connected to her as well."

"Did it help?" Olivia asked.

"It did. It gave me something to look forward to at night, my time with her, or so I came to regard it. When you came, I told her about you, and I started writing to you as well, as your doctor. But I found that I did not want to stop. Soon I was writing as much or more to you than I was to Anne, and the night before we were married, I penned my last letter to her."

Olivia leaned back to look at him. "I did not ask that of you."

"I asked it of myself. That I live in the here and now, in the present, with the woman I adore."

Olivia's eyes misted as he kissed her again. "What will you write about today?"

Elias paused, as if considering. "I'll say that another impulsive decision has served you—served many—well. Maime saved Ruth's life. She knew what I did not, and I will be forever grateful to her, and to you for coming. The baby was stillborn, and by her small size, I think she had been dead for at least a few weeks already. It was sad—always so sad to lose a child. But the thought of leaving all of those children in there motherless . . . It would have been so, had Maime not come when she did."

Olivia leaned into him, and Elias wrapped his arm around her. "I am glad to have been some small part of it and to have helped here. I'm a mess." She grimaced as she looked down at her dress that would probably never be the same. "But I feel better than I think I ever have. Is that what it feels like for you? Being a doctor and helping others?"

He nodded. "A lot of the time, yes."

Behind them, the sun streaked its last orange rays across the yard, lighting the run-down cabin and making it look a little better than it had earlier. Or perhaps it just seemed that way because it was better. A mother would live to raise her children.

Olivia brushed her free hand across Elias's brow as she stared at him and felt the same overflowing love that had encompassed her when she'd read his letters. *He is mine. We love each other. Together we have a noble purpose.* The last thought was new, a revelation. It pulled her back as an anchor might a ship, securing her to the life she had chosen. *I have a purpose, a plan.* Even beyond her love for Elias and Evie. Because she had more than enough love for them and for others she could serve as she had the children today.

As if he had read the understanding dawning on her face, Elias leaned close again. "I believe you are going to be an extraordinary country doctor's wife." He kissed her once more as the sun sank and the full moon rose to light their way home.

The end.

Michele Paige Holmes is the author of eighteen published romance novels and at least a dozen more, as yet unpublished books lingering on her hard drive. She has also written five novellas for the Timeless Romance Anthologies. She loves history and all things romantic, though the reality of her life is often less so, with piles of laundry to be folded, meals to be cooked, and dishes to be washed. She finds those blessings too, or evidence of the blessings in her life—her husband, five, mostly grown children, and five charming, high-energy grandchildren (four of whom reside in her home).

She is married to her high school sweetheart, a true Ironman who considers doing ultramarathons and triathlons fun. The only time Michele logs serious miles is at Disney theme parks, but she and her super-fit husband have been happily married for thirty-five years, in spite of her lack of coordination and lagging fitness levels. She is happy to continue her role as cheerleader and race support.

While her husband is out running, biking, or swimming, Michele's furry companion Sherlock Holmes—a Cavapoo strongly resembling a teddy bear—keeps her company and keeps her feet warm during the cold winter months in Utah.

In recent years Michele has enjoyed traveling to some of the locations she writes about. This summer she will be returning to Scotland to do research for upcoming Hearthfire Historical novels.

You can find Michele on the web: MichelePaigeHolmes.com
Facebook: Michele Paige Holmes
Instagram: Michele Paige Holmes
Pinterest: Michele Paige Holmes

www.ingramcontent.com/pod-product-compliance
Lightning Source LLC
LaVergne TN
LVHW011942060526
838201LV00061B/4180